DIGGORY TOWN
AND
THE CHILDREN OF PROPHECY

Dale Peplinski

Diggory Town and The Children of Prophecy

Copyright © 2016 by Dale Peplinski

This is a work of fiction. Names, characters, places, and incidents are used fictitiously, or are the products of the author's imagination. Any resemblance to actual events, organizations, locales, or persons, living or dead, are used fictitiously.

ISBN: 978-0-9976162-0-0

Cover Design by Michael Mittelman
Copy Edit by Ashley Turcotte
Painting by JD Speltz

To my brother, Jon Michael Hall,
whose life was too short,
whose laughter was endless,
and whose love knew no bounds.
I will miss you every day–
until we meet again.

Acknowledgements

My husband, Ed Peplinski, will never fully understand how much his love and life have inspired me. I want my daughters and their children to know that they are the reasons I was able to do the things I believed I couldn't do. To my husband and daughters, Brittani and Aaron, there is no form of gratitude I could give that would repay them for the life they have given me. I am eternally grateful to them, and for them. As if that were not a blessing enough, I would like to give special thanks to my sister, who is my life-long friend, Melissa Turner. She edits my ramblings with a sharp tongue, and stands by me even when every fiber of her body tells her to run. And how do I begin to thank my amazing copy editor, Ashley Turcotte of Brown Owl Editing, or Michael Mittelman of Michael Scott Photography who created this book cover that I love so well. Last but not least, JD Speltz of Speltz Studio of Wildlife whose marvelous painting on the cover of this book inspired the imagination of me and my grandchildren. His work will forever be embedded into my family history, and his kindness will never be forgotten.

Without these people there would be no Diggory Town.

http://www.michaelscott-photography.com/
http://speltzstudio.com/
http://www.brownowlediting.com/

CONTENTS

DIGGORY TOWN
AND
THE CHILDREN OF PROPHECY

My spirit is all that I leave behind when my soul departs This World. My name may be forgotten. Surely my body and possessions will decay. But my spirit will leave its mark on those who carry on. Before I die, I must build a good spirit.

GranMa

Chapter 1   Death

Grandma is dead and it's not the first time. The first time Grandma died was twenty-six years ago. She chose to die on a mountain that stood high at the edge of a range. Its breadth was small yet wide enough to hold a cave, a waterfall, and a small army. Distinct from the rest of the mountains, it stood on the edge of the valley like a finger pointing the way for Grandma. Even the mountain knew she was destined for heaven.

Still, the end of her life was far from heavenly. All around her swords cut through the air as raindrops of blood created rivers of death. She lifted her sword, and sailed out into a blaze of glory that flowed into an ocean of sorrow. Michael was seven the first time he fought beside Grandma. This was the same day he watched the enemy sword plunge into her heart, and bleed the life out of his.

Like a statue frozen in a field of blood, he remained motionless while the battle raged around him. He did nothing when the knight came down from the heavens, and knelt over his Grandmother's lifeless body. Entombed in sorrow's silence, Michael only watched as the knight removed his glove to caress her face, kiss her forehead, and then carry her into the heavens. He often wonders about the knight with the gold-faced armor helmet. But he no longer wonders why his Grandmother had to die in Diggory Town. At thirty-three, he finally knows what she always knew . . . it was her destiny. What haunts him now is that he knows why watching her die was *his*.

Chapter 2   The First Visitor

Unlike her grandson, Grandma never feared destiny. In fact, she pushed it along knowing that if she didn't get her eldest granddaughter to Diggory Town soon, it would be too late. Only the open-mindedness of a child could understand its complexity, and open the door to a world such as this. The day Alexis entered Grandma's home office looking for Grandma to mend her broken heart was the day Grandma seized her opportunity.

"Stop crying, child, and close my door."

Alexis didn't close the door. Acting the victim, she crossed her arms over her chest. An apish frown pasted itself across her fair face. Once again, Alexis was pouting, and had big, exaggerated crocodile tears drizzling to her chin. With indignation, she pushed her blonde hair away from her blue eyes and pled her case. "I don't fit in, no one loves me, and the babies get all the attention." Alexis quivered, babbled, and shook for effect. "Grandma . . . I think I'm Cinderella."

Grandma tried not to laugh at the theatrics. She drew Alexis into the comfort of her arms. "Everyone loves you Alexis, but the babies need attention like lungs need oxygen. Being ten when everyone else is less than five isn't really the best thing to be. But it isn't the worst either."

After a generous hug and a face load of kisses, Grandma whispered into Alexis's ear. "Go close the door like I told you."

Alexis went to close the door, but stopped when she noticed the crystal doorknob sparkling like a prism. There was no light in that corner of the room to cause the sparkle. Confused, she shrugged her shoulders, grabbed the handle, closed the door, and sat down on Grandma's soft, fluffy, red couch.

* * *

Grandma's couch was as soft and comforting as her arms, but it sure caused a stir the day Grandma had it delivered. Actually, there were five couches delivered to Grandma's before they finally delivered the correct one.

Grandpa didn't say anything when the first two couches were delivered and then rejected by Grandma. When she rejected the third couch, he only grunted. But when the fourth couch was rejected, he said, "Is your tushie so special that none of these couches will do?"

Grandma laughed. She loved Grandpa beyond words. It was more than his tall rugged good looks, dark complexion, dimples, and dangerous-looking jagged scar on his right cheek that drew Grandma to Grandpa. His kindness and good spirit caused him to maintain youthfulness well below his years. But her love for him had more to do with his good soul than his good looks. There wasn't anything in the world he could say that would cause her to get cross with him.

She simply replied, "I bought the couch from Magical Endings Furniture and Appliances. I bought a very *specific* couch and, so far, they have not delivered it. In order for a couch to be comfortable, it must fit you *perfectly*. Even the smallest detail can cause a couch to be incompatible with your tushie. I will go to the warehouse tomorrow, find my exact couch, and have it delivered." And that was exactly what she did.

The next week, two young men from Magical Endings Furniture and Appliances huffed, puffed, and struggled their way up the stairs with Grandma's fluffy new couch. They grunted and groaned as they made their way up to the first landing. Then they turned the tight hundred and eighty-degree corner, and struggled their way up the second set of stairs.

It was amusing to everyone, except Grandpa, when the fifth couch, which was *exactly* the right couch, did not fit through the door leading to Grandma's office.

With great exasperation, Grandpa said, "Well, this is a fine little mess!"

With the slowed speech of a southern gentleman and a long sigh, the taller, heavier, and most out of breath of the two deliverymen replied, "That's okay, sir . . . we'll take it back."

"I'm afraid I'll have to wrestle you to the ground if you try. I have been inconvenienced too many times by the delivery of couches. If the Mrs. says this is the one, I can assure you young man, *this* is the one!"

Grandpa had been working in his shed and happened to have a hammer in his hand when the deliverymen arrived. The swish of his hammer startled them when, without warning, Grandpa hammered the doorframe right off the wall. In no time at all, he had created an opening wide enough for Grandma's couch. For a moment, the young deliverymen just stood there with their chins hanging.

"Sir, do you have the skills to fix the mess you just made?" the tall, heavy one was bold enough to ask.

"Son, let me give you some sage advice. You can get a good carpenter anywhere, but a good woman is not as easy to find. Fortunately, I know how to fix this mess. But I would tear down this whole house if that lady asked it of me." And that's how Grandma got this extra special couch that Alexis was seated upon.

* * *

As she settled into the fluffiness of the red couch, Alexis began to feel better. Grandma and her couch had that effect on the children. There wasn't anything Grandma couldn't fix. And she was particularly good with broken hearts.

Grandma cupped Alexis's hand, and as they sat upon the couch, a tingle rose up Alexis's arm. She began to feel odd, like you feel in the morning when you're not fully awake, but you're no longer asleep. The tingling persisted as it traveled across every part of her body.

Within seconds, Alexis began floating on air and she could see through Grandma. It should have felt scary, but it didn't. Nothing about Grandma ever felt scary—a little crazy perhaps, often exciting, but never scary. Even when Grandma's lips and eyelids began to change to light purple with hints of violet sparkles, Alexis was not afraid. When Grandma's brown hair and eyebrows turned to Grandma's favorite color of periwinkle sprinkled with shiny strands of diamond hairs, Alexis was not afraid. She especially liked the way Grandma looked with her hair piled high on top of her head. The soft curls flowed everywhere. As Grandma's face became whiter, and her cheeks became pinker, her eyes began to almost glow violet, but Alexis was not afraid.

When the transition completed, Grandma's dark brown eyes were a beautiful shade of blue-violet with flecks of green. Her clothes had changed into a blue, purple, and scarlet gown that had something similar to silver woven into the fabric. Tight silver threads laced with jewels fitted around her forearms, ending at the elbow and attaching to the puffy billowing sleeves that extended to her shoulders. The waist seemed captive by midnight blue that poured up and down her gown as it gradually turned purple and then scarlet. The gown took Alexis's breath away. But what Alexis liked best was Grandma's magnificent eggplant-colored cloak with the crimson silk lining, and her crazy crimson boots. At that moment, she was certain Grandma was a queen.

Grandma reached inside her cloak and pulled out a scepter. The scepter was more ominous than beautiful. Despite the precious jewels that drizzled down its staff, it appeared more like a weapon than a symbol of royalty. Perhaps it was the ferocious look on the head of the lion atop her scepter that caused Alexis alarm.

Still, there was something beautiful about the way Grandma looked, and there was something . . . not quite right. It seemed appropriate that there be something not quite right about Grandma. Even in The World of People, Grandma is well respected, but everyone knows that something about her isn't quite right.

"Now Alexis." Grandma smiled the tender smile that she reserved for children needing comfort. "Tell me, how will you look in Diggory Town?"

"I don't know how I shall look in Diggory Town." Alexis could not believe the sound of her own voice, for it had changed ever so slightly. It was somehow more formal. Trying not to seem naïve, because she was all of ten, she said, "I'm afraid I don't know much about Diggory Town."

"Well, look at Grandma. How do you think *you* will look in Diggory Town?"

Alexis thought about her most fanciful dreams. The beautiful gowns, jewelry, and slippers she wore in all her fantasies. She was more interested in looking like a fairy or a pixie than a princess or a queen. She would love to have wings to fly anywhere, but the idea seemed ridiculous, and a bit indulgent. As her imagination went wild, things began to happen without her notice. What started as a small billow of odorless white smoke began to glow and swirl around her. She was too lost in thought to notice. It wasn't until she felt the tightening of material on her arms that she returned from her daydream. All the wonders that she had imagined were becoming real. Grandma turned Alexis to face the full-length mirror in her office.

"How do you like *Alexis of Diggory Town*?" Grandma asked.

Alexis didn't know the person with the golden hair and brilliant blue eyes who looked back at her in the mirror. She could not feel more beautiful, nor could she feel herself breathing. It was as if her beauty had made time stand still. For a moment, she just stood there wondering when she would wake from this dream.

"Well, what do you think, Alexis?" Grandma asked.

She gazed upon her beautiful dress and slippers, watching as a million stars sparkled in the fabric of her dress. She was speechless. The arms that had suddenly felt as if they had been squeezed into tin cans were covered with a silver, translucent material that Alexis could not identify. On each wrist was a bracelet made of three connected but distinctive bands. The top piece of the bracelet on her right wrist was a single gold band; the middle was platinum inlaid with a diamond about one inch in diameter; the final band was made of a material she had never seen before. Something about this third band was very peculiar. It played tricks on the mind. It changed from one precious stone to another so quickly that her eyes lost focus. There didn't seem to be rhyme or reason for the changes. On her left wrist was a similar bracelet, but the middle band was different. It had an antique watch exactly the same size as the diamond.

The bodice of her gown was a beautiful pink, silky fabric that shimmered even without the presence of light. It was soft, like the way she imagined clouds felt. The pearls sewn into the round neckline of her gown felt like stones around her neck, but they didn't weigh the dress down. Layer upon layer of purple silk chiffon ribbons, sewn into the braided silver band around her waist, hung unevenly just above her ankles. She tried to push her leg through the strips, but the unexplainable resistance of the silk weighed heavy against her knee.

Grandma caressed the fabric of the gown. "Ahh, silk," she cooed. "Did you know it's stronger than steel?"

THE CHILDREN OF PROPHECY

"I don't care what it's stronger than," Alexis replied in a songlike voice. "It's the most beautiful dress in the world." Alexis turned from the mirror to give Grandma a hug.

Grandma stroked the edges of Alexis's face as if touching a fragile, newborn chick. "Someday, my beautiful baby, you will need it to be strong as steel, and I will need you to be even stronger."

Before Alexis could ask the meaning of Grandma's words, Grandma guided her towards the old schoolhouse painting that hung above the couch. Framed in white, it came alive because of the two-inch matted strip of periwinkle that pulled the purple from the evening sky. Just inside the periwinkle, a thin strip of burgundy red caused the pink glow from the streetlamp to jump at Alexis. Bordering the edges of painting lay a one-inch white matte with words written at the bottom in beautiful black scroll: *"The Way it Was,"* and under that, *1901 - 1939.*

Before then, Alexis had never noticed the lady who was painted inside the snowman. She strained to see the faint image of the woman's tender smile. A tingling stirred in her heart, as if the lady was smiling just for her. Looking more closely, she discovered the faint image of a second woman in the street lamp smiling in the same endearing way. The tingling grew, and to Alexis's surprise, the smiles made her feel loved.

She had looked at this painting a hundred times, and still, she felt like she was seeing it for the first. Alexis had never noticed the slightly unfurled flag in the center of the painting, and there were more buildings than she remembered. Behind the No. 3 horse-drawn school bus, there was clearly an old white house, and a barn that she didn't remember. How could she have missed them? Most of the barren trees surrounding the house were not covered with ice, but the branches in the front, framing the painting, seemed a prisoner to it. The windows on the second floor of the old schoolhouse cast the glow of a fireplace, but the first floor windows were dark. *Why wouldn't there be a bell in the schoolhouse bell tower?* She wondered.

Was she imagining it, or were Debbie and Lightning waiting for her as they patiently stood hitched to the No. 3 school bus? Debbie's pure white mane was a stunning contrast to her majestic black coat. Her eyes stared straight forward, waiting for the call she had been born to hear. At any moment, "Giddy up," would cause her muscular build to jettison forward as if she were light as a feather.

Only the thunder of her hooves would give claim to her massive structure. Her snow-white partner, Lightning, stared back at Alexis, anxious for the command to be given. He was more than a coach puller. This enormous, pure white steed was a born fighter. Pulling this coach kept him in shape for the battles to come.

"They're always here waiting for us," Grandma whispered, as if hearing Alexis's thoughts.

While she looked into the painting, Alexis could feel herself being drawn in. Every molecule in her body jiggled as she transported through the glass. The cold of the winter night chilled her, and she gave an involuntary shake.

"There is a cloak waiting for you on the bus," Grandma said.

Confused and excited, Alexis said, "Grandma, when I passed through the glass, the molecules in my body seemed to change shape!"

"I thought I was the only one who could feel the change inside a transporter," Grandma said. "Never ever stop inside a transporter. There is no telling what you'll look like when you get to the other side."

"There are more of these?"

"Many more," Grandma replied, "and they're not all paintings, which can make them hard to find."

"Well then, how do you know how to find one?" Alexis asked.

"You know that feeling you felt when we moved into the painting?

Alexis nodded.

"Did it feel familiar?"

"Yes," Alexis said.

"Some people call it déjà vu. They think they've been here before, or felt this before, but they're just standing close to a transporter," Grandma said as a matter of fact.

"Then why don't they get sucked in like we just did?"

"Because they don't have a key," Grandma replied.

"What key?

"The ones in our swords," Grandma replied.

"We don't have swords," Alexis said.

"Yes we do."

"I don't see them." Alexis looked around with skepticism upon her face.

"You will when we need them," Grandma stated with absolute certainty.

They boarded the horse-drawn school bus, Alexis heard "Giddy up," and instantly they were airborne, leaving the snowy scene behind.

Flying high above the city, and still higher above the clouds, felt exhilarating. In no time at all, they were past the city and above the mountains. Things were moving ever so fast, but they were slow enough for Alexis to enjoy the journey with Grandma.

The horse-drawn school bus in the painting only had six windows on each side. Once inside, Alexis couldn't explain the full, fluffy couches of every color lining the many windows. Grand curtains hung, allowing the passengers to open, close, or enclose themselves at will. Alexis sat on a bright yellow couch in the back of the bus. Not being able to resist testing the curtains, she pulled and they encircled her like the kind you find in hospital emergency rooms. She was surprised when she opened the curtains, and there stood a woman seeming perturbed by Alexis's curious nature.

"Miss, I am the flight attendant. Can I interest you in a drink or a snack?" the attendant asked.

Alexis twisted her fingers and tried to avoid eye contact when she peeped back, "No thank you."

"Well then, if you change your mind, you can assist yourself in the dining car behind this door." The attendant pointed to a door that appeared to be freestanding. "In addition, you should know that if we come under attack, it is advised that you use your seatbelt." Seatbelts appeared on all the couches and then quickly disappeared. "Weapons can be found under your seat. In the event of an emergency, I will return for battle in full armor. Have a good flight." The attendant paused for a moment when she saw Grandma. "GranMa . . . I didn't know you were on this flight. Always a pleasure to see you."

"Thank you. And it's a pleasure to see you, too."

The attendant exited through the freestanding door. Alexis was quick to steal a peek inside.

"Wow, Grandma, that was interesting; a room inside a room!"

"Well, sort of," Grandma replied. "Don't worry about the attack thing. It rarely happens."

"Final destination!" the bus driver yelled from his seat in the front of the bus. He tugged the reins on the horses to slow them down.

The horses pulled in their wings that neatly tucked under their coats. Alexis couldn't figure out how the wings could be hidden this way since they were at least as large as the horses. And how was it they could fly so close together and not flap each other with their wings? Alexis scratched her head. The only thing she was certain of was that Bus No. 3 had landed.

The bus driver pulled the bus to a complete stop. A handsome cowboy riding a dark brown and black horse approached. "Whoa, Bump!" the cowboy instructed his horse. "Stanley, get away from those hooves or Lightning and Debbie will trample you into meat for tonight's stew!" he yelled to his constant companion, a golden retriever who had a small, brown, stuffed teddy bear in her mouth.

A sheriff's badge hung on the left side of the cowboy's vest, just above his heart. Like his horse, he was dressed in brown and black. His cowboy hat and long leather coat were black, but his chaps, vest, scarf, and boots were brown. His dark brown eyes, long hair, and beard complimented his disheveled good looks. There was something familiar about the aging cowboy, but Alexis couldn't put her finger on it. The chaps had large silver studs embedded all the way down the outside of both legs. The unique chaps were familiar too, but where had she seen them?

"Howdy, GranMa. I'm surprised to see you've brought Alexis since she's getting so old. Don't imagine she'll be making too many of these trips."

"Oh, Papa, don't count her out yet. There are many of us in *This World* who are much older than Alexis."

"Don't imagine there are too many in Diggory Town older than thirty-eight." Carroll "Papa" Whittaker chuckled. "Alexis, *This World* is full of surprises."

But Papa wasn't telling Alexis anything she hadn't already figured out. During descent, Alexis had noticed a drastic change in scenery. She could no longer be in sunny San Diego, that was for sure. Red, gold, and brown plateaus reached high above the ground. Then, without warning, she'd found herself descending into a deep crevasse. If playing with the curtains on the bus was her first mistake, then asking Grandma to explain where they were was her second.

"Grandma, are we in the Grand Canyon?"

"No, dear, we are in Gran Canyon," Grandma replied.

"That's what I said—Grand Canyon."

"Oh, sorry dear." Grandma smiled. "I thought you said Grand Canyon. In which case, we are not in Grand Canyon, we are in Gran Canyon."

"Grandma, that's what I said, *Grand Canyon*. I think, or maybe I'm saying it wrong. Maybe it is *Gran* Canyon." Alexis furrowed her brows. "Grandma, what are we talking about? Gran Canyon or Grand Canyon? I don't even know what it's called anymore."

"Well, if we are in *This World*, we are talking about the Gran Canyon, and if we are talking about *That World*, we are talking about the Grand Canyon. Since we are in *This World*, we are talking about the Gran Canyon."

"Grandma, I still don't know *what* we are talking about!"

"I know you don't, but soon you will. It is no accident that you are confused. In order to protect *This World* from *That World*, and *That World* from *This World*, we had to make things confusing. If someone were to accidently happen upon *This World*, it could be very dangerous for them. And if the evil of *This World* could easily find its way to *That World*, there is no telling how much harm could come to The World of People. We were chosen to protect the people of *That World*. If you are confused, or imagine that this is a dream, then Mimi did her job. Your Great GranMother created the security that exists between these two worlds. Eventually, you will not be confused. Eventually, if you have been chosen, you will understand."

"Grandma, are The World of People and *That World* the same place?" Alexis asked.

"Yes they are. See, you are already beginning to understand. By the way, in *This World*, I am GranMa, because in *This World* nothing is grand, not even grandchildren. In *This World*, everything is special, and one thing is not better than the other. Like there is no such thing as children and adults; you are either grown or still growing."

"Ohhh! So are we in *This World*?" Alexis asked, as if she had any idea what GranMa was talking about.

"We are at the gateway. Diggory Town is the center of *This World*," GranMa replied.

Alexis muttered under her breath. "Love her, but she's a nut." GranMa grinned without responding because, unlike in *That World*, in *This World*, GranMa could hear a pin drop.

Suddenly, Alexis's face lit up. "Papa! You are *my* Papa. You are GranMa's granfather. She flung her arms around the waist of the cowboy. "I love you, Papa." It surprised GranMa when the man not prone to demonstrations of affection, wrapped his arms around Alexis, rested his cheek on the top of her head, and closed his eyes. GranMa took in the moment before she interrupted.

"Papa, can you get us to the transport? I want to give Alexis a quick peek into Diggory Town." GranMa had waited a long time to share Diggory Town with her GranChildren. Tingling with anticipation and excitement, she could barely stay in her own skin. This was the beginning of prophecy.

"There have been a lot of disturbances. The Skelly has been quiet since the great Battle of Trafleka, but after all this time, he needs to be revitalized. I suspect the disturbances are coming from him." Papa shrugged. "I can get you to the transport, but I can't guarantee your safety.

"We'll go." GranMa was comfortable with this decision, but Alexis was not.

Alarmed, Alexis asked, "GranMa, do I get a say?"

"Of course you do, honey." GranMa smiled and smoothed Alexis's hair. "We'll have plenty of time to hear what you have to say on the way to Diggory Town."

Alexis could see GranMa's belly jump as GranMa fought back a laugh. She knew there was no point arguing, so she got back on the bus with GranMa.

In no time at all, they were standing outside the transport. Nothing eventful happened along the way. But now, Alexis could feel déjà vu. She stretched out her hands to find the entry to the transporter.

GranMa and Papa just stood back and watched.

"Do you think she'll find it?" Papa whispered.

"She's bright; likes to figure things out by herself," GranMa replied. "My guess is she won't give up until she does."

"How long you gonna let her fumble around?"

"Until she gets it," GranMa replied with her eyes fixed on Alexis's every movement. "I have to know how developed her instincts and powers are before I can let her exercise them."

Alexis closed her eyes and let déjà vu guide her to the transport. With arms outstretched, she extended both hands across the rock wall and began to be absorbed into the mass. She searched as if her eyes were open.

"Fantastic," Papa mumbled under his breath. "I don't think I've ever seen instincts like this."

GranMa's chest swelled with joy. Alexis was one of the Children of Prophecy.

Chapter 3   The Princess Dress

More than anything, Alexis wanted to take her brother, Noah; sister, Isabel; and cousin Michael, to Diggory Town. But days and weeks went by and Alexis kept her promise. She never uttered a word of the things she had seen with GranMa. She was bursting at the seams wanting to tell of her great adventures. But she feared the potential consequences GranMa had warned her about. The evil that wished to conquer Diggory Town could go wherever Diggory Town existed. Mere mention of Diggory Town in *That World* would give cause for evil to escape into it. The only way to keep the evil contained was to not mention it in other worlds. For safety's sake, Diggory Town was referred to as *This World,* and the world where Alexis grew up was referred to as *That World,* or The World of People. There was no better way to keep the evil of Diggory Town confined to Diggory Town. Unfortunately, wagging tongues filled with chitchat were harder to contain than the evil those wagging tongues sometimes produced. For that reason, it was very important to heed GranMa's advice and say nothing.

Before leaving Diggory Town, GranMa had cupped Alexis's chin in her hand, making sure she had her full attention. "We diminish our chance to conquer evil if we have to chase it through multiple worlds. For the safety of those we love, we must never utter anything of Diggory Town in *That World.* Such a grave error could doom humanity." GranMa had put just enough fear into Alexis to keep her from wagging her tongue.

Over the next few months, Alexis and GranMa made several trips between the worlds, always using Bus No. 3. With each trip GranMa learned more about Alexis's skills, and Alexis learned a little more about patience.

One day, GranMa calmly announced, "Alexis, it is time to take the children on an adventure."

Alexis could feel the tingling of anticipation. Finally, she would have someone to share her adventures, bewilderment, and excitement. A ball of knots formed in her stomach.

"When can we take them?" she asked.

"Right now," GranMa replied.

"Now! Without any notice or preparation? I need to get organized and plan how we'll do it. Figure out what they'll wear. There is plenty to do before we take them to Di . . . "

GranMa quickly cupped her hand over Alexis's mouth, almost choking her. "Unless you are prepared to pull your sword and save this family, I suggest we calm down and remember some words can never be spoken here. If you are not cautious, Alexis, I will have to remove any thoughts of *This World* from your brain for all time." GranMa was stern with Alexis, which had never happened before. GranMa let her hand slip from Alexis's mouth and then flattened and patted her clothes.

Head down and hands clasped in front of her, Alexis whispered, "I'm very sorry, GranMa."

"I know you are, Alexis, but please understand; I must take swift action if The World of People is compromised. They are innocents and we cannot let them be harmed. This is a lot to ask of a ten-year-old girl, but soon your responsibilities will become even greater. I must know that you can handle them, or I must remove you from the responsibility."

"What does that mean, GranMa?" Alexis felt her air passage constricting as a constant drum began pounding in her ears. "'Remove me from '*the responsibility*.' Does it mean what I think it means?"

"Yes. I will have to end your existence in the other place. Life will go on as usual for you in The World of People, and you will remember nothing of the other world. I know it is harsh, but it must be so that I can protect everyone, including you." GranMa turned her head so that Alexis could not see her eyes. "Try not to judge me too harshly. Being responsible is not an easy job, but it is necessary. I will do what I have to do to protect you, and everyone else I love."

"GranMa, look at me." GranMa looked upon the beautiful child's face. "We are a team now. I will do better, and someday, because *we* have overcome evil, you will leave *This World* of old age." Alexis couldn't contain the smile that stretched from one ear lobe to the other.

"I am very proud of you." GranMa pulled Alexis close to her and kissed her forehead. "Let's get the kids."

"Not yet, GranMa, I have one more concern. We're always home alone when you take me through the painting. When our parents and GranPa get home from playing golf, I'm pretty sure they'll notice we're missing."

"Don't worry about that. Alexis. We use apparitions to replace you. They're not perfect, but they do a good-enough job."

"Aren't apparitions ghost?"

"That's what most people think. Ours are life-like with flesh and bones, but they are not you, and yet, they are you." Grandma opened the door to her office and yelled down the stairs. "Who wants to go on an adventure?"

This usually meant it's story time, which all the children loved, but story time didn't compare with playing outside, or watching videos.

"No inside!" two-year-old Noah moaned from the backyard. "I play outside!"

Michael shouted from the living room, "I just want to finish watching Superman cartoons!"

And with a sound so sweet it could have sucked the sour out of a lemon, Isabel's voice rose from the living room. "I comin, GranMa. Michael won't let me watch *Princess and the Pauper*. I don't like him today, GranMa!" She had always called Grandma, "GranMa," almost as if she knew something was different about *Grandma*.

"Will you like him tomorrow?" Grandma asked.

"I fink so," the sweet voice responded, and Grandma smiled.

Soon, Grandma could hear the little stompings of Isabel's feet coming up the stairs. Isabel wanted to make a thunderous noise, but there is only so much noise you can make when you are only three. "I comin, GranMa," Isabel repeated, as if she thought Grandma had already forgotten. "You want me to get Noah?"

"That would be nice, Isabel. Thank you!" Grandma replied, and the stomping feet changed direction.

"Whaa whaa, leave me lone, leave me lone. Whaaaaaa!"

"What's going on?" Grandma called down to anyone who would answer.

From the second floor railing, Grandma could see Michael lying backwards on the oversized chair, watching television upside down. Michael's eyes shot in the direction of Isabel and Noah. "Isabel is dragging Noah by his arm on the floor." *BUMP! BUMP!* "Now they're going up the stairs."

"Oh, for crying out loud!" Grandma exclaimed as she headed down the stairs.

Alexis stayed at the top of the stairs giggling. She thought it so funny that Grandma could control an army, but she couldn't get a two-year-old, three-year-old, and five-year-old to come up the stairs.

"Michael, get up these stairs! I'm going to show you real life super heroes or I'm going to put you in time out! What is your preference?" Grandma wasn't usually agitated by anything.

Michael came running up the stairs and knocked over Noah, who had just managed to get on his knees. Grandma showed up in the nick of time to catch him.

"I helped you good, huh, GranMa?" Isabel's deep, brown, walnut sized eyes stared up at Grandma, awaiting praise.

"Of course you did," Grandma said as her agitation melted at the sight of Isabel's brown curly locks and bright smile. "Now let's go on an adventure, and later we'll teach you how to brush your messy hair."

"I like it messy, GranMa!" Isabel said as she tousled her curls.

"Of course you do." Grandma smiled

Getting the toddlers into her office was similar to herding cats, and once she got them there, that was when the fun began.

"Can I do it, Grandma?" Alexis asked.

This only started the pushing and chanting.

"I want da do it!" Noah begged.

"I want da do it!" Isabel pleaded

"I want to do it!" Michael insisted.

It didn't matter what *they* were doing; they all wanted to do it.

"ONLY ALEXIS CAN DO IT!" Grandma spoke above the noise.

"Then I not doing!" Isabel complained, putting on a dramatic pout and crossing her arms.

"Then *you* . . . will not get a princess dress," Grandma retaliated.

Isabel perked up. There wasn't much a princess dress couldn't fix when you were a girl of three. But for Michael, a boy who'd just turned five . . . well you could count him out. Michael headed to the door.

"Of course there's always a sword and a horse if that's your preference." Grandma's words glued Michael's feet to the floor.

"A real sword?" he asked suspiciously.

"That's the only kind *I* like on an adventure," Grandma replied.

"I want futbal." Noah smiled.

"Warriors don't have footballs." Michael was certain of that little detail.

Still, Noah knew what he wanted, so he gave Michael a little shove as Grandma handed Noah a small foam football. Everyone was getting what they wanted.

"Okay, Alexis, let's get these guys out of here before they start the potty thing." Grandma knew what would come next if she didn't move fast.

"Okay, everyone, look into the painting," Alexis said, but no one listened. "Grandma, they're not listening to me!" she whined.

"Make them *want* to listen to you, Alexis. If you are going to be a leader, you have to give people a reason to follow you. Barking orders isn't a sign of leadership. A *good* leader is followed because people feel a need to follow them, and not because they have to. Now think about how you can get them to *want* to follow you," Grandma instructed.

Alexis didn't like Grandma's lectures, and she *really* didn't like them when Grandma was right. She tried again. "Anyone who wants to pet the horsies has to tell me the colors of the horsies' eyes."

"I wanna pet the horsies!" Isabel said.

"No, I pet horsies!" Noah shoved.

"Oh brother," Michael said, then crossed his arms.

Alexis was determined to outfox these kids. "Well I'm definitely not taking Michael to pet the horsies because he thinks I'm making this up, so I guess he gets left behind. Noah and Isabel are talking instead of *doing*, so I guess they get left behind too. I guess I'm the only one who gets to pet the horsies." Alexis knew people always wanted what they couldn't have, even small people. Suddenly, these small people were intently trying to figure out the colors of the horsies' eyes.

"Coold, cooold, burrrr, cold, cold!" Noah moaned.

"Come to GranMa. I forgot you can't weather-transition yet." Everyone had made it through the transport.

Noah nuzzled into her neck and arms as GranMa wrapped her cloak around him. "Cold, cold, cold, Grandma," Noah said, shivering.

"Noah, here you call me GranMa."

"O-kay," Noah said with his sweet baby voice.

"Hey, I'm co . . . HEY! GranMa, how come I don't have a princess dress like you and Alexis?" Isabel was indignant. Being cold was not nearly as important as being a princess.

"Michael, approach those horses from the front so they know you're there! I don't want them kicking you!" GranMa shouted. "Isabel, give GranMa a minute and we'll get you a princess dress. As a matter of fact, we'll get you the best one."

"Okay, GranMa." Isabel just wanted to make sure she was being treated fairly, especially since they were talking about a princess dress.

Michael walked up to the black horse. "GranMa, this is Debbie, but she has a white mane."

GranMa halted as if she had run into a glass wall. She had forgotten that, since Michael was about two, he had told her many times of his imaginary pet: "I have a horse and her name is Debbie, and she's black." As far as GranMa knew, Michael had never been to Diggory Town. It never occurred to GranMa that Michael might have known what he was talking about. She thought he was just fantasizing, or perhaps had overheard his mother speak of Debbie.

"Michael, have you ever been here before?" GranMa wasn't sure she wanted to know the answer to that question.

"I think so." Suddenly he was speaking in a voice well beyond his years. "I think I may have gone into battle with this horse. But I don't remember her having a white mane."

Debbie rubbed her head on Michael's arm—a sure sign they had been linked in battle. Linking was what happened when you fought wars with another being and you became bonded as one. GranMa felt certain Michael had been here before, but what did he know, and who did he fight for? GranMa wasn't sure what to make of this.

"Okay, let's get my babies on this bus. You do want to see more don't you?" GranMa was getting everyone excited. Everyone, that is, except for Noah, who had managed to wiggle himself out of GranMa's arms. He was staring into the second floor of the school.

"Come on, Noah, we need to be going. What are you doing?" GranMa asked.

"I looking at da man in windo," Noah replied.

"Oh really . . . what's he doing?" GranMa asked.

"Nuttin," Noah responded.

GranMa watched for a moment, but saw nothing. "Where is he, Noah?"

"I don't know. He dis-da-peered." Noah shrugged.

"Okay, Noah, wave ba-bye. We have to be going."

"O-kay. Ba-bye." Noah waved.

As they flew away, GranMa kept a close eye on the second floor. She didn't tend to the children until the school building was well out of sight.

Controlling the children on the bus was a lot like controlling marbles on a spinning board.

"I want the blue couch!"

"No! *I* want the blue couch!"

"Then I want green!"

"You know I wanted the green!"

"I take lellow!"

"No, Noah! Yellow is mine!"

In the chaos, GranMa couldn't figure out who was shouting what.

"ENOUGH!" Alexis shouted.

The children stopped at the sound of her thunderous voice. GranMa smiled.

"You." Alexis pointed at Michael. "You look like the blue couch. Go sit over there; and that will always be your couch."

Although he had just been arguing over the blue couch, Michael pouted. "I don't like blue."

"Really? Huh? Blue is the color of the sky and the ocean. It symbolizes truth, peace, faithfulness, and loyalty," Alexis said. "Some Native Americans believe it is a symbol of great intuition. Policeman wear blue and great leaders have worn blue. I'm surprised you don't want it, but okay, Noah . . ."

"NO! I'll take it!" The words left Michael's mouth like a bullet train. He strutted over to the couch as if he were the ruler of the universe.

"You!" Alexis pointed an authoritative finger at Isabel. "You will get the pink couch. Pink is the color of love, and is a mixture of red and white. Red is the color of warriors, and white is the color of innocence and purity. Very responsible people wear white like doctors, nurses, and angels. You will fight with a warrior's heart, but have the compassion of angels."

Isabel pouted. "I just want to be a princess."

"Oh yeah, and pink is also a princess color," Alexis pointed out.

Isabel smiled as she tiptoed to her couch like a princess.

Noah sat cross-legged at Alexis's feet, waiting to see what his color would be.

"You, hmm . . . let me think about this one." Alexis tapped her finger to her lips. "What color is powerful and thoughtful? You are orange. Orange is red and yellow mixed together—warrior courage and a cheerful thinker. Orange is said to stimulate great thinking. I think you will not be afraid to fight, but you will want to solve problems with words to avoid bloodshed. Yes, you are most definitely orange."

"O-kay." Noah could not have cared less.

Alexis went to the yellow couch.

GranMa bent over and whispered in Alexis's ear, "Besides cheerful thinker, what else does yellow symbolize?"

Alexis's cupped her hand over GranMa's ear. "I don't know. I just *like* it."

"In the Asian culture, they believe it is a color that opposes evil." GranMa walked away smiling. Her Alexis was growing. As GranMa sat down on the red couch, she looked to the vacant green one. Natural and calming green that symbolized growth, renewal, and immortality; it was the color of the future. Green was the seat that *must* be filled. But what to make of the aubergine couch, she didn't know. Aubergine—a deep purple mixed from brown, blue, and red.

"Alexis, how do you make the color brown?" GranMa asked.

"You mix the primary colors together."

GranMa's attention was taken away from the empty seats by the flight attendant who had just appeared in the room. She looked into the small precious faces and said, "Oh brother! Do whatever GranMa tells you to do." She threw her hands into the air and walked out the freestanding door as the flight continued.

"GraaaaanMaaaa," Isabel sang.

"What, my precious princess?" GranMa sang back.

"I don't look like the best princess in this dress." Isabel beamed, and raised her hopeful eyes.

GranMa smiled as she gazed upon Isabel's bright eyes and ragged, over-worn, red velvet, ballerina/princess Minnie Mouse dress from last Christmas. "I like your favorite Minnie Mouse princess dress, but I guess it is time for a new one. What kind of dress would be the best kind of princess dress?"

"Ooh, ooh, I know! I know!" Alexis chimed in, wildly waving her hand in the air.

"Everyone gets to design their own princess dress, Alexis," GranMa said.

"Oh darn . . . " Alexis said with a snap of her fingers.

"Close your eyes and dream, Izzy," GranMa instructed her. "Dream of the best princess dress you can think of."

Isabel's pink little cheeks blossomed as she closed her eyes and widened her smile. Little billows of smoke began to swirl around her as her feet became laced in shimmering pink boots. She seemed to dance above the floor as her red Minnie Mouse princess dress transformed into a gown made in shades of yellow and pink. The pale yellow silk puffy sleeves flowed over her shoulders, then tightened on her forearms. The bodice clung to her ribs and tiny waist while yellow silk drifted down the middle front and back of her gown. The sides flowed pale pink, darkening to a brilliant silvery pink as the color spilled into the bottom of her formal dress. The skirt of the gown was tethered to a silver waistband, and elbow guards of the same odd silver, translucent material found on Alexis's gown circled each elbow. Dangling from the waistband, and hanging just atop the flowing skirt of the garment, were shimmering snowflake jewels that appeared to be painted with stardust. They hung unevenly from strings made of diamonds. No better princess dress could exist in all of the worlds.

But it was not enough that her dress be stunning. Her hands were covered with beautiful gloves made from the same strange silver, translucent material. Her pink princess boots sparkled just like Dorothy's *Wizard of Oz* shoes, except Isabel's shoes were pink and glowed yellow. Yet nothing was more perfect than her crown and scepter. *These* were the telltale markings of a real princess.

"Open your eyes, Isabel," GranMa whispered into her ear.

Isabel sucked in a great breath of air as she looked down at her feet. "Do I look beautiful?" she asked.

GranMa rang for the flight attendant. "Could we have a mirror, please?"

The attendant opened one of the curtains to expose a full-length mirror. Isabel sucked in another breath of air. Her three-year-old voice squeaked, "I am pretty! Look at my beautiful hair." In disbelief, she touched her dark brown curls piled on top of her head. The crown of diamonds woven into her hair caused a special glow on her radiant locks. She was perfect in her majesty when she looked into the flight attendant's eyes, curtsied, and said, "Ta-dah!"

"You look amazing," the usually curt flight attendant commented.

"May I please have a red princess dress too, GranMa? I love red."

"Yes, Isabel, you may have a red dress too. However, when it comes to matters of court, you must always wear this dress. Promise me you will."

"Okay, GranMa, but I want to wear this dress now so we can make the red dress later."

"Okay, Izzy," GranMa said.

"I need a new designer," the flight attendant said before she went out the freestanding door.

Chapter 4   The Arrival

The excitement built as each child became comfortable on their own beloved couches. Little tushies fitting perfectly and fidgeting endlessly as they sat in their own special places, anxiously watching the world go by. Even Noah, who was only two-years-old, knew most buses didn't fly. And as young as he was, he knew destiny awaited them just on the other side of mountains he could see in the distance.

The bus driver yelled back, "Everyone put on your seatbelts; we need to gain altitude if we're to get over those mountains! HIGHER! HIGHER!" GranMa liked his cheery, calming attitude, coupled with his big voice.

They rose over the mountains, but soon they were descending into the crevasse. Papa met them at the usual spot.

"GranMa! GranMa! I think I see Papa and Stanley!" Michael said. Besides Alexis, Michael was the only GranChild old enough to remember their adored great great granfather, and his beloved dog, Stanley. "You told me they died and went to heaven."

"They died in *That World*, Michael. They serve in *This World*. I also told you we were going on an adventure to see real super heroes. Understand that things are not the same here as in The World of People. You will need to open your mind, and change your way of thinking. I know you like rules, but in this place, the rules are different, so you are going to have to think differently. Can you do that?"

"Is it a rule that I do it?" Michael asked.

"Yes, it is," GranMa replied

"Then I can do it." Michael smiled.

Michael felt confused and invigorated. His belly was doing somersaults and his brain seemed to grow two sizes as he fidgeted and shuffled his feet. "GranMa, I'm so excited. This is much better than the cartoons I was watching!" Michael's voice returned to that of a five-year-old. "I'm going to learn all the rules, all of them!"

"That's my boy!" GranMa said, giving him a generous hug. "Now tell me how you know Debbie. I think she likes you."

Michael responded, "I don't know how she knows me, GranMa. She sure is pretty, and I know she likes me. She *told* me she likes me."

"Debbie talks to you?" GranMa had never heard of a talking horse. Not even in Diggory Town.

"Don't be silly, GranMa, horses don't talk. She thinks to me." Michael's round hazel eyes lit up as a grin spread across his face. He felt proud to have a friend like Debbie. GranMa did not ask another question, because she wanted Michael to be five for just a little longer. Soon, he would be doing things that were well beyond his years. As long as there was calm, she would get the information she needed gradually. Still, knowing Debbie could communicate with Michael through thoughts caused her alarm. She only knew of one other who could communicate in such a way.

Papa yelled into Bus No. 3, "You ready in there, GranMa?"

She hollered back once she got to her couch. "As ready as a bus filled with babies can be!"

"Fair enough!" Papa chuckled as Bus No. 3 lifted back into the air.

Once airborne, the children could not believe what they were seeing. Papa guided them past world after world, their heads turning left and right to see the faint imagines of distant worlds in the walls of the Gran Canyon.

"I think I saw Superman!" Michael screeched.

"Ah, the world of super heroes." GranMa smiled. "That just might be my favorite, besides Diggory Town of course."

"I see Belle and Cinderella!" Isabel could hardly get the words out she was so excited.

"Hooooly cow . . . " Michael murmured while rubbing his temples in a search for reality. "I think I just saw Hogwarts."

"I think I just saw Michael Jordon and Hank Aaron." Noah's voice could barely keep up with his thoughts. "What kind of world is that? These guys don't change the world! What are they going to do, fight evil by throwing a baseball or a basketball at it?"

The others couldn't believe Noah's mature speech pattern. He was a baby who could barely ask to go potty in The World of People. GranMa chuckled as she looked upon their stunned faces.

GranMa yelled to Papa and the bus driver, "Let's stop the bus for a minute!"

In a voice just above a whisper, GranMa said over Noah's shoulder, "Look closer and you will see Babe Ruth, Gretel Bergmann, Joe Louis the 'Brown Bomber,' Lou Gehrig, Tony Gwynn, Roberto Clemente, and Wilma Rudolph. There are a bunch of other sports heroes there too. Hey, there's Jesse Owens; he's one courageous man." GranMa knew all about them, and courage.

"Where are Ty Cobb, Lyle Alzado, or Barry Bonds? Are they in there?" Noah asked, while his siblings remained speechless and dumbfounded.

"Oh, they're in there," GranMa explained, "but they hang out with a *different* group of sports people."

Hardly believing baby Noah had a clue about these sports legends, Michael came to his senses. He asked GranMa, "Why is there a sports world here? I thought these are the worlds of *good* versus *evil*?"

"They are," GranMa replied. "These people and characters have taught The World of People much about good versus evil. Do you have any idea what risk Jesse Owens, a black man, took by going to the German Olympics in 1936 to stand up for what's right? Nazi Germany was no place for a black man during Hitler's reign. Maybe you didn't know that the boxer Joe Louis died with very little money because he was so generous and kind, he gave all his money away. What do you think the world learned about kindness from Beauty and the Beast? I could go on and on about sacrifices and lessons that have been learned from characters, sports legends, and super heroes, but we'll save this discussion for another time. We have much to do today. Okay, Papa, thank the bus driver for stopping, then let's get back on the trail to Diggory Town."

They hadn't noticed until they were about to started moving again, but when they stopped at the entrance to The World of Sports Heroes, the fog cleared. All the other worlds had dissipated and the only world that seemed to exist was Sports World.

Confused, Alexis asked, "GranMa, how come I never noticed these worlds before today?"

"First of all, we are usually moving too fast for your eyes to adjust to the opening of a cave. Secondly, the caves are normally closed like Diggory Town, so you may never see them again. They wouldn't be safe if they were revealed to all the worlds. Today was a special occasion because you are special children. These worlds are depending on you. Their futures lie in your hands."

"But GranMa . . . we're just kids," Alexis said.

"The greatest story ever told began with an infant," was all GranMa said.

Mounted on Bump, Papa reached over and grabbed the leads of the horses pulling the bus. "Is Stanley up there with you?" Papa asked the bus driver.

"Yup, lying under my feet as usual!" the bus driver replied.

"Then we're ready to take off," Papa said, looking left and then right as if he were looking for something very specific. "Ah, there it is," he said. "Come on, you two, let's get this bus back on the path." With that, he led the horses that pulled Bus No. 3 through the hazy circle. All at once, they were back in the haze moving down the Gran Canyon toward Diggory Town. It didn't take long before Bus No. 3 halted again.

Papa stepped inside. "Give me a minute, will you? I need to make sure we weren't followed." Papa hoisted himself back onto his horse, Bump, and in a flash, he was off. A few minutes later, he returned. "It's clear. Let's get you little whipper snappers into Diggory Town."

An eerie feeling surrounded the children as they left the comfort of their couches. GranMa's finger was pressed to her lips. "Shhh," she whispered. Everyone heeded GranMa's shushing, because everyone but Alexis was expecting monsters. And they weren't sure if the monsters were good or bad.

Chapter 5   The Cave of the Tired Souls

Alexis spread her hands across the rocks and they entered Diggory Town.

"GranMa, we don't look right," Michael observed of himself and Noah as the people of Diggory Town scurried along their way in clothing appropriate for *This World*. Dressed for their day's work, not all were in formal regalia. Many were farmers, blacksmiths, merchants, and the like, yet somehow, Michael's lighted Spider-Man shoes, jeans, and Spider-Man t-shirt still didn't fit in.

"Oh, of course, I should have dressed you properly on the bus," GranMa remarked. "Let's see, how does a young king look?"

"Ooh, ooh, I know, I know," Alexis said with flailing arms and hands.

"All right, Alexis, what do you think?" GranMa was ignoring the "everyone designs their own clothes" rule.

"Well, they usually have on yellow tights, and shoes that curl at the toes and perhaps have bells at the tips. They have fluffy shirts that are tucked into a belt, and they have big fat bellies, and a cloak with fur all around the edges." Her raised eyebrows and upturned lips teased Michael.

Michael grimaced. "GranMa said '*young* king,' not stupid looking king. GranMa, I'd rather wear a dress than Alexis's king's clothes."

Everyone, including Michael, laughed at the idea of seeing Michael with bells on his toes.

"All right then, a sword and sheath it is," GranMa said.

Michael began to fade behind a swirl of smoke as GranMa worked her magic. When the smoke lifted, a handsome noble prince emerged, dressed in a tight fitted long leather vest covering an oversized linen shirt. The black pants tucked into plain black, knee high leather boots that made him look more man than boy. Dagger straps, more functional than decorative, were built into the top of his boots. But it was the broadsword that hung in the sheath on his belt that gave him real distinction. Up the sides of his britches and down the front of his vest were steel studs like the ones on Papa's clothes. Michael didn't know it yet, but he had been outfitted for full battle.

"You are not quite a prince and not quite a king. Someday, you may be worthy of both titles," GranMa remarked.

Michael was pleased with the suit GranMa had created for him. In spite of his normally humble manner, he couldn't help but walk with the full chest confidence of a knight, or a warrior king.

Noah couldn't have cared less that GranMa had outfitted him in yellow tights and shoes that curled at the toes with bells at the tips. Wearing the fluffy white shirt covered by a cloak with fur around the edges, made him look like a marshmallow stuffed into a cookie.

"GranMa, that's not very nice," Alexis whispered.

"I know, but it *is* very funny. I'll fix it as soon as he complains."

"For his sake, I hope it's soon." Alexis giggled. "Where are we going?" she asked with the chime of little bells shuffling beside her.

"I'm taking them to The Cave of the Tired Souls. I want them to see Spencer and Tedde. I think it will be good on this first trip to keep them in familiar territory. They're still very young in *This World* and I don't want to scare them."

Michael's eyes were moving in every direction as they walked through the caves. Unlike Isabel and Noah, he knew this was *not* The World of People. "GranMa, what is this place?"

"This is Diggory Town," GranMa said with great pride, as if she had created the place herself. "It's the place where souls are made before they are sent to the infants in The World of People. In fact, it's the place where every soul is made for every world and universe, and you're going to help save it. It is why you are here."

"Me?" Michael asked.

"Yup . . . you, your brother, and your cousins, Alexis, Isabel and Noah. You're going to be heroes of epic proportion."

"Like Spider-Man?"

"Bigger than Spider-Man."

"Cool!" Michael said, but paused when it occurred to him, "GranMa, I don't have a brother."

"Oh, that's right. You don't."

The children were amazed at how the caves were transformed into cities, albeit small, old, medieval-looking cities. While some small areas seemed more Romanesque, others felt more contemporary. Buildings lined cobblestone and paved streets that sometimes gave way to dirt roads. Each neighborhood had its own influences similar to that of cities they had visited in New England. All and all, they had a feeling they belonged.

Finally, GranMa stopped outside a place that looked like a small mountain hidden inside the main chamber of the cave. Strangely, the mountain had a huge door with a rounded arch. Flanking each side of the door stood giant statues carved into the mountain. One of the statues was a handsome, muscular man, and the other a beautiful, muscular woman. Each had wings that rested upon their backs, but were only visible from their sides. They seemed alive, almost as if they were breathing and watching . . . but for what?

"Okay, this is it, The Cave of the Tired Souls. Any idea what happens in here?" GranMa asked.

"I fink peoples sleeps in here. I don't want to take a nap, GranMa!" Isabel declared.

"Then today you don't have to take a nap, Isabel. But someday, after training for a big battle, you are going to *want* to take a nap. You will be so tired that you won't be able to hold up your own head. Your arms will hurt and hang at your side as if they weighed as much as a mountain. Two of our bravest warriors will protect you while you sleep. Do you want to see who those warriors are?" GranMa asked.

"I do. I do. I do." The little ones all chimed in at once and jumped as high as their little legs would allow.

"Then we'll have to pull this very heavy door chime to get their attention." GranMa reached for the knob that had the face of a fierce lion, but before she could get her hands on the pull, Michael reached around and gave it a yank. A thick chain attached behind the lion's head rang the loud bell behind the door.

"That's not fair," Isabel insisted. "I wanted to pull it."

GranMa rolled her eyes at Alexis. "At least, in a few days, they will have grown and then maybe the nonsense will subside."

"Maybe," Alexis agreed, "but you have met Michael and Noah—the Kings of Nonsense."

"Point taken," GranMa conceded.

Within seconds, they heard, "HEY!" A voice pounded the air echoing in their brains. Their heads were touching their backs as they strained to look up into the face of the big voice.

"Very funny, Spencer! Get down here before I tell your mother you're goofing around on duty," GranMa threatened.

Instantly, Spencer was down to his normal size, which was still a whopping six foot four. "Auntie Dale, you'd never tell on me. I'm your favorite nephew."

"I'm sure your brothers will be glad to hear that, and don't be so sure about me telling your mother. Your mother and I are very close you know, and what's my name when we're in Diggory Town?"

"GranMa. Sweet, lovable, fearsome warrior, GranMa."

"You forgot adorable."

"Adorable," Spencer added.

"Mikey, you finally made it here. How do you like it?" Spencer asked. "It's pretty fascinating, isn't it? I love Diggory Town better than any place on Earth."

"Well, Spencer, this isn't *reeeally* Earth," Michael replied.

"Hahaha, you're such a stickler for details. I love that about you. You want to ride on my shoulders, or fly around between my wings?"

"Wings? You have wings?" Michael jumped up and down. "Yeah, yeah, I'll take a wing ride. Yikes! A wing ride!"

Spencer let one of his benevolent white wings slip out the side of his back just to give Michael a quick peek.

"He's such a show off!" Tedde, Spencer's sister, laughed as she appeared from nowhere.

"I'll see you in a minute. I need to give Michael a ride. Anyone else?" Spencer asked.

Isabel just hid behind GranMa's cloak. Noah violently shook his head no.

"No thanks, I'll wait until I can do it myself." Alexis was certain a pair of wings were coming her way soon.

"Okay, see you in a minute," Spencer said.

"Spencer, take him to see The Gates of the Fallen. Eventually, he will be responsible for securing them."

"No problem," Spencer replied.

"GranMa, it's so good to see you." Tedde embraced GranMa and gave her a kiss on the cheek. "Hi, you guys. How are you?" she asked the children.

"Where did you come from?" Alexis asked.

"Inside The Cave of the Tired Souls. You rescued Spencer from a merciless beating—we were playing chess. He always thinks he's going to beat me, but he never does."

"Are you the statues guarding the cave's entrance?" Alexis asked.

"Uh huh," Tedde replied

"So do you live in that statue?" Alexis asked. "Because it looks like it's alive."

"Yes, and it is," Tedde answered.

"So . . . how is it you are out here if you are living in the statue that is apparently alive?" Alexis could not wrap her brain around the idea.

"Crazy, huh? You're in Diggory Town. Forget what you think you know. That statue and me, we are one, but that statue needs me to live. I don't need it to live. It's the same with *This World* and *That World*; they exist in the same place in time, but they are different. I can exist without the statue, and the statue can exist without me, but it cannot be alive without me, so we are better together. If you die in *This World*, you will still live in *That World* and vice versa, but once again, they are better together."

"I think I'm finally getting it!" Alexis said. "Thanks!"

"My pleasure, but remember, learning takes time and patience. Shortcuts are not your friends when it comes to figuring this place out. Miss one thing and it could cost you your life."

"I'll try and remember that," Alexis said.

Spencer returned with Michael, whose face was red and chapped from the cold air pressing against his skin.

"That was great!" Michael said. "Will I get a set of wings like his?"

"We all get our own blessings, Michael," GranMa replied. "It is important to respect others' and appreciate our own. If we are too busy envying other people's blessings, we will not receive the gifts that our own blessings can bring. Trust me. Like everyone else, you will have fabulous blessings, but they may not be as obvious as wings."

Then GranMa turned to Spencer. "Can you take Noah and show him around? I need his skills to grow fast; his innocence will be dangerous to him here. He's powerful, even for a baby. Maybe you should start in the Hall of Warriors."

"I'd love to. C'mon, little buddy." Spencer took Noah by the hand.

"I love my brother." Tedde smiled at the sight of how gigantic he looked compared to her small cousin. His large body hunched to hold the tiny hand that would soon wield a sword. She felt it was a crime that such innocence would soon be stolen from both of them. "I wish he were more carefree, like our kid brother. Jackson doesn't worry like Spencer. Jackson just takes things at face value and then he deals with them. Spencer carries the weight of the universe on his wings."

"Perhaps that is why you love them so much," GranMa offered. "You love Jackson because of his lack of worry and his joyfulness, and Spencer because of his great concern for justice and tranquility. They are both admirable gifts."

"Yes, but Spencer's gifts harm him in *That World*," Tedde said.

"I know," GranMa agreed.

"How can they harm him?" Michael asked. "He's stronger and braver than anyone I know in any world."

GranMa chose each word carefully. "Spencer does not function as well in *That World*, but he is perfect in this one. I think his heart is too big for *That World*. He does not understand its wickedness. In *This World*, the evil is not hard to see, but in *That World*, it is masked in so many disguises. Even those who wear the cloak of goodness are sometimes bad, and our Spencer is sometimes confused by such deception."

"That doesn't make sense, GranMa. Spencer is a mighty warrior in *That World* too," Michael argued.

"I know," GranMa said. "But he is almost too good for *That World*. Because of his goodness, evil stalks him daily. He battles evil from the moment he wakes up until the moment he goes to sleep. I know he is your hero in *That World* and in *This World*; he is one of my heroes too. You need to understand that when he is there, he gets very little rest, which sometimes makes him weak. He cannot, and should not, use weapons in *That World*; it is against our law for him to do so. He must battle with his mind and with his heart, and those weapons are not always as strong as the steel in our swords."

"I don't understand. Why can't he use his sword and his powers in *That World*?" Michael asked.

"It is law and it is prophecy as defined by the Rule Book. In Diggory Town, good is good and evil is evil. He knows how to combat Diggory Town evil and he is good at it. But if he is to be part of prophecy, then he must understand the evil of both worlds. In *This World*, he must battle evil with power, but in *That World*, he must battle evil with wit. It is easier to swing a sword than it is to navigate in the treacherous waters of an immoral judicial system, or to function in a society that swims in the murky waters of unethical standards. Spencer is a perfect warrior here because his duty is clear, but in *That World*, things are uncertain and ambiguous."

"What is em-big-oo-us?" Isabel asked.

"I must try to remember that you are not fully grown, my little princess," GranMa replied. "*Am-big-u-ous* means that the directions are unclear, or something has two possible meanings so you can't figure it out."

"If your mother were here, she'd have you look it up in the dictionary." Alexis laughed. "She always makes me look things up in the dictionary."

"I can't read anything, not even the signs on the street." Isabel shrugged and wiggled her cute little shoulders.

"Someday, my little princess, you will read *all* the signs—every single one of them!"

Chapter 6   The Face of Evil

Weeks had gone by and the children shared with their friends fascinating stories of a magical place where children could be heroes. They spoke of riding horses with wings and swinging swords high over their heads. This place had princess dresses, castles, and temples where children were kings, queens, knights, or nothing at all. If you'd rather, you could live in caves, farm the land, or sail magnificent rivers. In this place, everyone was equal, and everyone was important. There was only one scary thing in this magical place, but they were not allowed to tell you what it was. Moreover, they were not allowed to tell you the name of *this place*.

"Really, Auntie, you *do* put crazy ideas into these kids' heads with your fantastical stories. Don't you worry that people outside the family will think our kids are crazy?" Amy asked Grandma.

"Of course they think our kids are crazy. Didn't they think you were crazy when I told you these wild stories? Isn't it a fact that everyone we know thinks our family is nuts?" Grandma asked her niece.

"Yes, they do think we're nuts," Amy agreed.

"So, sweetie, why do you think these same people are always hanging around our homes, coming to all our parties, and blending into our family any way they can?" Grandma asked.

"You got me, Auntie. I can't figure it out."

"It's because people love crazy. Crazy is fun. It isn't any more complicated than that. In our family, crazy is encouraged and appreciated. People need permission to let go of their worries and just be silly for a while. We give them that. When they are with us, they feel like kids again. Never underestimate the value of crazy." Grandma smiled.

"All I know is *I* love *this* crazy caboodle and so does everyone else." Amy chuckled.

"Then enough said. And remember, there was a time when you were part of my crazy stories too."

Amy lowered her voice. "I miss that time."

"Me too . . . " Grandma said with a broken heart, because between the two of them, only she understood what was really being said. Both her nieces, Amy and her sister Mindy, had died in Diggory Town, and GranMa stilled mourned their loss.

"I think it's time for more crazy. I'm going to go round up the kids." Grandma rose from the kitchen table, kissed Amy's forehead, and then shouted, "ANYONE WHO WANTS A GOOD STORY SHOULD GET IN MY OFFICE NOW!"

In a flash, the children were in her office staring into the painting above the fluffy, red couch. Once inside the painting, GranMa told the children, "Tedde says things are getting eerie. She can't put her finger on it, but things are not feeling right. She thinks there are saboteurs in our ranks."

"What does that mean?" Michael asked.

"She thinks there may be some warriors posing as friends, but who are really working for the enemy," GranMa replied.

"Can they get away with that? Wouldn't we know?" Isabel asked.

"They work with the same magic we work with, Isabel. If we can disguise ourselves, then they can disguise themselves. You've seen what we can do. Our only defense against magic of any kind is to use it better and use it for good, so that it remains little miracles. When they use the same magic for evil, it becomes someone's misery. Let's find Tedde and Spencer so they can help us figure out what's going on."

Once they got to The Cave of the Tired Souls, they found Tedde and Spencer standing at their post as always. Spencer began to describe late night disturbances, and things missing from the Court

Chamber and then suddenly reappearing. Things weren't making sense.

"Sometimes I can hear footsteps in the tunnels between caves but I don't see anyone," Spencer said. "Other times, when I scout The Great Beyond, I see people scurrying through the brush."

"So what?" Noah said. "People have a right to scurry."

Spencer gave a disappointed glance, and then knelt on one knee to be eye to eye with the little man. "The devil is in the details. Why would innocent people need to scurry? If you are going to be a great warrior, Noah, you need to observe the details. That is where you will find the truth about what's *really* happening. Be objective so that you are not derailed by your own experiences. When you are scouting, you must approach everything as if it were brand new. Do not let your own biases blind you to reality. Once you have collected the details, you can piece things together, and *only then* should you use your experience to make judgments. GranMa always says, 'Be careful of what it is you *think* you see.' These are words to live by. Until you have all the facts—the little details—you should assume nothing." Spencer stood, and the little man craned his neck, hoping Spencer would offer a more childlike explanation of what he meant. Spencer did not.

GranMa said, "You will do well to learn from Spencer. He is a great warrior, and his teachings will keep you alive."

Alexis was getting nervous with all this constant talk about "this will keep you alive" and "that will keep you alive." As far as she was concerned, they were just skirting the words "there's a good chance this will make you dead."

Michael was listening to Spencer, but watching GranMa. A curious little *thing* was flying around her ear and whispering something to her. It seemed to have come out from under GranMa's gown, or maybe just thin air. It was small like a pixie or a fairy, but it was dressed like a warrior with wings. *Hope*—it just popped into his head that her name was Hope, and she was almost one of a kind. How could she be *almost* one of a kind? Michael tapped his forehead with his long index and middle fingers. "Be careful of what it is you think you see." That's what Spencer had just said. He didn't have much time to wonder about these words before he was startled by a sound that could have wakened the dead.

GranMa reached inside her cape, pulled out her scepter, and raised it high in the air. It made a thunderous roar as she brought it back down to the cave floor. In an equally thunderous voice, GranMa called, "SENTURIES, GUARD YOUR POST!" Suddenly, GranMa floated several inches from the ground. Her regal gown was transposing into a suit of armor, and her scepter became a sword. The suit of armor was unlike anything Michael had ever seen. The silver threads on her forearms suddenly tightened as the jewels, like the ones on Isabel's gown only smaller, lined up vertically on the backside of her forearm just above her wrist. The material on her upper arms, chest, and legs changed into the same odd material found on Alexis and Isabel's gowns. A breastplate with the image of a woman with long, straight hair appeared on her chest, empowering her. Then the two large red jewels that were on the middle fingers of her gloves disappeared into the palms of her hands. The lion's head on the top of her scepter melted into the design in the handle of a magnificent sword. Appearing fiercer, his eyes narrowed, his jaw opened to show his dagger-like teeth, and he too prepared for battle.

Isabel began to shake. Stamping her feet and clenching her fists, she shouted at GranMa, "I can see it, I CAN SEE IT!"

Completing her transformation into a warrior, GranMa floated back to the ground. She rushed to Isabel, grabbed her arms, and knelt in front of her. "Calm down, Izzy, and tell GranMa what you see." Grandma's courage steadied Isabel's nerves. Her soothing voice caused Isabel to settle for a moment.

"He's riding on a white horse, but he is not a good guy, and the horse is not really white." Isabel whimpered as she tried to withdraw from the scene. "He wants me to think he's a good guy, but he's not!"

"What makes you think he is trying to deceive you?" GranMa asked as her brows furrowed and her eyes focused on Isabel's face. GranMa could not hide her concern over what Isabel was seeing. GranMa held tightly to Isabel's arms so that she could not withdraw.

Isabel began to shudder "I . . . I . . . can . . . I can just tell, GranMa. I can feel it! He's coming for me! He's . . . he's . . . he's coming for me, and he's going to destroy whatever gets in his way. He's looking at us. I think he can see through my eyes. He wants Noah and Alexis too! Oh no—no—no! He's looking for Auntie's baby! He doesn't know Auntie's baby hasn't been born yet." Isabel closed her eyes to protect her family from this horrid demon; but this put her face to face with an enemy who thirsted for her soul. This was the beginning of her long battle with The Skelly. Closing her eyes only put her closer to the grip of his evil power. She could feel herself being drawn into his darkness as he began to suck anything good or pure from her existence. GranMa's voice called her back.

"Tell me what he looks like, Izzy." GranMa's calm voice hid her concern for little Isabel's behavior, and what The Skelly might be doing to her precious GranChild. GranMa was not afraid to face this wicked demon. She had won many a battle with him. But in other battles, she never had so much to lose. This time, The Skelly was coming for the souls of her GranChildren.

Isabel's voice was quivering as she fought to overcome her fears. "He looks like a knight on a white horse. On the outside, he's handsome and courageous. But I can see through him."

"Do you mean you can see he's not really a good guy?" Alexis asked.

"NO!" Isabel snapped at Alexis. "I can see *through* him and he is not handsome. He is evil looking. It's horrible; I can see parts of his skeleton. His flesh is missing in some places but he has big-big muscles. Some of the muscles are not attached so they are flying like his cape. I can see the muscles around his black eyes, but there is no skin on his face. The blood is not moving in his veins." Isabel stared into his cold, evil eyes, and could see this monster was not quite man and not quite demon. "He doesn't have a good heart. It looks like the muscles around his heart are rotting."

"What about his hands and legs? Does he have hair?" GranMa persisted.

"No hair and his hands are just bones. I can't see his legs," Isabel replied. "Please GranMa; I don't want to look at him anymore!" Isabel's spine tingled, and the hair on the back of her neck rose. Her eyes filled with tears and a fear she had never known crept into her soul. Whatever The Skelly was, he knew a lot more about her than she knew about him.

"What about his horse?" Michael asked.

"His horse? Are you crazy? Who cares about his horse?" Isabel's fear was turning to hysteria.

"I do, Izzy!" Michael said. "We have to know how strong his horse is if we are to outride him."

"Okay, I'll look." Isabel's voice became a murmur. "He is big and he has all his muscles but he doesn't have fur."

"It's called a coat, Izzy," Michael corrected.

"Michael, do you *want* me to hit you?" Isabel tried to relieve her fear with sarcasm. But it didn't work. "GranMa, no more, please no more!" Isabel's toddler voice begged.

GranMa didn't approve of Michael's tactics, but she was impressed with his thinking. "Okay, just a few minutes more, sweetie," GranMa said. "What we are doing is *very* important! Look at his arms. You said he has big muscles. Are they big on his forearms too?"

"No, GranMa." Isabel begged, "Please, I'm very scared!"

"Okay, honey, GranMa will take it from here."

"I can't get him out of my head!" Isabel sobbed.

"Yes you can, Isabel! Look at GranMa!" GranMa's voice was calm, direct, and determined. "You have strong powers. Wish him out. He cannot defeat you and he knows it, which is why he must trick you. Wish. Him. Out!" Encouraged and convinced, Isabel wished him out.

"Spencer, take them inside The Cave of the Tired Souls. You and Tedde must protect them. I will provide reinforcements." And at the sound of her voice, seven large, muscular warriors with bows and arrows appeared. They had wings like Spencer and Tedde's, but they were much smaller. Three of the warriors were females who appeared to be slightly larger and more powerful than the males. Two instinctively positioned themselves on opposite sides of the cave door, about twenty feet apart. As if the laws of gravity did not apply to them, they rose thirty feet above the cave, and were barely noticeable as they blended into the background. The remaining five warriors entered the cave. Never again would they be fooled as they had been with the Missing One. It was a clever trap that was executed for the first time in The Cave of the Tired Souls. But that would never happen again. Diggory Town had learned from the Battle of Shame.

It was obvious Spencer and Tedde had dominion over the warriors, but Spencer protested being left behind to protect the cave. "GranMa, it is not reasonable that I be left behind. I should be going to battle with you."

GranMa moved Spencer out from earshot of the children. "Next to Hope, you and Tedde are the most powerful warriors we have. Protecting these children is the most important thing we must do. Hope goes to battle with me because I am the Responsible One. Her job is to watch my back. I cannot stay behind to defend the children. I must stop him from getting anywhere near them. If he gets their powers, we are all doomed. Make no mistake about this, Spencer: you and Tedde have the most dangerous job because he will stop at nothing to gain their powers. Nothing! Protect to your death and, if you must, kill them. He cannot have their powers or the universe is also doomed."

Spencer put his head down as his words fell softly to the ground. "I cannot kill them."

"You must." GranMa's words lay heavy across her tongue. "It is the only thing that will protect them in *That World*. They will go back to *That World* and life will go on, only without Diggory Town, and without the promise that the prophecy brings."

"GranMa, they cannot be the ones of prophecy." He looked pleadingly into GranMa's eyes. "The prophecy says *the victorious ones* will lead eight, but there are only four."

GranMa touched Spencer's hands, which were cupped in front of him. "The prophecy did not say they would all come at once. According to the prophecy, and according to what I have seen, they are the ones. They are the final bloodline. If we do not fail, they will be the rulers of the final days, and the fulfillers of prophecy."

Spencer's chest tightened, he stepped back, and he pulled his hands from GranMa's touch. "I SAVE LIVES! I DON'T TAKE THEM!"

GranMa brought down the invisible Dome of Silence, but Spencer's unhappiness didn't need to be heard; it could be seen. Isabel could see his rage and power, yet she felt safe in his presence. His great rage did not overshadow his great honor.

GranMa ignored Spencer's anger and answered calmly. "It may take killing them to save them, and a universe. If he gets their powers, there will be no life left anywhere; certainly not for the children. Take your post as I command. I leave you here because I trust no other with such an important job."

With that, GranMa lifted the dome. A special unit of one hundred senior warriors had assembled awaiting their instructions. One of the warriors handed her the reins of her trusted warhorse, Star, and she mounted him. The colors of her armor changed to a dull finish. She and Star began to blend in with the background. They were not exactly invisible, but they were certainly hard to see.

Noah, who GranMa suspected might be a warrior child prodigy, could not contain his curiosity, and yelled, "GRANMA, WHAT HAS HAPPENED TO YOU AND STAR?" He couldn't believe that such a wonderful weapon of war could exist.

"My beloved GranSon, the only ones surprised in a battle should be your enemy. If I battle in bright colors, I should be an easy target to see. Don't you agree?" And she blew him and the other children a kiss. Her heart could not have been more damaged than it was at that moment. The only way she would fail today was in death. She summoned all her powers. She loved these children more than life itself, and she needed every weapon at her disposal to save them. Soon they would become part of her weapons arsenal, but today, they were not.

GranMa snapped Star's reins, and they rode out of the caves, and into The Great Beyond. Unsure that Spencer could do what needed to be done—she quietly prayed to the Ultimate Ruler.

"Lord of all warriors, I beg you, help Spencer understand the battle at hand. Calm his anger. Put to sleep his rage. Let me not fail because your powerful warrior, Spencer, may have a heart too broken to do what must be done. The powerful exterior cannot hide from your eyes the tenderness of his soul. His love and kindness may blind him from the greater good. Help me succeed so that he will not need the courage to do what must be done. More than anything, I pray that you give him understanding to execute my orders. Grant him the forgiveness he will need for me and himself, should I fail."

What she had asked Spencer to do was nothing less than horrific. But it was now in the hands of the Ultimate Ruler.

As GranMa rode in silence, she thought about her early years as the Responsible One, when she tried to explain her reasons for the decisions she made to those who would argue with her. She tried to comfort others who could not understand her need to hold fast to what she knew to be the correct course of action. There were always bitter consequences when she compromised in order to make others happy. She had learned early that doing the right thing was not always popular. But right, after all, was *right*. Nothing good ever happened when she compromised to appease someone else's opinion. In fact, that effort is what had cost her most.

Today was a perfect example of what it meant to be responsible. If she failed, and the children were not killed in *This*

World, they would surely be killed by The Skelly in both worlds. It was simply the lesser of two evils, no matter how much it broke her heart. These were the burdens of a *Responsible One.* It was often a hated and lonely title to hold, but in these lonely moments, she found her strength.

For now, she must remove distracting thoughts such as these from her head. Soon she would be engaged with the enemy. She needed to face The Skelly and his Skull Warriors with a clear mind. The Skulls were either mercenary warriors motivated by personal gain, or victims being mind controlled into doing The Skelly's business. Either way, she knew them to be predators void of conscience.

With each beat of the hooves, GranMa and her warriors got closer to the sting of evil. She began to smell the rot of wicked souls as the air became thick and foreboding. She did not fear The Skelly nearly as much as she feared the possibility of failure. She listened to the pounding of the horses, and her heart began to beat to the tempo of war. She funneled her thoughts and set her sight on the battle ahead. Her focus became sharp, and the old feeling of victory began to enter every muscle of her body. Ah, victory . . . she could smell it. Soon, she would *taste* it.

"IF HE SMELLS YOUR FEAR, HE WILL CAPTURE YOUR SOUL! IF YOU CANNOT ENTER THIS BATTLE WITHOUT FEAR, I WANT YOU TO FALL BACK NOW!" She shouted above the pounding of the hooves, but all horses remained on pace.

"HOPE! REPORT TO ME!" GranMa commanded, and suddenly little Hope was flying just above her head, and shouting into her ear.

"They're in The Great Beyond, just over the next hill. There are about a hundred horses. I don't see any foot soldiers. I don't think he knew the children were coming. He probably found out just before he took control of Isabel's mind. I'm sure he wants to see if the ones of prophecy are really here. He hasn't had time to prepare. He won't be looking for a battle."

"Well, he's going to get one, isn't he? Do you think he has any clue we're coming to meet him?" GranMa asked.

"I don't think so," Hope reported as the familiar winds of war passed between her and GranMa. "He's leading the horsemen. If he thought you were coming, he'd be in the middle of the pack."

"What about his Protectors?" GranMa asked.

"I don't see any indications of their presence, but they're there," Hope replied. "They are always there."

"Do you think you can get close without being spotted?" GranMa asked, her voice tuning itself to the pounding hooves that created a familiar melody of war. Too many times she had heard this music that soothes the beast called Fear.

"Maybe. It's just those Protectors that worry me. I don't want to give our presence away."

"Well, don't do anything to compromise us or yourself. I'm not much good without you." GranMa smiled. The wind blew the newly forming sweat beads across her forehead. "He's very sneaky, so I won't underestimate him. I need you close to his men to listen and look for signs of a trap. But stay as far from *him* as you can. His Protectors will sense you if you get too close."

It wasn't long before Hope returned. "I don't sense that they know we're coming. But at this pace, we will meet at the top of the hill. Should we keep pace, pick up the pace, or slow down? How do you want to fight this battle?"

"If they're not expecting us, we can put the element of surprise to full advantage. I can't throw my light for long, but I can throw it long enough." GranMa slowed Star, which caused all the other horses to slow. Warriors ride wild horses, and in a herd of wild horses, there is only one leader, and their leader was Star.

"PULL IN!" GranMa shouted. Without hesitation, each rider and horse closed ranks to get within earshot of GranMa. She brought down the Dome of Silence. This allowed all within the dome to hear as she explained the plan.

It wasn't long before they could hear the thunder of The Skelly's horsemen, but as planned, her team of wild horses kept pace with Star. There were plenty of trees flanking the meadow that crept over the hill, but GranMa decided on a full frontal attack. She would use their momentum against them. At the moment she smelled *his* rotting flesh, she knew he had crested the hill. One didn't have to see The Skelly to know he was there. She lifted the dome and instantly her right hand rose, palm stretched before her, and a red flash of light filled the horizon. The Skelly's men were stunned. The light blinded them and their steeds. It splashed past them, filling the horizon with yellows, pinks, and reds before everything went dark as night.

"NOW!" GranMa yelled, and Star kicked forward. This time, the thunderous sounds were created by *her* horses. Swords were drawn but slashing downward instead of ahead as her plan enacted its gruesome deed. Blinded by the light, The Skelly's men found themselves hurling to the ground as their horses lost their footing. The Skulls never got to their feet as swords put an end to their villainous ways. One by one, GranMa's warriors removed their horrible souls from their treacherous bodies, but there was one who would live another day. GranMa felt the tremendous wind of his horse's wings, and she knew he was gone.

When she heard the last groan, GranMa lifted her left palm, and the sun returned to the sky. She was not surprised to see all were dead except the one that mattered most.

"HOW MANY DID WE LOSE?" GranMa shouted.

"NOT A ONE!" Hope shouted back. "SHALL WE BURY THEIR DEAD?"

"LET THE VULTURES HAVE THEM!" GranMa replied.

She and her warriors headed back to The Cave of the Tired Souls. The rumble of victory was heard amongst the chatter of her warriors, but GranMa didn't say a word. She rode in thoughtful silence, wondering what would she say to the children?

As they rode on, the beauty of The Great Beyond masked the ugliness of the lives just lost. However, the ugliness was not hidden from her view. Even the rolling hills, the beautiful forest, the smell of flowers, and the sounds of babbling brooks and animals going about their day could not wash the evil from her mind's eye.

Through it all, the voices of her loved ones in the distance brought a smile to her face. But her smile did not dim thoughts of how most children would never learn of horrible acts executed by *their* grandmothers. She was not one of *those* blameless grandmothers. GranMa would have to explain the blood on her hands. And with her hands cupped over her saddle's horn, she sat rubbing the top knuckle of her left thumb. She knew the day was fast approaching when she would be judged for the sword she had just swung.

"GranMa . . . GranMa . . . GranMa!" Happy little voices called to her.

"I was afraid, GranMa!" teary-eyed Isabel exclaimed. "I was really afraid for you!"

GranMa dismounted to hugs and kisses. "So you left the safety of the cave to come greet me at the edge of The Great Beyond. That's so sweet." She gave Spencer a glare out the corner of her eye. He shrugged palms out, and gave her an apologetic look.

"Can I go next time?" Alexis asked, to GranMa's surprise.

"Did you win?" Noah shouted. "How many did you kill?"

"GranMa, did you get the bad guy?" All Michael cared about were big results. Details mattered only in that they led to an outcome. Follow the rules and get the job done—that was it. Who could argue with his logic?

GranMa addressed Michael's mature question while she walked toward the cave's opening. "We won the skirmish, but I knew we would not win the war today. What happened today is not part of the prophecy."

But Isabel's question was more ominous than the others. With trepidation, she asked, "GranMa, who were all those men with that bad man?"

"The bad man is called The Skelly and they are called Skulls," GranMa replied. "Most are his mercenary warriors. Some are victims being forced to fight for him."

Fearful of the answer, Isabel asked, "What does that mean, 'mercintary warriors'?"

"It's pronounced mer-cen-ary and it means people who fight battles that have nothing to do with them, but they fight for personal gain like money or power. In fact, The Skelly promises the Skulls that they will get some of what they loot, and he will make them very powerful. Let's go back to the safety of the caves and I'll explain."

As they walked towards the caves, GranMa continued, "We will win and lose this, and many other skirmishes. But the war can only be won in the Omega Battle, after other battles are fought. Each battle will get us closer to the ending of war. However, each time we engage The Skelly, we must worry of what is foretold in *his* prophecy. We are not invincible and neither is he."

"So, we can kill him?" Alexis asked.

"If we can find his prophecy, we can learn how he is destroyed. I know how the war can be won in the Omega Battle, because the end has been written. What I don't know is how it is we may lose. You see, he has a battle plan for victory too, and that is his prophecy. As yet, we do not have access to his foretelling. To our knowledge, he has never found ours. It is hidden in the ark. The Sealed Books will lead us to the ark."

"Where is his prophecy hidden?" Michael asked.

"If they knew, he'd be dead by now," Noah piped in. "Isn't that right, GranMa?"

"Yes, Noah. That is exactly right," GranMa replied. She headed to the stables with Star and little feet followed close behind.

Spencer nudged Noah. "Little details . . . " Spencer smiled.

Michael would not be deterred. "What are the other battles?"

"Eventually, you will read the entire prophecy, because you *are* the prophecy, and you must fulfill it. The Battle of Shame and the Battle of Trafleka have been fought. The Battle of Destiny is what we will prepare you for. When you are ready, others, who have known war, will come to fight with you in the Omega Battle. This is the battle that will end war forever, but that is enough for today. A brain can only learn so much at one time."

"I'll say," Isabel squeaked out. "I like The Great Beyond, GranMa. It's prettier than the caves and it smells better."

"Yes, it is, sweetheart. But it is not as safe there," GranMa said as they left The Great Beyond behind them and headed into the caves, past The Cave of Tired Souls, and towards the stables.

Once inside, the warriors and the guards went about their business. The coolness of the caves comforted GranMa's tired muscles. As she walked, she watched the daily life in Diggory Town once again become her reality. Most of the time, she paid no mind that she was in a cave. Except for the torches and the absence of a sky, it seemed like any other small city of old. It was good to put the battle and the pitiful lives she had just taken behind her. What she couldn't remove from her thoughts was the idea that weighed heavy on her heart. She was the Responsible One. It was her job to take the innocence from her GranChildren, and make them warriors.

"C'mon you little rascals," GranMa said. "I need to get you back to *That World*." No one wanted to leave; they were having such great fun playing with the horses. "Stop your giggling and nonsense, and let's get you back to your mothers in *That World*. I'm sure there are baths to take."

"Darn it!" Isabel stamped her feet, but it was time to get her home and get her mind away from her fears.

"C'mon you little knuckleheads." This was GranMa's final warning.

As the GranChildren conceded to GranMa's demands, GranMa whispered to Hope. "They are growing, which does my heart good, but we are ending their innocence, and that pains me."

GranMa knew she could not allow herself to cradle the children and protect them from the cruelties of war. She could make no allowances for youth or weakness because such allowances would cost lives. She must treat her precious babies like instruments of war. There would be no day of *future* judgment for these sins. GranMa's judgments and punishments were harsh, immediate, and self-imposed. She knew a day would come when she would no longer be able to bear the sorrow of her sins.

Instead of flying near GranMa, as was her custom, Hope expanded her size as much as she could, and put her feet on the ground. She wrapped her arm around GranMa's arm, then leaned her head just under GranMa's shoulder. The two friends walked in peace and quiet for a while, and the children walked nearby in thoughtful silence. Alexis couldn't help but notice that, when expanded, she and Hope were nearly the same size. She thought about this almost all the way home.

Chapter 7   What to Believe

Papa was waiting for GranMa and the children at the Gran Canyon transport that would take them back to *That World*. He watched the children quietly mosey their way to the No. 3 Bus. They said nothing. There was no pushing, no teasing, and no laughing. He was given a silent hug by each child before they entered the bus. A soberness hung over them, as if all the childish energy had been sucked from their little bodies.

"Today was too much for the children. We need to get them home," GranMa said to Papa in a voice just above a whisper. "Poor Isabel was a mess. Let's take them by way of Narnia and past Harry's world; maybe that will distract them from what they've just seen. It wouldn't be wise to let their last experience of the day be a scary one."

"Why don't we put Stanley in the bus?" Papa suggested. "She'll be a good distraction for the kids."

Without one ounce of enthusiasm, GranMa said, "Good idea."

Papa asked, "You think the baby has much of a future in Diggory Town?"

"Aaron's having a boy," GranMa said. "They have decided to name him Gavin. And yes." GranMa turned her back to the bus and lowered her voice again. "I think Gavin *is* the future of Diggory Town, because without him, the rest of this is just a waste of time. What good is a future if there is no one there to build it?"

"Good point," Papa said. "And if The Skelly can stop him, then the other kids pose less of a threat. We'd better make sure that little guy stays safe. I wouldn't want to lose a one of them, but I imagine The Skelly will target our new baby first. That's what I'd do if I were as evil as him."

"Well, let's get these kids home before Gavin's mother kills me for getting his brother home so late." GranMa smiled. "Gavin is due to be born any day and Aaron is often tired at the end of her pregnancy. But she won't be sleeping until I get Michael home. Unfortunately, we'll have plenty of time to think about The Skelly later."

Each child had silently found the way to their most special couch that fit their tushies perfectly. However, none felt comforted. Each sat lost pondering the day's events, and what might lie in their future. Even Stanley's constant prodding for a hug, or a pet, did little to distract them. They blindly ran their hands down her smooth chestnut-colored coat, and dully stared in thoughtful confusion.

"Can we bring Gavin next time?" Michael asked suddenly.

"Not yet, he'll be too young," GranMa responded in monotone.

"Does my mother know about Diggory Town?" Michael asked.

"Not anymore. She no longer has a life in Diggory Town," GranMa responded.

"If she doesn't know, how can she kill you for taking us there?" Michael asked. Apparently, Michael's ease dropping skills were as good as his deductive reasoning skills.

"You've met your mother right?" GranMa responded.

"Yeah . . . you're a goner if she finds out."

GranMa thought about Gavin. Even before the other kids were born, there were telltale signs of their connection to Diggory Town, but she saw nothing in Aaron's pregnancy. Not a hint of any kind of power seemed present. She began to doubt her own instincts. What if she was wrong and misreading the children? Could it be that she was leading the children to their doom? Of course, she did witness Alexis's amazing ability to find a transporter, but what if Alexis was just responding to the déjà vu? She pushed these thoughts from her head. Doubt is not a warrior's friend. She changed her focus to the present, because for the moment, that is what she could control.

Suddenly, Alexis jumped up and asked, "What's that?"

"Narnia. It's the highest of all the worlds," GranMa said, "because all worlds exist in Narnia and Aslan is the ruler of all worlds."

Alexis pondered GranMa's words for a minute, then asked, "Does that mean Diggory Town does not exist in Harry's wizard world?"

"That's correct."

"But there are some worlds within worlds?" Alexis asked.

"That's correct. There are a few. Like the World of People exists in most other worlds." GranMa smiled as her sweet, brilliant Alexis began to piece together the truths about the worlds. GranMa thought about the kind of intelligence it took to reconcile these concepts and ideas. It's not the kind of intelligence that is gained after great study, but the kind of intelligence that is gifted by the ruler of all worlds.

"GranMa, are you telling me that Harry is real?" Alexis asked.

"I'm telling you that some authors record history while others tell stories. Diggory Town isn't like Harry's world because his world is very old, maybe as old as time itself. Diggory Town is new like the Americas. Oh, it looks old, but old is relative to what it is being compared to."

"So how old is everything?" Noah asked.

"Well, not more than six thousand years old," GranMa replied.

"My teacher says things can be millions and billions of years old," Isabel said.

"I know. Isn't that funny! People want to believe anything except that Diggory Town exists. I don't know where they think souls come from. I can assure you my soul is anything but random. It was especially created for me in Diggory Town, and when I was born, it was carefully placed in my heart. Did I ever tell you that's why Diggory Town exists?"

Michael responded, "You mentioned it, but that was the first time we came here. I'm not sure we understood the importance of what you were saying."

"I don't even remember you saying it," Noah chimed in.

"Well, creating souls is *mostly* why it exists. It's also a waiting place for our souls."

"What are they waiting for?" Michael asked.

"To go home," GranMa replied.

"Where is home?" Noah asked.

"It's where the Ultimate Ruler lives," GranMa replied.

"Are all souls perfect?" little Isabel squeaked.

"They start out that way. But sometimes, bad things happen as they make their way to a person's heart, and sometimes they get damaged while they are in a person's heart."

"Why?" Isabel asked.

"I wish I had a good answer for that. But the truth is, I don't know. I try to love the broken souls too, because they are the ones who need love most. Be careful not to confuse a broken soul with an evil soul. They are not the same thing."

"How will I know one from the other?" Michael asked.

"If you pay attention, you will know. Don't overlook anything, and don't take anything for granted. Broken and evil souls are different. When a person can tell the difference, they are said to be a good judge of character. It would be wise to learn that skill."

"Can you do it?" Michael asked. "Judge broken from evil?"

"No, she stinks at it!" Tedde said, walking out the freestanding door.

"I didn't know you were on the bus," GranMa said.

"*I* need to get home to *That World* so I can feed Maggie and Molly. Tim and Mom have been busy in the Square, so they asked me to feed and walk the dogs. I was a little hungry myself, so when I got on the bus, I headed to the dining car," Tedde said.

"Can we go in the dining car?" Michael asked, more curious than hungry.

"Sure you can! Eat lots of ice cream! I'll have you home at about the same time the sugar kicks in," GranMa said.

"Yippy! Yippy! Yippy!" Michael, Isabel, and Noah shouted.

"I've wanted to see what's in that room!" Alexis said as GranMa rang for the flight attendant.

"Please take the kids to the dining car and give them any ole sugar thing they want," GranMa said to the flight attendant.

"Yippy . . . " the flight attendant said with barely any interest. "C'mon let's get this over with," she added, herding the children to the freestanding door that Tedde held open while the children happily danced through it.

GranMa smiled from her seat on her fluffy, red couch while Tedde watched. When the last child walked through the door, GranMa asked, "So Tedde, when are you going to tell me what's on your mind?"

"What? There's nothing on my mind."

"I might 'stink in the judging character department' but I can read people like books. You've been perturbed for several weeks, so fess up. What's been hanging over your head?"

"Okay, since you asked . . . *You*, GranMa. And you're not hanging over my head. You're getting under my skin with your Ultimate Ruler, your holier than thou attitude, and your cute little sayings. 'There are no accidents. Teach if you are there to teach. Learn if you are there to learn. Do *that* for which you have been chosen. There are no accidents.' Let me tell you something, GranMa, he doesn't believe in *me* and I don't believe in *him*!"

"Well," GranMa said in a voice that lacked surprise. "Now that you've got that off your chest, I hope you feel better."

"Not really," Tedde said, flopping herself near GranMa. "Actually, I feel worse."

"Maybe it's because you spend a lot of your time defending your position on something you believe doesn't exist," GranMa said, taking Tedde's hand. "I don't believe in aliens and I don't spend *any* energy on them. And they never make me mad." GranMa started to laugh.

"I hate you," Tedde said, giggling.

"I hate you too," GranMa said, gently squeezing Tedde's hand.

"It's just that, well, look at my brother Spencer. How does this happen to him? He is a good man who seems lost to your Ultimate Ruler. Look at how hard things are for him in *That World*. He doesn't belong there, GranMa! They don't love or appreciate him, and I fail at protecting him from them." Tedde turned her back to GranMa, but her heaving chest gave her away. She took a deep breath to gain her composure as her words stayed prisoner to her broken heart.

"Try to understand what I'm telling you." GranMa spoke softly while Tedde composed herself to hear GranMa's words. "Failures do not cancel a life, and they are not the sum of who we are. Don't get swept away by their evil. As for the people of *That World*, they don't know it, but they need Spencer. They don't understand him, they don't appreciate him, and they often break his heart, but they *need* him. They need his gentleness, his kindness, and his strength. *That World* would be less without him."

Tedde's voice was a tone above whisper. "Why is that his problem?"

"Because *That World* may not even survive without him. He seems to have dominion over evil there. He does not control it, but he keeps it under control. I don't know why the evil of *That World* fears him; I only know that it does."

"Once again, GranMa, why is that *his* problem?"

"Because he has made it *his* problem. Do you think soldiers want to die in war? No. But they go to war because they must; it's in their souls. In fear, but with courage, they do what they must to protect their loved ones. That is our Spencer; he knows what he is up against, but his heart won't let him walk away. He is not forced to be in *That World*. He chooses to be there helping the good as well as the ungrateful. Some days he wins, and some days he loses, but there is never a day when he gives up."

"He's a better person than me." Tedde snorted as she took in another deep breath trying to find the calm that eluded her.

GranMa hugged Tedde and dried her tears. "No, my princess, he is a better person than most of us. He believes in, and is guided by, the Ultimate Ruler. You will believe too . . . when believing is all you have."

"Is that what it takes to believe? You must be void of everything else?" Tedde did not look into GranMa's eyes, fearing the conviction that might be there.

"No," GranMa said, lifting Tedde's chin. "One atom of true belief fills all voids. One tiny atom of unyielding faith conquers fear, wins wars, and opens our minds to the knowledge of the universe. It is said that seeing is believing. But the truth is . . . you cannot see . . . until you believe."

Chapter 8   The Missing One

Once again, Michael beat his cousins to the door chime that had the face of a fierce lion. And once again, Isabel moaned, "That's not fair. I wanted to pull it!"

"Then you should move a little faster." GranMa grinned, and wondered how long it would be before Isabel would take charge of her own destiny.

The children had never been inside The Cave of the Tired Souls. Alexis entered the arched doors eclipsed by muscular rock warriors who flanked the entrance. She felt even smaller than usual. Little heads bobbed behind her, turning in every direction, trying to capture the vastness of what lie behind the arched doors. From the main chamber, one could head toward tunnels in any direction.

"Just walk straight ahead, Alexis," GranMa said, herding the children from behind.

Noah entered the tunnel and dragged his hand along the cold, rough wall until he reached an alcove. He stopped and peeked his head around the opening to see men and women dressed in battle gear resting on couches and listening to Mozart. He looked across the tunnel hall to see another alcove, so he snuck a peek into that room to discover the same sight, only Beethoven played in the background.

GranMa came up behind Noah and whispered in his ear, "I prefer Tchaikovsky after a good battle. Come. Let's see what other comforts we can find in The Cave of the Tired Souls."

Alexis came to a fork in the cave. A set of stairs to her left went down, and the set of stairs to the right of the fork went up. "Which way should we head, GranMa?"

"Well, that depends. Are you hungry, or do you want to play games? If you head left you will find lots of fun things to do, like play chess or horseshoes, and if you head right, you will find all the food you can eat. There are many tunnels and rooms in this cave that go up and down many levels. It is an endless surprise that is very hard to defend during a battle."

All the children were excited, except Michael, who worried because his mother was in so much pain in *That World*. He didn't know what she meant when she said, "False labor hurts as much as the real thing," but he knew that the false labor thing wasn't good. He felt anxious and excited that soon he would have a new brother. His mother told him not to worry because the pain was "worth it," but Michael would wait until Gavin was born before he decided if it was "worth it," or not.

"Will Gavin come to Diggory Town?" Michael asked.

"Yes." GranMa's violet eyes twinkled.

"Does everyone in our family come to Diggory Town?" Michael needed information as much as he needed oxygen.

"It's the duty of the Responsible One to make sure that all direct descendants of the first Responsible One know about Diggory Town. Occasionally, especially in the case of marriage, we bring others to Diggory Town. However, it's rare that we take that kind of risk. So yes, most family members come here . . . but not the fallen ones." The twinkle left her eyes.

"What does that mean?" he asked.

"The fallen ones are those we lost in battle. In Diggory Town, they are no more, but they still exist in The World of People. Come into this cavern. I'll take you to our family Thanksgiving nine years ago."

GranMa motioned the children into a cavern with several couches. Once seated, each looked deep into GranMa's violet eyes as her soft voice transported them to Aunt Melissa's house. Aunt Melissa's transporter was a mirror near the front entrance of her home. It was a nice, unassuming mirror. One would never have guessed it to be a transport. Once transported, the children were surprised to find a bunch of Pilgrims and Indians eating in a modern home.

"GranMa, where have you taken us?" Alexis had a dull, confused look on her face.

GranMa smiled remembering this day with fondness *and* sorrow.

"This is the time before you. Aunt Melissa and Uncle Tim had just moved to San Diego from Manchester, New Hampshire. They decided to host the family for every Thanksgiving now that they had moved to San Diego. They wanted *this* Thanksgiving to be special, so they asked that each person dress as either an Indian or a Pilgrim. It was a wonderful first Thanksgiving. "My sister, your Great Aunt Melissa, and her husband, Uncle Tim, were great warriors and, together, they were almost unstoppable."

Isabel asked, "What happened?"

"It was the great Battle of Trafleka where they drew their swords for the last time. Perhaps you've noticed their images on the canvasses in the Chambers of Defense building. They are part of the great legends. Aunt Melissa is the gallant warrior mounted on the royal chariots; she almost always has her sword drawn in the paintings and canvasses that line the walls. Uncle Tim is the soldier you see strategizing and thinking of great plans to outwit The Skelly. He's usually depicted leaning over a map. Together, they accomplished the work of a thousand men. But something happened at Trafleka that caused them to lay down their swords. War has a way of bending souls in ways they shouldn't be bent."

"GranMa, that doesn't tell us what happened," Isabel said.

"Be patient, princess. I have so much to tell you today." GranMa smiled and kissed the top of Isabel's head.

GranMa turned their attention to the Indians. "Many of the Indians do not belong in *This World*."

"Where do they belong?" Noah asked.

"They belong to *That World*. Although all souls are created in Diggory Town, not all souls end up in Diggory Town. It's only the place where souls are created. Once the souls are delivered to their body, most stay in the world where they were birthed. Very few return to Diggory Town. Most of the people in Diggory Town were birthed here. Some, like you kids, were not.

"Do you remember the first time you came to Diggory Town and you saw the other worlds like Sports World?" They all nodded. "Do you remember I told you they are all depending on you?" Heads nodded. "There are some people, like you, who are aware of the other worlds. People aware of our worlds can die in one world and not in the other. However, most people in Diggory Town are unaware of other worlds. The legends of *This World* who die here are left to live in peace in *That World.* For instance, have you ever had that feeling that you have met someone before, but they assure you that you have not? Still, your feeling doesn't go away. The truth is, you *have* seen or met them. However, once dead in Diggory Town, the aura is gone, and in *That World*, they have no recollection of Diggory Town, so they cannot know you."

"Then how do *you* know them?" Michael asked, as if he thought GranMa was trying to trick him.

GranMa smiled. She knew one day Michael would grow up to be a great counselor, but he would need to develop his diplomacy.

"Because I have fought beside them for many years in many battles, and I cannot forget the sacrifices they made. They were valiant beyond anything you can imagine, and that kind of courage is not soon forgotten. I knew them when they were alive in Diggory Town, and they will always be *my* warriors. As long as we have shed blood together, they will not be forgotten by those who loved them while they were alive in Diggory Town. Those born after their death will only know the legend, but when in *That World,* they will not know who these people once were."

Michael did not like this answer, but he didn't challenge GranMa. It seemed to him like once a hero always a hero, no matter what world you were from.

GranMa pointed to the two most beautiful Indians. "We lost Amy and Mindy to the No Ones. The No Ones are hard to defend against because they only harm to get what they want *right now*. Once they have what they want, they settle back down into a normal life as if they have done no harm. But they do plenty of harm to their victims. Unfortunately, they strike, get what they want, and settle back down as the nice neighbors. They blend in and most people are fooled by their cordial ways. We were fooled by their cordial ways, but that won't happen twice.

"Amy and Mindy's father, Uncle Dennis, was lost in the Battle of Shame too. I wish you could have seen Amy and Mindy. They were the sentries at The Cave of the Tired Souls. They were majestic in every way, and strong beyond your greatest imagination. They had round muscular shoulders to help carry their wings, which spread eight feet across. Mindy's wings had taken on beautiful pastel colors because she was the gentlest of the sisters. Amy's wings were bold and beautiful, because in battle, she was the fiercer of the two. During a battle, their beauty shone so brightly that the enemy could not bear to look upon their faces. For years, they stood post protecting our most tired. We had no cause to worry about our resting warriors, because we had Amy and Mindy at the post, and it was there that the No Ones came looking for the Missing One. This day would be our greatest shame."

"Did Amy and Mindy not do their jobs?" Michael wanted details so he could learn from the Battle of Shame. He was certain that an army was only as strong as its weakest link, and that army could only become stronger if it learned from its past.

"Amy and Mindy were most admirable and fought to the death. Our shame is that we never saw what was coming. We had just lost your mother, but we should not have been defenseless. In our grief, we let evil enter our camps because we never saw it coming. We all let our guards down. That is why there was little any of us could have done to protect the tired souls from the No Ones. The leader of the No Ones had spent six years targeting the Missing One. He took advantage of us, and in the last two years, he strategized and successfully executed taking her. He had befriended us, and he was with her inside The Cave of the Tired Souls when the battle began. Amy and Mindy never had a chance. They did not know the enemy was among us. None of us did."

"And how do you know this?" Michael asked.

"Because it is what the leader of the No Ones told me while he bragged. He had outwitted us to steal one of our most precious members. I can still hear the evil in his words and laughter. Because we let the enemy into our camp, because we were not vigilant, because he tricked us so easily, it is called the Battle of Shame. It tore our family apart, and there are scars that we can never mend. Oh, certainly the wounds have healed but . . . ."

"GranMa, why don't we just go get her back?" Isabel asked.

"It is not that simple. We cannot just go take her because only love can bring her back."

"If love can bring her back, and you love her, why isn't she back?" Isabel asked.

GranMa's loss rode upon her voice. "It is not our love that can bring her back. Only her love for us can bring her back."

"Why doesn't she love the family?" Isabel asked.

"She doesn't love us because of the enchantment. It will take strong love to break the bonds of pride. Pride is one of the deadly sins and one of the greatest enchantments, but it is not the only enchantment. There is a bubble of deceit that entraps as well as enchants her. Some of the deceit was created by the No Ones, and some has been created by her own foolish thoughts. Do not underestimate the enchantments of the No Ones. They are extremely charming, and that is how they enter our lives. Most of us will never see the evil because it is hidden under a veil of charm. But those of us who have seen it, will not soon forget it. Your only defense is to never let them near, because without prey, they will eventually self-destruct, but it seems there is always prey."

"That doesn't explain why we're not going after her." Alexis, who grew wiser every day, wanted a better explanation for this nonsensical response.

"Only No Ones can take you from the bond of the family, and only you can bring yourself back. Our ways are not simple, but they are there for a reason. If we rescue her, she will not be here of her own free will. Her love for us should have protected her to begin with, but for reasons only she understands, it did not. We will fight to bring her back as soon as she calls us to arms. But it must be she who calls. It is cowardice that keeps her from calling us, and it is her cowardice that will cause her sorrow, if there is any sorrow left."

"What is she called?" Noah wanted to know whom it was he felt he must save.

"She is only known as the Missing One."

"Then how are we to save her?" Noah persisted.

"We are not to save her. She must save herself, and how are you to know that she requires saving? How do you know that she is not there of her own free will? We cannot choose for others. It is the rule of our world. We are where we choose to be, and only *we* can decide what path we will take."

"How do you know she's not a prisoner?" Alexis asked.

"Because I did not hear her call. Know this, Alexis: If the No Ones take you, when you need or want us at your side, all you need do is call. There is nothing in all of creation that can keep us from you once you call. And there is no barrier in all of creation that can stop us from hearing it."

"Will things ever be the same?" Isabel asked.

"What's done is done." GranMa had nothing further to say on the subject. But all the children could feel her loss.

Chapter 9   The Battle of Trafleka

As the days passed, the secrets of Diggory Town began to unravel before the children. The Great Beyond, although not entirely safe, was entirely beautiful. And whether it was or not, it *felt* peaceful. GranMa had taken the children there for a picnic, and a revealing.

"Preparing a warrior for a victorious battle has more to do with thinking than fighting. A hard fought battle can still be lost if your enemy is better prepared." That was GranMa's motto regarding a battle. She was always outmanned when she fought The Skelly, but she was never out-skilled. Her soldiers were taught to think, and were given the responsibility of protecting each other. The Skelly's soldiers were either prisoners of his dark magic and forced to fight, or they were evil and self-serving. Whichever the case, his soldiers fought for the wrong reasons. Had they fought for the right reasons, there was little doubt in GranMa's mind that she would have lost every battle to them. It was imperative that the GranChildren knew *how* to fight, *why* they fight, *who* they fight, and *what* they were fighting for. *When* to fight was going to be a little trickier to explain. *When* was not always something they could control. There was much to learn, but today the GranChildren were to gain knowledge of *who, how, and what* had cost so many lives at the great Battle of Trafleka.

The children sat forward, hearts pounding while they hung onto every word GranMa had to say. The sense of foreboding kept them leaning forward with fists clenched, needing to hear but not wanting to. No matter how much the children wanted the words to stop, GranMa continued.

"The stench of The Skelly can be smelled for miles. His constant need to rejuvenate the deteriorating flesh and muscles that encapsulate his evil soul leaves an endless path of destruction. Try as we might, any effort to destroy his body seems meaningless, since it is his soul that is so dangerous.

"From the beginning, we knew that our only hope was to destroy his body over and over again until we could figure out a way to destroy his soul. But with each rejuvenation of his body, his ability to murder for gain and pleasure becomes more and more effortless. Before Trafleka, his victims would hear the thunder of his horses as he and the Skulls quested for their blood. With courage and resolve, they took arms and stood waiting for the thunder to turn into a horde of murderous warriors. Sadly, the militias they formed were no match for The Skelly and his men. The last sound they would hear was the swish of one quick movement as they were slaughtered by swords, axes, and other weapons, including bad magic. With each kill, The Skelly gained power both in mind and in body. I and my soldiers were the only things that stood between The Skelly and his dream of endless power. But we were not his charge.

"His goal is, and always has been, to steal your powers, because *you* are the keepers of Diggory Town. Once he has absorbed your powers and bodies, he will be granted power beyond anything you can imagine. Your charge is to see that he never gains your powers. Know this: he will not take your souls quickly; he will absorb them slowly as he delights in your pain, anguish, and destruction. There is nothing crueler or more criminal in any world than The Skelly. He will use your fear as a weapon against you, so you must not fear him. You must outthink and outfight him. Your death will be nothing compared to the horror that will occur should he defeat the prophecy. Humanity as we know it will be gone forever because he will be indestructible."

As GranMa told the story of the Battle of Trafleka, each GranChild could feel the prickly hairs rising on the backs of their necks. Cold tingles drifted down their spines when they began to hear a story they didn't want told. They were his ultimate victims, and soon they would smell his rotting flesh. They would hear the thunder of his horses. They would look into his evil eyes. The Battle of Trafleka would be nothing compared to the battle they would have to fight. Soon, they would taste the blood of war. They must learn from the Battle of Trafleka, and build on the knowledge gained. Each knew that in the Omega Battle, they must destroy The Skelly's soul, or lose their own. They listened to every disquieting word GranMa had to say.

"As difficult as it may seem, you must not fear The Skelly," GranMa continued. "We learned much at the Battle of Trafleka; but the most important thing we learned is that he will destroy you from within. He has mastered evil, and with no effort at all, he will gain control of your minds." GranMa stared them down and tapped her finger to her temple. "The only way to stop him is to not fear him." She moved her hand from her temple and balled her fist over her heart. "A brave heart is what you will need. Courage works like a shield against his mind control."

"How could that be, and how did you discover it?" Michael asked.

GranMa smiled. She understood that Michael's powers came from his uncanny ability to get strength from information. He could figure out anything with little information, which is how he would outmaneuver his enemies. He was so much like his Uncle Tim. GranMa felt sad when she thought of how Tim was harmed at the Battle of Trafleka. He and GranMa's sister, Melissa, demonstrated courage beyond anything she had ever seen. These two Titans sacrificed much, and were broken, in exchange for the information that empowered GranMa's warriors. They had survived the battle, and still, the ravages of war had claimed them as victims. But because of them, and Michael's mother, The Skelly no longer had the upper hand. Because of the Battle of Trafleka, the warriors of Diggory Town knew how to defend themselves, but they still didn't know how to kill The Skelly.

GranMa gazed upon her GranChildren, who sat cross-legged and hypnotized by GranMa's words as she divulged the details of an ill-fated battle. She began slowly because the story of Trafleka was not easy to tell, nor was it easy to hear.

"The answer to Michael's question is the key to defeating The Skelly, so listen carefully and learn."

Each set of innocent little eyes stayed fixed on GranMa.

"Some would say that too much was lost at Trafleka. I would be hard pressed to tell you that either side won. And although the costs were high, what we gained was invaluable. It wasn't like we were careless. We had prepared for weeks. Many sources had informed us that Trafleka was The Skelly's stronghold. I was amazed that he would make such a grave error."

GranMa paused and took a long breath. "Trafleka was an old training camp for us inside of Tulum. We knew all the secret passages and we had control of them. It made no sense for him to hold up there. Knowing it was unlikely The Skelly would error in this way, I suspected a trap. It wasn't until Professor Panaid came to me suggesting a strategy to overtake Tulum that I began to feel confident we could use this new information to our advantage. But I had misgivings about the professor.

"Professor Panaid had taught at Trafleka for many years. She never seemed to trust anyone. She had many associates but few friends. We trained at Trafleka together when we were young. After warrior school, I would see her occasionally, but then she left for many years, and I was never sure why. One day, out of nowhere, she appeared at Trafleka looking for a job as a teacher. Her sword skills and knowledge of the magic arts made her an excellent teacher, but I couldn't understand why anyone would *want* to work at Trafleka.

"The buildings were made of dark quartz stone, which didn't let in any light. There were few windows so the smell of burning torches was everywhere, and the halls echoed. It seemed the perfect place for evil to lurk. It was chosen as a warrior training camp because it was so dreary and unpredictable. Since the primary training was battle, Trafleka's dark and cold environment was ideal for recreating the darkness of war.

"However, it didn't make for a very pleasant place to live. Teachers were forced to live on the premises. You could choose from any building including Tulum Castle, but no matter where you chose to live, it would be dreary. You taught at Trafleka because it was your turn and for no other reason.

"Professor Panaid volunteering to be there was nothing less than suspicious. Despite that, she was a good teacher for many years. Curiously, shortly after the Battle of Trafleka, she disappeared as quickly as she came."

"Why was the training camp shut down?" Michael asked.

"We could no longer defend the perimeter. A wall surrounded it on every side but the east. We didn't need a wall there because of the ocean cliffs and Tulum Castle sat directly above them. We felt fairly secure since we could see for miles, but even if it got foggy, the ocean waters are treacherous. They can easily make toothpicks out of any ship. And if the ship survived the tumbling of the unforgiving ocean, it would never survive the razor sharp rocks.

"Over time, the pounding water carved the rocks on the east, creating an entry point for an enemy meaning to do us harm. All they had to do was get up over the cliffs to kill anyone not inside the castle. You'll see when I take you to Tulum. Inside the fifteen foot walls, there are eight buildings, and Tulum Castle. There is a labyrinth of secret passages that lead everywhere including outside the property. For the safety of everyone, we decided it best to move the warrior training camp."

"Where is it now?" Michael asked.

"Everywhere, we train everywhere. After the Battle of Shame, it was decided we could no longer afford to have so many warriors vulnerable in one place."

Michael smiled and nodded at GranMa's words, but not Noah. "Aren't we more vulnerable in small groups?" Noah asked.

"Ahh, my little soldier, you think with a warrior's heart. Our new strategy is to have our training camps aligned in a circle. We are never very far apart. I can bring you together in an instant. The strategy is to let the enemy inside the circle and then we close ranks to snare them."

Noah smiled as his thoughts slowly oozed from his mouth. "Great thinking . . . "

"Anyway, Professor Panaid came to me with an idea. She thought we could use the secret tunnels to see how The Skelly was positioning his men. We knew there would be a lot of risk, but if we could determine how The Skelly was using Trafleka, and determine any patterns in his procedures, we could execute a secret attack. The idea was to silently capture as many of the Skulls as possible, and bring them into the tunnels. If we could capture enough of them, we could weaken their position, and then attack in full force. It was important to execute the plan over time so they didn't notice their force getting smaller. By the time they noticed, we should have the upper hand. We only had three problems.

"One, The Skelly might read one of our minds and extract the plan. Two, I didn't trust Professor Panaid. Three, once the full battle began, The Skelly would be engaged and we could never battle him for long. His mind control was more powerful than any weapon we had.

"Professor Panaid's plan was sound. It was the only chance we had to deplete the enemy forces. Whatever I thought about her didn't change the fact that her plan was good. Unbeknownst to the professor, had she betrayed us, a second brigade of warriors waited to be dispatched. Their orders were to kill her first, and then engage in a full force battle. We would do as much damage as possible to The Skelly's army before retreating.

"It seemed she had not betrayed us. Our attack was executed to perfection, except The Skelly was able to read many minds, slay many warriors, and absorb many souls. He grew extremely fierce as his powers grew during the battle. I watched as muscles began to grow on his body. He grew hair and the muscles around his eyes were no longer bare. He became so strong that he was able to block my command to withdraw with mind control. My warriors had no idea I was sounding a retreat." GranMa's voice grew hollow and distant until it was a murmur. "It was a horrible bloodbath. Uncle Jon's head injury . . . it's a miracle he survived . . . "

GranMa's eyes drifted in thought and her expression changed as if being painted by death. The muscles in her neck tightened as she swallowed hard, like she was choking down a golf ball. Lost in the bowels of hell, she was overcome by the memories she relived. The children became hypnotized by her presence, and images of that night began to pass before their eyes. Before long, they could hear the cries of fallen warriors.

"I can do it!" Aunt Melissa yelled back to Uncle Tim.

"Not yet! I think I have something. I think he's trying to read my mind. He's having trouble. He can't get through to me. COME BACK!" Uncle Tim shouted to be heard over the thunder of the battle. "I THINK I'VE FIGURED IT OUT!"

Aunt Melissa kicked Lightning in the ribs to get him higher into the clouds. She needed to get turned around but the clanging swords, the flashing arrows, and the venomous spears made it impossible from the ground. "HIGHER!" She yelled. "HIGHER!" Her sword was gripped in her right hand, ready for whatever came her way. Lightning, true to his name, had her turned around and at Uncle Tim's side in quick time. As she dismounted, the blood that had spat onto her leather smeared against Lightning's already bloodstained white coat.

"GET YOUR ARMOR!" Uncle Tim bellowed.

"I can't fight in that thing and I can't carry my bow and arrows! I need flexibility. I won't last a minute in armor," Aunt Melissa spat back.

Uncle Tim's voice softened. "I'm sorry. I don't want to lose you tonight." He lowered his tone. "Others fight in armor. You are not in this alone."

"I know." She smiled. "What have you figured out?

"I think he can't get to me because I don't fear him," Uncle Tim said.

"We need to test your theory. I'm going to have to go after him," Aunt Melissa said.

Before she could mount Lightning, Uncle Tim grabbed her arm. "I'm going with you."

"You can't. You're a Commander, and I am a Warrior. You have to strategize a winning battle so that the rest of us will live." Aunt Melissa was determined and her argument made sense.

"First, you are my wife. Where you go, I go, especially if it means death!" His grip was firm.

"You don't have a horse," she said.

"As you pointed out, *I am* the commander. AARON, BRING ME A HORSE!" he barked.

Within a moment, there appeared Michael's mother, Aaron. She was beautiful in every way. Long, straight, brown hair with shimmers of gold streaming like a river down her back. Her torso protected only by a metal plate as her unprotected, muscular legs held tight against Debbie's black ribs. She too was a powerful warrior like Aunt Melissa, and the flexibility they needed for battle would prove to serve them both in the same way.

"Here you are, sir!" she yelled above the roar as she tossed Uncle Tim the reins to his horse. "You'll need this shield since you don't have a metal jacket. Debbie and I are at your service."

Uncle Tim commanded Aaron, "Stay to the rear. We're going after The Skelly. I believe that he cannot read our minds if we do not fear him. If I'm right, we'll be able to slay many of the Skulls, and he won't be able to stop us. If I get close enough to see his bloody eyes, I'll cut them out and feed them to him. We have to get close to prove my theory. Your job is to get this information back to GranMa should Aunt Melissa and I not survive the test."

"Uncle Tim, let me go. You're too valuable," Aaron pleaded.

"Do you think you can face The Skelly without fear?" he asked.

Aaron shook her head no.

"I'm glad you can't. I love you too much to watch you die in this battle." He smiled at his beloved niece.

"Let's go!" Aunt Melissa shouted, raising her sword, and heading into battle.

Blood spewed everywhere. Aaron could taste the beads of blood that landed on her lips; she could smell it in the air, and hear it in the cries of the dying warriors from both sides. Aunt Melissa and Uncle Tim rode steadfast ahead of her, but she never let them out of her sight. Together, they cut down the rotting souls of The Skelly's evil men, but in a flash, it happened. They were closer to The Skelly than anyone had ever gotten. Fearlessly, they swung their swords as they proved Uncle Tim's theory.

How could they know about the invisible Skulls? No one had ever been this close to The Skelly. Aaron couldn't believe her eyes as she watched a sword that seemed to be floating in thin air pierce through Aunt Melissa's side. As if time started moving at a snail's crawl, Aaron watched as a second sword cut across Uncle Tim's unprotected chest while the sound of his scream echoed in her brain.

"NOOOOO!" He screamed before the sword hit his chest, as he watched the love of his life fall into the neck of her steed, Lightning. As if mocking her, her blood mingled with the blood of the evil Skulls she had killed.

Aaron turned fast because this information had to get back to GranMa. "HIGHER!" she yelled, to get Debbie above the battle. It was too late . . . a sword swung across her leg, slicing her femoral artery. The blood coursed through her veins, exiting her sliced artery, never to return to her heart, yet all she could think was, "I have to get back to GranMa."

Long ago, Aaron linked to Debbie. Their thoughts were exchanged in a language only they understood, and they both knew this was Aaron's last ride.

"Debbie, take me back to GranMa; no matter what the cost, get me there alive. GranMa needs to know The Skelly controls our minds through our own fear, and about the invisible Skulls protecting him. Hurry! We're being chased!"

Debbie's high-pitched neigh cried through the night air because her sorrow overwhelmed her as she carried her dying rider. She vowed to Aaron, "I will not let you down, and if I survive, Michael will ride in your saddle."

Aaron fell forward, grasping at Debbie's mane and tangling her fingers into the long hairs to prevent a fall. Debbie's black mane was turning white as blood rushed from Aaron's body. The Skulls were not far behind and Aaron was losing her grip.

Aaron heard hooves thundering too close behind. She turned to see Uncle Jon, GranMa's brother. "Hang on, Aaron! I can keep these Skulls away. You need to hang on and get to GranMa! She'll save you!" Uncle Jon gave his steed a good kick, turned him around, and with sword drawn, he rode directly at the Skulls.

Debbie pleaded, "Don't let go, Aaron, hold on. I cannot communicate with GranMa; you must live long enough to tell her." She continued to jostle Aaron to keep her alive as the cold night air whipped across their faces. Aaron was grateful to spend her last breaths on the horse that had served her so well.

"I am dying a warrior's death, aren't I?" The words struggled to leave Aaron's thoughts. Tears rolled down her face when she finally accepted that this would be her last ride in Diggory Town. "Take care of my children, Debbie. Love them the way I have loved you."

Debbie's large brown eyes burned with sadness as she strained to make it to GranMa in time. Her tears splashed back off her face, hitting Aaron's as pearls of Aaron's blood floated into the wind created by Debbie's massive wings. "Just a little farther," Debbie begged. "Don't die yet . . . not yet . . . you and I are not done. Stay with me, please stay with me. Do it for your children and Diggory Town."

It was enough. Debbie had said just enough to bring Aaron back, and in no time they landed next to GranMa.

"My baby . . . Oh, my sweet baby!" GranMa cried as Aaron's battered body slid off Debbie, past the rod strapped to her saddle, and into GranMa's arms.

Aaron had suffered so much blood loss that she struggled with every sentence. "I'm sorry Ma . . . I didn't make it . . . they got me . . . I didn't see them coming. He has invisible Skulls . . . they protect him.

Aunt Melissa . . . Uncle Tim . . . and I . . . we never saw them coming." Aaron's listless body pushed on. "The Skelly uses fear . . . to control our minds. Courage . . . can overpower his control." And with her last breath, she uttered the only words that might save Diggory Town. "Protect my babies . . . "

GranMa brought Aaron's head into the crook of her arms as she rocked her baby into the silence of death. "I know, my sweet angel. I watched it all. Today my powers were not a blessing; they were my curse. I watched you in battle." The battle raged around her, but GranMa was broken. She did not fight. All she could do was cry, and rock her baby into heaven.

Michael's voice trembled with pain and anger as these images washed over his eyes, but it was rage that kept them from tearing. "GranMa, he will die at my sword, or I will die at his, but his terror will not go unanswered. What happened next?" To formulate the next plan of attack, he needed details about Trafleka. He couldn't afford to make the same errors and have the same results in the next battle. Too many lives had been lost at Trafleka.

"Michael, not today. Cut GranMa some slack. She's had enough," Noah said.

"Easy for you to say, it wasn't your mother!" Michael lashed back.

"Noah, Michael needs this information and so do you. The more you know about what went wrong, the less likely you are to repeat it." Unlike Noah, GranMa knew the value of Michael's questions.

"I thought you considered it a victory," Isabel said.

"It was a victory, but we paid dearly for it. Maybe when I finish my story, you will understand what it cost us, and why it is difficult to view it as a victory." GranMa continued with her story. Her voice began to visually transport them back to the battle.

The first thing they saw was Aaron's lifeless body as Brittani knelt at her mother's side. "Ma? Ma?" Brittani's voice cracked and salty tears drifted into the crook of her mouth. She quickly wiped her eyes to disguise her vulnerability.

GranMa lifted her head, but she did not respond to her eldest daughter. GranMa was finding it hard to breathe, let alone speak or think.

"I'm so sorry, Ma." The words were choking Brittani, but she knew she had to get her mother out of the battle. "Ma, let me carry her."

Brittani's incredible strength did not match her womanly physique. She appeared delicate, but few men could match her in hand-to-hand combat. Brittani gently took her sister's lifeless body out of the cradle of her mother's arms. "Ma, pull your sword, grab Aaron's rod, and let's head to the caves. I will carry her. We need to get to safety."

GranMa just sat there.

Brittani couldn't bear to look upon GranMa—not while "the woman who couldn't be broken" sat before her breaking. In the midst of a battle, Brittani had discovered her mother's kryptonite. Up until then, Brittani believed it was the GranChildren who would prove to be GranMa's Achilles' heel. The walls came closing in on Brittani as she discovered it was her mother's daughters that owned GranMa's heart.

"Mother! Look at me! I am my mother's daughter; Aaron was her mother's daughter. We do not cry. We do not lose control. We do not fear, and we do not lose faith. I hurt too, but she knew the cost, she chose to be here, and she paid the price. Do not dishonor her by losing this battle. We must win this battle and we must protect the children. Anything less dishonors her and all that we have fought and sacrificed for. Now get up and do the things you taught us to do . . . otherwise . . . all you did was lie to us!"

Britt stood and held her sister's lifeless body close to her chest. She walked carefully as she cradled her precious cargo. GranMa could not see the tears marking Brittani's armor as she walked away. She could not feel the burning in Brittani's chest, or the need for revenge that was ravishing her soul. Brittani knew that her day of reckoning would come, but it was not today. Today, Brittani needed to finish *this* battle, because at the next battle, she would exact her vengeance with the rage of a hurricane.

What GranMa couldn't feel, Aaron felt all too well. Her body lay lifeless in her sister's arms, but her soul did not. She felt all that Brittani felt and wanted desperately to comfort her sister who walked away. She needed to say all the things she should have said while her body still breathed. But that moment had passed with so much left unsaid.

"Regret is a terrible thing to take to your afterlife," a beautiful, melodic voice said.

Aaron turned to see a shorthaired, blonde beauty who looked like an angel from the roaring twenties. Full red lips, unblemished pink skin, striking blue eyes—Aaron would know her anywhere. Yvette's picture had graced Aaron's bedroom wall for years. A gift given to her by her mother as nothing more than wall decoration, or at least that's what Aaron thought—until now.

"So I must be dead if pictures are speaking to me," Aaron commented.

"I am anything but a picture, and you are anything but dead," Yvette responded.

"Are you my guardian?" Aaron asked.

Nodding her head in GranMa's direction, Yvette said, "Yes, I have had the privilege of guiding you all your life. She entrusted me with that job on the day you were born."

"So if I'm dead, you failed?"

Yvette chuckled, then said, "I love your sarcasm. However, destiny is destiny, fate is fate, and all I can do is help make the path easier. But the path does not change because of me. It only changes based upon the choices you make."

"Am I dead because I made bad choices?"

"Dear, sweet Aaron. You have not always been easy to guide, but you have always learned from your errors. Because of that, in time, you became wiser than she could have hoped. You have fulfilled your destiny and all your mother's hopes for you. You are dead in *This World* because it is your time."

"So my mother wanted me dead . . . "

Yvette laughed again. "You don't know what you don't know! Your mother only wants to save you. Sometimes we have to die to live. You are only dead in *This World,* and it is my job to get you safely back to *That World.*" Yvette extended her hand to Aaron. "Come, I will tell you of your future in *That World,* where I will continue to guide you."

Before Aaron left, she cupped her hands over her mother's head and gently kissed her. Then she took Yvette's hand and began to float as if on clouds.

GranMa felt a gentle calm settle over her and she came to her feet. She turned to grab Aaron's rod from the saddle, but the rod was missing, so she drew her sword and followed Brittani back to the caves and tunnels. By the time they reached the command post, GranMa had composed herself. She called upon Spencer. "Take your cousins back to The Cave of the Tired Souls. Stay on your guard; The Skelly's greatest victory during this battle is that he has broken my heart. He will want to savor the victory, which puts you and Brittani in mortal danger. Do not hesitate to draw your sword or to call upon magic."

"GranMa, calling upon magic is forbidden. Magic guides us. We do not guide it. I am greatly saddened by our loss, but we should not challenge the Ultimate Ruler. We will be judged by *our* loyalty, not by the loyalty of others. We must do what *we* know is right, and I must protest for the sake of us all."

"Spencer, I would never deliberately cause you to be disloyal. I am not suggesting that you draw upon magic; I am demanding that you call upon the Ultimate Ruler to perform it." GranMa was stern; there was no time for discussion, and she needed Spencer to follow her command. "Take Debbie with you. She belongs with my fallen warrior, and she mourns with the rest of us."

"I understand, GranMa. You will not have to worry about us. You can trust that no harm will come to Brittani or Debbie. I am faithful to the Ultimate Ruler, and I will call upon him if needed." Then Spencer leaned into GranMa and hugged her with protective arms. "I would die if you asked it of me," he whispered.

GranMa stood on her tiptoes and pulled Spencer down so she could whisper in his ear. "I know." Then she gently kissed his cheek. "Go with the Ultimate Ruler's protection."

The visions began to fade as GranMa drew the children back into the present. Her voice cracked as she battled her own weaknesses. Watching her child die for a second time was almost more than she could bear, but GranMa pushed on. "Michael, you are not Debbie's rider. Debbie's rider is with the angels, so she must be communicating to you through Debbie. You must learn to channel your thoughts so that you are linked to your mother while riding her horse. Your powers are connected as long as you are on Debbie. I suspect Debbie's mane has changed color to disguise her from The Skelly."

"GranMa, how did Uncle Tim and Auntie Melissa survive?" Isabel asked.

GranMa took a deep breath and gave a sober smile. "Uncle Jon," was all she replied.

Michael opened his mouth to push for more information that would feed his power. But before any words could leave his lips, Isabel grasped his hand.

"Not now Michael, another day. Grandma will give you more information on another day," she whispered.

Michael understood GranMa's pain, but he was growing fast and required information to complete his growth for battle. He would not let this lie for long.

Chapter 10   Cherith

Bus No. 3 was beginning to feel like home away from home for Noah and Michael. Many countless times they had transported through the painting in GranMa's office, but never before had they done it without permission. And no matter how many times they boarded Bus No. 3, Noah could not escape the uneasy feeling caused by the lights on the second floor of the schoolhouse.

"Where's Lightning?" Noah asked.

Michael shrugged. "I don't know."

"Well, he was in the painting before we transported through it," Noah said.

"Of course he was. You don't think the painting changes in *That World*, do you? What would people think if the painting kept changing every time we were here? Don't you think they might get suspicious? Debbie can pull the bus by herself. All the flying horses can."

"You sure are smart. How do you figure everything out?"

"Little details bud. Pay attention to the little details."

"Michael, why do you think those lights are on in the schoolhouse? That's a little detail." Noah knew this question would make Michael's ears burn, but he couldn't resist harassing him. Besides, he hated not knowing.

"Not that again! GranMa said we're never to enter the school. Never, ever, ever, it's a rule. Why do you have a problem with that?

Do you think GranMa makes up rules just to drive you crazy?" Michael shook his head and rolled his eyes.

"C'mon, Michael, you know it's driving you crazy too. You love information. How come you don't need the answer to this question?"

"You know what I love more than information, Noah? I LOVE RULES! Why do I love rules? Because there are reasons for rules, and rules are created to keep people safe. The only time I need information is when the rules are not keeping us safe, or if someone like The Skelly is breaking the rules. I've never known GranMa to do things just to annoy us. Have you?"

"Well, no . . . " Noah stalled while he tried to think of a good reason for Michael and Noah to get to the second floor. "But I also know that GranMa will do anything to protect us, including risk her own life. What if whatever is up there is a threat to GranMa? Shouldn't we find out and do something to protect her?"

"No argument here," Michael replied, "and as soon as I see a threat coming from that light, I'll do something about it. In the meantime, you keep your curiosity in check, or I'm going to execute the *it's okay for older cousins to clock younger cousins in the head* rule. You got that?"

"Yeah, but—"

"No buts, Noah . . . you got that? But, but, but . . . no buts."

"All right, you big cry baby! But I'm telling you right now, something is odd about that light. Sometimes it's on. Sometimes it's off. You can't tell me there's no one in that room! Besides, Mr. Rules Guy, I'm pretty sure coming here without permission is breaking a rule." Noah wasn't telling Michael things that didn't already concern him.

Michael shot Noah the *you may be strong but I can still clock you* look.

"Okay, okay, I'll lay off," Noah said aloud, but then whispered, "For now."

Soon after Bus No. 3 took off, the lights shut off and the woman slipped out into the cold, dark night. The door creaked. Her eyes darted across the road, making sure the door had not betrayed her. *I need to get that fixed before it becomes the death of me*, she thought. It was hard to tell whether it was her nerves, or the cold, causing her to shake.

"Ma, you out there?" she queried the night air.

Nothing—not a sound. She waited a few more minutes before she turned to reenter the school. But before the door shut behind her, she heard the soft cry of an infant. Her lips widened across her face with a grin touching from ear to ear. She had waited a long time to hear that sound.

As she turned and pushed the door back open, there he was in outstretched arms. "Gavin," she said as both joy and sorrow flowed over her heart. She removed her nephew from the arms, pulled him to her chest, took in a deep breath of his baby fine hair, and kissed him. "How long do I have?" she asked her mother.

"Not long. His parents are trying to get some much-needed rest. Fortunately, he's been keeping them up at night, so they're exhausted. I told them I would watch him for a while so they could sleep. I'll need to get him back to *That World* in a few hours. Take him to Cherith; he must begin the growing process. Have you found a transporter in Cherith?"

"No, I'd like to take Alexis with me. Taking Gavin from here is not safe. I need her to find a transporter for us in Cherith. This is too great a distance for us to travel; it wastes time, and gives evil a greater opportunity to discover him. Without him, there is no future. If anyone finds out about Gavin, danger will erupt everywhere. Evil will stop at nothing to kill him, and stop the future that rests in his tiny little hands."

"Alexis is not good with secrets," GranMa said. "It's risky."

The strong arms cuddling Gavin caressed the silky smooth baby hairs across her chin and cheek. He cooed and smiled at his auntie.

"I know," Brittani said, "but Alexis has grown a lot in a short period of time. She will understand the importance of this secret, and besides, we won't be able to stop Noah's curiosity for long. Eventually, he's going to enter this schoolhouse, and that's another problem we need to deal with. But right now, if word gets out about Gavin . . . well, you know what the results will be. One person leaks information to another, and so on, and so on, and before long, the enemy knows he's born."

"I know how dangerous this is. Maybe I should go to Cherith and find a transporter," GranMa suggested.

"You need to stay here and keep an eye on everyone. We cannot afford to take you to Cherith with no one to monitor the activities of the children. Finding a transporter could take a long time. Who knows what kind of trouble our little heroes could get into while you are gone?"

"Get Gavin to Cherith as soon as possible," GranMa told Brittani. "The more time he is there, the faster he will grow. Go as fast as Lightning will fly, and I'll talk to Alexis."

She mounted the horse and GranMa handed precious Gavin to her.

"She knew, you know," GranMa said. Brittani could not see GranMa's tear-filled eyes in the dark of night.

"Who knew what?" Britt asked.

"Aaron . . . " GranMa choked. "She knew she was pregnant. She said, 'Take care of my *babies*.' She knew Gavin's soul had been delivered to his heart."

"Ma, I . . . "

"There's nothing to say, Britt. Do as she asked. Take care of her babies." The tears that were teetering on the edges of GranMa's eyes finally trickled down her face.

"I will." A loud clicking sound filtered past Brittani's lips, and she said the words Lightning longed to hear: "Giddy up!"

Lightning's hooves were no sooner off the ground when GranMa went after Michael and Noah. They were surprised to see her walking towards them as they made their way to The Cave of the Tired Souls. "So, you boys having a nice trip?"

"Oh—oh!" Noah said, while stumbling over his own feet.

"So, where you goin'?" GranMa asked.

Michael smiled. "GranMa, we've grown a lot and, these days, we feel pretty confident about our skills. Eventually, you're going to have to treat us like men."

Noah threw his chest out. He was fairly certain Michael knew what he was talking about. To Noah's surprise, GranMa smiled at Michael, which caused Noah to throw his chest out even farther.

As GranMa turned to Noah, she crossed her arms over her chest, which was never a good sign. "I don't know what you're feeling all high and mighty about?" She scowled at Noah. "It looks to me like Michael has grown enough to stand his ground. At what point will you stand yours? All I see you doing is hiding behind your cousin's courage."

"That's not fair, GranMa . . . " Michael started, but was abruptly shushed by GranMa.

"Let me tell you what's not fair, young man! It's not fair to jeopardize other people's lives because you are confident you can defend your own. It is not fair to hold eternity in the palm of your hand, and show disregard for it. It is not fair to assume you are ready for battle, and yet, you have passed no test. And it was not fair for me to leave you unprepared for what should happen next. Now let's get your courageous little fannies over to The Cave of the Tired Souls. I know just the man to prepare you for battle. I have a big job for you two, and I must know you can handle it. You may be little men in *This World,* but you are children and toddlers in *That World*. We can ill afford to guess at your skill set."

Tedde and Spencer's brilliant statues stood guard outside the opening. To no one's surprise, Michael pulled the door chime. Once inside, GranMa lifted her scepter, and tapped it to the ground. Immediately, the tunnels came to life with people and blessed creatures going about their daily business. The unseen was now seen in the well-lit tunnels and caves. The energy created in The Cave of the Tired Souls was felt as it shivered into the core of their being. Unlike any other place, whether you are resting in a cavern, or chit chatting in a meeting chamber, vitality is poured into your soul.

Spencer came around a corner, and ran smack into Michael and Noah. "Hey, little buddies. My statue told me you were here, but I wasn't expecting you. What's up?"

"They are courageously breaking rules and defying GranMa," GranMa replied for the boys.

"Well, there's always a fine line between courage and stupidity," Spencer noted.

"Yes, and I believe my two handsome GranSons have crossed it."

"I have sometimes been steep in stupidity myself, but then I make a mental correction, and all is well with the worlds." Spencer laughed while the guilty boys cowered. "So how can I help you torture them, GranMa?"

"Glad you asked. It seems our two heroes have volunteered to venture out on their own at a most opportune time. I need you to train them to protect you-know-who because he has been born, and he will need their particular talents to begin his own growing process."

"Hey, I think Tedde would love this job. She's really good at torturing men." Spencer smiled.

"No, I think we need your talents for this job," GranMa replied.

"GranMa, I'd love to help, but I'm pretty busy right now."

"Doing what?" GranMa challenged Spencer.

"Well I've been doing work around the cave and I have some practicing I need to be doing. I just think she's a better choice is all," Spencer lied.

"Spencer, please tell me this is not about the significance of your job. How many times have I told you? One job is not more or less important than the other."

"Yes, GranMa, but some jobs are more or less exciting than others!" Spencer shot back.

"Oh, really! Why don't you tell that to Amy and Mindy, who gave their lives for a job such as yours? Perhaps they were not aware of a more exciting way of life. Perhaps giving their lives to try and save someone they loved was not exciting enough," GranMa snapped. "Let me remind you of the cost."

"Please, GranMa, don't!" Spencer begged. "I don't want to relive that day."

GranMa gently grabbed his hand. "I know you don't, Spencer, but I need you to do more than understand. I need you to believe that every job, no matter how insignificant it may appear, is important. I also need you to believe with all your heart that the people who do these jobs are as important as any other person. It is exciting to be where the action is, but it is *more important* to be where you are needed. No matter what job you are assigned, you must treat it as if all the worlds depend upon you doing it well. You must always work as if someone's life depends upon you doing the seemingly insignificant job well. And never underestimate what impact your job may have on someone else's ability to do theirs. I know most GranMas would not show children the gruesome realities of life. Most GranMas would shield children from harsh visions and let them remain protected and naive. I am *not* that kind of GranMa. I want the boys—"

"Men!" Noah piped in.

"I want the *men*—" GranMa shot him a half-scowl, half-smile kind of look, "—to know about the importance of doing a job well.

How every detail matters. We must all learn from the Battle of Shame." Her melodic voice began taking the three *men* back in time. They could see the Missing One resting, eyes closed, and a gentle smile across her face when suddenly chaos broke out. In a moment, lives were changed or ended. In a moment, serenity transitioned into a bloodshed. In a moment, history was made, and the future became uncertain.

"It's amazing the difference a moment can make," GranMa whispered, but suddenly raised her voice in authority, which brought them back to the here and now. "Spencer, I need you to teach your cousins how to develop battle skills such as yours. They must learn the importance of developing catlike reflexes through practice, repetition, and trusted instincts. I came to you because I believe that no one has your heart, or your determination. Teach them to feel what you feel. You are a man of honor. Teach them about honor that commands respect and esteem because it is earned through courage, integrity, and trustworthiness. That honor is a demonstration of high moral character, and nobleness that is without compromise. Honor is not a word. It is a state of being. Teach them to be humbly worthy of it."

"I will," Spencer said with a renewed sense of worth.

GranMa looked at Noah, and it was obvious to her that he had grown in *this* moment. "You two boys—pardon me Noah, but you will always be *boys* in my heart—have a very important job to do. Soon you will be assigned to protecting and defending the future," GranMa said.

"I don't understand, GranMa. I thought you said the prophecy says we *are* the future," Michael said.

"It does, and you are. However, everyone has a part, and you are each one fifth of a whole that is equal to the sum of its parts," GranMa replied.

Noah grimaced. "What does that mean?"

"Very funny, fresh face." GranMa tapped his nose. "It means that anything can have pieces, but in order for the *thing* to function, all the pieces must be in place. Think of it like a ball . . . "

"What kind of ball?" Noah asked.

"Any kind of ball, goofis!" Michael replied for GranMa.

"Yes, any kind of ball," GranMa agreed. "Now think of the ball in five pieces and pull one out. How good is that ball now? Will it still throw? Maybe. Is it still catchable? Probably. Will it still bounce?

Doubtful. The point is, it will never function in the perfect way it was intended without all its parts. Therefore, it is only as good as the sum of its parts."

"Ahh," Noah sighed. "I get it!"

"Good! Now you two go with Spencer and don't waste a moment on nonsense. You have a job to do." GranMa didn't believe for a second that they wouldn't be wasting time on nonsense; that was why she asked Spencer to handle their training. Spencer was all fun at play, but at work, he was no nonsense, and the two clowns he was training would be made to toe the line. She knew her *boys* were going to be two *very* tired and overworked souls when they headed back to *That World* tonight. She also knew that, in spite of their teasing and bickering, their love for one another would see them through it.

Over the next couple of months, the boys spent many nights wishing Spencer were not so good at his job.

Chapter 11   Making of a Man

Brittani sat in the shade of a full tree, feeling the cool breeze caress her with a thousand little tickles. The early morning sounds of the Jordon River sang to her ear as its water rippled across the nearby rocks. She cradled the baby higher in her arms to take in the full breath of his powdery smell. He cooed as she mourned this moment that belonged to her sister, and yet she rejoiced in the inheritance of its grace.

"Soon I will tell you a love story about two sisters," Brittani whispered into his ear. "You will learn of two women with one heart, and their dedication to one another. We were not perfect, and neither will you children be perfect, but soon, you will learn that you are perfect together . . . like we were." Thoughts of her sister rolled through her head. She did not try to clear them, but instead, she embraced them. She knew her sister was with the Ultimate Ruler, and that Aaron would be rewarded for her sacrifice, because that was the promise of the prophecy. She was proud that, when given the final test, her sister had not failed.

The solitude of the moment was disturbed by the swishing of branches.

"GranMa, why did you have me meet you here?"

"Shh! Noah be quiet!" Within the blink of an eye, GranMa had Noah in a headlock. Her fingers surrounded his lips and dug into his face, preventing any chance of a sound.

"Whaah, whaah," the baby began to cry, but Brittani was already alarmed to a noise she could not attribute to the child. With weapon drawn, she moved in GranMa's direction.

GranMa threw Noah to the ground and pulled her cloak over both of them. Instantly, they camouflaged into the surroundings. Trying not to breathe, their hearts pounded as Brittani's boots crackled the branches under her feet—branches only inches from their heads.

Once satisfied the area was clear, Brittani took Gavin back to their makeshift home. She entered the cave and tended to his needs.

"And that is why you are here," GranMa said to Noah in a low voice when she felt Brittani was no longer within earshot.

Ignoring GranMa's words, he asked in an equally low voice, "Why didn't she see us under your cloak?"

"Because the cloak camouflages us the same way my armor camouflages."

"Did it make us invisible?"

"No . . . it's more like a chameleon. We blend into the background, but if you look close, you can still see us."

"Can I get one?"

"Cloak or armor?"

"Both."

"Have you had any signs that you will be getting either one of them as part of your gifts?"

"No."

"Then it's a good thing I'm here to help you hide from your mother. It sounds like you won't be getting a camouflage cloak, or armor."

Noah pursed his lips and shook his head, knowing this conversation was going nowhere. "Why are we hiding from my mother anyway? Isn't she one of us?"

Continuing in a low voice Granma responded, "Of course she's one of us! I need you to think about this. You have just spent a couple of months with Spencer honing your battle skills, but there is more to war than a fist and a sword. There is *strategy*. The thing that determines if a war will be won or lost isn't how powerfully you swing your sword. It is deciding when, where, and how you will swing your sword. Preparing a warrior mentally is as important as preparing him physically. So why do you think I don't want your mother to know we are here?"

"Got nothin'," Noah whispered, and shrugged his shoulder.

"What did she do when she thought she heard a noise?" GranMa asked.

"She immediately put the baby in his Moses bed and started looking around."

"Did she have her sword drawn?"

"Ohh yeah! For a moment, I thought I might get beheaded by my own mother!"

"So you'd say she was pretty alert," GranMa commented.

"To say the leas . . . all right, I get it. You don't want her to know we're here because you want her to be on her toes. But that doesn't explain why I'm here."

"Follow me. Star is in a field not far from here. Brittani won't hear us over there." GranMa led Noah away from the cave.

"You're here because you are going to secretly protect the perimeter. You will be the first line of defense for your mother. I don't want her knowing because I don't want her to relax and put her guard down," GranMa told Noah.

"Protect her by myself?" He swallowed.

"Yes," GranMa replied.

"GranMa, I don't know. I'm not ready for something like this."

"We are never ready for that first call of duty, Noah. It is the first step to becoming a real warrior. Prior to this moment, you were a warrior-in-training. Now, you will be a warrior applying his newly learned skills. Only experience will make you a great warrior, and experience only comes from doing the things you have trained to do."

"How do you know I can do this?" Noah paced and rubbed his temples and forehead.

"I don't. We only find out who we are when we are tested. Banging your chest and telling people how great you are doesn't make you great. We are defined by what we *do*, not by what we *say*. All that running around yelling and pretending to fight that you and Michael used to do was untested bravado. Boys declare their honor, but as men, you must prove it. A person can say all the right things, convey a heart of gold, and promise you the world, but in the end, it's what people *do* that matters."

"So you're going to leave me in this wilderness with no food or supplies and you expect me to protect my mother and cousin without my mother knowing it?"

"Yes."

"No supplies."

"They only weigh you down."

"GranMa, this is crazy!"

"No Noah, this is life."

"What about Michael? He's older, bigger, smarter, and more resourceful," Noah begged, allowing his voice to raise slightly.

"Actually, Alexis would probably be a better choice, but she was not chosen for this job, you were."

"I wouldn't put either one of my sisters in harm's way. It's my job to protect them." Noah paused as he considered the hypocrisy of what he had just said. "Okay, that doesn't make sense. Saying I would protect my sisters but not my mother and baby cousin, but you know what I mean . . . don't you GranMa?"

"I've been in your shoes, Noah. I know exactly what you mean."

"Good, then you know I'm not the best choice."

"You are my only choice. No one will do a better job than you."

Noah began to have a conversation with himself. He paced like a wild cat in an eight foot cage. Rubbing his temples, his forehead, and then brushing his hands through his hair. "Crazy talking. This is just crazy talking." He continued to mumble to himself.

Once they reached a clearing, GranMa mounted her winged horse, Star, who had been waiting patiently, and Noah continued to lose his mind.

"GranMa, how can you leave me out here alone? I will die! This isn't a brilliant idea! You don't know as much as you think you know! I am not ready for this!" Noah was pleading more than he was complaining.

"Surely you don't think I am brilliant, Noah, because I am not." GranMa leaned forward in her saddle; her confident eyes stared back into his ridiculing glare. "I know that in the immense scope of the universe, I know nothing. I am but a pin-dot in the night sky, limited by the things that make me human. I start everything with the assumption that I know nothing, and from there I learn. I am wise because I know I know nothing, and it is that wisdom that you interpret as brilliance. If I thought you were not capable of defending my daughter and my youngest grandson, you would not be here. There is nothing to discuss. You will be the warrior I know you were born to be. You are more than your heart tells you you are. You are not here because I want to test you. You are here because I believe in you, and you are too good a man to waste." With that, GranMa snapped Star's reins and began to fly away.

In a final desperate attempt to change his fate, Noah yelled, "GRANMA, WHAT IF I CAN'T DO THIS?"

GranMa stopped as if her winged horse had been caught in a snare. She turned in her saddle to look upon the boy/man who she loved so well. Her face tightened as a sad, nervous smile made its way from her heart to her face. "WHAT IF YOU CAN?" she shouted back before she headed into the sun-filled sky whose light only gave her further cause to hang her worried head.

But Noah's head was lifted skyward and his worries had just begun. "What did he say? What did he say? WHAT DID HE SAY?" Noah pounded his head as he struggled to remember all that Spencer had taught him. "First don't panic . . . first don't panic . . . first don't PANIC! Are you kidding me? Arrrrrgh!" Noah pulled at his hair. "I can't think of anything to do but panic."

"Think about what matters to you most," Noah heard Spencer's calm voice say. "What could be worse than the situation you are in right now? What will happen if you don't do your job? Who will do it if you don't? Can you live with yourself if you don't try to do what must be done? Who would you rather see dead? The person you are protecting . . . or you?"

A sudden calmness overcame Noah. Suddenly, the haze had lifted. He could think because fear had completely abandoned him. He knew the answer to the final question. The woman who had given him life was too beautiful to die. He couldn't imagine a world without her long curly hair, bright eyes, big laugh, and beautiful smile. He would defend her and that sweet, innocent baby with every ounce of strength and courage he had. Of course he would, and he would be smart about it too. What did Spencer say?

"Don't worry about what you don't have. Determine your assets and know your liabilities. Have at least two plans, but three is better. I can teach you how to swing a sword, but only you can decide when the right time is to swing it. Sometimes the best weapon you'll have is good judgment; make sure you use it."

Noah began to take stock of his assets and liabilities. "I'm strong, and no matter what my cousin says, I'm smart. I have my sword, my dagger, and my bow and arrows." Noah stroked the cold steel at his side, reached down to ensure his dagger was in his boot strap, and shifted his shoulders to feel the bow and arrows on his back. "I have plenty of weapons, but I don't have a horse, and I can't make a fire to cook any food I might gather because my mother will notice. My mother has Lightning. How am I going to keep up if she moves? What did Spencer say?" Noah rubbed his head as if trying to massage Spencer's words from his memory.

"Unless your life depends on it, you don't need to address every liability immediately, but you must know what they are immediately. It's better to give real thought to your predicament and make the best decision, then to jump to a ridiculous conclusion."

"Okay, I don't need a horse this minute, but I'd better come up with one soon."

As the sun began to set, Noah felt the chill of the night air move over his skin. The Jordan River was beautiful by day, but by night, the humidity it caused laid against his skin like a cold, wet rag.

"Oh man, I'd better add bad weather to my liabilities. Shoot! Let's see . . . check out my surroundings, address the immediate need, which is warmth, and maybe stop talking to myself before my mother hears me." Noah walked in a large circle around his mother's cave so that he could survey and understand the environment he was up against.

All right then, he thought, *I'll make camp on high ground so I can get a better view of what's coming up the hill and stay out of her line of sight. I'll make a debris blanket like Spencer taught us, and then I'll hunker down for the night.*

When he found the right spot, he pulled his dagger from his boot and stabbed the ground repeatedly. Then he used his bare hands to dig out the area he had stabbed. The topsoil was easily removed, but before long, his hands began to ache, as the soil became dense. He stopped digging to rub the ache out of his hands, and happen to see a broken tree branch with an end resembling a shovel. Using the tree branch, he dug a clearing about four feet long and two feet wide. "Not too big," Spencer had said. "It contains your body heat better if it's cozy. Remember the debris blanket is about warmth, not comfort."

After he dug down about eighteen inches, he began filling the hole with fallen leaves, moss, ferns, and anything cushiony he could find that might work as an insulator. Then he found some long, lanky branches and began weaving them together. Once he created a frame, he wove soft, pliable, branches with leaves into the frame to create his blanket. But this did not distract him from his real mission. He kept one eye on the valley and the cave below.

There, he thought, *it's not my Superman comforter, but it'll do the job.* He took one last look around the circle, and then turned in for the night.

He woke to a clear blue sky, the smell of bacon, and an angry, crying baby. *Mmmm, bacon.* He stretched. *Darn! It's not for me. Thanks Mom for torturing me with your breakfast. This is just cruel and unusual punishment*, Noah thought. *I shouldn't have made GranMa mad, and then it would be Michael sleeping under this rat's nest. Now, what to eat?*

Spencer said avoid white and red round berries. Water hemlock is the most poisonous plant in the area and can kill you with one bite; I hope I can remember what it looks like. Protein . . . yum, I love fish and the Jordon is right there. I can eat it raw . . . yuck! I can also dry the fish out in the sun so that will make it easier to carry and stock. I'll create a dam to trap the fish then I'll make a spear with a stick and my dagger. How do I do that without my mother seeing me?

Just then, he spotted some blueberries and wild prickly gooseberries sitting right near some mint leaves. *Yum! Thank you, Ultimate Ruler, at least someone is showing me compassion.*

Shoot, Spencer said don't eat the food closest to your camp. Save that for emergencies in case you find yourself in a situation where you can't move from the camp. Well, maybe I'll find the same kind of food fifty or sixty yards away. With that in mind, Noah began using his good judgment, and the survival skills Spencer had taught him.

"Wow, Spencer taught us a lot. I don't remember paying this much attention to him. Huh!" He rubbed his head, unable to resist saying this aloud.

Around lunchtime, Brittani mounted Lightning and headed down the hill with Gavin cradled to her chest in the papoose she'd made for him.

Noah panicked because he hadn't expected her to leave so soon. *What to do?* Noah asked himself. *Think . . . don't reach ridiculous conclusions. GranMa said protect the perimeter as if she expected Mom to stay here. Mom didn't take anything with her except the baby; that means she's coming back. Of course she is. She has to get Gavin back to That World since Auntie Aaron isn't aware of Diggory Town anymore. She can only keep Gavin here for short periods of time. Oh Ultimate Ruler, please make that true. Don't let me reach ridiculous conclusions*, Noah begged as he massaged his head.

Noah spent the rest of the day worrying, but not wasting time. He began surveying his mother's camp but touching nothing. He engaged in all the noise-making activities he couldn't do when she was in camp. Surveillance was a long, silent, boring job, and most of the time was spent sitting and watching. He had to do what he could when she was gone. If his mother were to come back tonight—no, when his mother came back tonight, he would be better prepared.

Day turned into night and still nothing. Noah was fast becoming panicked. *Don't do it . . . don't do it*, he thought as he rubbed his hands. *Panicking will get you nowhere.* As he gazed into the star-lit sky, he noticed three brilliant lights. *Huh, those are odd lights*, he thought, as one started moving towards him. He ran and cowered into his debris blanket as old fears and innocence crept back into his two-almost-three-year-old mind. *I don't belong in Diggory Town with all these monsters*, he rationalized when his instincts became more powerful than his realities.

The brilliant light whispered out to him, "Noah! Noah!"

From under the cover, Noah stared back into the small but brilliant light whose center was like the pupil of an eye, only whiter than any white he remembered. His eyes burned as they strained to look into the core of the light sprays that flew from the pupil. There was something familiar about the voice, but he didn't want to be tricked by the harsh beauty of the light.

"Noah, it's me Jackson. C'mon, stop being a chicken. GranMa sent me."

"I'm no chicken! I'm just trying to be smart!" Noah shouted back as he jumped from under his blanket. "Your sister and brother taught me to be cautious. You want me to tell Tedde and Spencer their *baby* brother, Jackson, is trying to undermine my training."

"Shhh. Okay, okay, you're a big strong hero, now quiet down before someone hears you, tough guy. Jeez Louise," Jackson's voice called back. "Listen up before Cousin Brittani gets back. GranMa wants me to let you know she's on her way so don't jump her or anything. She needs to bring Alexis out with her to find a transporter. Your mother is in real danger each time she travels with Gavin, and riding horseback is a big time waster. Gavin will be a slow grower and he needs all the time he can get in Diggory Town. Something to do with him being a preemie or something."

"What's that?"

"What's what?"

"Preemie . . . "

"I don't know, Noah. Maybe it's something magical or girly, but that doesn't matter—listen up. Anyway, Katie, Nicky, and I are here to let you know what's going on before Brittani gets back."

"Jackson, c'mon. What's takin' you so long? This is dangerous," one of the other lights said.

"Noah's like Cousin Michael. He thinks he needs to know every little detail," Jackson responded to the light.

Noah took it as a compliment, and said, "Hey, Jackson! Spencer, told me to pay attention to details. You want me to tell him his *baby* brother is undermining him?"

"No! And stop saying *baby*. Just shut up and listen," Jackson's hurried voice said. "They'll be here soon. Alexis will be everywhere looking for a transporter, and you need to stay out of sight. Got it?"

"Yeah, I got it," Noah responded.

"Ouch! Cut it out, Katie, let go of my ear!" Jackson moaned.

"Oww! Let go of my ear, Katie, I didn't do anything," Nicky groaned.

"What part of get in there, update Noah, and leave quickly didn't you two clowns understand? I thought GranMa was very clear about this," Katie said to her brother, Nicky, and her stepbrother, Jackson. "Sorry you had to hear this, Noah. It's my job to keep these two knuckleheads out of trouble. Now quiet down, you two. See you, Noah, and good luck. We'll be watching you from up here. We can't do much in this form but communicate and move at the speed of light. Just know you're not alone; at least not for tonight."

"Thanks, Katie. Good luck, knuckleheads." Noah chuckled.

"Noah!" Katie whispered as loud as she dared.

"Yeah?" he whispered back in the same tone.

"Let the ravens and the bees feed you."

Before the lights returned to the sky, Noah could hear the swishing of Lightning and Star's wings. He raced and jumped under his debris blanket. While he lay quietly on the debris mattress, and before the Star Riders had flown too far away, he heard Katie say to her brothers, "She's coming. We might as well deliver the final soul tonight." Noah was stunned at the words "*the final soul*." What did that mean, and who was *she*? Then he heard his mother's voice.

"Were those the Star Riders?" Brittani asked, casting a quizzical glance in the direction of the debris blanket. Noah's heart nearly jumped out of his chest, but then his mother turned back to GranMa.

"Yes," GranMa responded. "I asked them to scope out the place before we returned. You know, make sure it's safe."

"Good thinking. Will they always be here?"

"No, can't do it. We only have three of them, and they can't be everywhere, but they'll be checking on you often," GranMa lied. "Alexis, slide down off of Star so I can dismount."

"I can't wait until I get my own wings." Alexis smiled as she glided down Star's dark, silky rump.

"What makes you so sure you're getting wings?" GranMa asked.

"I can just feel it." Alexis sang the words as she twisted her arms behind her, and ran the tops of her fingers over her shoulder blades, contemplating the silky smooth softness of the feathers she would soon find there. "Ahh, the freedom of wings. My legs will no longer be a slave to walking," she mused.

"Well, get your slave legs moving. We don't have much time before you have to get back to *That World*. We need to find a transporter as soon as possible." Brittani chuckled.

"You're assuming there *is* a transporter, Brittani," Alexis said.

"Of course. There's always a transporter," Brittani responded.

"Not necessarily, Britt," GranMa said. "You've always had one at your disposal because the closer you get to the center of Diggory Town, the more there are, but we are on the fringes of the kingdom. There aren't as many out here because we don't want any crossovers from the other worlds. We can't assume transporters are everywhere."

"Can't they be created? Surely someone created the existing transporters."

"Someone did. Your GranMother, Mimi, created the transporters, but she's no longer with us in Diggory Town. I don't know of anyone else capable of creating a transporter, so we need to find an existing one. Alexis and I will get to work."

"Ma, I didn't know Mimi could perform magic. She never told me she was blessed with magic."

"She wasn't, honey. She was a great scientist like you and your sister. Not everything is magic. Some things are just good science, and in Diggory Town, you call me GranMa."

"Yeah, sorry, forgot!" Brittani grimaced.

Alexis chuckled to see Brittani getting into trouble like a little kid. She was even happier to be a crucial part of protecting the future. She felt like a superhero as she walked around the area with her arms spread, waiting for the feeling of déjà vu.

Brittani's chest also pushed out as she watched Alexis with her outstretched arms, demonstrating courage and maturity that Brittani had never seen in her before. Brittani was bursting with love for the child who once thought she didn't have a place in the world. This kid had a place of honor in two worlds, and for the first time, the child believed it. Yet Brittani couldn't help but notice that while the other children were growing taller, Alexis actually appeared to be getting smaller.

"GOT IT!" Alexis yelled with great pride.

Noah was happy to see that the transporter was inside the cave and not next to his blanket. Unfortunately, it also meant that he would not have a visual of the transporter. It would be more difficult for him to monitor his mother's comings and goings.

Cradled in Brittani's arms, Gavin cooed as if he were congratulating Alexis on her wonderful find.

"Ahh, the sweet smell of success, huh buddy?" Brittani said to Gavin as she took in a deep breath of his sweet baby smells. At exactly that moment, a rather loud sound came out of a rather small baby's bottom.

Alexis said, "How does that bit of success smell?"

Chapter 12   The Humbling of a Man

Over the course of the next few weeks, Noah realized many things, including this would be a long-term assignment. As instructed, he did not travel far from camp, and he certainly did not head upriver. Outside of a half-mile area, he knew little of what was south of him, and nothing of what laid north.

He built an excellent debris hut atop his debris blanket. It provided him with a small, six feet long, four feet wide, two feet tall shelter, where he could store his limited supplies and camouflage himself when needed. Built against the edge of a small rock incline, it was unrecognizable, and the false door he created was undetectable. Noah felt grateful to Spencer for being a tough, and demanding, trainer. Noah was sure Spencer's discipline was saving his life—that and Katie's advice.

"Let the ravens and bees feed you," Katie had said.

It was three days of eating nasty raw fish, live bugs, and choking on wild garlic, onion, and other assorted vile roots and weeds, before he finally found out what she meant. On the third day, he walked into the woods, not finding any food fifty to sixty yards from his camp, when he saw a raven carrying a berry branch. *Yum, if I could catch you, I'd take those berries from you*, he thought. Then it struck him, that's what Katie meant: the ravens will take you to the food. He kept his eyes on the ravens, and before long, they led him to fields of berries and edible plants. If they ate it, he ate it, and if they stayed away from it, he stayed away from it. Once, he even found robin's eggs for protein. Mixed with the honey, he found the eggs didn't taste as bad raw as you might think. Finding the bee hive was a stroke of luck, and once he learned to harvest from it without being stung, he was set. Honey is delicious; even worms taste good with honey on them. This place was beginning to feel like home—a lonely home, but home.

Brittani's days were random. Sometimes, she spent many hours in Cherith with the baby, and sometimes only a few. Occasionally, she and Gavin would stay there for three days in a row and he grew a lot during those times. Still, Gavin's growth was as slow as Jackson had predicted. Fortunately, there was no activity on the Jordon River that concerned Noah, or his mother.

The days were lazy, but Noah never let his guard down for fear of being caught by his mother. This caused him to be mindful of everything. Had he not feared being caught by her, he may have become complacent, and less aware of his surroundings. He suspected that GranMa understood this phenomenon, which was precisely why she'd created the anxiety. The more he grew, the wiser GranMa became in his eyes.

Gavin, on the other hand, lacked everything: wisdom, intellect, motor skills, and the ability to go potty anywhere but in his own pants. But you don't need to know anything when you're as cute as Gavin. His face was finally filling out, and his huge, bubbly gray eyes drew you in like a black hole. You couldn't help but wonder what greatness lie just beyond the void.

Prophecy told them Gavin was destined to greatness; but first they'd have to get him to sit up on his own. His giggly little personality was a big asset to Noah. Gavin's giggles always warned him that Brittani was seconds from transporting into the cave. Until this assignment, Noah was completely unaware that noise could be heard in the transporter seconds before the transport was complete. It was good information to have.

In *That World,* Gavin couldn't keep his own head up, but in *This World,* he was wobbling his way to an upright position. Auntie practiced with him regularly, and Gavin would giggle and giggle at the little game. Drooling, chewing on his fingers, even figuring out he had fingers, was all so much fun. Noah loved knowing that his mother had fawned over him in exactly this same way. He loved seeing this side of his warrior mother, who was the model of strength and power in Diggory Town. It pleased him to know that her nurturing gentleness transcended both worlds.

But this play was part of a bigger picture. GranMa instructed everyone to get Gavin growing fast. "It is everyone's responsibility," she said. "We cannot begin training him until he reaches the physical age of two." Noah surmised that at the current rate of growth, they would need at least another nine to twelve weeks in Diggory Town.

Nine to twelve weeks, Noah thought. *Jiminy Cricket! How much more will I grow in nine to twelve weeks? I'll be as old as the hills, for crying out loud; assuming I don't accidentally eat water hemlock. Heck, if it gets any lonelier out here, I just might make myself a hemlock stew*, he joked. *Gosh, I hope I'm not going crazy.*

In the middle of Noah's crazy thoughts, his mother stood up in alarm. Her body constricted as she gazed across the valley and, without hesitation, she grabbed Gavin and his things. In haste, she made sure to minimize any evidence that they had been there, and then she headed to the transporter.

When Noah was certain she was gone, he stood up and cupped his right hand, fashioning it into a telescope. During the boring moments, he'd discovered that when he placed his *hand-telescope* over one eye, it allowed him to focus better on the areas he was scouting. In the distance, he could see it—the speck that had alerted his mother to danger. How was this possible? He could barely see the figure moving, so how did she know it was there? He was certain that the figure was unaware of his presence.

"Yeah, there's no way he knows we're here," Noah heard his own voice whisper as his right hand slid down his face but stopped at his chin. His right hand's middle finger and thumb gripped the sides of his chin as his index finger began to tap repeatedly upon its center. "I can get him. I can stop him before he does any harm," his voice whispered as his fingers and thumb mashed, pulled, and tapped at his chin. He could feel his own heart slow as he began to devise a plan. His chest breathed with a calm he had never experienced. A heaviness found itself in the middle of his body, creating a center of gravity. The eerie warrior's calm that would soon become a part of him, told him he was in control.

I have no horse. I must bring him to me. He searched the cave for anything to signal the rider; he found a tin cup. He brought it to the daylight, but had difficulty getting a downward reflection that would alert the rider. He was starting to panic that his opportunity was slipping away, when suddenly, the rider turned in his direction. Noah threw himself down near the edge of the cliff, and allowed the cup to dangle in his fingers as if he had died with his fingers in a curled position.

With a vise-like grip, the rider thrust his heels into the sides of his horse and headed up the small mountain at a gallop. Noah could hear the rhythmic pounding of the hooves as the rider got closer, but he did not budge. His breaths were shallow to keep the rider from observing the rise and fall of his chest.

You're not a very smart one, Noah thought as he heard the sound of boots approaching his body. He wanted to yell as a sharp kick came to his side—but he didn't yell. The boots had provided Noah with what he wanted to know—the exact location of his victim.

When Noah heard the sound of the foolish man's boots sliding across the gravel in such a way as to kick him again, Noah turned precisely as Spencer had taught him. He then twisted his legs around the man's legs, causing him to lose his balance, and in the blink of an eye, Noah brought him to the ground with a thud. The man was no match for Noah's power, and before the man knew what hit him, Noah's weight was crushing his chest.

Looking up at the weeks-long weary and disheveled Noah, the putrid, filthy man—who smelled of rotting flesh and infected pustules—just assumed Noah shared his destiny. "I'm just like you!" the man shouted. "I'm just like you! I work for the Master."

"Which Master?" Noah spat back.

"The Skelly!" the man retorted.

"He's no master of mine!" Noah bellowed as he reached down with the swiftness of a falcon and grabbed his cold, sharp dagger from its sheath, raised it high, then plunged it into the side of the man's throat.

Noah's face began to pound as he sat, stunned, upon his victim's chest while life gurgled out of it. The man made a final gasp for air by lifting his head. His thick tongue slid down his chin and blood drizzled off it. His rotting, jagged teeth, corrupting the air with their essence, barely caught Noah's attention. Motionless, he stared down at the man, and wondered about the man *he* had become. What foul twist of fate separated him from his victim, or did it?

"Noah."

He did not turn to look at the face of the familiar voice. He just continued to stare at the man.

"Noah!" This time, she was certain he had heard her. "Noah, get up and look at GranMa." Her soft-spoken but commanding voice insisted, but he remained a statue.

Her armor only tinged slightly as she moved closer, bent, and touched his arm. "Do you know who this man is?"

His stunned face turned left and right, and then left and right again, but his voice remained trapped in his throat. Tears teetered on the ledges of his bottom eyelids, longing to betray his youthful masculinity.

"I've been tracking him for weeks," Tedde's voice offered.

Finally, he turned to see who and how many were there. There were only the two.

"How did you know?" Noah asked.

"The Star Riders . . . " Tedde's voice drifted as she pursed her lips and shrugged her shoulders, as if offering condolence. She remembered her first kill. One can never forget their first kill—no matter how they try. It visits them in their dreams, playing over and over again, as if trying to give them an opportunity to change the past. To never have killed—how peaceful that must be. However, she had killed at the Battle of Shame, and under the same circumstance, she'd do it again, even though it didn't stop Mindy from dying. She had killed Mindy's murderer; it was a justified kill, but that didn't stop it from hunting her in her sleep.

"Noah, he's a very bad man. Hope identified him as one of The Skelly's men. I was tracking him hoping he'd lead me back to one of their camps. I lost him just outside Maranatha Valley. I think he discovered me in the sky and fled by night. This man would have killed you, your mother, and Gavin had he found you. It was just a matter of time before he killed someone you love. Then you would have to live knowing you didn't stop him!" Tedde knew this sorrow too well. The one that hunted her, choked her, paralyzed her with the fear that she could fail again. She was determined that this demon would not know another victim—at least not one in her family. "Get up, Noah! Do not mourn this rotting mass of depraved humanity!" Suddenly, Tedde felt contempt and anger the same way she always did after a kill. She resented that evil forced her to also do evil.

Recompense to no man evil for evil, is what the Rule Book that judged her so harshly said. Well, she would not stand idly by and watch evil do its work. She *would* recompense evil for evil.

"Noah, you didn't kill a good man. Now get up!" Tedde demanded.

Noah looked at the man in disbelief. He had killed and it didn't matter if the man was good or bad. What does one do after he has killed? Do you go make lunch and take a nap? Do you go for a leisurely swim to wash the blood away? What precisely is it that one does immediately after he kills?

"Noah, help me get this body out of here before your mother returns. GranMa, where should we put it?" Tedde asked as Noah finally stood.

"We'll take it back with us in the transport, then see if anyone knows anything about this guy," GranMa responded. "Noah, did he say anything to you about what he was doing or where he was going?"

"No."

"Did you see anyone else?"

"No."

"Darn! This is Bill Hight's horse. Look at the markings on the saddle. We haven't seen Bill for many weeks. He'd never give up his horse to this guy. This creep must have killed Uncle Jon's best friend." With that, Tedde walked over and gave the dead man a tremendous kick to his already dead ribs." *CRACK!* The rib snapped. "Good!" Tedde spat.

Noah walked up to the horse and stroked its stocky neck. "It's an odd looking creature. It looks like a Frankenstein horse. The face is unbalanced with brown, black, and white markings everywhere. Huh, one side of his face doesn't match the other. I'll bet if I took pictures of each side of him, you'd swear it was different horses." Noah ran his hand down the horse describing each feature as he came to it. "His neck and shoulders are brown and white; front legs are brown; white and brown hindquarters and midsection; white back legs; a black tail; and his mane is mostly white except behind and between his ears its black." Noah ran his hand across the other side of the exhausted, barely cared for horse, and continued to state the obvious. He'd rather talk about anything, then answer the questions he was sure would come next. "It's like someone took pieces of multiple horses and put this horse together. The only things that match are his hooves. At least they're all blond. What's his name?"

"I don't know," Tedde responded. "Do you know, GranMa?" Tedde called to GranMa, who was surveying the area.

"No, umm, no I don't," GranMa called back, trying not to lose focus. She searched the horizon for clues as to why this man was here. Were there others, and what was his mission? Did he even have a mission, or was he just unfortunate enough to wander in this direction? Worst yet, why did he look so familiar?

"I'll call him Frank," Noah said. "Can I have him, GranMa?"

GranMa replied while still looking for clues. "I think Bill would be proud to have the man who avenged his death ride his pride and joy."

Noah couldn't help but notice that GranMa had called him *a man*.

"Do you think he's an appaloosa or pinto?" Noah asked no one in particular.

"Neither. He's an Abaco Wild Horse from the Caribbean. His markings help him blend into the surrounding trees in the Bahamas. He's extremely rare and Bill was a proud owner. I just don't remember him calling the horse by name, but I'll bet Bill would like the name Frank," GranMa said.

"I can ride him back if you'd like," Tedde suggested.

"If it's okay with you, GranMa, I'd like to keep him here, with me. I don't have a horse, and I'm always wondering what I'll do if I need one."

"It's kind of hard to hide a horse." GranMa smiled.

"No, there's a field on the other side of the mountain where I get my food. I can keep him there. She'll never hear him." Noah became hopefully excited.

"Good enough," GranMa consented with a whole heart. It seemed to her that this horse and Noah had much in common. This horse was handsome with a sturdy, compact body and strong legs, just like his new owner. He also did not cave to his dire circumstance, just like his new owner. *There is honor in this horse*, GranMa thought as she stroked him. She loved the long, lustrous, mostly white mane and extremely long, black tail; it reminded her of another horse she knew. More importantly, the horse seemed to sense that Noah was rescuing him, and with any luck, they had linked.

Now that she had Noah in a different state of mind, there was more serious business to tend to.

"Noah, I know this is difficult, but we must have this conversation—"

Before GranMa could finish, Noah interrupted. "It's okay, GranMa. Spencer explained this part to me. A warrior learns more after a battle than he will ever learn during. We discuss what went right, what we did wrong, what was gained, what was lost, did we serve the Ultimate Ruler with honor, and how can we do better? I *am* sad that I killed this man, but I am a warrior. I must live with all that I do and make sure that all that I do serves a greater good."

"Wow! *My* brother, Spencer, taught you that?" Tedde mused. "Tall guy, big wings, thinks he's smarter than everyone else?"

"Yup," Noah responded.

"Well, maybe he is smarter than everyone else." Tedde laughed.

"Okay, you two clowns, let's get down to business. We need to figure out why this guy is here," GranMa said. "Noah, what *exactly* did he say to you before, well, before you erased his existence?"

Noah lowered his chin to his chest and mumbled, "He said something like I'm just like you. I work for the Master."

"I know this isn't easy, but you must look at me as we speak, and raise your voice please," GranMa said.

"I . . . um, I believe he said I was *just like him*." The words rang in Noah's ears. "And he . . . um . . . said he worked for the Master." Noah wrung his hands as he struggled to drag every word from his vocal cords.

"You're nothing like him! Nothing!" Tedde said with complete authority.

"Maybe, or maybe I'm more like him than I knew," Noah muttered with complete shame.

"It's times like these that test men's souls," GranMa said. "Good men sometimes do bad things because that is the nature of humanity. If this were not true, then there'd be no use for shame because only evil would beget evil, and only good would beget good. What causes us to misstep is we forget that sometimes good men do bad things, and sometime bad men do good things. However, one act does not cancel out the life that has been lived. A person is the *sum* of their life; they are not summed up by one moment in their life. Before your life is over, I believe it will be summed up into something good and wonderful." GranMa rubbed Noah's shoulder.

"You're my GranMa. You have to say that." Noah smiled.

"Haven't you noticed? I'm not that kind of GranMa." She smiled.

"I'll say!" Tedde chuckled.

"Now let's get on with this. We need to dissect what happened so we can figure out how safe Brittani and Gavin will be here," GranMa said.

With renewed vigor, maturity, and authority, Noah began to dissect the scene. "He was coming from the west, which is why I had to squint to see him; the sun was in my eyes. Using my hand-telescope—" (Noah demonstrated) "—I could see him riding along the river heading north through those trees." Noah pointed to an area where the trees were sparse. "I was alerted when my mother jumped up. How could she hear him from here? She had her back to the sun."

"Star Riders," Tedde said. "They're hard to see in the sun, but they were here."

"Oh yeah. Well anyway, I was up there were I usually sit while my mother moves around the camp. I like to sit there because I get a pretty good view of the camp but, as you can see, it's not visible from down here . . . " Noah went on to tell the story of how he overcame the man.

"Well, there's not much there," GranMa concluded. "I'll send the Star Riders upriver to see what they can find. Let's see if there's something Frank can tell us."

"Frank has a lot of dried mud on his coat," Tedde said as she licked her fingers, then ran them across Frank's chest and licked them again. A heavy salt lay across her tongue.

"Yuck!" Noah squirmed.

"This from a guy who eats worms." Tedde laughed. "He's been ridden hard," she said as she began lifting each hoof. "When did Bill come up missing?"

"Three, maybe four months ago," GranMa answered.

"He would have never let Frank get this run down. Look at these shoes. Custom shoes, flat, embedded with rocks, and imbalanced; this horse has been ridden hard for long distances over a short period of time. Looks like the start of an abscess on this hoof. I'm surprised he's not lame," Tedde said, and then whispered into

Frank's ear, "Poor thing," and kissed the side of his face. "The dead guy has been up to something and my guess is it wasn't good. Noah, hand me your dagger." She wiped the blood on her leather skirt, and then began digging the crud out from Frank's shoes, catching it in her hand.

"Do you have anything we can collect this stuff in? Maybe Brittani can analyze it for us. It might tell us where Frank has been." Tedde was looking at Noah.

He picked the tin cup off the ground, and handed it to her.

She poured the crud into the cup, and then she opened the saddlebag to rummage through the dirty belonging of the dead man. She crinkled her nose and clenched her teeth at the lingering body odor that smelled like dumpster juice mixed with blue cheese. Cringing as her fingertips touched the grime that had become part of the fabric, she removed the contents of the saddlebag. Near the bottom, she found something precious. It was a child's embroidered handkerchief tucked into the corner of the bag. The pink letters called out Bill Hight's place in the universe: "World's Greatest Father." Tedde once again walked over to the corpse and, with a great thrust, kicked his ribs. Only this time the force was enough to cause daylight to peek between the man's dead carcass and the ground.

"You keep that up and there'll be so much damage, we'll discover nothing further from this insidious piece of scum," GranMa warned.

Tedde tossed GranMa the handkerchief. Upon close inspection, GranMa immediately walked up to the man and kicked him so hard that Tedde thought she heard the dead man groan.

"Let's get back to finding out why a good man lost his life to this rotting vermin. My brother, Jon, will seek revenge that far exceeds an eye for an eye. This vermin's life doesn't begin to pay the debt owed."

Noah asked, "Does Bill's family travel between the worlds?"

"No, only Bill," GranMa responded. "Uncle Jon brought him here before Bill ever married. They were working in Albuquerque, New Mexico, when mountains of evil stirred in Diggory Town," GranMa said while continuing to look around the camp for any evidence that might help them discover this putrid man's intentions. "Uncle Jon went to Santa Fe to see if he could figure out where all the disruptions were coming from; Bill secretly followed him. Bill's instincts were strong and he knew his best friend was heading into harm's way."

"GranMa are you saying that all the evil of Diggory Town started with Uncle Jon going to Santa Fe?" Noah's voice creaked, causing GranMa to remember he was only a child in *This World,* and still a toddler in *That World.*

"No, don't be silly." She chuckled. "His being there was just a coincidence. Wait until we have all the children together and I'll tell you how evil walked into Diggory Town." Tedde shot GranMa a look that begged her not to tell.

"C'mon, Tedde, get back to business," GranMa insisted.

Tedde ran her hands under Frank's undercarriage to find it still damp and warm. "Was he running when you saw him near the river?" Tedde asked Noah.

"No, it was a leisurely trot."

"Did anything about the man tell you he was alarmed?" Tedde asked.

"I didn't pay that much attention. I was busy trying to figure out how to get him up here so I could stop him," Noah replied.

"Next time, consider taking a prisoner. We don't have much to go on. I can't tell much about this guy," Tedde continued. "GranMa, let's just see what Brittani and the Star Riders can figure out. This horse has done a lot of traveling this past week, but I don't think the horse was riding past here regularly, or Noah and Brittani would have seen him."

"Not necessarily," Noah piped in. "When my mother would leave, I knew I had at least a couple of hours to get things done around here. So I'd go down to the river and bathe, catch some fish, and go over the other side of the mountain to get my food. Are the Star Riders always here?"

"No. Darn it!" GranMa responded.

"Then we don't know much about where this horse has been," Noah said.

"True," GranMa responded.

"Spencer said it's better to think things through than to reach the wrong conclusions. I think we—"

"We know. Spencer's a genius, probably gonna save the world, blah blah blah . . ." Tedde complained as she dragged her feet over to the dead man so she could pick him up for transport.

GranMa just shook her head. "Siblings. No matter how old they get, they never grow up." She chuckled. "Let's get back to Diggory Town and get this checked out so Brittani can get Gavin back here as soon as possible. He has a long way to go before he is grown enough. Noah, you can go back with us; the Star Riders will keep an eye on the camp. Your mother thinks you're training with Spencer. It wouldn't be a bad idea for her to see you with him. Why don't you go tie up Frank and we'll get out of here."

"GranMa, Frank needs some tending first. I'll meet you back there," Noah suggested.

"You don't know how to transport. Do you?" GranMa asked.

"Yeah, I think I can manage," Noah said.

"It will bring you right outside the stables. I want you to transport for me. I don't want you lost in space forever. Transport there and back right now."

Tedde yelled over her shoulder, "You'll know if you transported to the stables because you'll smell them long before you see them."

Noah walked over to the transporter and placed his hands on the cave wall until he found the déjà vu. Then he let the rock absorb him. When he ended up near the stables, he turned right back around. "Ta-dah!" For GranMa's benefit, he spread his arms and took a bow.

GranMa was not impressed with the *ta-dah*, but she was impressed with his skills. As GranMa entered the transporter with Tedde, in those last few seconds, Noah heard her say, "He's such a paste eater. I had no idea his skills were so impressive."

Noah wasn't sure if he had just been complimented, or insulted.

Tedde and GranMa found Brittani waiting for them on the other side of the transport, and wondered if she had seen Noah transport.

"Hi there. Glad to see you made it back! Is this the guy?" Brittani asked, sneering at the dead body at their feet.

"Yes," GranMa said. "Can you help us analyze what we've found? We have some stones and clay that were on the horse's shoes. I'd like to see what we can find on this guy."

"Sure, let's go. Is everything okay? You seem uneasy. Who killed this guy?"

"I killed him," GranMa responded, in a way that told Brittani she didn't want to talk about it.

Tedde rolled her shoulders up. "She doesn't want me to talk about it either." Tedde wasn't lying. Besides, if GranMa was going to concoct these elaborate schemes, it was up to her to defend them. Tedde adored GranMa, but she wasn't getting involved, especially since it was Brittani's son who was in so much danger.

Tedde had no trouble keeping up with Brittani as they dragged the putrid man behind them; however, GranMa looked like a little kid running beside her mother. GranMa's steps were two to one, and with Brittani at a rushed pace, GranMa was practically running to keep up. Her armor wasn't helping much, and it certainly wasn't designed for Olympic sports.

Once at the lab, Brittani got to work. The scientist was in her element, barking orders and working at a feverish pace. She felt as exhilarated as she had in the days when she worked beside her GranMother, Mimi. It was at times like this that she missed Mimi most.

"Oh, this is not good, Ma," Brittani said.

GranMa chose to ignore the error regarding her name. "What is it?"

"This soil is from the place that is not Diggory Town."

"Do you mean?"

"Yes, I do mean."

GranMa placed her fingers over her lips and puffed out a breath. "Well, the camp must be close to *That Place*."

"Ma, it's not a problem as long as we don't go in there."

Again, GranMa ignored the error.

"Does anyone want to clue me in?" Tedde asked.

"NO!" Their combined voices sounded like a shout.

"Ma . . . " GranMa shot a look at Brittani that caused her to pause. For the third time, Brittani had called GranMa Ma. Recognizing her error, Brittani continued, "I mean, ahh . . . look, it's only dangerous if we enter, so we just don't enter."

"No, we just don't enter," GranMa repeated, as if doubting their ability to follow through with the suggestion. "But still, we have to wonder why this guy was anywhere near there."

"Yeah!" Tedde said, hoping someone would clue her in.

GranMa looked at Tedde. "Ah, my beautiful warrior." She stroked Tedde's face. "I already ask too much of you. There is no way I am including you in this horrible tragedy."

"But—"

Tedde was cut short by Brittani. "Tedde, trust me on this one, I wish *I* didn't know."

That seemed to be good enough for Tedde. She had come to respect Brittani just about as much as anyone. And her history as an intelligence officer told her there *were* things you were better off not knowing. For now, she was happy to let things lie. "If you need me, in a moment's notice, I will awaken to whatever dark secret you keep."

"We all know we can count on you," GranMa said. "Okay, let's go find out what the Star Riders know." Just then, Noah and Spencer stopped by to say hi to Noah's mother.

"Hi, Mom, bet you weren't expecting to see me here," Noah teased.

Brittani smiled. "You didn't think my mother would bring you to Diggory Town without me knowing, did you?"

"Yeah. I think she would," Spencer said.

"Me too." Brittani laughed. "What are you two doing here?"

"Just taking a break. I thought you'd want to know how your boy is doing," Spencer said.

"I do."

"Well, he's doing great!" Noah reported.

"He's a real legend in his own mind." Spencer chuckled and rubbed Noah's head hard enough to let him know who was boss.

"Ow! Someday I'll have you calling 'uncle' out to me while I hold you down to the ground," Noah said.

"I look forward to it." And Spencer truly meant every word. "We'll see you later, Brittani."

Noah was now in a headlock, so he mumbled to his mother, "Love ya!"

"Love ya back. And Spencer, take it easy on my kid. He looks terrible." She laughed.

"Not gonna happen, Britt." Spencer replied.

"I love these kids and their nonsense. I love everything about it and what it implies," GranMa said.

"Me too," Tedde said.

"Yeah." Brittani agreed. "Now, besides this piece of human waste, what else did you bring back?"

"I scraped the horse's coat to see if you could analyze what might be on it." Tedde was proud of the detective work she had done.

"Great! Where's the horse? Maybe I can find something in his teeth or feces."

"Yuck!" Tedde curled her lips down.

"Hey, it's part of the job. Where's the horse?"

GranMa piped in, "We let it go."

"Why?"

"Couldn't transport it," GranMa responded.

Tedde started looking around the lab and fiddling with the things on the tables to avoid Brittani's questions.

"Hey, don't mess with my stuff. What's up with you? You look like I just asked you to gather the feces and dig through it. Don't worry; I'm not going to ask you to do that—unless, of course, you run into the horse again," Brittani joked.

"Great . . . just great." Tedde said and crinkled her nose.

GranMa thought it was time to get Tedde out of there. "We're going to find the Star Riders. Where's Gavin?"

"I took him home to make sure he's safe," Brittani reported.

"Good thinking. Let's go Tedde." GranMa led Tedde down the torch-lit hall. "It didn't occur to me she'd ask about the horse. I think she knew we were hiding something."

"Everyone is always hiding something in Diggory Town. She knows the rules. If you're not told, it's because you don't need to know."

"Yeah, well, that makes one person who obeys the rules." GranMa laughed. "But in this case, I'm sure she'd feel a need to know if she knew her son, who is still a child I might add, is left in harm's way."

"I don't want to think about what she'll do if she finds out. She's always in control of her temper, but I have a feeling that will end if she finds out what we're doing," Tedde said.

"Who could blame her?" GranMa was making an observation, not asking a question.

Once they were out of the narrow halls and in the open space of the cave, GranMa yelled, "Star Riders!"

At the speed of light, Jackson was the first to arrive. "Hey, GranMa."

"Tell me what you've discovered," GranMa said.

"Well, it looks like he rode from Diggory Town caves through the kingdom to Maranatha Valley, and past Mount Carmel. At one point, he makes camp and we see a second set of hoof prints. This horse doesn't wear shoes, so we're assuming it flew in. Only one set of prints leave the camp, so whoever stopped by didn't ride out with this guy. The putrid guy's trail ends at the edge of the kingdom where Noah takes care of him."

"Any clues to who the visitor might be?" GranMa asked.

The two straggling Star Riders finally showed up. Their Stars were easier to see inside the cave, but still dulled by the bright lights of the cave. Two small lights grew from a spec to four feet tall, white, glowing, sparkling balls before they rolled to the ground. As they rolled, Katie and Nicky stepped out of their respective balls to their full size.

"That is so cool!" Tedde said. "I wish I had a cool gift like that."

"We all have the gifts we need," GranMa said.

"We kept scouting for a few seconds after we heard your call. Sorry, GranMa, we just had a hunch," Katie explained.

"It's almost always good to follow your instincts," GranMa said.

"It sure paid off this time! Look, we found a black feather and this looks like blood on this leaf. Do you think it's him?" Nicky could hardly contain his excitement.

GranMa took the leaf and the feather to inspect them. "Let's not jump to any conclusions. A few of the horses have black feathers, and this may or may not be his blood. Have Brittani take a look at it. Was this all?"

"Yes," Katie responded.

"You did great work. What about beyond Brittani's camp; did you see what was up the river?"

"It was what you expected," Jackson reported.

"Okay, you did great work as always. Let's see what Brittani has to say about your findings," GranMa instructed.

Tedde searched GranMa's face for signs that would tell her what was upriver. As always, GranMa's deadpan face didn't give way to a hint.

Tedde scraped the dried blood off her leather skirt and rubbed it into a handkerchief. "Here, have Brittani compare the blood you found with this blood. It belongs to the creep Noah killed."

"You could be a little more sensitive," GranMa suggested.

"To the dead guy!" Tedde grimaced.

"Of course not!" GranMa shot back. "To the fact that Noah has killed; it was a little hard on him, don't you think?"

"Yes I do, and I'm truly sorry," Tedde said.

"Me too," GranMa said. "Now get out of here you three—time's a-wasting." She smiled, hugged, and left her lipstick mark on the cheeks of her three teenage Star Riders.

The Star Riders went galloping off, pushing and teasing. All the usual nonsense being greatly exaggerated by how anxious they were to know what they had discovered.

"They're so silly, but you couldn't ask for better warriors," GranMa remarked, smiling as she watched them fade into the crowds.

"What's upriver?" Tedde asked.

"You don't want to know. Just stay away from *That Place*."

"Okay," Tedde said in a lowered voice as she walked away.

Before Tedde could take two strides, GranMa gripped her arm. "Don't test me on this one." GranMa put a stern eye on Tedde. "It will not be me who punishes you if you go upriver."

Tedde stared back into GranMa's serious eyes. "I won't test you GranMa, I promise."

Chapter 13   A Second Sacrifice

Noah and GranMa were in her office in *That World*, preparing to transition through the painting. She needed to finish a few more things and they would be off. Noah learned a long time ago that a few more minutes in Whittaker Women terms meant he had a good thirty minutes before he needed to do a thing. It also meant he would be hanging around waiting, and doing nothing. Nothing but thinking of things to do, which almost always led to someone yelling, "Noah, what were you thinking?" His toddler fingers traced the outline of the lamp he was "never to touch." He pushed just a little harder to see if it were truly made of metal, or that resin stuff.

"Noah, how many times have I told you not to touch that lamp?" GranMa scolded. "Let's go before your mother gets in here. I don't want her seeing you head back to Cherith."

The lamp began to fall from the small end table GranPa had built. The cord was caught around Noah's foot. Before he realized what was happening, GranMa dove to catch the lamp before it hit the floor. When she rose from the floor, her face was pale, as if someone had stolen her blood.

"Sorry, GranMa! You okay?" Noah asked.

GranMa's hands trembled as she held the pewter-colored lamp shaped like a knight in armor. Noah's eyes fixed on the lamp. Knowing he was in trouble didn't stop him from wondering what made this lamp so special. The knight knelt beside a sword that was half the knight's size. The sword was plunged into the rock that functioned as the base of the lamp. From a kneeling position, the knight's right arm was placed across the guard, appearing to hold the sword in place. His head was lowered, as if in reverence, while he guarded a place of honor. As fancy as it was, it was still a lamp, and Noah was still in trouble.

"GranMa, I'm reeeally sorry!" Noah was almost begging for forgiveness.

"This may be the most crucial thing in my office," GranMa said. "It is not your fault that it almost broke, but I must make sure this never happens again. I will place it where you cannot harm it and *it* cannot harm you."

Her last words shocked Noah. But before he could ask what she meant, his mother's footsteps could be heard coming up the stairs.

"Hurry! Get through the painting!" GranMa clenched Noah's shirt at the shoulder and pulled him through the portal.

After a couple weeks of observation, GranMa felt comfortable that Brittani and Gavin could return to Cherith. The testing Brittani had done yielded little results, but what it did reveal shocked her. Brittani was not about to tell GranMa whose blood she had found on the leaf. She had not reported anything further to GranMa, and precious time growing Gavin had been lost. He needed to grow for his own safety. The blood she'd tested on the leaf made her all the more wary. GranMa and Noah barely made it out of Brittani's sight before Brittani entered GranMa's office with Gavin.

* * *

Noah felt revived after the short vacation from his debris hut. GranMa had agreed that, occasionally, Michael could fill in for Noah so that Noah could become more acquainted with Frank. Besides, it would give Michael a chance to put his new skills to good use. Michael would spend a day or two watching Noah to learn the ropes around camp, and then he would take over. It had become too dangerous for Michael to learn the hard way like Noah had. There was a new air of caution everywhere in Diggory Town.

"So what have you been doing while I've existed like a wild animal?" Noah asked Michael.

"Don't worry, Spencer has been brutal. He says I don't understand my sword, and until I do, it's of little use to me."

"What does that mean?" Noah asked.

"I don't know. I think I'm every bit as good with a sword as you," Michael said.

"I do too. But he didn't say you were using it improperly; he said you didn't understand it. Show me your sword."

Michael pulled his sword from his back sheath and presented it to Noah.

"When did you go to a back sheath? Didn't GranMa give you a side sheath?" Noah asked.

"Yeah, but while working with Spencer we decided a back sheath would work better because of my swing. It's also easier for me use when I'm on Debbie. We designed this sheath to carry two swords with a crossbow and arrows down the middle. I doubt I'll ever carry two swords, but we needed to balance the harness." Michael turned to show Noah the engineering he and Spencer had done.

"Nice! I like the way it crosses, but I'm a more traditional guy. The standard sheath works for me." Noah patted his sheath.

"That's because of your brute strength. Spencer said it was easier to train you because you and he are a lot alike physically," Michael said.

"Yeah, only he's a giant and has long legs." Noah laughed.

"That's true for now. You're still growing and who knows where you'll stop."

"Wouldn't it be great to end up like Spencer?" Noah dreamed aloud.

"Yeah . . . " Michael sighed.

Noah turned Michael's sword in his hand and admired its simple beauty. The pommel at the top of the seven inch gold hilt lay perfectly balanced with his family crest inscribed on the top. Noah liked the assuring way it felt in his hand; he was certain it would not slip in battle. A simple guard, whose ends pointed forward, threatening its victims, lay between the hilt and the twenty inch stainless steel double-edged blade. However, it was the stone centered in the middle where all pieces crossed that caught Noah's eye. "Did your sword always have this stone?"

"Yup."

"I never noticed it before," Noah said. "It's weirdly beautiful, and it goes all the way through the center to the other side of the guard. Won't that compromise its strength? I thought all swords needed to be solid."

"I thought so too. Spencer said this stone is special and actually makes the sword stronger," Michael replied.

Noah handed Michael back his sword, and pulled out his own sword. It too was simple and powerful in its beauty, but in the center where all parts met, his had a simple white crest with a red cross upon it. On the guard to the left, engraved in beautiful script, it read "*The*" and on the right guard, "*First*."

"I wonder what this means," Noah said, thinking aloud.

Michael grabbed the sword that was much like his own and turned it over to see the identical inscription on the other side. "I don't know, but everything here has a purpose, so I'd find out if I were you."

"Well, the more I know here, the less I want to know," Noah said as both boys/men laughed like old friends, except these friends were not old.

The next few days were easy. Brittani had not returned with Gavin until the third day, which gave Noah and Michael a better chance to scope out the place. The Star Riders were assigned to keep watch from above, and best of all, Noah was able to eat food cooked on an open fire. This peace would not keep for long.

On the third day, Noah heard the giggles coming from the transport. "Hurry! I'm heading to Frank. Good luck to you, buddy. I'll see you in a day or two."

Brittani came through the transport without a hitch and began setting up camp. Supposedly, she was taking care of Michael and Gavin for the weekend so their mother and father could get a well-deserved weekend away. *This means two days of growth for both boys*, Brittani thought, and then she wondered why she hadn't seen Michael for a while. "Huh! I didn't see him in Diggory Town," she said to herself. "Things aren't adding up. His mother thinks he's with me."

In *That World*, Aaron told Brittani that Michael was with his grandmother for the day, and Grandma would bring Michael back home later. Brittani wasn't worried exactly, but she did feel a tinge of concern. "Well, little buddy, at least there's a nice breeze up here today." She smiled and hugged the baby.

Michael looked over the edge, wondering why his aunt was talking to herself and what it was she was discussing with no one. He didn't notice the horses far in the distance, and neither did the Star Riders. The horses in the distance were about to stop. Their riders were making camp until nightfall to ensure they went unnoticed.

"We'll rest here!" the vile, creaky voice commanded in broken tones. The voice projected the words loudly enough, but the deteriorating vocal cords had trouble forming the sounds.

Despite the lack of skin, and without regard to the missing or misshapen muscles that hung from the frame, the strong skeletal hands hoisted the body down from the horse. The creature walked towards his men as his cloak of muscles blew behind him. "Get these horses rested!" he barked. "I don't want any excuses for failure tonight, or there'll be more dead than just my enemies!"

"Yes, your Majesty!" one of his officers responded. "Hurry up, you men, and get this camp ready or I'll skin you myself. Get food ready for our Master!"

"NO, YOU FOOL!" The master flung his powerful, boney backhand at the man. "Do you want to alert them to our presence? We'll be eating tack, fruit, water, and not another thing. Make sure their weapons are ready, then get these men and horses rested. Tonight will be a long, tiresome, slow ride, and we'll be attacking at first light."

"Master . . . "

The master pulled a dagger from his belt and slid it under the officer's chin. "Not another word; the wolves out here will eat anything—even you!"

The man kept silent about the rumors he had heard of the fabled Star Riders.

A horse and rider appeared from thin air. The rider ran to the creature and knelt. "Excellency." He bowed his head and then rose. "She appears to be alone with the child, and a youth seems to be standing guard above her. I stayed high and didn't see anything other than the three. She seemed to be enjoying the breeze I created." He laughed.

"Yes, just how we want her—happy, and unalarmed." The creature laughed back. "Did the youth take note of anything?"

"No, your Majesty, he appeared confused. I watched him for a long time, but there is nothing remarkable about the boy. He looked bewildered, which I found odd since he was obviously guarding the woman and the child."

"GranMa doesn't make mistakes." The creature growled. "Do not underestimate this youth. Get your horse rested. Tomorrow, we'll need him in the air where he is invisible. Once again, you have

THE CHILDREN OF PROPHECY

impressed and honored your ruler." The muscles on the creature's face moved as if to smile, but the missing lips hid his evil insincerity. "Go! I need my rest."

"Shall I have food brought to your Majesty?"

"I have no need of food, only rest."

"Shall I bring you drink?"

"No, I have no need to taste. Today is not about pleasure; it is about victory. Now leave me." The Skelly was not interested in consuming the unnecessary food he loved tasting. His nutrients came from the souls he absorbed, and tomorrow he would be full. He closed his eyes and waited for the sun to go to sleep.

Under the cloak of darkness, The Skelly's men moved. It was their good fortune that cloud cover made them even more difficult to see. Only the light of the mysterious three stars made them hide in the shadows. The men spread out as instructed and made little sound as they moved toward their victims. The Skelly could barely contain his excitement, as he was certain that, within hours, all eternity would belong to him alone. Once he owned eternity, he could control time, and the queen he longed for would once again be at his side.

Just before dawn broke, The Skelly's men made it to the rallying point. "You will all be rewarded handsomely by day's end." The Skelly enticed the men as he paced before them, casting a deadly stare. "You are here to honor me and to fill your own pockets. Once I am in charge, we shall be the rulers of the universe, and *nothing* shall be kept from our desires." The void in his dark, soulless eyes showed a small glint of delight. "We can have everything . . . everything! We'll have no need of money because everything will be ours. When you have power, there is no need for commerce. When you control time, there is no need to concern yourself with it. When you control souls, then you have all the love and adoration you need. By the end of this day, our thirsts will be quenched," he said as he mounted his muscular but coatless, black-winged horse.

"Commanders, take your positions!" he shouted, without concern for who might hear. It was too late for GranMa to stop his victory. He only needed one soul, and today he would consume that one.

"Protectors, at my side! Execute as ordered!" He raised his sword and motioned the Skulls forward.

As he did in all perilous battles, The Skelly held back, leaving his men to be the first to fall. He layered them the way one layers clothing to protect oneself against the cold. He built a protective wall with his followers who didn't understand that they meant little, if nothing, to him. They were diluted by fear, or greed, into believing that their positions in this unholy union could lead them into paradise. They fearlessly moved forward, drastically underestimating the youth standing guard on the hill, and the woman he protected.

Michael jumped at the sound of the creaking voice barking commands. "Brittani!" he yelled, all formalities being cast aside.

Brittani ran out from the cave. "Michael?" she yelled to the familiar voice.

"They're coming!" In the short distance, Brittani could see a flying horse, but it was too late. A pair of wings she couldn't see hovering in front of the entrance blocked her from reentering the cave.

"Debbie!" Michael yelled as he jumped from above the cave entrance. The unseen Skull on the invisible horse was thrown to the dirt when Michael grabbed the air, guessing where the Skull might be seated. The instant the Skull hit the ground and became visible, a dagger was stabbed in his neck. Michael's ability to deduce much from little information was proving to be an asset of war.

"Get Gavin!" Brittani yelled as she pulled her bow and arrows from her quiver. Michael pulled his dagger from the man's neck and slowly the horse that blocked the cave entrance became visible. Michael tugged the horse's reins and pulled it from the opening. He grabbed the screaming baby from his Moses bed. Flying high, Debbie responded to Michael's call, and with a sharp whistle from Michael, she landed.

"Get on Debbie and go!" Brittani yelled.

"I can't leave you!" Michael's youthful eyes begged.

"Go! This is prophecy! Go!" Brittani demanded, and at that moment, the transport opened with GranMa and a small army. Brittani yelled some final instructions before Michael mounted Debbie with the baby tucked in his shirt.

"Debbie, fly as fast as you can."

And in his thoughts, he heard her respond. "You are safe with me. I will keep my promise."

Once in the air, he could see Frank and his rider peek over the mountain. Without leaving the ground, Frank moved nearly as fast as

Lightning did in flight. Noah's powerful legs held tight to Frank's massive ribs. They became one because Noah's mother's life depended on it.

Noah lifted his head to the sky. "MY MOTHER!" he yelled.

"SHE'S FIGHTING!" Michael yelled back as Noah entered his first battle.

The Skelly's men were dropping like flies as the arrows being shot down the mountain from the cave hit with deadly accuracy. But the sheer volume of Skulls made it impossible for GranMa's warriors to stop them from getting close to the cave. It wasn't long before the first sword was pulled from its sheath.

Brittani stepped in front of the blow that was meant for GranMa. Her sword clanged against the downward thrust of the Skull's sword, but he was no match for her powerful arms. Soon he lay at her feet.

"Ma, what should we do?" Brittani yelled above the roar.

"STAR!" GranMa yelled. "Take Star. They'll be tracking Michael! Go! He and Gavin are what they came for! You're faster and stronger than I am. They'll have a better chance with you behind them!" GranMa shouted as her sword clanged in response to her enemy. "Be safe! I love you!" GranMa yelled to the only child she had left in Diggory Town.

"I love you too! I won't fail!" Brittani assured her mother as she cleaned her blade in the stomach of another Skull.

The Skelly raged in the midst of the battle as his plan began to unravel before his eyes. In his rage, he lifted his sword, and removed the head of the unfortunate officer who was close enough to suffer his wrath. The head rolled off the shoulders of the one who wished he had been brave enough to tell his vile master of the fabled Star Riders.

"Excellency, there she is! The one with the child! She's getting away!" the favored Protector yelled.

"She is not the mother. Are you sure she is the woman?" the creaking voice asked.

"The child's mother was removed from Diggory Town by my sword, Master," the Protector reminded.

"Yes she was . . . " The Skelly delighted in the memory and, for a moment, his rage was appeased.

"After her!" he yelled as his rage rekindled and he joined the men in the chase.

Brittani heard the ominous sound of many wings behind her. She needed to lead them away from Michael and Gavin. Flying over unfamiliar territory, she changed course, uncertain of whether she was leading them away or towards Michael. Not seeing the boys in the distance she thought, *from here on, if I don't turn left or right, we should be moving away from the boys.*

Star was a true and faithful horse who had seen GranMa through her childhood. He was the oldest horse in Diggory Town, and before long, his age began to show. Brittani knew she must land and fight. Knowing there could only be twelve flying horses in Diggory Town at any one time, Brittani began to account for each flyer. Star, Lightning, Bump, Debbie, the flyer back at the cave whose rider Michael had killed; with five out of twelve accounted for, seven at most could be behind her. She knew of other flying horses in Diggory Town that belonged to white knights. *Remember, remember*, she tried to force herself. *If there are two more flyers being used by the white knights, then that only leaves five behind me. Five at most. I can fight five. Sure . . . I can fight five.*

She looked for a clearing that would give her the best advantage. *I need to land on high ground to make them come at me from below. What if they stay in the air? I'll need shelter too.* She saw a mountain with two large boulders atop separated by a small space. *Perfect*, she thought, *If they don't land, I'll be protected here. If they do land, I'll have the advantage of high ground. Oh, Ultimate Ruler, protect me, guide me, and if my life must end today, make my end meaningful. Keep Michael and Gavin safe.*

Completing her prayer and summoning her courage, she landed Star and immediately released him to the sky. It wouldn't take long for her assailants to land, but at least *she* would have the advantage of high ground. Looking to the sky, she saw The Skelly with only two others. She laughed at how easy this was going to be, but when they landed, she saw the two hidden Protectors lose their invisibility. She needed to live now more than ever, because knowing how the Protectors could be seen could lead to The Skelly's downfall.

As he approached, The Skelly grinned at the beautiful face that had been a thorn in his side once before. After today, she would no longer cause him concern. He stopped to keep a safe distance between him and the beautiful warrior.

"Master, shall I take her down?" the favored Protector asked.

"You played with her sister. I see no reason to keep you from further entertainment," The Skelly said to his favored Protector.

Brittani lifted her sword in the direction of The Skelly's stare. A menacing grin spread across her face, she shifted the point of her sword toward the Protector, and waited for him to come closer. Her day of reckoning with the evil that killed her sister had come. It was as if everything else melted away. She could only see the favored Protector. He held the sword that had ended Aaron's life. Her gaze pulled to the murderous weapon like metal to a magnet. *CLANG*! Her sword screamed of revenge as it burst against its intended victim. She danced him into the small space between the two boulders. The others ran to the back of the boulders in an effort to trap her. It was too late; her sister's murderer lay gurgling in his own blood. *CLANG*! Her second victim was chosen. This was going to be easier than she thought.

The Skelly watched as the muscular beauty flung her sword as if it were weightless. He almost felt sad that such an artful creature would have to be laid down. *CLANG*! *CLANG*! Her weapon shouted as every offensive move was made by the beauty. How worthless were his men, he wondered, that this elegant creature took down her second victim while staying a third. He marveled at her footwork as she advanced at all the appropriate times and then retreated in a lovely waltz. He found himself loving her the way he loved her GranMother. Fixed on her every move, he could almost hear music playing in the background. Her legs flexed, strong but delicate, while her arm carved the air with confidence and precision. He found himself sinking into the magic of her beauty, when he heard an ugly voice from deep in his dying soul yell.

"ENOUGH!"

Angered by a dance that the beauty performed so elegantly with her sword, he found himself being captured by a love betrayal that tasted so bitter. He would not denounce, Carol, the queen he loved so well, with thoughts such as these.

"ENOUGH!" he yelled once again as he threw his dagger firmly into Brittani's chest, just below her left shoulder.

To his surprise, this only seemed to enrage her, and with one swift swing, her third victim was down. "Oooonly two more," she moaned, as her determined eyes stared into his.

He'd kept the distance between them, so before she could advance, he was back on his coatless horse, being followed by one of his cowards. Brittani fell back against the boulder as the blood was absorbed into her shimmering, long curls.

"Star! Star!" she wailed. The faithful servant was at her side, ready to do her bidding. "Take me to Michael!" she instructed as she struggled to get herself on the horse. She fell forward, leaving the dagger in her chest, fearing that a removal would cause her to bleed more, and die sooner.

Raindrops of blood fell from the sky as she flew high above Maranatha Valley in search of her nephews. They were nowhere in sight, and Star could sense his rider was failing more each second. Soon there was nothing for Star to do but bring his rider to the ground.

The battle continued to rage outside the cave as Noah proved to be as powerful as Atlas. He swung his sword with grace as his muscular build danced with the agility of a ballerina. He was music in motion, and GranMa was confident he and her army would have this under control in no time. She needed to rescue Brittani, Gavin, and Michael.

"LIGHTNING!" she called, not knowing that her daughter's fate had been sealed, and her GranSons' futures were being formed.

Several miles after Michael had watched Auntie Brittani steer the villains from his path, he decided to let down in the woods. The baby's hysterics needed comforting, so he sat under a large tree and began rocking. But the baby would not be calmed. Michael's eyes welled and the pain of a million fears spilled across the children's bodies. Without warning, every monster that stalked Michael in his dreams seemed to haunt him now.

"I cannot save us, Gavin. I'm just five; I'm not brave like Mumma. I'm just a boy. I'm sorry, but you will not be safe with me." The five-year-old's tears fell across the boy and the baby as the futility of it all consumed Michael. His rhythmic motions began to sooth Gavin, but did little for the child who was asked to be a man.

As Michael rocked, Gavin found peace in the powerful arms that surrounded him in love. These were not just any arms; they were the arms of an all-consuming love that comforted the baby as the boy/man cried an ocean of fear. Soon, Gavin curled his tiny legs under his belly, and nuzzled himself to sleep in the crook of his brother's neck. Michael reached up and wiped the snot dripping from his nose onto his sleeve, and then cupped the baby's head in his hand.

"I'm sorry, I'm sorry," he hummed into Gavin's ears. "I'm sorry I'm not courageous and strong like Mumma. I'm bigger now, but I'm still only five. Mumma would know how to protect you. She would not be afraid." He chanted, shivered, and rocked. "She would know what to do."

Debbie stood above the two children, keeping watch for the evil that had led them to this place. Remembering the promise she made months earlier, she knew something must be done. She nudged Michael.

"Michael . . . Michael," a small voice whispered with each nudge from Debbie.

Michael looked left and right, and then stood with the baby, being careful not to wake him. He looked through the trees and down into the hills. No sign of anything. Once again, Debbie nudged the boy whose fear was rising as if to burst through the top of his head.

"Michael, put your head on Debbie," the voice said.

"Mumma?" a small voice whispered back as the tears once again rolled down the broken boy's face. Cradling his brother, he placed his forehead on Debbie's neck. "Mumma, I need you." Michael's large, round, hazel eyes cried.

The crackling, broken voice of Mumma answered back. "I know, my sweet son, I need you too." There was a moment of peaceful silence as the boy nuzzled his head into the horse's neck, searching for the comforting arms of Mumma.

"I'm afraid, Mumma. I'm not brave like you." Michael's thoughts traveled through Debbie to Mumma's soul.

"Oh, my sweet boy, your courage doesn't come from me; my courage came from you. For years I was lost. I wasn't strong and courageous like my mother, or sure like my sister. I tried so hard to be like the other women in our family, but I didn't have Mimi's determination, or Auntie Melissa's resolve. Outside, I was every bit as tough as any Whittaker Woman, but inside, I was stumbling to find my place in the world."

"I think you're just saying that to make me feel better," the boy/man interrupted as his fear began to subside.

"I know," Mumma's voice whispered back, "but it's true. Nothing could convince me that I was every bit as good as any one of them. The weight of a thousand men couldn't give me the courage and resolve I needed to become a true warrior. Then something happened nearly six years ago, on October thirteenth at 1:54 am, that would change me forever. It only took seven pounds and fourteen ounces for me to become the strongest, bravest, most determined person I know. Suddenly, I was important, fearless, completely alive, and completely in love."

"Mumma," the embarrassed boy whispered, "that's when I was born."

"That's right! Your courage doesn't come from me. My courage came from you. After you were born, I was a better warrior than I had ever been. Ask anyone. They will tell you how much you changed my life. After you were born, I could move mountains. We were alone for a long time, just you and me, and there wasn't anything I couldn't do with you by my side. You are better and more powerful than you think."

"Look at me, Mumma, I'm crying like a baby. How can Gavin trust me to take care of him?" Michael suddenly felt shame.

"You are a man. A little man, but a man nonetheless, and you will learn what all good men know. Some days you will be the victor, and some days you will be the victim, but this will always be true . . . you will not be judged by how you fell down, but by how you got up. Do not be afraid to fail, because that is where most of your learning will occur. An untested life is hollow and meaningless. How can you claim to have any value, or be anything, when you are untested? One thing I am certain of is that, as a young man, you will fail more than you will succeed. If you do not learn from your failures, that will never change. If you are afraid of failure, then you can live a cautious life. This will minimize your risk of being harmed, but a cautious life is a life unlived. You were not born to be that man; you were born to greatness, and if it means a short-lived life, then that is what it means. It is better to live one day of sheer joy then a million days of nothing special. Son, do you understand what I have told you?"

With his head held high and a smile on his face, Michael responded, "Yes, Mumma!"

"Then go do what you are destined to do. I am *very* proud of you, and Debbie will always be your link to me. This is very hard on Debbie—" Michael raised his head to see an exhausted horse, "—so I must leave you now. I love you. Take care of our baby."

"I will, Mumma," a tear-filled boy/man responded. "I will."

Just then, Michael heard hooves touch the ground behind him. He swiftly turned, stepped away from Debbie, pulled Gavin to his chest with one hand, and pulled his sword with the other.

"GranMa, you scared the heck out of me!"

"I'm sorry, Michael; I didn't mean to scare you." GranMa looked at Debbie and knew what had just happened. She didn't ask for details, knowing that Michael would share whatever he thought she needed to know; still, she was curious.

"Where is Brittani?" she asked

"I don't know. I saw her drawing off the Skulls."

"How many followed her?"

"She was far off, but I only saw three," Michael responded.

"Good, she can easily manage three," GranMa said.

"I think one was The Skelly," Michael said. "Shouldn't we go back for her?"

"No, our job is to protect you children, not vice versa. Don't underestimate your Aunt, because she is an amazing woman." GranMa's voice was convincing, but her heart was not as sure as her mouth.

"You don't have to convince me of how amazing the women are in my family. Truth be told, I think you're all a little scary too." Michael was glad to have something to laugh about. The past two hours had taken their toll on him.

"We *are* a little scary!" GranMa smiled. "Let's get you boys out of danger." GranMa gave Michael and Gavin a hug and a kiss. "I'm going to get the horses some water, and then we'll get you out of here." GranMa surveyed the area as the horses drank from the nearby tributary. She decided that it would be best to head north since greater danger lay south. She knew the risk of heading to *That Place,* but Michael was smart and she was certain he could make it through.

"Okay, time to mount," she announced with more confidence than she was feeling. She'd tell Michael about *That Place* while on their journey. But before they had traveled very far the horses landed and stopped.

"GranMa what's happening?"

"The horses know better than to come into this area," she whispered to Michael.

"GranMa, are we upriver?" Michael asked.

"Yes. Lower your voice."

"Is this *That Place*?" Michael asked as they both dismounted.

"Yes."

Without warning, GranMa used the tip of her dagger to cut into Michael's chin.

"Ouch! GranMa, what are you doing?"

"Shhh . . . Michael, be silent. I'm sorry, but there is precious little time for explanation. We are no longer in Cherith. I know it looks the same, but trust me, this is an evil, deceptive place. Now, as long as you are bleeding—" GranMa took Michael's free hand, dipped his index finger in the blood, and showed it to him, "—you are alive. If you touch your chin and there is no longer blood, you are dead. And if you are dead, do not continue with Gavin because you will be taking him to his death—assuming he is not already dead. Once you have determined you are dead, do exactly the opposite of what your instincts tell you to do. It will be Gavin's only hope, since The Skelly will now be guiding your instincts."

"If I'm dead, what becomes of the prophecy?" Michael asked.

"If you are dead, my sweet prince, then you need not worry about prophecy. If any one of you children becomes dead, it marks the end of time." GranMa touched the precious blood on his chin. "I have marked you forever as the man who saved time."

"What if . . . " GranMa raised her hand to his lips and stopped Michael from finishing his sentence.

"There is *no* 'what if.' You will *be* the man who saves time. You *must* become the man who saved time. This too is prophecy." GranMa fed her GranSon courage, because it was all she had to give. "Follow this path. When you get to the end of the trail, you are out of this evil place. Call for Debbie; she will find you. Now take your brother and go. Be safe, my beloved GranSons, and take your mother's spirit with you." GranMa kissed both heads, took in full breaths of their sweet aromas, and slid her cheek across theirs, as if painting them in courage. Then she took a dab of Michael's blood and placed it over her heart. "Go."

With that, GranMa turned and raced back through the woods in the direction from which she had come. She needed to find Brittani and help her out of Cherith. One daughter had already been lost to death; she could not bear to lose another. She decided to short cut through the woods, but the deeper she got into the woods, the harder it was to make time. The bushes gave way to the heavy cuts made by GranMa's sword, but it was a long and slow process. Her arms began to ache under the weight of her sword as beads of sweat rolled into her eyes. She was beginning to think that running around the mountain would have saved her time. "Lightning!" she called, but he was nowhere to be found.

She worried if Michael could find his way out of *That Place,* and get Gavin back to safety. She had to trust that Spencer had done his job as though someone's life depended upon it. Finally, she got through the woods and climbed the top of the mountain that overlooked Maranatha Valley and down into the Jordon River. From here, she could see the small dots of The Skelly's Skulls retreating, but she could not see her precious daughter. "Lightning!" she shouted across the mountain. This time she was in Cherith, and this time, Lightning came.

"Take me to Brittani!" she commanded as she mounted the steed who would take her to her first-born child.

Brittani lay on the ground as the little blood she had left trickled out. She prayed for Michael's safety, and that he would be strong enough and wise enough to get his brother to safety. "Take your brother to Maranatha," was her last instruction to him.

With tear-filled eyes, she watched as his and Gavin's shadows disappeared in the distant horizon. She strained for a final glimpse of her beloved nephews; their dark images appeared to be returning, but she was not at the cave. She struggled to remember; she had been in the skirmish at the cave, sent her nephews to safety, then faced The Skelly, but in her weakened state, her mind played tricks on her. Blood was no longer bringing oxygen to her brain.

It wasn't the boys returning. Her heart raced. It was a Black Jaguar coming nearer and nearer, but a giant *ROAR* turned the Black Jaguar into a Lion. She did not fear the Lion that came to her as she lay dying. He curled around her listless body as his muzzle lifted her head and nudged it into the crook of his massive front legs.

As she felt her life streaming from her body, she thought, *Today I will die.*

The Lion's thoughts entered her consciousness. "Today your body will be lifeless, but you will not die. You will walk with me in my place of peace, and there you will rest until the Omega Battle."

"What about my children?" Brittani asked.

"You will spend your life in *That World* with your children until your final days there, but your days with them in Diggory Town are over." His furry mane nuzzled her neck and comforted her until she finally broke rule number three and gave up.

Soon Brittani found herself floating as if the clouds were pulling her in no particular direction. She felt calm as all anxiety bled from her body. She raised her head that seemed to weigh a thousand pounds, and in the distance, she could see a beautiful woman watching her. The women's aqua blue eyes sparkled against her skin, which was the color of night. Brittani called out to the woman, "Do I know you? You seem familiar and yet you seem a stranger."

The woman floated closer to Brittani with her right hand extended. "Come with me. I am *your* Hope, and I will guide you from *This World* back to *That World*. You no longer belong here."

"Who are you?" Brittani asked.

"I am Elizabeth," she replied.

"Why do I know you?" Brittani asked.

"You know me because I have always been here watching and guiding you. Now I must guide you to *That World*, where I will continue to watch over you. I will be that little voice in your head that you are always so willing to ignore." Elizabeth smiled.

"Where did you come from?"

"I didn't come from anywhere. I was given to you by your mother, and you have always been in my care. I am your guide." Elizabeth's smile widened.

Brittani snapped, "Well, apparently you are not very good at your job since I appear to be dead."

Elizabeth's smile seemed to widen, if that were at all possible. "You still have that little temper of yours. When will you be happy to give it up? It has never served you well. I did not say it was my job to *protect* you. I said it was my job to *guide* you. I'm that voice in your head—the one that says don't do that, keep your head down, something's not right with that person or place. Some people like to call us a conscience or instincts, but the souls like me, our job is to sharpen your instincts. You have never been confused about the *right thing,* but you don't always have the good sense to do it." Elizabeth laughed. "I have always loved you, even when you ignore me. C'mon, take my hand; I need to get you safely to *That World*. You still have an important job to do there. You are raising heroes like the other Mothers of Prophecy."

"Will I remember *This World*?" Brittani felt that pinch in her nose—the one that lets you know you're about to cry.

With a heavy heart, Elizabeth responded, "No."

"Why will you stay with me? What will you do in *That World*?" Brittani asked.

"I told you. I will be your conscience," Elizabeth responded. "My job will not change. I will whisper the three rules in your ear when you cannot find your way. Trust the Ultimate Ruler. Be a good person. Never give up. I will not let you forget that you are a Whittaker Woman. You are a part of the legacy, and as such, you may fall, but you will always get up. You may break, but you will always mend. Troubles may cause you to bend in ways you never anticipated, but you will never shatter under the pressure. When you think you cannot get up, or believe you will not mend, if for a moment you believe you just might shatter, I will remind you who you are. Your bloodline is filled with courage and faith, and that is your legacy."

"So you will give me all these things?" Brittani asked.

Elizabeth laughed. "Of course not. Why would I give you what you already have?"

"It seems I'm lacking in rule number three. Apparently I am willing to give up since I gave up my life in Diggory Town." Brittani rubbed her forehead as reality settled in.

"You don't understand, 'Never Give Up,' do you Brittani?"

"I'm pretty sure it means NEVERRR. GIVE. UP!"

"It means never give up on a valuable idea. Never stop fighting for the things worth fighting for. Never accept failure as a result. If you're not getting the results you need to accomplish a worthy goal, then you find another way. Don't beat your head against the wall just because you don't want to *give up* on a plan that isn't working. That would be foolish! Never give up is about worthy accomplishments. It's about building a world you can be proud of. It's about helping your fellow man. It's about finding joy in every little thing. Do you understand that?" Elizabeth implored.

"Yeah! Yeah! Rah! Rah! Blah! Blah! Let's go, Elizabeth. I'm dead in Diggory Town; you can cheerlead later."

"Man, you're a pain!" Elizabeth jerked Brittani's arm as she guided her back to *That World*. "You're going to do fabulous things in

That World, and I'm going to help you do them even if it takes every ounce of rule number three in me to get it done."

"Really? What am I going to do that's so great?" Elizabeth had Brittani's attention.

"You and Aaron are responsible for giving birth to prophecy. Now you must raise these children to be the kind of people who can fulfill it. You and Aaron may be the two most important mothers in history. You drive me crazy, but the Ultimate Ruler doesn't make mistakes. He has chosen you for this most important task, and it is your destiny to accomplish it. Even if it kills me!" Elizabeth guided Brittani through the painting in GranMa's office. "We're here."

"Although you won't know it, you have now become a legend who generations will honor. Try not to mess it up!" Elizabeth directed Brittani.

"Are you mad at me?" Brittani asked.

"I have *always* loved you, but that doesn't mean you are not a pain in my bottom," Elizabeth replied. Then she kissed Brittani on the head and raised both her hands, as if praising the Lord. Her actions caused Brittani's body to float horizontally as Elizabeth laid Brittani down on GranMa's fluffy, red couch. Brittani tried to resist Elizabeth's magic, but Brittani's days of communicating with anyone from Diggory Town were over.

"You will wake from this nap and you will not remember us, but you and your courage will be remembered in Diggory Town for all of history. Sleep well, my beautiful pain in the bottom." Elizabeth blinked back the tears that signified the end of an era.

Before Brittani's eyes were completely closed, she heard the lonely, agonizing, painful screams of the woman who could not be broken. It was at that moment that a second image of a woman with long, curly hair appeared on GranMa's breastplate.

Chapter 14   Three Sisters

The children sat on the fluffy, red couch, waiting for GranMa as she had instructed. "Isabel, stop kicking the couch," Noah complained.

"It isn't me!"

Noah looked down. "You and I are the only ones with legs short enough to kick the couch with our heels, and I know it wasn't me."

Izzy gave Noah a devilish smile, so Noah gave her an elbow.

"Cut it out, you two," Michael whispered. "Do you want our parents coming in here and seeing us? The apparitions can only do so much to cover for our absence." Michael was distracted from his chastising when an image appeared on the wall. It started small, like a bubble filled with clear gel, changing shape as if someone were poking it, causing the edges to move. As it grew, the bubble continued to jiggle. The children leaned forward, squinting their eyes to see inside. It was GranMa waving them in.

"Jump in. Don't be afraid," GranMa whispered.

The children smiled. They were anything *but* afraid when they let the bubble suck them in. It took them out of GranMa's office in *That World* to another location in *That World* by using the universal transport in The Cave of the Tired Souls.

GranMa said, "Never show anyone this transport for any reason. If someone does not know about this, it's because they don't need to know. If they *do* know about it, but *don't* know where to find it, it's because they are not supposed to know where it is. Never, ever show or discuss this transport with anyone. It is a universal transport and it can take you anywhere, but it is very dangerous. Mimi designed it that way to ensure amateurs didn't try to fool with it. It can take you to any of the worlds, and anywhere in those worlds, but it always returns to its original location. It will abandon you, and if you use it wrong, it *will* kill you."

Big eyes focused on GranMa's scary words. "Are there any others?" Alexis asked.

"There are seven, but only three are in use because they are so dangerous," GranMa responded. "There is this one at The Cave of the Tired Souls, the one in The Great Beyond, and the one in my chamber."

"The one above the fluffy, red couch?" Noah asked.

"No," Michael responded, "she said her chamber, not her office. Where is your chamber?"

GranMa smiled at the boy who paid great attention to details. "My chamber is in the center of town in the Chambers of Defense building. You haven't seen it yet. I can get to my chamber from my home office, but I use a different transport to get there."

"Are you talking about the one in the—" Alexis tried to ask, but GranMa clasped her hand over Alexis's mouth.

"I should have known you would figure that out. Did you try using it?" GranMa asked.

"I tried but nothing happened."

"Then count your lucky stars and stay out of that transport!" GranMa responded. "I'm taking you kids to the Three Sisters in *That World*, and then we will travel through to *This World* again using another transport just beyond the Temptress. Pay particular attention to what we do today, because this training is going to save your lives someday."

"What's the Temptress?" Alexis asked.

"In due time, Alexis; let's learn the fundamentals so that we don't fail as a result of the simple things. Fundamentals are not always the most interesting part of learning, but make no mistake about this: they are *always* the most important part." GranMa continued to speak as the universal transport released them. "We are at the base of the

Three Sisters." She began leading the children through the lush, tropical forest.

"Why are fundamentals the most important?" Alexis asked.

"Let's say you are going to a ball and a seamstress made you the most beautiful ball gown in the kingdom. That would make you happy, wouldn't it?" GranMa asked as she pushed through the dense forest.

"Oh, yes!" Alexis smiled as if she thought she would be getting one.

"What if you didn't get measured and the dress was made two sizes too small?"

"Hahaha . . . I would see your booty. I would see your booty," Noah teased.

"Knock it off, Noah." GranMa gave him *the look* before she continued. "You get my point, right? The most basic thing he should have done, he forgot, and the project failed."

"*He*?" the boys chimed.

GranMa stopped, crossed her arms, and shot the boys the stink eye. "Oh, do you think sewing is *women's work*?"

They mumbled and fumbled, but they knew better than to answer that question.

"I thought so," GranMa said while secretly chuckling inside. "*He's* usually called a tailor anyway," she said as she moved on.

"I knew that!" Michael said.

"Yeah, sure you did." Alexis chuckled.

"I didn't!" Noah said.

"No kidding?" Alexis chuckled again, mocking her kid brother.

Isabel, lost in thought, didn't join in the nonsense. "If something bad happened in Diggory Town, would someone come to get us in *That World*?" she asked.

"Maybe, Isabel. We try not to cross the worlds because there's potential for great harm to come to *That World*. It's just a precaution," GranMa said.

"Most of the time when I'm in *That World,* I question whether Diggory Town exists, or is it just the imagination of a child. When I'm in *That World,* I don't feel like this Isabel of Diggory Town. I feel like four-year-old Isabel of The World of People, and I think like four-year-old Isabel."

"That's a device we use to keep you safe. As you mature in The World of People, you will probably become more certain of Diggory Town, but not everyone does. Some people have an acute awareness in *That World*, but for most, it's almost like a dream. They know it's real, but there's a certain amount of skepticism that keeps them from believing. That disbelief keeps people from talking about Diggory Town in *That World*. They're afraid others will think they're crazy, and others will. Yet when we need them to be in *This World*, something happens in their brains that triggers Diggory Town. Mimi deliberately designed the transports to confuse people. But how she got the brain to trigger, no one knows. She was one smart lady."

"It's hard for me to think of Mimi that way," Isabel said. "In *That World*, she's my great grandmother who looks like Santa's wife, and makes Robert Redford cake, jumbo pudding, and potato casserole. I can only imagine her with a carving knife that cuts ham and turkey, not a sword that cuts . . . well, you know."

GranMa laughed. "I know. But your Mimi, Mrs. Claus, was more powerful than any of us, and that's no exaggeration. She stood up and fought when the rest of us couldn't even figure out we needed to fight. There were no rules of engagement when Mimi picked up her sword to protect us. She made up the rules as she went along, and everything we are, we owe to her. The only thing that ever caused her to misstep was love. Mimi didn't have the best man-picker, if you know what I mean."

"No, GranMa, I don't." Isabel's little voice had returned.

GranMa looked down to see confused faces. *Note to self*, she thought, *try to remember they're still toddlers and children in That World*. "Well, it's not important now," was all GranMa said.

GranMa herded the kids in the direction of the Third Sister. The Three Sisters (three tall, very steep, narrow mountains) were detached from the Blue Mountains, and jutted out in a row with the third Sister standing at the farthest point. "Okay, stay close to me. I don't want you separating, and then I'll need to run up and down the mountain to get to you. However, I do want you to keep a safe and comfortable distance from each other for two reasons. The first is if someone falls, I don't want them causing the others to fall too. The second reason is that, during a battle, if you huddle up, it makes it easier for the enemy to shoot, and hit a target. In hand-to-hand combat, it's smart to stay close to each other for safety, but when traveling, it makes more sense to keep some distance between you because it makes you a harder target."

"Yeah, that makes sense," Noah said.

"Good!" GranMa said. "You're going to have to learn to use good sense when deciding if you should huddle up together, or keep a distance apart. The more experience you gain, and the more you are tested, the easier these decisions will become. It's all about practicing the Art of War."

"It all sounds scary, GranMa!" Isabel's voice quivered, although she wasn't certain why.

"It is scary when you are not prepared, but the more you know about things, the less you need to fear them."

"Why?" Isabel asked.

"Have you ever heard anyone say 'I conquered my fear'?"

"Yes."

"How can you conquer what you don't understand?" GranMa asked.

"I don't know." Isabel's big eyes told GranMa that Isabel had no idea what she was talking about. Alexis could only laugh at the futility of it all.

"Let's try this. Have you ever lain on your bed at night afraid of what was under it?"

"Yes," Isabel replied.

"Do you think you would be afraid of what was on top of your bed if you were lying under it?"

"That's pretty tricky, GranMa!" Isabel said.

"Yes it is, but what is your answer?"

"I don't know my answer," Isabel said.

"When will you know your answer?" GranMa asked.

"I fink when I lay under my bed tonight."

"So you're going to lay under your bed tonight?" GranMa asked.

"Yes," Isabel replied.

"Why?"

"So I'll know if it's scary on top of my bed," Isabel said.

"If you discover it's not scary, will you then be afraid of what's under your bed next time you sleep on top of it?"

"I don't fink so, because I'll know there's nothing to worry about," Isabel said.

"You'll know because you'll have lain on top and beneath your bed, and you'll have conquered your fear?" GranMa asked.

"Yes."

"So the more we know about ourselves, our limits, and our surroundings, the less we have to fear. Right?"

"I fink you are right, GranMa!" Isabel said with confidence.

"I know I am right, Isabel. Fear is a good thing, because it keeps us alert and out of harm's way. However, too much fear is paralyzing. It keeps us from doing anything because we think everything is going to harm us. It takes a lot of courage to get past fear, but once we do, the fear no longer controls us. There are only two things my mother told me to always fear. Always fear a person who is fearless because that person is crazy, and always fear a person with nothing to lose. A person who has nothing to lose can do anything, because they have nothing to lose. The Skelly has everything to gain and nothing to lose, and in some ways, that makes him pathetic."

"What does that mean—pathetic?" Michael asked.

"It means you feel some sadness for him, but he's still a villain, so he makes you angry at the same time."

"I don't feel sorry for him. He's very bad!" Michael said.

"I know. It's hard to understand, but sometimes you can feel sad for a bad guy, yet you still have to get rid of him. I guess that's what separates us from him. We still have humanity in us, and he has no humanity."

"I don't know what that humanity is either. But if it makes you feel bad for The Skelly, I don't want any," Michael said.

"You better want some," Isabel said. "It's what makes us *different* from The Skelly."

"Okay, I'll take some, but only because I don't want to be like The Skelly," Michael said.

"I think that's a very good idea," GranMa said.

"I'll bet you're glad you opened this can of worms," Alexis joked with GranMa.

"Every opportunity to learn is a good opportunity, even when it includes worms." GranMa laughed.

"Then you've never eaten worms!" Noah said.

"I don't know what that means, Noah, but please *don't* explain," Alexis said, casting a suspicious eye his way.

GranMa and the children reached the base of the Third Sister and began a climb up toward the steep peak. The boldness of the day was bearing down on them and it wasn't long before their cloaks were shed. A sky void of clouds began to bake them in a blistering heat. With each step, their calf muscles became tighter and tighter as pebbles of red and yellow clay rolled across the toes of their boots. The final straw for Noah was the bead of sweat that rolled into his eye, only to roll out with the tear it created, and then dripped over his upper lip and into his dry, parched mouth.

"Jiminy Cricket!" Noah spat. "GranMa, why don't we just transport to the top of this mountain?" Which seemed like a perfectly good alternative to this hot, clammy mountain climb.

"What will you learn if you don't have your feet firmly planted on the ground?" GranMa asked.

"I don't know, but with my feet firmly on the ground, I'm learning I don't like this dry, treeless mountain peak. I don't like the gravel getting in my boots. I don't like the way I'm perspiring, the sun beating down on my head, the lack of water, the boulders in my path, the lack of shade, that there are few places to hide, and that it takes incredible strength to get up here." Noah moaned.

"Good, that is *exactly* what I wanted you to learn." GranMa smiled.

"How about a rest?" Noah asked.

"Okay, where would you like to do that? The enemy will be on your tail and you will stop where?" GranMa asked.

Exhausted little Isabel responded, "I suggest we rest before we start up the mountain."

"Well, that's fabulous input, Isabel. It's only two hours too late!" Noah spat.

"GranMaaa . . . Noah's being mean to me!" Isabel sang as only she could.

"Honey, that's because Noah wants to carry you the rest of the way up the mountain," GranMa said as she huffed and puffed.

"I'll shut up," Noah said.

"Good thinking." Alexis laughed.

"Okay, let's stop here. Tell me what you see," GranMa said.

The children threw their cloaks to the ground and leaned forward with their forearms on their knees to catch a moment's rest. GranMa stood with one leg in front of the other since the grade made it impossible to stand with one's legs together. GranMa waited patiently until Isabel stood up and cupped her hands over her eyes to block the sun.

"Well, GranMa, the view is terrific. I can see forever, but it's hard to see the ground below because the brush is so thick."

"Very good, Isabel! What else can you tell me? What would happen if we were running from an enemy?"

"Well, the thick brush would make it hard for them to get to us, and it may interfere with their shooting arrows. Their daggers and spears wouldn't be much good to them unless they found a place to make a clear shot. Still, the number of places where they could take a shot at us is limited. These three mountains are tall, but they're round and narrow, so we could easily run to the other side for protection. They, on the other hand, would have trouble moving to the other side as quickly or easily because of the thick brush. They would be forced to chase us up the hill, and we would have the upper hand because we could easily shoot arrows down since the mountains are treeless, and it's easier to shoot downhill than up. Since the three sisters are in a row, and there is little distance between them, we could easily climb the mountain on the sides where they face each other, and then it would be *really* hard for anyone on the ground to get to us. The brush and flowers are especially beautiful from here, and I'll bet it's cool under all those tropical trees and bushes."

"Is that little commentary supposed to be helpful in this miserable heat?" Noah jeered.

"GranMaaa . . . " Isabel searched for justice. If she were lucky, maybe GranMa would crack Noah for being mean.

"Noah! If you have enough energy to pick fights with your sister, then you have enough energy to carry her up the mountain," GranMa barked.

"Okay! Okay, I'll be good," he pleaded with GranMa. "Big cry baby!" He sneered at Isabel, who stuck out her tongue. Alexis and Michael just stood by and giggled as the two were heading into the kind of trouble they had seen before. GranMa was short on patience when it came to arguing, and Noah and Isabel liked to test her limits.

"Isabel, I'm very impressed with everything you've learned. Tedde and Spencer have done a wonderful job training you," GranMa said.

"Oh, I've been learning from everyone, GranMa. It has been so much fun. I especially like my sword class, and I like learning how to use the weapons in my armor. It's like I'm magical," Isabel said, amazed by her own accomplishments.

Noah stood behind GranMa. "It's like I'm magical," Noah's lips mocked, mimicked, and teased.

"Still, the work you've accomplished is impressive. Your war-skill thinking is more mature than I anticipated." And as GranMa made these comments, Isabel turned her head toward Noah, but out of GranMa's line of sight, and slowly, tauntingly, and with an ugly, mean face, stuck her tongue out at Noah. It had a certain bratty, victorious, vengeful appeal as it slid down her bottom lip.

"Noah, how do you think this heat could work to your advantage?" GranMa asked.

"Well . . . " He stalled for time. "I think . . . "

"Oh! Oh!" Alexis's arm shot up.

"Not this time, Alexis. I need to know how Noah's strategic training is going. I'm impressed with his physical training, but there is more to war than big muscles. This is a hard question, so let's give him time to think," GranMa said, but it was only a few seconds before Noah had an answer.

"If this mountain is part of your strategy, you should make sure you're properly hydrated and completely rested before you lead your enemy in this direction. A trap that looks like warriors retreating is a work of art. Having to look up towards the sun will put them at a huge disadvantage. If you have prepared properly, you can easily exhaust them, which will make them easier to defeat."

"Perfect!" GranMa applauded Noah.

"No, GranMa, that's not all. If you didn't strategize this plan, but by some twist of fate you fall into this situation, it will be to your advantage that you've trained under these conditions. War is not an act of coincidence, is what Spencer tells us. War is about understanding the most likely terrain, people, and events that you'll come into contact with, and then train under those conditions." Noah's smile said he was done.

"I'm proud of you, Noah," Isabel said.

"Yeah! Wow! Nice job, Noah," Michael said, without one ounce of sarcasm.

"Man, I was completely off base," Alexis said.

"A sharp mind is always better than a sharp sword." GranMa patted Noah's shoulder. "Let's get to the top of this mountain. I have more to show you."

As they were making their way up the final quarter of the climb, little Isabel struggled with each step. Not one to complain, or show weakness, she just pushed through her exhaustion. Her struggle did not go unnoticed.

"Hey, Iz, why don't you jump on my back and I'll give you a piggy back ride to the top?"

"No thanks, Noah, everyone is tired, and I can hold my own," Isabel said.

"It's not for you. I want to show GranMa how much I've grown. She'll see how strong my muscles are."

"Okay, then I'll do it for you, so GranMa can see your big muscles," Isabel consented and jumped on his back. But the only big muscle GranMa could see on Noah was his heart.

"I think you've grown as much as a good man can," GranMa said, to Noah's delight.

"Too bad he didn't carry water on his climb up instead of Isabel. I think water could show off his muscles and make the rest of us happy," Michael joked and everyone laughed.

"I think you'll be pleased at what you see when we get to the top," GranMa responded.

The kids were deceived by the layers of barren red-and-gold-layered sandstone that had formed into three towers. These Sister Towers were not two hundred and thirty million years old like the geologists claimed. They were much younger based upon the carbon-14 found in the fossilized wood, and it wasn't years of erosion that had carved the towers. It was one massive flood and sediment that built these towers, which explained the terrain in the valley below and atop of these monuments to the flood.

To the delight of the children, on top of the Third Sister, they found a small lake and a climate nothing like that on the side of the mountain. It was lush and cool like the terrain below. The cool air felt refreshing as it brushed against their skin, while the sound of a nearby waterfall lulled them into euphoria.

"Do not be caught by the Temptress," GranMa said.

"Who's she?" Isabel asked.

"She's that sweet sound you hear humming to you from the waterfall. Can you hear her sing to you?" GranMa asked.

"I don't hear any singing!" Isabel said.

"Listen carefully. Are your eyes feeling tired? Do you wish to lie down and sleep? Don't you just feel so peaceful and secure?" GranMa's hypnotic voice whispered.

"Yes I do," Isabel whispered back in agreement.

"That is the Temptress brushing away the exhausting heat from your long journey," GranMa continued to whisper. "She cools you, soothes you, and does what a temptress does. Leads you to a false sense of security, and then WHAM!" The children jumped. "You regret your actions!" GranMa's voice was sharp and threatening. "Make her your ally, and she will be a great weapon used against your enemy. Make her your enemy, and she will be the weapon used against you. The Temptress cannot be trusted because she has no honor. All she cares about is getting what she wants, and having control."

"What could a temptress want?" Alexis asked.

"Control! She wants to be adored, honored, loved, and she wants to make a slave of your soul. She doesn't care about you or anyone else. She cares about the Temptress. So don't underestimate her and what she can do *for* or *against* you. She is disloyal, but most are unaware of her charms, so they will not know how to control her. Now that you know about her, use her against your enemy."

"I still don't get it?" Isabel said.

"You will, little one." GranMa patted her head. "You will."

"Follow me. I want to show you how we will enter *This World* from up here." She took them across the large, gray boulders to the far side of the mountain where the waterfall flowed. "See the other two sisters to the east of us?"

"Yes," they all chimed in.

"The few who are aware of a pass-through from one world to another just assume the pass-through is on the first sister, because she is mysterious and the hardest to climb. But they are wrong. The pass-through is on the third sister. See the waterfall, how the falls split like pant legs?" GranMa pointed to the dark spot where the glistening water didn't flow. "Well, you dive in the middle, and if you hit it just right, you get to the other side. It is a passage to take you out of *That World* and into *This World*. Even the ones who find this location miss the entry point because they believe the transport is inside the cavern under the waterfall. Mimi was careful to create many deceptions. We could not have anyone accidentally, or purposefully, finding this transport."

"Well, I would think most people would want to dive into this water if they managed to get up here. Wouldn't it be more likely that they would find the transport?" Alexis asked.

"Good thinking, Alexis, and since you're our expert on finding transports, let's have you go first," GranMa said.

Michael jabbed Noah in the ribs. "I could have told her not to say anything." He laughed.

"I know, but she just can't help herself," Noah said. "She always has those arms flailing in the air, wanting everyone to know how smart she is. Well, I'll bet she doesn't feel too smart now." They both laughed.

"I don't know what you two are laughing about. You're next," GranMa said.

"I could have told you that too," Michael whispered.

"This is why I was so determined to make sure you were all good swimmers. Now Alexis, I want you to dive straight as an arrow between the pant legs of that waterfall. Make sure you hit the darkest spot. The reason the entrance has not been discovered is because you must dive exactly right. Do *not* close your eyes. You must see the other side once you hit the water. If you do this just right, you will swim from the Third Sister in *That World* to the Third Sister in *This World*, and you will be completely dry," GranMa said.

Alexis made a graceful dive exactly to the center of the pant legs. Before a minute passed she came to the top gasping for air, wiping her face and choking on the gallons of water she had swallowed. The boys were laughing with delight, but Isabel did not find this particularly amusing knowing that her turn would soon be coming.

"Well, that didn't work out for you did it?" GranMa said to the drenched and humiliated Alexis.

"Nope." She choked between gasps for air while trying to wipe her eyes.

"What do you think went wrong?" GranMa asked, while the boys laughed and poked fun.

"I didn't keep my eyes open." Alexis finally caught her breath and began treading water in earnest.

"Why don't you get out and let these knuckleheads give it a try," GranMa said.

"No problem, I'll go first," Michael said as he helped his cousin out of the water. "Sorry, Alexis, I hope we didn't hurt your feelings, but it was so darn funny."

"That's okay; I spend plenty of time laughing at you. It's my turn to take what I've been dishing out." Alexis smiled as GranMa looked on with great satisfaction.

Michael took his sword off and laid it on the ground. "Oh no you don't," GranMa said. "You have to take everything with you. You may need this on the other side."

"Yeah, that makes sense," Michael said as he put his equipment back on, then turned and, without warning, made a beautiful dive in exactly the right spot.

After a few minutes, GranMa said, "Next." Isabel cut Noah in line. "You can do this, Isabel."

"What about my princess dress? It's awful big."

"Alexis didn't drown and neither will you." GranMa assured her.

"Okay," Isabel responded and, within seconds, she had her hands together, pointing towards the sky. She arched her little body, splashed, and she was gone.

To GranMa's amazement, Isabel didn't come back out of the water.

"Greaaat!" Alexis moaned.

"I'll go next," Noah said and, once again, the act was perfectly executed.

"GranMa, I'm the oldest cousin and I couldn't do this. I feel like a jerk!"

"Honey, they learned from your mistake. I'm proud of you because you tried and you took a leadership role. Never apologize for having courage. It's better that you failed while trying instead of failing because you never tried."

"You always say the right things, don't you, GranMa?"

"I suppose it's because I believe all that I say. After all, right is right. So always do and say the right things, and then you don't have to apologize for anything. Got it?"

"Yeah, I got it."

"Good," GranMa said as she gestured for Alexis to make her grand exit. This time, Alexis's execution was perfect.

"Isn't that the coolest thing ever?" GranMa heard Michael say upon her arrival to the other side. "It's like you're in a bubble, and you can see the fish in the crazy blue water. I've never seen water that color."

"What about the sparkle?" Isabel asked. "It's the best ride I've ever been on."

"I know, and you can feel the cool of the water, but you can't feel the wet of the water," Noah said.

"I wouldn't know about that!" Everyone laughed at Alexis's words. "But I agree it is the best ride ever. The only thing is now my mouth tastes like fish."

"Nothing's perfect," GranMa explained. "Let's get moving. You are now in Diggory Town, on top of the Third Sister. Everything is pretty much the same except there is no First Sister. Mimi chose this location for a transport because she knew the missing sister would confuse people who *shouldn't* be using this transport."

"Did Mimi remove the First Sister?" Michael asked.

"No, she was already missing," GranMa said as she gestured the kids to go back the way they'd come, except this time they were heading to *This World,* not *That World.*

"GranMa, these clothes aren't much fun when they're wet," Alexis said of her pink and purple fairy gown.

"No, they're not," GranMa said and, with that, she tapped Alexis with her scepter.

"Wow . . . you look great!" Isabel perked up. "Can I have clothes like that?"

"No, my princess. You have a different job, which requires different clothes."

"Darn!" Isabel snapped her fingers.

With great difficulty, she tried not to envy Alexis's new battle clothes. They weren't made of heavy armor complete with headgear and weapons. On the contrary, hers barely covered her skin. The only weapons she carried were the daggers attached to her leg straps, and the sword that lay directly down the middle of her back. The leather straps of a most unusual sword sheath crossed her chest and shoulder blades, with a bottom strap that wrapped around her waist, securing her weapon upon her back. The bracelets made of three connected but distinctive bands were still on her wrist.

Her chest was covered with a tan, leather-like material that extended over her shoulders, and draped around her arms just below each shoulder. A small piece of fabric made from that same strange material on Isabel's gown flowed majestically below the leather piece on her chest, covering her stomach. A small glimpse of bare skin separated her top from her bottom. A short skirt made of the same leather-like material wrapped around her waist, hanging about halfway between her knee and her hip. The soft curls of her hair were held back by a jeweled band that tied at the base of her neck. The jewels sparkled, as if daring the hair to go wild. Everything about her was breathtaking.

"What? What?" Alexis shrieked at her mesmerized cousins.

"You really have no idea how beautiful you look . . . do you?" Michael regretted saying it as soon as the words left his mouth.

"Ew, creepy." Alexis squished her face as she trudged along.

"Eck! I know!" Michael responded back.

"She looks so good, I almost want warrior clothes like that for myself," Noah said.

"Hey, that's pretty creepy too, especially coming from you!" Michael said.

"I'm just sayin'. We don't always have to follow the rules, you know. Besides, I'm all man and I don't need masculine clothes to tell me who I am." Noah smirked, knowing this would drive Michael crazy.

"Yeah, well, I do, and I suggest you just keep wearing man clothes if you're going to hang out with me." Michael sneered at Noah.

"All right, macho man!" Noah said as he cracked Michael a good one on the shoulder. "Is that manly enough for you?"

Michael's big, hazel eyes responded with a dirty look as he rubbed his shoulder.

"I still think I got gypped!" Isabel pouted.

GranMa didn't miss a beat. As if nothing had just happened, she said, "C'mon, we need to get down this mountain. Now that you've learned how to get up, and what to do when you get here, you need to learn how to get down."

"Perfect," Isabel said. "Insult to injury!"

The heat going back down the Third Sister wasn't any more pleasant than going up.

"Okay, how do we use the mountain when we're heading in this direction?" GranMa asked, without stopping for a rest.

"Seems to me," Isabel said, "we should be at a disadvantage if we're chasing an enemy down the hill . . . ," She paused for thought. "Because they will have the advantage of cover when they hit bottom. It would be easy for them to shoot us . . . but hard for us to see them."

GranMa raised an eyebrow. "Go on."

"I would think it would be to our advantage if we could move to the other side of the mountain and get down as quick as possible. Then we could ambush them from the bottom." Isabel bit her bottom lip, waiting for GranMa to respond, but she did not.

"It would be even better if we had an army waiting for them. We could attack them in the retreat mode and have them surrounded," Michael said.

"Yeah, and if something went wrong, and they chased us to the top, we could make a run for the transport, or hold up in the cavern beneath the falls. That would give our army time to get up the mountain and attack. Either way, the ambush works," Noah said.

"The real trick is to get them to take the bait," Alexis said.

GranMa did not interrupt while the children brainstormed. She listened as they formulated the strategies of warriors until they got to the bottom of the mountain. There, they checked out the terrain as if they knew there was something special about this place. Each headed in a separate direction, just looking to see what they could see.

"Okay, you guys, we need to head back," GranMa said, and the children came back from the surrounding woods.

"GranMa, there's a lot of hemlock around here," Noah said.

"Could make for good poison arrows, don't you think?" She smiled.

"A small person, like Hope, could easily slip behind enemy lines with all this cover," Alexis said.

"That's true," GranMa said.

"We need to remember this place," Michael noted.

GranMa said nothing.

Michael's intense curiosity got the best of him, and although he knew it would unsettle her, he had to ask. "GranMa, why is it when we passed through Three Sisters from *That World* to *This World*, the Three Sisters became only Two?"

"There is a legend," GranMa began, "about three sisters who were so linked that nothing could separate them. Their love for each other was nearly invincible. When together, they were the most fun loving, gentle force in nature. This force had served them all their lives, and it kept them safe. It is said that their hearts were woven together by a single golden string that only they could break. This bond was admired by most, but some envied their relationship, and jealousy from others crept into their lives. The jealous ones wanted what the sisters had, and thought that if they could get one of them, they would have the power of love that the sisters possessed only when together. Their brother was a strong warrior who loved them, and he had managed to protect them from jealousy for many years. But even he could not protect them forever.

"One day, a great sorcerer, posing as a prince of peace, enchanted the most beautiful of the sisters. He convinced her she would find more happiness with him. She believed him and she cut the golden string. From that day on, when we pass from the Three Sisters in *That World* to the Three Sisters in *This World*, we find only Two Sisters. The First Sister is missing, but not forgotten, so in *This World*, we still call these mountain peaks the Three Sisters."

"Why can't the other two sisters just go and take her back?" Isabel asked, since the solution seemed so obvious to her.

"It sounds easy enough, doesn't it? But it's only a legend. Perhaps there was no golden string. Maybe we just want to believe there was one," GranMa responded.

"They look lonely without her," Alexis observed.

"They are," GranMa replied, with an unmistakable sadness in her voice.

It was easy to see that a soft spot in GranMa's heart had been breached. The children did not pursue the conversation any further. They walked on in the deadening heat with deafening quiet.

It was Noah who finally broke the silence. "That old bat is going to kill us!" he whispered to no one in particular.

"Noah!" Isabel growled low.

"Well, it's true. I don't want to be mean, but c'mon!" Noah groaned back.

"Don't you know what this is about?" Michael whispered.

"Yeah, I'm sure she's preparing us for some battle . . . "

"Not *some* battle, Noah; *the* battle. And not us, but *you*," Michael whispered.

"What do you mean *me*?"

"Noah, haven't you figured out you're *the warrior*?" Michael asked.

"So are you."

"No, I'm *a* warrior, but you, you're 'The Warrior' warrior."

"Get out of here, Michael. You're always messing with me, but I'm not in the mood for your stuff right now!" Noah bit back.

"Noah, you're such an idiot," Isabel whispered.

"Immediately after birth, he was put in an oxygen tank," Alexis whispered. "I'm sure it did some brain damage. I blame the oxygen tank." Alexis giggled.

GranMa smiled as she led the pack. The children assumed since she was old, she was also deaf, and their underestimating her was proving to be to her advantage. She was learning much of how the children were developing, but Michael's gift was developing beyond anything she had imagined. He was given very little information, and with it, he accurately assessed their circumstance. He was becoming powerful, but his information would mean nothing without the gifts of the others. Weaponry and power had been established; it was the less obvious gifts that concerned her.

Chapter 15   Act Like a Lady—Fight Like a Warrior

Alexis preened herself in the mirror that was carved into the cave wall.

"What do you think, Isabel? I look pretty snazzy in this warrior outfit, don't I?"

"Yeah, snazzy!" Isabel replied, without looking up from her scepter that spun in her fingers.

"I like our room in Diggory Town," Alexis commented as she looked around the large, torch-lit cave. The four-poster bed they shared, with the over-stuffed feather mattress, stood regally in the middle of the room. Striped curtains of gold and red that matched the bedding hung under gold and red-draped valances. Behind the curtains were paintings known as frescos. They'd been painted on flat surfaces ground into the walls in an effort to create the illusion that one could see outside.

"I wish I had asked for more than one dress. You were smart to ask for the red gown; at least now you have choices. I wear the same gown every day. Don't get me wrong, I think it's beautiful, but c'mon, the same gown every day! I think that's crazy, don't you?"

"Yeah . . . crazy," Isabel mumbled back.

"Are you listening to me?"

Without looking up, Isabel said, "I'm listening! I'm just wondering what our powers are and why don't we know. The boys seem to know what they're capable of doing."

"Well, how hard is it to flex your muscles and swing a sword? We can do that and I think we're pretty good at it," Alexis responded.

"I know, but they have just a little something more. Take Michael—he can figure out anything with just a few bits of information. It's like he's a mind reader or something. And look at Noah. He has survival instincts that are amazing. I'm pretty sure he could strategize and fight a battle all by himself. What can we do? Swing a sword and fight. Who cares?" Isabel flipped her scepter on the bed and, as she did, she noticed for the first time that something inside was spinning. She picked it up to take a closer look as Alexis went on and on about how she liked her warrior outfit and what she thought her power was going to be.

"This outfit is so different from everyone else's," Alexis commented.

"Not Hope's," Isabel pointed out as she watched the thing in her scepter spin.

"Sure, but Hope's isn't cool looking like mine."

"Hope's was created a hundred years ago. What do you think it's going to look like after all these years? I think styles change in a hundred years," Isabel responded.

"Wow, that means mine is going to be out of style in a hundred years."

"I think if you live a hundred years, you don't care what your clothes look like. Heck, I think if you live thirty years, you don't care what your clothes look like. Look at our parents." Isabel made a good point.

"Well, I guess you're right about that! In thirty years, I probably won't care either. I can't wait to fly like Hope."

"Come over here and look at my scepter. There's something spinning in the top," Isabel said to Alexis.

Alexis looked carefully into the scepter as Isabel held it up to her face. The same lion's head that adorned Michael's sword was carved in gold on the top of the scepter. Around the edge of the gold was the same odd stone that was in the third band of Alexis's bracelets. Drizzling down the silver staff of the scepter were sparkling diamonds that weaved all the way to the bottom. Alexis moved her face closer to the odd stone to see something spinning inside.

"Wow, that's pretty interesting!" Alexis noted as she reached for the staff. "YOWEE!" she yelled as electricity arched from the scepter to her bracelet. "WHAT KIND OF EVIL SCEPTER IS THAT?" Alexis screamed.

Isabel tried to cram the chuckle back down her throat, but it was determined to be heard. Her stomach launched it forward into unrestrained laughter.

"You're sick! This thing practically kills me and you laugh." Alexis glared at Isabel.

"C'mon. That was funny! You should have seen your face." Isabel crunched her eyes and tried to move her nose and lips to the space between her eyebrows as she tried to mumble through her lips. "You looked like this." She laughed until she fell over on the bed.

Alexis couldn't help herself and fell onto the bed, joining her sister's sadistic laughter.

After settling down and wiping away the happy tears, Isabel asked, "What do you think that was about?"

"I don't know."

"Try it again." Isabel held the scepter out for Alexis.

"What, are you crazy? There is no way I'm doing that again."

"Why? Is it because you're afraid?" Isabel challenged.

"NO! It's because I'm smart."

"Let's go ask GranMa and see what she thinks," Isabel said.

"Yes, I think that's a much better idea," Alexis said as she pulled her kid sister off the bed, avoiding her vicious scepter.

As Alexis pulled her up, Isabel said, "By the way, if you're gonna fly, you're gonna need wings. Have you noticed? You don't have any wings," Isabel said.

"Still," Alexis said, with full confidence as she reached behind and ran her thumbs across her shoulder blades, "I can feel something going on back there."

Isabel thought she could see something changing too. But she didn't want to be wrong and then be the cause of Alexis's terrible disappointment.

Isabel expressed herself with caution, not wanting to give Alexis false hope and yet feeling her pain. "GranMa says we get what we get and all that we get is perfect for us. I think that's true, but all the same, I want something fabulous. Something that will make the boys jealous!"

"What? Like another warrior skirt?"

"No, that's been done." Isabel snickered as she closed the cave door behind her.

The cave hallway looked like a college dorm, except the doors were round at the top and made of steel. Isabel walked down the hallway toward the large cavern with her arms spread, so that her fingers touched both walls.

"How old do you think this place is?" Isabel asked.

"Well, we know it's at least a hundred years old," Alexis responded.

"I'll bet it's a least a thousand years old," Isabel speculated.

"Maybe two thousand," Alexis guessed.

"Well, not more than six thousand. GranMa said nothing created for humans is more than six thousand years old."

"Imagine, six thousand years old. How old do you think GranMa is?" Alexis asked.

"Well, I'd say she's about a hundred years old, but she doesn't look a hundred. I'd say she looks forty or fifty years old. Still, that's very, very old—almost dead," Isabel pointed out.

As they rounded the corner and entered the large cavern, they found many warriors sitting around talking about the skirmish at Cherith. "Noah was amazing," they heard one person say.

"Did you hear about Michael jumping from the top of the cave and knocking the invisible Protector from the flying horse? How on Earth did Michael know he was hovering there?" asked another.

The conversation ceased when the warriors looked up to see Isabel and Alexis standing there. Alexis's eyes were filled with tears as she remembered the day two months earlier when her courageous stepmother selflessly gave her life to a greater cause. She looked across the great room where many warriors sat on large, stuffed leather and wood sofas. The glow from the wall torches and candle-lit chandelier above illuminated their stunned faces. They looked like they had just been caught in the middle of the school gym naked. Some tried to scatter to avoid the sad expressions on the girls who had been reminded of a dreadful day.

"Stop," Isabel whispered. "Stop moving!" she repeated with more conviction.

The embarrassed warriors stopped in their tracks, but the silence continued.

"My mother died and we buried her body, but let's not bury her spirit too. It hurts us to remember, but it will hurt us more to forget," Isabel said through the blur of moist eyes. A faint smile made its way across her lips and she said, "Please don't let her legend become quiet." Her voice trailed, but only for a moment as she gathered her thoughts. "Her sacrifice should not become a whisper. It should become a proud voice spoken for all eternity. She loved you, as do Alexis and I. Keep us in your thoughts, your prayers, your words, and your love, because that is where we keep you." Then Isabel walked past the uncomfortable faces, through the great cavern to the large steel double doors that led to the streets of Diggory Town.

"Thank you," Alexis whispered to Isabel. "I didn't know what to say."

Isabel opened the large steel door. "They need us to lead even when it's uncomfortable," she whispered back.

Once outside, the challenge would be to find GranMa. Without cell phones, they depended on another communication network. They went inside Mrs. Ballam's dress shop, because she knew everyone and everything. She wasn't a gossip so much as she was a friendly soul with whom people liked to share information.

"Hi, Mrs. Ballam! Have you seen GranMa?" Alexis asked, while stopping to admire Mrs. Ballam's incredible creations. It puzzled Alexis that a dressmaker had a store in Diggory Town. Who was buying this stuff since everyone wore the same style dress day after day? Each dress was unique, since it was created solely for the individual, but still, wearing the same creation every day.

"Oh, that's one of my favorites," Mrs. Ballam said of the dress Alexis held out from the rack. "The greens and blues just scream of royalty, and I like the material. Do you know it can't be burnt," she proudly announced. "It matches this suit in the corner." She pointed to the formal man's suit that hung on a mannequin.

"When do people wear these clothes?" Isabel asked, as if reading Alexis's mind.

"Special occasions," Mrs. Ballam said.

"Like when?" Isabel asked.

"Parties, weddings, coronations—events like that," Mrs. Ballam said.

"Really!" Alexis said. "When does that happen? I'd love to attend a coronation in Diggory Town—preferably mine." Alexis smiled.

Mrs. Ballam didn't smile back. Her eyes made their way to her shoes as the normally cheerful tone in her voice drained away. "Because of The Skelly, it's been a long time since we've celebrated. That awful creature has robbed us of coronations, weddings, and any other kind of party. Maybe someday we will be able to live and love like we used to, but until that time, we must live in the shadows. Well, enough of that talk." She raised her head. "I think your GranMother is in her chamber."

"We've never been to her chamber," Isabel said.

"My . . . " Mrs. Ballam touched her lips. "How could that be?"

"We don't know. I guess we've been so busy, there's never been time." Isabel covered for her ignorance because she was afraid Mrs. Ballam wouldn't tell them what they wanted to know. Isabel was suspicious as to why GranMa kept her chamber such a secret, so it didn't surprise her that Mrs. Ballam was alarmed.

"Perhaps I should check with . . . "

Isabel cut her off. "GranMa keeps us pretty busy with training, so there's never been a reason for us to go to her chamber. I think it's just one of those silly coincidences."

After a moment's thought, Mrs. Ballam said, "Well, you'll never find it on your own. Ed . . . Ed, Sr.," she yelled.

"Yes, my beautiful bride," the tall, dark, handsome, hair thinning Mr. Ballam answered as he entered the store from the stockroom.

"Would you take these young ladies to the Chamber? They are looking for GranMa, and I'm afraid they'll never find her on their own."

"The pleasure would be mine!" The content Mr. Ballam smiled.

As they left the store, Isabel couldn't resist pulling the shop bell. She was growing, but something about the Whittaker family caused its members to never fully grow. There was a childlike quality that stayed with them no matter how many candles were added to their birthday cakes. GranMa liked to refer to it as being "gracefully immature."

Mr. Ballam led the girls down the streets of Diggory Town, and with each step, they began to feel a change in the air. They were going someplace where they had never been. The streets were becoming brighter, and something resembling a sky hung above them. They could almost feel a sun beaming down upon their heads, and before they knew it, they were coming upon the heartbeat of the kingdom—the Town Square.

As they approached the Square, (which was how the locals referred to the Town Square), they could see a massive white marble building that was built into the north marble wall. It was not quite a cathedral, not quite a castle, and not quite a fort. Having qualities similar to each, but not exactly resembling any, the building laid shroud in mystery. Dead center of the building, spreading several feet left and right of center, the wall was pushed back to make way for an extremely large bronze statue that had turned green, as old bronze statues often do. A magnificent lion with wings stood poised for revenge, its vicious canines daring its predator to attack. Behind the lion stood a humble, dignified woman dressed in regalia, her purpose unknown. The scroll in her right hand was inscribed with the name Anita Whittaker. There were few windows on the massive wall behind her, and none were close to the ground, but all seemed an excellent lookout.

Mr. Ballam led the girls south, past the two iron gates that were decorated with pearls. They opened into the Town Square, which lay just beyond the Community Chambers Building where one could find the Chambers of Education, Commerce, Government, Healthcare—the fine institutions that made sure the day-to-day life in Diggory Town was cared for properly. The letters carved boldly into the white marble read "Community Chambers."

To the east was another significant white marble building that housed the Judicial Chamber, Department of Defense Chamber, Council Chamber, Joint Chiefs Chamber, and Chamber of Responsibility (GranMa's chamber). Above the columns that so proudly supported the structure, and carved deep into the white marble, were the words "Chambers of Defense."

From their position on the northeast corner of Town Square, they had a full view of the activities. Cobblestone streets lined the park in the middle of Town Square, which teemed with people who rushed about their daily lives. There was bartering on park benches and on every corner, tradespeople hocking their skills, and politicians offering an insightful view of world events—which all seemed contrary to the life within the narrow halls of the caves where the warriors lived.

The buzz and friendly chatter of neighbors loving and respecting neighbors told the story of what the warriors fought to defend. The young warriors of Diggory Town were fighting to preserve a person's right to live without fear. Alongside them, a militia of townspeople fought without the benefit of training, or proper weapons, because an uncertain evil gave them no choice. It was up to the Diggory Town warriors to secure the safety of the militia and restore peace.

Isabel watched the children as they played in the park. These were the true heirs of Diggory Town. She felt envy for their innocence; they had no knowledge of another world that might harm them. They didn't have any obligation for responsibilities beyond their years. They were not asked to (nor would they) grow overnight. Each year, they would place only one additional candle on their birthday cake, because they had no debt to pay. They were not the inheritors of prophecy. She found herself wishing she knew less, but understood her need to know more. Like all heroes, she felt her position was a blessing and a curse.

She gazed upon the stores scattered throughout the park, and admired the window dressings that gave the impression that all was normal. Neighborhood co-ops, a bakery, a town hall clock, and an information center, all gave claim to the charade. But the secret legislative council war room proclaimed a truth that nothing was normal in Diggory Town.

"The Chamber will be this way," Mr. Ed Ballam, Sr. said, interrupting her thoughts. He led the girls toward stairs in front of the building, leading to the towering white columns.

"There must be fifty steps," little Isabel said, as she stretched her legs between each step. She enjoyed the way her gown dragged across the stairs.

"Nope—seventy uneven steps," Mr. Ballam corrected.

"Why so many steps?" Alexis asked. "And why so uneven?"

"Easier to defend," was his matter-of-fact response.

The top stair gave way to an unobstructed view that supported what Mr. Ballam claimed. On the west side of the Square stood the Chambers of the Arts that housed the Historical Archives. To the north lay the Community Chambers, and to the south lay the Chamber of Faith in all its glory. Three steeples towered over the Town Square as if reaching into the heavens, trying to grasp the hand of the Ultimate Ruler in an effort to touch eternity. A bridge connected the two front steeples where twelve statues stood guard, protecting all who entered the doors that lay beneath the stained glass windows whose art told a story of sacrifice. The predominantly white marble building stood out from the others not only because of its magnificent gothic steeples, but because of the rare lavender and pink marble stone that traced the building. Yet, with all the appearance of innocence, it had a foreboding that caused one to pause with awe.

"Is this where my GranMother does her business?" Isabel asked.

"This is where everyone does their business," Mr. Ballam responded. "This way, ladies." He extended his hand toward the heavy gold doors that opened into a grand vestibule. The arched, tiled ceiling looked more like an upside down, overly decorated egg carton, except where each round spot came to its conclusion, a marble beam extended to the immaculate floor.

Their eyes could not leave the ceiling, despite the regal surroundings, because the tile ceiling told stories like those told by the canvases in the caves. The same battles were depicted as the woman on the chariot raised her sword and the same general labored over maps strategizing a battle. Somewhere amidst the tiles came an unexpressed feeling of something horrid, illicit, and undefined. It was ever-present, stirring fear and rage in the eyes that beheld it. Hidden in the maze of tiles was an untold story waiting to be written by history. But the one thing that never escaped their notice was the two beautiful women. They stood with purpose and conviction, distinguished only by the long straight and long curly hair that separated them. Isabel longed for their passion, and needed their respect. She was not confused by the stories in the tiles. She knew she was looking at the Battle of Trafleka, and the Battle of Shame, but it was the blurred images of the Battle of Destiny that concerned her. That story had yet to be told, but as sure as she was standing there, the blurred images were the foretelling.

"Which chamber is GranMa's?" Isabel asked.

Mr. Ballam looked up, his neck stretched back as far as it would go. "Top floor. Her chamber sits just below the bell tower. It's the large door with the lion's head on it. You can't miss it."

"Is there some kind of lift to her chamber?" Isabel asked.

"The only lift to GranMa's chamber is if someone carries you. Otherwise, I only know of one way to get there." His eyes moved to what looked like an endless staircase. "I'll be wishing you well from here." Mr. Ballam winked and extended his hand.

"Thanks to you and your lovely wife. I hope we see you again soon," Alexis said as she and Isabel thanked the kindly man.

"We'll all get a chance to meet again someday. Some will be meeting in the Lake of Fire, and some will meet in a better place. Good luck to you ladies." He smiled as he walked away, because he was not as naïve as his missus, and he had not been played by these little ladies.

"We think we tricked the Ballams into taking us to the Chamber," Alexis said, "but I get the feeling the only suckers here are you and me." She laughed.

"Maybe," Isabel replied. "So how is it that GranMa's chamber became *the Chamber*? No one hesitated when they were told GranMa was in *the* Chamber. Shouldn't they have asked which chamber? Perhaps her chamber is like a heartbeat that all other chambers sync to."

"Aren't you being a little dramatic? Get up the stairs." Alexis pointed then murmured under her breath, "A heartbeat that all others sync to. Oh, brother!"

Huffing and puffing, they finally hit the top stair. "Go bang on the door, will ya?" Isabel asked.

"No, I won't."

"What . . . are you afraid?" Isabel rasped out as she bent forward to catch her breath.

"Yes," Alexis replied with equal exasperation.

"Seriously?" Isabel blew out.

"Yes!"

"Chicken!" Isabel accused as she walked to the door and craned her neck in an attempt to look into the eyes of the lion. *KNOCK! KNOCK!*

"Come in, Isabel, and bring Alexis and her bug eyes with you."

Isabel entered with confidence while her sheepish sister stepped on her heels.

"Back off, will ya." Isabel sneered at her sister.

"Alexis, what on Earth are you afraid of?" GranMa asked.

"Are you mad at us for coming to your secret place?" Alexis's sheepish eyes only glanced at GranMa's, for fear she would be turned into a pile of ash.

"Secret place! Who told you this is a secret place?"

"Well, it seems like a hallowed place, and you've never taken me here before," Alexis said as she glanced around a room that resembled the entryway below.

"I never had a reason to take you here, so I guess that's why I never did." GranMa shrugged.

Isabel pursed her lips at Alexis in an upside down smile. The kind of look you give that says, "I told you so," without ever having uttered a word.

Alexis retaliated with the shrug of the shoulders that said, "So what! You know it all!" She too had not uttered a word. This fruitless communication was not lost on GranMa.

"I suppose you came here for a reason," GranMa said as she rested her elbows on the arms of her Queen Anne chair, and deliberately tapped her fingers upon the ridiculously large, overly ornate desk.

"Yes, Isabel's scepter attacked me, or maybe it bit me. No, I'm going to say it attacked me."

"Really? And what did you do to provoke the attack?" GranMa asked, then quickly added, "I've never known a scepter to be vicious."

"Well, maybe I'm exaggerating a little, but no kidding, GranMa, the thing was throwing sparks at me. What do you think is going on?" Alexis asked.

GranMa rose and extended her hand, and Isabel placed the scepter in it. Then GranMa grabbed Alexis's wrist with the watch and pulled it to the scepter. Things began to move in slow motion as GranMa brought the two together. GranMa's deliberate motion was equally slow and steady as she watched Alexis's face move from fear to curiosity. Then GranMa took the bracelet with the diamond and began to move it toward the scepter, and sparks began to fly. It was not chaotic sparking; it was controlled and deliberate like a fireworks display, not random and unyielding like a lighting storm. It was almost as if Alexis had the ability to control weather with Isabel's scepter. Finally, GranMa put the diamond to the watch. Nothing. Well, maybe something, but what, the girls didn't know.

"Now you try it," GranMa said.

Alexis pulled the scepter toward the watch and things began to move fast and then slow, and fast again, slow again over and over as she lost control. She wanted to vomit the way you want to vomit when you get on a ride that moves and jerks in such a way that your stomach moves from your brain to your feet with the momentum of a bouncing ball.

"Augh!" Alexis gagged as she and Isabel ran to hurl chunks of lunch into GranMa's umbrella stand.

"Well, I don't suppose you'd like to try the lightning?" GranMa asked.

"DON'T! Augh! DON'T!" Isabel gagged through her vomiting. "She'll probably set us on fire!"

"All right. Good enough then," GranMa said. "Wipe yourselves up in my private facilities, and we'll start your training in earnest."

"We've been training. Spencer and Tedde have spent hours with us," Isabel said as she wiped the drippings from her lips onto the hand towel she found in GranMa's bathroom. Then Isabel threw a cool, wet facecloth to Alexis, who had discovered a nice, cool spot on GranMa's marble floor to settle her stomach and nerves.

"No, that was warrior training. You need gift training."

"It's about time." Isabel threw her hands to her lips, as if trying to stuff the sarcasm back into her mouth. GranMa pretended to be the old deaf person the children were content to believe she was.

"Follow me then," GranMa said, without the slightest concern over their nausea recovery.

"Can we have a minute please?" Alexis asked, certain that GranMa was unaware of the gravity of their situation.

"How many minutes will you need to recover during a battle?" GranMa's question was meant to be sarcastically rhetorical and required no answer.

The girls collected themselves and skirted out behind GranMa, whose chamber door closed itself with a low growl. They turned right, heading north towards what seemed like an endless hallway. Unlike the caves, the white marble cast a glow that made the hallway bright.

Occasionally, they passed a chamber on the left, or a hallway on the right, but mostly they looked forward, trying to keep pace with GranMa.

"How long is this building?" Alexis asked.

"Including the outside walls that protect the Square, it is 2,640 feet."

"Wow, that's half a mile!" Alexis noted.

"Yes it is," GranMa said as she continued to move the children along at a trot. "The building itself is 2,008 feet long, as are all the buildings lining the Square," she added as she made a brisk right turn at the end of the hall.

Before they began to descend the white marble staircase, Isabel caught a breathtaking view out the back of the building. For as far as her eyes could see, the view was peaceful, almost heavenly, as the land stretched to the ocean. On the tip of the horizon, she could see what may have been a ruin, or a very old castle.

"What did I see on the horizon, GranMa?" she asked.

"Tulum."

"Isn't that where . . . " Isabel's voice fell short.

"Yes," GranMa replied.

Alexis knew that the Battle of Trafleka had been fought there, but she felt no need to get involved with the unspoken conversation being shared by Isabel and GranMa. *How awful it must be*, she thought, *to look upon such a peaceful view day after day, and know that your daughter's life had not been spared under that sky.* She felt herself growing up. She was thinking adult thoughts, and she didn't like it. She didn't like it at all.

"We're here," GranMa said as they walked across the impeccably manicured lawn. "Please take a seat, ladies." She gestured to the garden bench. "So, my dear friend Dottie told you where to find me." GranMa crossed her arms and said, "Isn't she sweet?" Not concerning herself with *why* the girls had found her chamber as much as *how* they had found it, GranMa probed to uncover the weaknesses in her ranks.

"Well . . . " Isabel twisted her fingers. "We kinda tricked her."

"You don't say?" GranMa let her gaze linger upon Isabel for an uncomfortable moment.

"Not me," Alexis defended herself. "Isabel did all the talking."

"So you're going to let her sink on this ship by herself?" GranMa was not amused.

"Well, no. but . . . Well, I just thought you wanted to know the truth," Alexis responded.

"What truth? The truth that Isabel tricked my good friend or the truth that you are not standing by your sister?" GranMa glared at Alexis and let her fidget, because she knew there was a good lesson in the midst of this tomfoolery.

"You know what, GranMa, you're right!" Alexis said as she stood, planted her feet on the ground, and crossed her arms. "I'm the older sister and I should have taken charge. It's not Isabel's job to get things done for me . . . it's mine. We all need to be responsible for our own actions. We need to become better warriors, and we need to figure out what our gifts are, and if that means making you mad . . . well . . . then that's what it means."

Isabel couldn't remove the smile that pasted itself across her face. She especially couldn't wait for GranMa to respond to this insanity. Alexis was spinning like a top, and digging herself into a cesspool of trouble in the process. Watching this was more fun than the time Alexis tried to get through the waters in the lake at Three Sisters. The next words that flowed out of Alexis's blabbering mouth delighted Isabel even more.

"I'm watching the boys grow and learn about their gifts, and I'm wondering, what about me, what about Alexis. I want some wings. I want some answers. I want to develop into a Warrior of Legend. The time is now for Alexis to find her place in the universe!" Alexis folded her arms and gave her head a good jerk for emphasis.

Oh, this is good, Isabel thought. *GranMa is going to eat her for lunch.*

GranMa said, "All right, let's get started."

Isabel stood, flapped her hands palms up, and stammered in confusion. "Le-le-let's get started? Let's get started! What about, 'The truth that Isabel tricked my good friend, or the truth that you are not standing by your sister,' what about that?"

"It was really a question about taking responsibility. You could learn something from Alexis, you know," was all GranMa said regarding the matter.

"Life is not fair," Isabel muttered.

"The correct statement is 'life is not always fair,' because sometimes life turns out exactly the way it's supposed to," GranMa said.

"Well, not today." Isabel moaned with disappointment.

Alexis laughed, draped her arm around Isabel's shoulder, which seemed higher than usual, and said, "Better luck next time, sis."

Isabel just rolled her eyes.

"You two are as silly as those two male clowns who constantly test my patience," GranMa said. "Follow me. We need to go find out about Alexis and her gifts before her head explodes."

"I'd rather wait around and see her head explode," Isabel said.

GranMa gave Isabel "the look."

"Okay . . . Okaaayyy!" Isabel moaned as she danced her little pink shoes across the white marble stones in the garden path. The tips of her shoes created little pink sparks that she could feel tingle her toes.

"Guard!" GranMa called to one of the warriors who stood vigil throughout the chambers and gardens. "Please take Isabel to the Historical Archives Chamber. Isabel, I need you to learn about our history, culture, and judicial system."

"What?" a stunned Isabel asked, as if her ears must be mistaken, but GranMa didn't bat an eye.

"GranMa, are you kidding! Michael gets to predict the future, Noah gets to be a powerhouse super-hero, Alexis gets magical bracelets, and I get to be a librarian! I don't care what you say, this isn't fair." The guard unsuccessfully tried not to crack a smile as Isabel went on her rant.

"Look!" Isabel pointed to the guard. "Even this guy knows I'm getting cheated!"

Shaking her head, Alexis threw Isabel a sad, sympathetic glance; because she knew this time Isabel was right.

"Be careful of what it is you *think* you see, Isabel!" GranMa said. "Guard, please take her to the Historical Archives Chamber. Isabel, you'd better have filled that beautiful little head of yours with knowledge by the time I get there." GranMa wasn't about to feed Isabel's rant. This conversation was over, so Isabel stamped her feet in the direction the guard led.

"GranMa, this will kill her," was Alexis's only comment.

To which GranMa retaliated, "There's an old saying, 'What doesn't kill us only serves to make us stronger,' and I think Isabel may end up stronger than any of you." GranMa couldn't help but chuckle at her own dim wit.

"C'mon, Alexis, we need to get going if we're going to walk to Tulum."

"Tulum?" Alexis's voice barely croaked a whisper.

"That's right, Tulum," GranMa said as she began her walk.

"That's a long walk—it could take hours."

"Yes it could, but it will take less time if we walk fast," GranMa said.

Alexis had long ago learned that arguing with GranMa was akin to barking at the moon. You can do it. But why? So they walked on through the beautiful woods of The Great Beyond, smelling the clean air, and discussing the days of Diggory Town before The Skelly. As they passed the ruins of Ek Balam, GranMa pointed out some of the buildings and their significance. They also discussed how far north and south The Great Beyond stretched. GranMa hinted at *That Place* in the north, and how ironic it was that something as beautiful as The Great Beyond could border a place as hideous as *That Place*. She suspected the contrast was created so that those who loved The Great Beyond would appreciate what they had, as opposed to its alternative. "Everything is created for a reason," she said. "Even *That Place*."

Alexis was surprised at how quickly they had passed through The Great Beyond to reach Tulum. GranMa's stories were so captivating that she hadn't noticed the passing of time. Within a couple of hours, they had walked from the brilliant white streets of the Square to the cool, mist-filled ocean breezes of Tulum.

"What now?" Alexis asked.

"See that axe over there?" GranMa pointed to a long, narrow stone passage that ended with a stack of hay holding an axe, and a thick piece of wood with a target painted on it. "You're going to throw it at that target." GranMa perched herself on a haystack a good distance from the haystack with the axe. With a grunt, Alexis lifted the axe from its haystack, and returned to GranMa.

"Okay, throw it," GranMa said.

Standing straight as an arrow and using both hands, Alexis pulled the heavy axe behind her head, took a deep breath, and heaved the axe forward . . . only to find it at her feet.

"I believe that is how Uncle Dennis lost his left toe. You may want to make some adjustments," GranMa said as a matter of fact.

Alexis spread her feet to shoulder width before she made her second throw. This time, the axe ended up in the same exact spot, but nowhere near her toes.

"You might consider letting the axe go a little sooner," GranMa said as she crossed her dangling ankles, and swung them up and down.

Alexis continued throwing for the next hour, until she thought her arms were going to fall off. But with each throw, she adjusted until, finally, the axe hit the target.

"GranMa, you and I both know you could have taught me an hour ago how to do this properly . . . " Alexis just let the incomplete thought sit there, waiting for GranMa to finish it.

As if picking in the air for just the right words, GranMa contemplated for a moment before she completed Alexis's thought. "You and I both know that a day will come when I am not here to lead you by the hand. When that day comes, I want to go to my resting place knowing that you can think and adjust without me. I want to know you are safe because *you* are all that you need."

Alexis lifted the axe over her head and continued throwing it, though she wasn't sure why. She had worked past the pain in her arms and was now hitting the target with a high degree of accuracy.

"GranMa, why is flying Hope's only gift?" Alexis asked.

"What makes you think that Hope's gift is flying?"

"Well, what else does she do besides fly?"

"Hope *is* the gift, Alexis. So tiny, yet so brave . . . when I am afraid, she moves me forward. She anchors my heart with her sure and steadfast ways. When I think there is no possibility of victory, she reminds me that if I quit, I have already failed; but if I go on, I may still smell the fruit of victory. She does not tire because she does not believe in hopelessness. She reminds me that hatred always loses, and love always wins. When all is said and done, it is always Hope that encourages me to do what I believe impossible."

"Doesn't that make her a slave to you?" Without malice or sarcasm, Alexis asked the question whose answer she feared.

"Don't underestimate the power of Hope. I am a slave to her. She is not a slave to me." Alexis's ego required no further appeasing. She was now as powerful as she would ever need to be. There is victory and honor in the tiniest bit of Hope, and if she were correct, she would soon be a new Hope.

GranMa knew her work with Alexis was almost complete. She had taken her as far as a teacher could. The road ahead would be filled with discovery and development. However, it was a road GranMa would not walk with Alexis. The final test was the distance that lay between GranMa and Alexis's freedom.

Isabel, on the other hand, had far to go. GranMa needed to spend many hours on Isabel's difficult road before she set her free. Although significant, Isabel's job was no more, or no less, important than anyone else's; however, her job was not as clear or well routed as the others', either. It did not manifest itself with well-defined rules or obvious choices. Someone would have to make the hard choices, and that someone was Isabel.

"You and I are done," GranMa said. Alexis knew the message that lay between the lines. GranMa did not mean we are done for today. She meant *we are done*. You are ready for battle; you are ready for the future; you are ready to take on your own training; you are ready to perfect yourself. Alexis knew without GranMa ever uttering the words. They were done.

"Let's go find your sister and see what kind of damage I can do there."

Chapter 16 A Gift by Any Other Name

Alexis headed home and GranMa went off to find the thoroughly frustrated and disappointed Isabel. She checked everywhere but found no sign of her little princess. She headed to the Historical Archives Chamber on the off chance that Isabel would still be there, and that is where she found her, burning midnight oil. Seated at a large library table, lit by a single lamp, Isabel was immersed in her family's history. Distracted only by the sound of GranMa's crazy red boots echoing as they tapped their way down the long, book-lined halls, she sat addicted to the rows of books towering high above GranMa's head. They were reciting Diggory Town's history to tiny, tired, sweet Isabel.

"What are you still doing here? It's so late. I thought you would have left by now." GranMa said.

"Well, you instructed me to fill my head, but I had no idea there was so much to know. Do you know about Papa?"

"Yes, I do."

"He's not just any guy, and that dog of his, Stanley, well, she's pretty amazing too. I started out resenting every moment of this, but then something happened, and these stories started speaking to me. I find I can't know enough, and the more I read, the more I want to read. That Papa guy and his Great GranMother are like the beginning of all this stuff; he's been a farmer, a city builder, a council member, a general, and he and that dog fought creatures as bad as or worse than

The Skelly. That lady with the lion statue, that's his wife Anita, and she's pretty amazing too. They just didn't fight bad guys in Diggory Town, either. Do you know they've been in other worlds? Very few have been allowed to live in other worlds—not even you. Look at this book; it's all about you." Isabel reached for an old leather book that laced up the sides. Words were flying out of her mouth like she had no control of them.

"You don't say," GranMa said as she ran her fingers through Isabel's messy hair.

"And look. Not everyone can unlace this book about you. That lady who works here told me she's never looked inside this book. This funny lace they call a seal, and when she pulled on it nothing happened. I gave a slight tug and it practically fell open in my hands. I can't believe this, GranMa, it's so exciting."

GranMa lifted the little face with the big brown eyes. "You look exhausted," GranMa said as she pushed Isabel's crazy curls away from her face. "I'm going to take you home now, but I want you to always keep this thought in mind. It doesn't matter how much I teach you, or how much you learn; information is only valuable when we do something good with it. Do you think you can always remember that?"

"I promise I will, but I'm not tired. Can't I stay just a little longer?"

"No, my princess, not tonight. I'll let you take a book home if you promise not to read it until you've had a good night's sleep."

Isabel promised and grabbed the book about GranMa.

"There is one more thing. The books are protected in the Historical Archives, but they are not protected outside these walls. Never leave the books unsealed."

"But I've seen it seal itself. Won't it do that outside the Archives?"

"Yes it will. But if someone enchants it before it can seal itself . . . well there's no telling what harm will come. Just don't leave it unsealed, and we won't have to worry about it. Deal?" GranMa asked.

"Deal." Little Isabel smiled.

GranMa tapped the book in Isabel's hand and said, "Altogether, there are seven books such as this one. Eventually, you will read them all, but you will not be able to open their seals until you have enough information in your head to understand the next book."

GranMa grabbed her chin and gently shook her sweet little head. "You are the gentlest and most innocent of all my babies." Isabel's naïve smile showed she thought GranMa was complimenting her, but GranMa was reprimanding herself. The guilt of harming such innocence was almost more than she could bear, and these tender moments were harmful to Isabel's safety. GranMa could not allow herself to be compromised by her own heart. She must do what needed to be done.

"C'mon, GranDaughter of mine, let's pick up this mess. I need to get you home so you can get that rest we're talking about."

"Can I take this book to *That World*?"

"Sure. It changes form in *That World,* so pay attention when you cross over, otherwise you won't know what it looks like when you get to the other side."

"What about my mother and the others?"

"When they look at it, they'll see a school book, a story book, a Bible, something like that, which is why I want you to pay attention to what it looks like when you transition through the transport. You won't see what they see when you cross over. You'll see exactly what it is, but during the transport, it will show you what form it is taking in *That World.* You'll only have a few seconds to see it, so pay attention. Otherwise your mom might say something like, 'Hey, when did you start reading Dickens?' and you'll say, 'I'm not,' and she'll say, 'Don't mess with your mother, I can see it right there in your hands.' See what I mean?"

Isabel giggled. "That would be funny."

"If you find yourself in a spot, you'll have to ask the boys or Alexis for help because they'll see what the others see."

"Why will they see what the others see?"

"Because they don't have your gift."

"Wow, this is *my* gift?"

"It's one of them."

"WAYYYY COOL!" Isabel said.

"Remember, in *That World*, Noah is still a toddler, so he will not be as much help as Alexis. And Alexis is a preteen, which means she has a little brain damage."

"Alexis has brain damage?"

"Honey, all teenagers do!"

"GranMa, you're just joking with me."

"Yeah, I'm just joking, but remember, in *That World*, the knowledge of Diggory Town is limited, and your awareness is present, but dulled. You'll think of Diggory Town as if viewing it through a cloud. It can be confusing."

"I'm not confused in *That World* anymore. I remember everything about Diggory Town."

"I thought you might get that unfortunate gift, which is sometimes a burden."

"It doesn't feel like a burden," Isabel responded.

"I know, princess . . . but it will." GranMa's tone had a foreboding that Isabel did not want to pursue at that moment. She just wanted to bask in the glory of her newfound gift.

"GranMa, what is your gift?"

"It's wisdom."

Isabel puckered her face. "That doesn't seem like a gift."

"It's the one I asked for. C'mon, I'll transport you from here," GranMa said.

"There's a transport here?"

"There are a couple in each of the buildings around the Square."

"GranMa, how is it we get to spend so much time in Diggory Town? Aren't they suspicious in *That World*?" Isabel asked.

"They're not suspicious because your apparitions are exactly like you in appearance, and *similar* in personality."

"Does that mean Alexis doesn't *really* go to school?"

"Well, we send her to the important classes, but it's a balancing act. Save the worlds—go to school. Go to school—save the worlds." GranMa smiled and shrugged. "If we don't save the worlds, then the school thing won't matter much, will it?"

"Guess not, but I like going to daycare, and that's kinda like school." Before GranMa could comment, Isabel added, "But I like being here way better than daycare!"

As they walked down the rows of bookcases that lined the halls of the Historical Archives, Isabel put her arms out like an airplane tipping its wings from side to side. The laced book in her right hand caused it to tip more as she began with, "Save the worlds—go to school. Go to school—save the worlds. Save the worlds—go to school. Go to school—save the worlds." She continued in this manner until they arrived at the transport.

GranMa cupped Isabel's cheeks in her hands. "I'll see you in the morning."

"Okay, I love you. Goodnight," Isabel said, stepping into the transporter.

"I love you too. Goodnight." GranMa blew Isabel a kiss before she became vanishing molecules.

CLANG! The sound of metal falling sprang GranMa to action. She banged her scepter to the ground and immediately transformed into battle gear.

"Who's there?" she shouted into the darkness of the ill-lit Archives.

A cold, hallow, creaking voice whispered, "Wouldn't you like to know?" The voice rolled in waves that echoed back against GranMa. "Let's just say I'm old, but I'm no friend."

Heart pounding, GranMa drew her sword and turned in all directions straining to see, but her eyes failed to find their target. The sounds echoed around her, causing confusion as the voice continued.

"I see your precious GranChildren are becoming strong," the vibrating voice continued.

GranMa did not respond as she eased her way down the rows of books and dark halls, waiting for the voice to falter. Courage guided her as the voice taunted in an effort to disrupt her concentration.

"I am coming for *you* first. Then I will devour the innocent ones before they are no longer innocent. Ohhh . . . that's . . . right . . . " the slow, methodical voice taunted. "There are two who are no longer innocent. How ugly your soul must feel to know that they have killed because of your teachings. But fear not, most beautiful one, I will punish them dearly for their sins, and then I will absorb their souls . . . I will show no mercy! Ha ha ha . . . " The haunting laugh drifted throughout the halls.

GranMa closed her eyes in an effort to feel the position of the evil voice. She had trained to fight with her eyes closed because it heightens the senses, but it was of no use. The moment she heard the ting of cracking glass, she knew the voice was gone. She also knew that the voice was the only thing that had been with her in the Archives.

She ran out the front doors and commanded the twelve statues that stood guard on the bridge, "Sound the call!" The statues lifted horns that appeared from nowhere. Simultaneously, each horn made a separate noise, as if calling their own. Soon, the Square was alive with activity. GranMa made her way to the bridge and, before long, she was joined by Tedde and Spencer.

"Someone left a chatter box in the Archives," GranMa said.

"Who was with you in the Archives at this late hour?" Spencer asked.

"Isabel and the librarian, Beatrice Bryer, but anyone could have left it during the day," GranMa replied. "The wooden box can take on any box form before it changes to metal and grows legs. Once it was done speaking, I heard it change to glass and break."

"Did you see the glass before it disappeared?" Tedde asked.

"No. I looked, but I wasn't sure if the clang I heard was a sword being dropped or a chatter box. It wasn't until I heard the glass break that I knew what I was dealing with."

"What did the chatter box say?" Spencer asked.

"It was *him*. He said he was coming for me first, and then the children. He wasn't providing information. He was taunting me."

"GranMa, my job in The World of People is to decipher code for the Marines. Even little details can be significant. Please tell me *exactly* what happened," Tedde said.

GranMa recounted the events in the Archives, including the day Isabel spent there until the moment she heard the glass break.

"I'll need to speak with Isabel," Tedde said.

"No!" The word raced out of GranMa's mouth. "Isabel is at a critical crossroad. I don't want anything compromising her at this moment. You need to do this research without her and get back to me. You two get your warriors organized, assign them duties, put them on high alert, send out a reconnaissance party, and debrief me before dawn. Spencer, you're the High General; I'll expect you take over Tedde's warriors so that she can process the intelligence. Are you confident that The Cave of the Tired Souls is secure?"

"Of course we are. Our spirits protect it, and we can be there at the speed of light if need be," Spencer said.

"No need to be so defensive, General," GranMa said.

"Sorry, GranMa, I can't help myself."

"I know. It's in your blood." GranMa laughed.

"It's not that funny, GranMa. I've been putting up with it all my life." Tedde was not amused.

"Oh, get over yourself, Ms. Intelligence Officer," Spencer spat back.

"Are you two kidding me? Honestly . . . sibling rivalry! Will you ever grow up?" GranMa countered.

"I promise as soon as you, Uncle Jon, and my mother grow up, we will grow up," Tedde said.

"Touché!" GranMa replied. "Let's get serious, go do our jobs, and pretend we're adults."

The rest of the night was spent anxiously anticipating The Skelly's next move, and preparing Diggory Town for *its* next move. By morning, conclusions were reached, but little was known.

Spencer reported first. "Uncle Jon will take a battalion of warriors to the perimeter. They'll keep watch in case The Skelly tries to attack from all sides, but I suspect he'll be attacking from the inside, like what happened to us at the Battle of Shame. If he does, we've still positioned Uncle Jon properly because he'll have The Skelly surrounded."

Tedde said, "I agree with Spencer, which is why I think we need to lure The Skelly away from Diggory Town. We want him to think he's on the offensive so that we can lead him to a place we can easily defend. Our problem is we have a spy on the inside, but I can't figure out who or how many."

"I have three concerns. One is Uncle Jon wants revenge for Bill. Is he thinking clearly, Spencer?" GranMa asked.

"He doesn't let his passions get in the way of his good sense. He'll be fine. I think he functions better when he has a clear-cut goal. His rage gives him focus; it's why I put him there."

"You're right," GranMa said. "My second concern is the only thing that will lead The Skelly away from Diggory Town is the children or me. You're exactly right about our leading The Skelly to a place away from Diggory Town that we can defend, but it's very dangerous for my GranChildren."

Spencer spoke to GranMa as her General. "Of course it is, GranMa. I've trained your babies for what we know is inevitable. This will be the battle that tests their skills. The prophecy says 'the battle that *she* cannot bear'; it's their destiny. I'm sure Mimi had trouble letting you fulfill your destiny. But the time has come, and you must let them fight this battle. It is not the Omega Battle."

"You don't know that, because prophecy also says '*He* will not interfere with destiny because fate is in *their* hands. *They* must rebuild a nation and secure their rightful place among the heavens.' Spencer, we can lose if we don't do this right." GranMa's trepidation rarely showed its ugly head, but it rarely had so much to lose.

"You trusted Spencer to prepare them. Trust that he has done his job," Tedde said to GranMa, then turned to Spencer. "Are they ready?"

"They are as ready as I can make them. It is time we test the results of our efforts. There is only one way to know if they are ready," Spencer said.

GranMa nodded her reluctant head in agreement. "My third concern is we don't know who we can trust. Be cautious regarding who knows what, and keep a keen eye for telltale signs of a traitor. What should we be looking for, Tedde?"

"Everything and everyone is suspect, GranMa. I'm guessing a less obvious person could be our traitor, but a less obvious person tends to have less access to critical information. I hesitate to profile our possible traitor because it could throw us off track. I have a few people in mind, but I'd rather not say right now in case I'm wrong."

"Good enough. I trust your instincts, but promise us if it gets dangerous, you will let one of us know immediately," GranMa insisted.

"I promise. Now I need to get back to my research," Tedde said as she headed back towards the Square.

"She'll wait until she's in mortal danger and then she'll sound an alarm. You know that, don't you?" Spencer asked.

"Yes, I know. She's always worried about protecting the family. Keep a close eye on your sister. If you have to, follow her," GranMa said.

"Are you suggesting I spy on my sister?" Spencer asked, cocking one eyebrow.

"Stop acting like you won't enjoy every moment of this. Your job just became twice as hard. Remember, tracking your sister is a secondary objective. Your primary focus is protecting and defending Diggory Town."

"I'm good at my job, but sometimes it's mundane. It just became very interesting." Spencer rubbed his hands as if warming them.

"Focus!" GranMa warned. "Now go about your business. I need to meet Isabel."

"See ya," Spencer said.

The sun was now full in the sky, but morning had come much too soon for GranMa, and not nearly early enough for Isabel. GranMa headed to the center of the Square, where they had agreed to meet.

"So how was your night?" GranMa asked Isabel.

"It was so exciting. I could hardly sleep waiting for morning to come so that I could read. How was your night?" Isabel asked.

"Oh . . . pretty typical," GranMa lied as she draped her arm across Isabel's shoulders while they walked.

"Today, we're going to work on making sense of your gift. Now that you know what you have, you need to know what to do with it, but first I want to discuss another gift you have."

"Another gift! I have two! Ohhh, Michael is *not* going to like this." She laughed.

"Isabel, first off, that's not nice. And second, you have no idea the extent of Michael's gift, and neither does he," GranMa said.

"Okay, but still, two gifts for me! WHOO HOO!"

"You can do something with the palms of your hands, and it's very dangerous. Very dangerous!"

Isabel's face became serious as GranMa explained, "There was a time when I was greatly underestimated and, for a time, you will be greatly underestimated. Take advantage of your enemy's error. This will not be a time for pride. Pride is not a warrior's friend. Many have died at the feet of pride because pride is determined, overconfident, and reckless. If you are to become a great warrior, then your pride must be put away, and a confident but humble servant must take its place. Your gifts will mean nothing if you do not respect them. Reading the information in the sealed book is only one of many gifts you possess."

"Many!" Isabel squeaked like a mouse.

"What did I just say about pride?" GranMa scolded.

"Sorry . . . " a reluctantly humbled Isabel replied.

"When you are in armor, you can throw light, fire, and, if you pick up a rock, hot lava," GranMa said. "You must be very careful with these gifts, because as I am sure you have already imagined, they can be dangerous to unintended victims. For this reason, you and I will go to Tulum to practice your gift. It is near the water, and it is an established training ground for such gifts. Have you flown yet?"

"No, I'm not sure I want to."

"Well, you'd better get sure," GranMa said, then yelled, "Star! Lightning!"

The two horses appeared. "Isabel, I want you to fly in armor, and I'd like you to spend more time in your armor since that is what you will wear in battle."

"Is the battle coming soon?" Isabel worried.

"If we knew when the battle was coming, we'd all know exactly how to prepare. We have to hope for the best, and prepare for the worst, because that is all we can do for now. I have warriors whose only job is to figure out if a battle will come to us, or we will go to it. The only thing we have control over is if we will go to it; everything else is speculation."

"Am I spetulated?" Isabel asked.

"Not spe-tu-lated. Spec-u-la-tion. It means we're making the best guess we can based upon what we know, and yes, you were speculated. We were fairly certain that all of my granchildren would be here in Diggory Town. Now watch GranMa. I'm going to show you how to get into armor." GranMa tapped her scepter to the ground and began to spin in a swirl of white smoke a few inches above the ground. Her gown turned into a suit of armor, her scepter a lion's head sword. The silver threads on her forearms suddenly tightened as the jewels lined up vertically on the inside of her forearms, just above her wrists. A breastplate with the image of two women appeared on her chest. The two large, red-jeweled rings that were on her middle fingers and attached to her sleeves, disappeared into the palms of her hands.

Once landing on the ground, GranMa asked, "Did you see how slowly I changed into armor?"

"Uh huh," Isabel replied.

"That is because I do not feel threatened. If a battle were imminent, or I felt threatened, my heart would race and my armor would appear much quicker. Sometimes it happens on its own. I want you to be aware of these things because I want you to expect and anticipate certain events. I don't want you confused by your own equipment; this would be dangerous in a battle."

"That's what Spencer said when he was training us," Isabel responded.

"Didn't he show you how to change into armor?" GranMa asked.

"No, he said I could learn to fight in whatever I wanted. Sometimes I fought in my jammies, but never without a shield. Spencer said we have to be flexible. Sometimes during practice, he would raise his sword and yell, 'BLESSED ARE THE FLEXIBLE BECAUSE THEY CANNOT BE BROKEN!' I like that saying," Isabel said.

"Come to think of it, I do too." The more GranMa learned about Spencer, the more impressed she became with him. "Now you try it," GranMa said.

Isabel tapped her scepter to the ground, but nothing happened. She looked at GranMa with big, confused eyes.

"Here's what happened. You didn't believe you could change into armor, so you didn't. Normally when you walk, don't you occasionally tap your scepter to the ground?"

"Not very often. I don't want to damage it," Isabel replied.

"I understand, but all the same, you do tap it once in a while, don't you?"

"Yes," Isabel admitted.

"Why do you think you don't change into armor when that happens?" GranMa asked.

"Because it doesn't work for me?" Isabel responded cautiously, unsure if it was a trick question.

"Good guess . . . but wrong. The scepter knows when it's time to transform by the commands you send it. Now tap it like you mean it!"

Isabel gave her scepter a convincing tap on the ground. Suddenly, she was airborne, spinning in a puff of smoke decorated with shimmering stars. Her silvery pink and yellow gown began to transform into a suit of armor. The odd metallic material from her gown began to melt across her body. Her silver waistband that the shimmering snowflake jewels hung from became a flexible yet impenetrable chest guard. The elbow guards from her dress moved to her shoulders as the material moving across her chest crept its way down her arms. The snowflake jewels that once hung from her dress's waistband were now making their way into each wrist guard, and her scepter became her sword. The sword was much like Michael's, except the pommel of her sword looked the same as the top of her scepter. On the left side of the guard, engraved in beautiful script, it read "*The,*" and on the right side of the guard, "*Last.*"

The crown of diamonds that had adorned her head was now weaved into a single braid that twisted around her head.

"It feels like a helmet," she said as her little fingers danced over her head.

"Your crown has weaved itself into your hair to protect your head like a helmet, but you won't have the inconvenience of a helmet. You look as beautiful as ever, only more powerful," GranMa said as she preened Isabel. "In Diggory Town, our clothes are like our fingerprints. They're not fashion statements. They house our weapons, our gifts, and they establish authority. We don't have rank like the armed forces in *That World*. Authority is established by the job that needs to be done, which is usually determined by the gift required, or weapon needed."

"You always seem to be in charge. At least, everyone listens to you," Isabel said.

"Things are not always clear cut, and when the right choices don't present themselves, it is up to someone to be responsible for the ultimate decision. Today, that someone is me. It is a position that has been handed down through our GranMothers."

"So you're a queen."

"No, a queen is always in charge. The people are not allowed to decide for themselves how a kingdom should be run. A parliament, on the other hand, or a congress, decides as a group how a city or kingdom should be run. But in Diggory Town, everyone is responsible to be good citizens and do the right things; for the most part, they do. It's in times like these, when our livelihood is threatened, that the Responsible One must take charge. Trust me, in a civilized culture like Diggory Town, no one wants this job, and that is why it must be inherited."

"Being the Responsible One doesn't sound like much fun."

"It has its rewards," GranMa replied.

"Like what?"

"Love, for one."

"You do it so people will love you?" Isabel felt shame casting a shadow over her. She never knew GranMa to be self-absorbed.

"No, silly! I do it because I love *them*. When you do difficult things for people that they cannot do for themselves—because *you* love *them*—it's the best feeling in the world. I've had days when I've felt frustrated and angry at their inabilities because I'm human. But mostly, what I feel is great joy when I serve my fellow man. I like it best when I can do something for them without them knowing about it. Real love comes from the heart, and the only reward it needs is knowing that you have helped someone you love. If they don't know you did it, then they are not beholden to you. Now that's a real gift."

"Yes, I suppose it is." More than clothes had changed for Isabel. She reached up for the horn on Lightning's saddle and effortlessly pulled herself into the seat. "C'mon, GranMa, there's only so much time to practice. Pull yourself onto Star."

With the energy of a young woman, GranMa pulled herself onto Star. She wasn't about to be outdone by a smarty-pants four-year-old. "Tulum!" GranMa said in a louder-than-normal voice, and the two horses were airborne. After several minutes had passed, GranMa pointed down to some ruins in an open area that was surrounded by woods. "That is Ek Balam; it is an important place in our history. When you read, make it a point to learn about Ek Balam."

"Okay," Isabel said. "Is there something special or important I should focus on?"

"Everything about Ek Balam is special and important," GranMa said.

From high in the air, the world appeared peaceful. No threats, no sadness, no death, and no fear. In the past, that was the life of Diggory Town and, for the most part, that was still a true existence. It was the calm before storm. From up there, Tulum was just a castle ruin that sat on cliffs high above the ocean. The Great Beyond was just beautiful wooded rolling hills with meadows sprinkled here and there, the Gran Canyon was just deep, Maranatha Valley was just lush, and the Square was just a neighborhood. Yet all had seen their share of bloodshed.

"It's beautiful!" Isabel shouted to GranMa.

"It is, but we cannot afford to get lost in the romance! We must always be on guard. So appreciate the beauty, but remember who you are, and what it is you must do!" GranMa shouted back, and then took a sharp dive to descend. Isabel was just behind her, but made a gradual descent, choosing not to be as show-offie as GranMa.

"Well, here we are. I want to take you to the top of Tulum Castle and let you shoot from there," GranMa said.

"Shoot?" Isabel asked, surprised. "Like guns?"

"No. There are no guns in Diggory Town. Shoot, like magic." GranMa smiled as she headed up the deteriorating granite steps of Tulum. Once they reached the wall walk, GranMa shot her wrist towards the sky and darkness fell. "Now throw your wrist and let's see what happens." A few moments later . . . nothing.

"Are you throwing your wrist?" GranMa asked from the dark.

"I guess so," Isabel said.

GranMa felt around in the darkness. She grabbed Isabel's arm and followed it down to her wrist. "Flip your wrist over. You're not Spider-Man. Now leave your arm in front of you, but raise the palm of your hand just over your head. Good. Now pull it back to your side, only this time when I say 'throw your wrist,' push it forward like we had it and think light.

"THROW YOUR WRIST!" GranMa said, with such conviction that it scared Isabel into action. Her little wrist jerked forward with the strength of a tornado, and then there was light.

GranMa beamed as little Isabel, who was growing slightly each day, stood there with a stunned expression. "Feels pretty powerful, doesn't it?" GranMa wasn't expecting an answer, which was good, because Isabel was too stunned to give one.

"All right, now we're going to throw fire and lightning," GranMa informed Isabel, who just stood there looking at GranMa as if she was crazy. GranMa ignored the look she had seen so many times before. "Now this time, I want you to think fire, but make sure your wrist is facing the ocean. We don't have to do this in the dark unless you want to."

Isabel shook her head no, because her mouth wouldn't open.

"THROW YOUR WRIST!" GranMa repeated her last command.

Isabel jerked with the same involuntary reaction and fire shot from her wrist.

"Now, isn't that easy?" GranMa said as she ignored Isabel's stunned silence. "You want to try lightning? THROW YOU WRIST!"

Isabel's little body jerked and her knees shook as a bolt of lightning shot haywire across the sky.

"You are doing better than I thought possible. I'll be out of here in no time. You'll need to stay and practice."

"By myself?" a little voice squeaked.

"Of course by yourself! Warriors don't just fight in a clan; sometimes they fight alone. I need you to learn how to fight alone—without me, without Spencer. Your gift is special, but it means you will often be alone. I need to know you can survive *alone*." GranMa's voice was as forceful as it had been, but her heart tried desperately to compromise her. GranMa knew the consequences of such a weakness, so she ignored the pain in her heart.

"It's important for you to know that all your weapons are built into your daily Diggory Town clothing. When you transform into your armor, decorations become deadly. The snowflakes on your princess dress are an ignition switch for your next weapon.

"Okay, hot lava!" GranMa announced with a smile. "This one is a little trickier, because you have to pick up a rock. It melts into lava in the split second before it is thrown, and if it has a chance to cool before it hits something . . . how do I explain this? Normally, friction caused by speed will cause something to heat up, but in this case, nothing in this process is hotter than the melted lava. As soon as it leaves your palm, it starts cooling even though it is moving at an incredible speed. If it doesn't hit a target immediately, it becomes a lot like a bullet, but it's harder to control, and it can travel greater distances. Because it is harder to control, you will have to practice it more. I don't use it very often, but I practice it a lot, because in the few times I've needed it, it has been the only weapon that would get the job done."

"Why don't you use it more if it's so useful?"

"What makes it useful is it performs like a gun, but not a very well calibrated one. That's what makes it dangerous to use."

"Why don't we have guns in Diggory Town? We could transport them over."

"They are not allowed here."

"Why not?" Isabel asked.

"The Ultimate Ruler does not allow them."

"Why not?" Isabel repeated.

"His ways are not our ways. We do not understand all there is to know, and based upon what I do know, I'd just as soon keep it that way. The one thing I don't need is more responsibility, and with information comes responsibility. You want more?"

"No thanks!" Isabel replied.

GranMa smiled. "Well then, let's focus on what we are responsible for. I'm going to leave you to practice. You'll know when you're done. If you think you can control your gifts enough to save someone's life, then you are done. Otherwise, keep practicing. The one that will take more time to learn is lava throwing. Don't expect to learn it in one day, but do spend enough time with it so you feel comfortable throwing lava."

"Okay, I'll see you back in the Chamber?" Isabel asked.

"Yes. Check in with me before you head home. I want to see how your day went."

GranMa mounted Star and headed back to her chamber, and Isabel went about learning her new skills. It wasn't long before Isabel could darken a sky and then reignite it at will, but what she found limiting was the amount of time she could maintain the dark. Changing the sky from light to dark, and vice versa, was taxing. Creating lightning required a little more skill, because she needed to control its direction. However, it didn't tire her the way darkening the sky did.

Throwing lava was another matter altogether. It was exactly as GranMa said it would be, and after several hours, she felt comfortable with the day's training, and decided to head to GranMa's chamber. Instead of flying, she walked back with Lightning so that she could practice the most difficult skill of lava throwing. The long walk to the Square led her from the openness of Tulum through the wooded areas and meadows of The Great Beyond.

On her journey, she was tempted to stop at Ek Balam, but the hour was getting late, and GranMa would be waiting for her. She was enjoying the lava throwing as she practiced her way along the path, but was concerned with the noises she started to hear ahead. They were well in the distance beyond the trees, but they were constant and unnerving. Fear caused the child inside her growing body to take control. She started to imagine the monsters that stocked her dreams in *That World*. She pulled Lightning's reins closer to keep him from being hit by the lava she started to throw in all directions. Fear had caused panic, panic caused terror, and terror caused confusion. Anything she had learned as a warrior went right out the window. She was operating on fear-induced instincts, which was never good.

She thought she heard screams ahead, and she had. People were running everywhere to avoid her lava bullets. Isabel had forgotten GranMa's warning. A horn on the church bridge called for Spencer.

"The child known as Isabel is shooting lava bullets in all directions," a statue on the bridge reported.

"Why hasn't someone stopped her?"

"The bullets are in all directions. No one can get close," the dry voice of the statue reported.

"Jiminy Cricket!" Spencer spat as he headed to the Chamber.

Out of breath, Spencer's exasperated voice reported Isabel's journey to GranMa.

"Anyone hurt?" GranMa asked.

"Elvis was shot in the behind."

"Elvis!" GranMa couldn't believe her ears. "Elvis, our dog?"

"Yes . . . but she . . . "

GranMa raised her hand for silence and took a moment to glare at Spencer. The sheepish look on his face told GranMa there was more to come.

"But! The only 'but' I want to know about is '*but*' why you thought I didn't need to know someone was bringing things from *That World* to this one. You are my General. Your job is to *inform* me, not keep information *from* me!" GranMa glared at Spencer as she pushed herself away from the desk. "Hope, wake up!"

Hope startled from her sleep on the round, silk cushion that perched in a custom-built nook in a corner of GranMa's chamber. In a split second, she was full size before GranMa with her sword pulled.

"Oh, put that away. We are drenched in stupidity—nothing as reasonable as a battle!" GranMa erupted. "Please head to Ek Balam. Along the way, you will see a small, dangerous girl shooting lava bullets at the good people of Diggory Town. Please stop her and bring her here."

"Oh my!" Hope chuckled.

"Be careful! You are tiny and will make a small target, but apparently she can shoot a flea off the rump of a dog!" GranMa glared at Spencer, as her sarcasm was not intended to be funny.

Hope left and GranMa directed her frustration at Spencer. "You—big guy—continue with *your* 'but . . .' I want it to be followed by the name Michael and include something about a dog named Elvis."

"Well, Michael has been coming to *This World* with Ninja Stick and Elvis."

"Ninja Stick too!" GranMa snarled.

But this was not just any old ninja stick or any old dog. The ashen old bamboo stick had once stirred the imagination of a five-year-old boy into believing it was a *Ninja Stick*. And Grandma's back yard, in *That World*, was a dangerous forest. Together, the boy and the stick fought battles against an imaginary, but formidable, enemy. That enemy was Elvis. A five-year-old, blonde Chesapeake Bay retriever who the rest of the family unwittingly knew to be nothing more than a family pet. Michael knew better, but Elvis did not. She was no match for the fearsome boy/stick duo.

For months, poor Elvis was forced to do battle with the boy and the stick. Her only peace was Grandma, who occasionally shouted to Michael, "If I catch you poking or prodding that poor dog again, I'm taking that stick away!"

This only caused Michael to go underground to the secret imaginary caves on the side of the house, where Grandma couldn't see him. There, he and his loyal dog continued to learn the secrets of the *Ninja Stick* that had magically appeared in his Grandma's yard one day.

The dog would remain loyal and endure many humiliations caused by the boy's imagination. Why? Dog Cookie Treats. The boy would always reward the dog for her part in the adventure by giving her Dog Cookie Treats. But if that were not enough, the dog knew the boy loved her better than anything, and the dog loved him back twice as much.

Frustrated by what she was learning, GranMa said to Spencer. "So he's shopping in *That World* and bringing his favorite things to *This World*?"

"No, GranMa, you should see what happened to Ninja Stick in *This World*. The bamboo stick he fantasized with in your back yard in *That World* has become an amazing weapon here. It's gold and it can penetrate anything, and Elvis was meant to be here with Michael like Stanley was meant to be here with Papa. Elvis is fearless, which is why she went after Isabel. She understands every command Michael gives her. Do you remember how the first thing Michael did every morning in *That World* was put his head on Elvis, and kiss her good morning? I think they were actually communicating. He wouldn't even look at the rest of us until he wished her a good day."

GranMa made her way back to her desk and rested her chin on her folded hands as she listened to Spencer. It was a twisted story, in that it was filled with deceiving her, and yet, the benefits of such deceptions were clear and obvious. She decided to move on.

"Where are Jon's men? Why aren't they at the perimeter? They should have stopped Isabel!"

"Be reasonable, GranMa. Uncle Jon's men don't have guns. They are defenseless against lava bullets."

"Is that what you will tell me when The Skelly's men come with something equally as threatening?" GranMa accused.

"No." Spencer thought for a moment. "I will tell you that I have met with Uncle Jon, and we have corrected the problem we had not previously been prepared to address. I will tell you that Uncle Jon is as creative a warrior as I have ever witnessed, and between the two of us, the problem is solved."

"Good answer. This is precisely why I selected you as the General." GranMa's eyes met Spencer's with respect and approval.

"Thank you for your confidence." He smiled back.

"Please, go get your sister for me while we wait for the little terror to arrive." Just then, the little terror entered the room with Hope, who immediately went chuckling back to her perch.

"So . . . " GranMa rose and placed her hands on her hips. "You've been a busy little girl," GranMa said to Isabel, whose eyes were beginning to swell. "I guess you forgot one important instruction."

"I'm sorry, GranMa, I didn't mean to hurt Elvis and I certainly wouldn't want to hurt anyone in town. I . . . "

"You also knew about Elvis being here?"

Isabel looked to her shoes as a hiding place. "Yes," she whispered.

GranMa began to rant to no one in particular. "That dog loves me! In *That World*, I feed her, I bathe her, I give her bad haircuts, and I play ball with her. I do everything for her. Why didn't she come looking for me?"

"Michael told her to stay clear of you," Isabel responded.

"Of course he did!" GranMa said.

"GranMa, I was afraid . . . I didn't mean to . . . "

"No, Isabel, that is of no interest to me!" Isabel's face puckered and her lip began to quiver as GranMa's words cut through the air. "I know what went wrong, and I own most of that, but what I want to know is what you have learned about fear."

A tear fell out of spite. Isabel wasn't prepared for GranMa to be understanding. She was expecting a tongue-lashing. "I don't know what you mean."

"What are you going to do the next time fear begins to consume you? Panic is obviously not a good choice. Someday, you may be up against The Skelly, and if you cannot control your fear, it will cost you your life. It may even cost the lives of others."

Just then, Tedde walked through the door with Spencer in tow.

"Good," GranMa said, and took her seat. "Tedde, you are the first one through the door, so it's your job to make sure Isabel is trained not to panic. I don't want her gifts terrorizing Diggory Town again. Problem solved, Isabel. Tedde will be teaching you the proper reactions to fear."

"Perrrfect!" Tedde said. "Just what I want—more work. I knew I should have let you go in first." Tedde jeered at Spencer.

GranMa ignored Tedde's complaint and said, "Isabel, over the next few days, I want you reading. I'm pretty sure the Kingdom will be safe if all you do is read. I'm going to *That World* to ask your mother if you can spend the weekend with me. That will give you plenty of time to submerse yourself in our history and culture. Tedde will train you regarding fear next week."

While slowly backing out of the room, as if escaping a clan of villainous thugs, Isabel said, "Well, that's good news. I look forward to working with Tedde. I guess I'll get out of here and get started then. See you later." She prattled as she closed the door and made her escape.

"GranMa, what do you want me to do about her?" Tedde asked.

"Do what you know is right. Fear is good because it triggers our instincts. Uncontrolled fear . . . well, I think we've all just had a pretty good glimpse of what it does. Teach her how to use fear to her advantage, and how to overcome it so it doesn't kill her. If she doesn't learn to manage her fear, The Skelly will use it against her. I didn't call you here for that, though. I want to know how your investigation is going."

"It's still drastically inconclusive. I have a lot of data, and I'm close, but I'll need another week," Tedde said.

"That assumes we have another week," GranMa responded. "If he's contacting me, he's getting ready to attack."

"I know," Tedde said. "I'll put all my energy on this, and training Isabel. There's no reason she can't work with me. It will be good for her. It's time to give the muscle between her ears a little flexing."

"Spencer, you keep an eye and ear to the wind. We're trusting you to keep us alerted to any activity. Do whatever you can do to buy us time," GranMa said.

"I'm on it," he replied.

"Tedde, next week I'm going to want to know what you know regardless of its accuracy. I'm *very* uncomfortable with the fact that only you have information that could lead to our traitor," GranMa said.

"I understand. I'll be prepared to give you all the information next week."

"By next Friday!" GranMa said.

"Next Friday."

"Okay, go get some rest. It's not fruitful to work when exhausted. A good night's sleep brings a clear head." GranMa was certain of this since she had not slept in two days.

"Goodnight," Tedde and Spencer said as they excused themselves for the evening.

"We've waited a long time for this," Hope said as she stood in the doorway with GranMa, arms crossed, watching the children leave the Square.

"They're doing better than we expected," GranMa said. "They protect each other and they cover for each other. Heck, even the dog took a bullet for Isabel. There's a good chance they might actually beat The Skelly."

"Prophecy says, 'if their hearts are pure, and their souls connected, no evil can conquer the Five,'" Hope reminded GranMa. "What do you think they are whispering about?" Hope asked GranMa as she watched Tedde and Spencer.

"I'm not sure, but they've been very secretive lately and it's not feeling right. I think Tedde knows more than she's letting on."

"I guess we'll know by Friday," Hope said.

"I'll be anxious to see what kind of catastrophe that brings," GranMa said.

But she was not given a week before the next time she was summoned to action. She was given two days.

On Sunday night, GranMa opened the door to Isabel's troubled face. Her puffed red eyes and runny nose told a story GranMa was all too familiar with.

"Take it back," Isabel said of the book that lay in her extended hands. Her arms were half bent as she held the burden of the world at the ends of her fingers. "Please . . . take it back," she repeated as the tears of pain carved sorrow into her swollen face. "I know where this leads and I cannot go there." A broken voice that didn't belong to her pleaded with GranMa.

But GranMa knew she could not reverse the damage that had been done when she said to Isabel, "You cannot unknow what you know, and I cannot take back a gift that I did not give. If that were possible, I would have given this gift back to my GranMother many years ago. If you do not accept the gift, it will mean the end of time. The story is being written, and how it is written depends upon you; open the book."

Isabel opened the seal and looked at the first page. Just above GranMa's entry, in big, bold English script, it read "*The Times of Isabel.*" The next line indented and began, "Her arms were extended and the fate of the worlds rested in her hands. It was too much to ask of a four-year-old, but she was not just any four-year-old. She was the last of the Whittaker Women who would ever hold the position of the Responsible One—a position of honor, goodness, and contrition. She knew, like her GranMothers before her, that she would not always be loved or understood. This would often be a lonely position, as being responsible often is. Like her GranMothers before her, she would need to choose. And like her GranMothers before her, she would need courage beyond any reasonable human expectation. As she offered the book back to her GranMother, she anguished over the insidious knowledge that there could only be *one* Responsible One."

Isabel began to shake and GranMa caught her as she crumpled to the floor, a small, shattered, emotional wreck. GranMa cradled her and rocked back and forth as the normally-sealed book lay open at their feet. No matter how hard GranMa rocked, she could not bring calm to this moment.

"What should I do? What can I do?" Isabel's barely-audible voice asked.

"Today, you will cry," GranMa responded. "You will cry for many days, and then you will become angry. Over time, you will seek understanding. When you accept that the fate of the worlds rests in your hands, you will do *the responsible* thing. Just as all your predecessors have."

"*Predecessors?*" Isabel whispered.

In a voice just above a whisper GranMa said, "Many years ago, I crumpled to the floor on this exact spot. My Grammy Whittaker rocked me and said these words: 'The fate of the world does not lie in your hands alone. There are others. What lies in your hands is the responsibility of deciding life and death, and knowing where those choices lead. If you believe in your heart, and not just with your mouth, that the Ultimate Ruler is real, then you know death cannot take the good hearted. The Black Angel can only take those who have volunteered to go. It will be up to *you* to make the difficult choices, and do the things that must be done, because most cannot. It will often be lonely, and you will be judged harshly by others, but you will have given your life to a greater good. It is easy to carry a burden such as this when your love for others gives you the strength to do what they cannot.' I didn't make my choice that night. I didn't make it for many nights. But I continued to read until making a choice was all that there was left to do."

GranMa wiped the last of the tears from Isabel's cheeks, kissed her forehead, and continued. "I won't be here forever, and you may not need to choose in my lifetime, but a day will come when you must answer the call . . . even if the answer is no."

Chapter 17   Tracking Traitors

Several weeks passed and Isabel could do nothing but read and follow Tedde around. The more she read, the less she wanted to know about her choices and the Rule Book. Today, she was glad to be distracted by Spencer and Tedde's arguing. It gave her a break from her own hideous problem.

Isabel liked reading in her mother's lab, which Tedde had taken over since it was in the Healthcare Chamber. It helped Isabel work through her mother's loss and it put Tedde close to everything she needed—including a few suspects.

"I told GranMa about everything except the blood on the leaf," Tedde told Spencer.

"She knows you think the leak is coming from Mrs. Ballam's dress shop!" Spencer accused.

"I told you, the evidence doesn't exactly point at the Ballams. Mrs. Bryer hasn't been cleared either, but yes, GranMa knows I think it's one of those two."

"And you're going to ignore the blood on the leaf?" Spencer accused more than asked.

"I don't believe for one minute that he could have anything to do with this, and neither do you!" Tedde snapped at Spencer. They both shot a look at Isabel, who didn't look up from her book.

Spencer lowered his voice and spoke through his teeth so Isabel, who was sitting in her usual corner of the lab, couldn't hear him. "No, I don't believe it, but we can't ignore it."

Tedde lowered her head but kept an eye on Isabel and whispered, "Have you been trailing him?"

Spencer turned his back to Isabel and whispered back, "Yes, but I have to be careful; the dog is always picking up my scent. I've had to throw treats into the woods to get her off me. It won't be long before I'm caught following him. I'm exhausted because I'm not getting any sleep between leading the warriors, tracking him, and tracking you . . ."

"What?" Tedde snapped, as Spencer considered cutting out his own tongue.

"No, well I'm not exactly, I mean . . ."

"Tracking me! Are you kidding? Who told you to spy on me?" Tedde pressed her fumbling brother for answers.

Oooh, this is getting good! Isabel thought as she closed the sealed book, giving her full attention to Tedde and Spencer.

"Keep it down, she's watching us. Let's talk about this later." Spencer's low voice begged for mercy.

"Oh, no!" Tedde's voice rang, clearly not interested in offering mercy. "We'll talk about this right now! WHO HAD YOU TAILING ME? Is that low enough for you?"

"GranMa, GranMa did it," Spencer blurted.

"Well, it doesn't take much to crack this big, strong warrior, does it, Isabel?" Tedde asked.

"Hey, keep me out of this. I'm just here for the entertainment," Isabel replied.

"Look, GranMa had every right to have you tailed," Spencer said. "You and I both know you take far too many chances. We were concerned for your safety."

"I said I'd call for help if I needed it!" Tedde reminded him.

"That's always the big lie," Spencer said. "You're so afraid to compromise the family, or show us your delicate underbelly, that you wait until you're drowning in your own mess, and *then* you call for help! There, I said it and I'm not taking it back."

"Wow . . . is that what everyone thinks of me?" Tedde's bubble of anger had been popped, and a new bubble of disappointment emerged.

"Just the ones who love and worry about you," Spencer said.

"It's okay; don't bother to cover your tracks," Tedde said as she sat down on the lab bench and leaned her head into her hands. "I thought I was a pretty good warrior."

Spencer put his hand on Tedde's shoulder, but Isabel decided it was time to step in before he put his other foot in his mouth.

"There's no shame in being courageous, *or* being loved. No one meant to harm you," Isabel said. "But sometimes that's exactly how it ends up. Our family is this big chain of know-it-alls, and we smoother each other with all that caring stuff. It's imprinted on our brains and we just can't seem to stop it. We have to protect each other to the point where it becomes a trust issue. It wasn't a matter of them trusting you to do the job. It was a matter of them trusting you to protect what they value most, and what they value most is *you*."

"Why didn't you just tell me?" Tedde asked Spencer.

Spencer and Isabel gave her the, *you know our family, don't you*, look.

"All right, I get it. Don't tell GranMa I know," Tedde said.

"I won't tell her if you tell me about the leaf," Isabel said to their dumbfounded faces. "I'm only four in *That World,* but in *This World* I've grown considerably, and I'm not deaf in either world. What's the deal with the leaf?"

"Okay," Tedde said, "but we're in this together, and we're sworn to secrecy. *I* decide when GranMa will be told. Do you understand?"

Everyone agreed.

"Do you remember the first man that Noah . . . " Tedde hesitated. "Do you remember the guy who was riding Frank before he became Noah's horse?"

"Yes. I know the story," Isabel said.

"Were you told about the Star Riders finding his camp from the night before? They discovered two sets of hoof tracks and blood on a leaf?"

"Uh huh, sure." Isabel's eyes narrowed.

"The blood was Michael's!" Spencer spat out.

Isabel's eyes nearly fell out of their sockets while a great silence thudded to the floor. It was as if someone had just jerked her heart out of her chest while a veil of disbelief strangled her.

"I don't believe you!" Isabel's lips barely parted as the bitter words left her mouth.

Tedde said, "It's true, Izzy! I didn't want to believe it either, but after I read Brittani's lab report—"

"Brittani! You're telling me MY MOTHER reported Michael as a criminal!"

"No, no. I'm telling you that her lab test showed the blood matched Michael's. We don't know anything beyond that. Don't speculate. Only evidence can speak the truth. We have no idea what your mother did or didn't do with this information." Tedde rattled on and on, occasionally shooting dirty looks at Spencer.

Isabel leaned forward against the brilliant white lab table, tapping her fingers and taking exaggerated breaths. "We need to clear Michael. Has anyone spoken with him?"

"Isabel, don't do this," Tedde pleaded. "Patience is what is required here. We all know Michael would never do anything bad. He just wouldn't. What we need to do is figure out what he's doing, and why he's doing it. We've been tracking him." This time, Spencer shot Tedde the evil eye. "Michael goes off on his own a lot, so *Spencer* started tracking him. Michael takes too many chances, but it's leading us to good information. We think he may be getting close to The Skelly's camp. However, there's evidence that someone besides us is tracking him too."

"Then he's in danger," Isabel said.

"Yes," Spencer said, "but I'm with him most of the time. I should have more time now that I won't be tracking Tedde."

"You got that right!" Tedde spat.

"How do you know someone else is tracking him?" Isabel asked.

"I heard noises, saw hoof tracks, and well, I've seen fresh . . . some, ah . . . "

"Oh, for crying out loud, Spencer, just tell her . . . horse dung, manure, poo, whatever you want to call it; it was fresh.

"Have you seen Michael talking to anyone?"

"No," Spencer said.

"So what does he do?" Isabel asked.

"He uses Elvis to track. She's good at listening to his commands and she's very protective. I saw her take down a Skull who was riding straight toward Michael. Elvis jumped off a boulder onto his horse and sunk her teeth into his neck. It was over in seconds. It was actually pretty scary. I've never seen Elvis act like that before. Her yellow eyes were glowing, her canines were extended beyond her jaw, and the color of her coat made her look like a lioness. I'm sure that's what the Skull thought had attacked him."

"Someone else also saw her attack the Skull," Isabel said.

"Why do you say that?" Tedde asked.

"Because Alexis and I have been talking to Mrs. Ballam about dresses, coronations, and balls—girl stuff," she said to Spencer, and he rolled his eyes. "Anyway, she said the town is abuzz over a large cat in Diggory Town that kills people. Do lions live in this area?"

"No," Tedde said.

"According to Mrs. Ballam's description, they do now. Which means someone else saw Elvis attack that Skull. Anyway, she said Beatrice Bryer was all amiss wanting to know what Mrs. Ballam knew. She came to the dress shop asking Mrs. Ballam what she knew of the large cat that attacks people. Of course, Mrs. Ballam only knows what the gossip chain brings her. If the gossip's true, Elvis weighs about a thousand pounds, and can disappear after devouring men with one bite. At least that's what the rumor mill says. Honestly, I just thought it was a bunch of hysterical old ladies making up tales. I had no idea they were talking about Elvis."

"You think the rumor started with Mrs. Ballam?" Spencer asked.

"No, that sweet old lady is only a story teller. She hears gossip, adds a little something spicy to the story, and retells it. She's no more dangerous than I am. Oh, wait a minute, there's that whole lava bullets thing. No more dangerous than Gavin," Isabel said, shrugging and adding a bright smile.

"What about her husband?" Tedde asked.

"Can't speak for him; he seems nice enough," Isabel said.

"When was Beatrice at her shop?" Tedde asked.

"I don't know," Isabel said. "One afternoon shortly after the lava bullets incident."

"That's just after Elvis jumped the guy," Spencer said.

"Who was watching the Archives while Beatrice went to the shop?" Tedde asked.

"I don't know. Who usually watches the Archives when Mrs. Bryer isn't there?" Isabel asked.

"Me," Tedde responded.

"She has lots of help in the Archives. I've seen other people helping her," Isabel said.

"She does, but there are certain people assigned to protect the Archives at all times. The only exception is at night when the Archives are protected by an alarm and an enchantment. I am the next in line. If I can't be at the Archives, *I* report to GranMa, who assigns another guard," Tedde said.

"Maybe she went directly to GranMa," Isabel suggested.

"Sure, that's possible," Tedde said, "but why? Protocol says she comes to me, and I go to GranMa if needed. Mrs. Bryer should only go directly to GranMa when something critical is happening. I wouldn't call going to the dress shop critical. GranMa is too busy to handle routine matters and that's why she doesn't."

"Why don't we ask GranMa if Mrs. Bryer asked her to send a guard so that she could go to the dress shop during working hours?" Isabel suggested.

"Because lately, GranMa has been asking Michael to help out in the Archives. We don't want to risk exposing him. I think she'll have our heads if she finds out what he's been up to and we knew about it and didn't tell her," Spencer said.

"That's for sure!" Isabel said. "What a mess!"

"Oh, what a tangled web we weave, when first we practice to deceive!" Tedde chanted.

"You got that right," Isabel said.

"Wasn't me. I think it was Sir Walter Scott who said it."

"Well then *he's* very smart. We should have listened to him sooner," Isabel said.

The three sat in the overly clean, overly white lab for nearly an hour. Not much was said. Mostly, they sat lost in thought, or poked around in Brittani's files, hoping something would jump out at them.

Spencer was most entertained by the gory things he found in the lab, like jars of slimy pigs' eyes, slippery livers, and bloody stains that formed images. The bacteria collection was interesting, although he didn't know why some were marked *This World* and some were marked *That World*. Obviously, her medical research was not confined to *This World*. He wondered if she'd ever taken anything medical or scientific from Diggory Town to *That World*. Even his thoughts were grasping at straws since no obvious course of action was presenting itself. The only interesting thing he found in the file marked *"That World"* was a name: Larry Florio. Before he could dig deeper into the file, he was distracted by Isabel.

"I have an idea. We need to get closer to the center of all the gossip if we're going to find out who was in the woods besides Michael, Elvis, and the Skull that day. There's a green and blue dress with a matching man's suit in the dress shop. Mrs. Ballam said the matching dress and suit are worn at formal parties. I'm certain that neither the dress nor the suit would fit either one of you. I think you should go buy them and . . . "

"You want me to buy a suit that I am certain I will not like, to go to a party I am certain will not happen, and you are *quite* sure the suit will not fit me. Of course!" Spencer said. "It's an excellent idea. Why didn't I think of it?"

"Wow! I'm the Intelligence Officer; I should have thought of that," Tedde said. "For a little person, you're very smart, Isabel!"

"What?" Spencer's head moved forward as if someone hit him from behind. "What kind of crazy idea is that?"

"Crazy like a fox," Tedde said. "Mrs. Ballam will be all astir if she thinks there's some reason for us buying the clothes. Tongues will start wagging, and we'll have every reason to be there all the time because the clothes will need altering. Then Isabel and Alexis will have a reason to be there because they'll need new dresses too."

Isabel began piecing together the plan. "What shall we tell her the occasion is? She's going to ask."

Tedde's mind began working at the same pace. "Tell her she's sworn to secrecy and we can't tell her because we don't know. Tell her not to tell GranMa we said anything because we aren't supposed to say anything. All we know is we were instructed to get formalwear."

"This is a great idea. Mrs. Ballam will never tell," Isabel said. "She doesn't create gossip; she just passes it along. She is always careful to say, 'Now this is just a rumor,' before she passes the rumor along. She would never betray a secret. It's not in her character. She spreads rumors, not secrets."

"Precisely," Tedde said.

"Pardon my stupidity," Spencer interrupted, "but I have no idea what we're talking about. Can you explain this plan to me like *I'm* the four-year-old?"

"It's simple!" Tedde said. "One: we need to be in the dress shop often, but we don't want Mrs. Ballam telling GranMa what we're up to. So we make her swear she won't tell GranMa we've been in the shop. Two: we still need the gossip mill talking about the cat, so we encourage Mrs. Ballam to have discussions with everyone coming and going, including us. Three: if she doesn't know who was out there watching Michael that night, her husband might. We haven't eliminated anyone as a suspect. Either way, we will know how the information is traveling, and who's passing it around. Trust me on this, you two; it's my gift. I *am* the Intelligence Officer."

"Yeah, you don't have to tell us five hundred times," Spencer said, rolling his eyes.

"All right," Isabel said, "but let's agree if something doesn't stir in the next week with Mrs. Ballam, we'll need to start setting traps. Tedde, do you want to give Mrs. Bryer the bait or should I?" Isabel asked.

"I think it would be more believable coming from you. If she's the spy, she'll think it a rookie error if information were to leak from your mouth. She'll underestimate you," Tedde said.

Isabel smiled, remembering what GranMa had told her about the benefits of being underestimated.

"Now that we have a plan, I'm going to see what Michael's up to since I'm done tracking you," Spencer said, and gave Tedde a little punch in the arm.

"I'm tired. I need to get some sleep. What are you going to do?" Tedde asked Isabel as they headed out of the lab and into the marble halls.

"GranMa and I have been discussing my gifts, and some decisions I need to make about them. I think I'll stop by her chamber before I head home," Isabel replied as she turned towards the park and the seventy marble steps. "Good night, Tedde."

Chapter 18   Facing Demons

Isabel climbed the seventy stairs of the Chambers of Defense building, and then hauled herself up the endless set of stairs that led to the lion's head doorknocker. She stood before the door wondering what she was going to say to the woman who was asking her to do the unthinkable.

"Come in," GranMa said as the door opened before Isabel knocked.

"How did you know? I didn't even knock."

"Hope, can you give Isabel a demonstration please?" GranMa asked.

Hope came buzzing from her perch and headed outside. "Close the door please," she instructed Isabel.

When the door closed, Isabel heard a low growl.

"Show me." GranMa barely spoke.

To Isabel's surprise, the backside of the lion's head doorknocker turned into a hundred and eighty-degree peephole about the size of a basketball. Hope made faces into the room while she awaited GranMa's next command.

"Open the door . . . but do not let her in," GranMa said with a grin.

As soon as the door opened, Hope flew into the invisible shield, then slid down to the ground where she became her full size.

"GranMa, that wasn't very nice!" Hope giggled.

"No, but it was very funny." Isabel had begun laughing the moment Hope's face smashed against the shield. "I can't believe you didn't see that coming," Isabel blurted out between fits of laughter.

"Lift shield," GranMa commanded as she extended a hand to Hope, pulling her up and into the room. "Sorry, my good friend; I couldn't resist."

"That's okay. I would have done it to you," Hope admitted, flying to her perch. Her pride was bruised, but still intact.

"Take a seat. What brings you here at this late hour?" GranMa asked Isabel.

"I was over in my mother's lab with Tedde, thinking. All I do is think. Since I read the sealed book, I can barely sleep or eat. When I'm with Tedde, I spend a lot of time looking over my mother's work. She dedicated her life to science. I wonder, knowing what she knew, how could she believe in the prophecy?" Isabel asked.

"Your mother raised you to believe, but she didn't raise you to be a fool. You are not the first to question the Rule Book. Most wise people do. But I'm curious, why now?"

"GranMa, from what I can tell, science doesn't support the things we have been led to believe."

"It doesn't disprove it either," GranMa said. "Lack of evidence is prevalent on both sides of the argument. Science is not infallible."

"I've been reading while I've been in the lab with Tedde, and it seems like it to me."

"Ahh! So you are facing the demon that we all eventually face. The evil one plants that seed of doubt. However, the Ultimate Ruler is not limited by science. He is the creator of all that you see; therefore, the rules do not apply to him."

"Why don't they apply to him?" Isabel challenged.

"Look at it this way. When you read a book, are you limited by the content of the book? In other words, do you get to change the story by reading it?"

"Of course not!" Isabel said, waiting for GranMa to set the trap.

"The authors are the creators and can add, delete, or edit the books in any way they choose, because they own the story."

"I think that's obvious," Isabel said.

"But the reader is completely limited by what the author decides the story will be. In the same way, the Ultimate Ruler is not limited by science because he created science. What he can do is limitless, but what we can do is limited by the laws of science created by the Ultimate Ruler, and our own mortality."

"Then why did he create bad guys?" GranMa's explanations weren't helping her cause, and Isabel found herself in more doubt than ever.

"He didn't create bad guys, Izzy. He gave us free will to become whatever character we want to become. The bad guys created themselves. Every writer knows that eventually the characters, and the story, take on a life of their own. There comes a time when you have to let the characters become who they are, even if you would like them to be something different. Free will allows us to become good, or bad, characters."

"If the Ultimate Ruler controls everything, then why doesn't he stop the bad guys?"

"That's the thing about free will. If he interferes, then it's not really free will, is it?"

Isabel inhaled a full breath, blew it out through puffed cheeks, and then said, "Free will is really hard isn't it, GranMa."

"Yes, it is. But how else would you test the human spirit? How would you know the good from the bad?"

Isabel shrugged.

"The Ultimate Ruler's ways are not our ways, Izzy. Someday, we will understand, but for now, we must trust in his ways, learn his rules, and then abide by them."

"Even the ones we don't understand?" Isabel asked.

"*Especially* the ones we don't understand. Do you think that something bigger and smarter than us can exist?"

"Maybe," Isabel said.

"You trust me, don't you?"

"Of course I do." Isabel's voice rose. "I have never doubted you!"

"Why?" GranMa asked.

"For one, because I can see you, and two, you've never let me down. Even when I thought you had let me down, I found out later that you were right, and I was wrong."

"Odd that you would give me the benefit of the doubt. If you're wrong about me, life will go on. But if you're wrong about him, an eternity is a long time to pay consequences," GranMa said.

THE CHILDREN OF PROPHECY

"Why do you believe blindly?" Isabel asked.

"I'm an old lady and I've seen things no one should have to see. The thing that always carried me through is believing that all things work for good. When I got to the other side of whatever tragedy, or evil, was placed before me, I was all the better for it. His ways are not our ways, but I have never been sorry that I followed them. I was only sorry when I didn't. I can't give you my life experience; you can only create your own. But ask yourself, why is it people like me seem to fare so much better than those who have nothing to believe in?"

"I don't know," Isabel said quietly.

"I think it's because we have hope," GranMa said. "It causes me to wonder why people who don't believe in anything spend so much time trying to take away my hope. Why do they care? They don't want to take the Easter Bunny away from me, or Santa. I wonder why they take issue with my beliefs."

"I don't know," Isabel said again.

"Do you agree that if you don't believe in something, then it doesn't exist?"

"It doesn't exist for the people who don't believe. Sure, that makes sense," Isabel said.

"If it doesn't exist, then it is nothing. Correct?"

"Yup," Isabel said.

"Why do you think some people waste their time, money, and effort on nothing? There are plenty of good causes in both worlds; yet they decide to spend their time on nothing."

"That's crazy, isn't it?" Isabel observed.

"It is to me."

"So you're saying if I'm not going to believe, then I need to at least leave the rest of you alone?" Isabel asked.

"Absolutely not! I am saying if you are not going to believe, then without a doubt, what you will end up with *is* nothing. What does anything matter, if it all ends up nothing? I'd rather spend my entire life believing a blissful lie, then knowing a sad, empty truth. I don't know how they do it."

"You don't know how they believe in nothing?" Isabel asked.

"No, I don't know how they live without hope, which is the essence of believing nothing. It makes me sad for them, and that's why I never give up on anyone. I have enough hope for all of us."

Isabel said, "I don't want to live in a world without hope that ends in nothing."

"You don't have to, Isabel. But the problem with a belief is you can't see it, touch it, or fake it. You can only *have* it. Something happens to believers that keeps us going. But we can't explain it to the non-believers, because it defies explanation. It's like explaining the color beige to a person who was born blind. You can try, but beige is not like red." Then GranMa reached over and gave Isabel a good pinch under her bicep that nearly bled.

"OUCH! Why did you do that?" Isabel asked with words like 'you crazy old lady' staying locked behind her lips.

GranMa shoved her hand over Isabel's eyes. "That's how I would describe red to a blind person. Are you seeing red?"

"Keep your hands to yourself!" Isabel said as she pushed GranMa's hand away. "And for goodness sakes, don't try and show me how you'd teach a blind person blue." Isabel laughed through her irritation. "Do you ever lose faith?"

"We all lose faith sometimes."

"How do you get through it?" Isabel asked.

"I remember that I have lived through miracles," GranMa replied.

"Miracles like Diggory Town?"

"Goodness no! My miracles are much better than that. When friends and family pull together to help us get through a tragedy—that's a miracle. When I hold a newborn baby—that's a miracle. When I pray and something bad still happens, and then something better happens as a result of the bad—that's a miracle. When someone I love dies without suffering—that's a miracle. The biggest miracle comes when I need courage to go on, and a little knot forms in my chest reminding me that I am not alone. I hear a quiet voice in my head that says, 'Even if your body stops, you will never die, because I am with you.' When I push through my fear, that is when I believe the most," GranMa said.

"Why would the Ultimate Ruler create a reason to fear?" Isabel asked.

"Ah, another age-old question. The skeptics love this one because it proves that they are either right, he doesn't exist, or he does exist and *he's* a bad guy. My response to this is always the same: 'According to the Rule Book, you can't believe in an Ultimate Ruler without believing in an Ultimate Evil Spirit, so who do you think is doing the bad stuff?' When a natural disaster happens, I believe it is sent by an evil spirit. I think the kind souls who are sent to help clean up the disaster, and help the victims, well, they are sent by a good spirit. Every time I see one of those good souls helping an unfortunate one, they rescue me a little too. It's good to see love in action. If you observe closely, you'll see that love always shines brightest in the middle of a tragedy. I know you want more than this, but I can't make you believe, and I can't rescue your soul. You have to do both of those things yourself."

"GranMa, you *did* just rescue my soul."

No further words were needed. They both knew what was being said. Isabel had found the faith, hope, and courage she would need to do the horrible thing that must be done. Perhaps facing her demon would be her greatest gift of all.

Chapter 19 Mimi in Diggory Town

Bus No. 3 left the school with the green couched filled. Gavin was sitting up, strapped into his seat, having the most wonderful time waving to everyone. His big gray eyes surveyed the brightly colored couches with obvious approval.

"Ha-ha-HI!" he yelled to the bored flight attendant, who entered from the door in the middle of the room.

"Well, ha-ha-HI to you, cutie," she said, forgetting herself. "Ahem." She cleared her throat, regaining her composure. "Well, you know the rules: do what GranMa says." She threw her hand with casual annoyance.

"Ah, wait a minute please," Isabel spoke up. "I'd like a 7UP, please."

"A what?" The flight attendant's dull tone was in full force.

"A 7UP. I'll take a Sprite if that's all you have." Isabel smiled with her most sincere gratitude.

"GranMa, would you kindly translate?" the flight attendant requested.

"She'll have a Sweet Bubbly Lemon, please," GranMa said matter of fact. Before the stampede started, she quickly added, "They'll *all* have Sweet Bubbly Lemons."

"Darn!" Alexis snapped her fingers as the flight attendant went back through the door. "I wanted to see what else we could make her do."

"I know what you wanted," GranMa said as she shot each of them the stink eye.

"By the look of her dress, she has a new designer, and she looks wonderful," Isabel said, just as the door in the middle of the room swung open.

All the Bubbly Lemons were handed from the tray in an orderly fashion. Alexis frowned at her half full glass. Apparently, Isabel's kindly comment was not wasted on the normally surly flight attendant. Inside Isabel's Sweet Bubbly Lemon was a mountain of maraschino cherries.

"Ohhh! I love cherries!" Isabel lifted her voice slightly higher than normal.

Realizing the error of her ways, Alexis pursed her lips. "Never bite the hand that feeds you," was what her stepmother often warned. GranMa caught the surly flight attendant smiling just before the door closed behind her, and felt pleased that she had triumphed twice. After all, a lesson is a lesson.

"How is it you have all of us on Bus No. 3 today?" Michael asked.

"Well, your Auntie Brittani is visiting your mother in Portland. I suggested I come and take care of you kids, so they could go on a weekend trip. All your parents are vacationing for an extended weekend in Vancouver, Canada."

"So where are we supposed to be?" Noah asked.

"We're over at Whidbey Island. GranPa and I have rented a cabin near Deception Pass, which gives us full access to the Pacific Ocean."

"Are we having fun?" Noah asked.

"I don't know." GranMa pulled her scepter out from under her cloak and pulled the top of the scepter up to her eye. "Let's see." The lion's head that usually sat on the top flattened out into something similar to a telescope lens. "Oh, yes, we are having a great deal of fun," GranMa reported. "Oh, look at you, Noah, diving off the raft and into the large hole in the middle of a black inner tube. Wow, it's so large that all four of you can sit around its edge. Hey, Isabel, I didn't know you and Alexis knew how to water ski."

"Neither did I." Isabel pouted.

"Can I take a look?" Noah asked.

GranMa placed her scepter in Noah's hand.

"I wish I were an apparition." Noah said.

"Can I take a look?" Alexis asked, more curious about the scepter than the fun the apparitions were having with GranPa.

"I wish I were an apparition too," Alexis agreed once she pushed her eye onto GranMa's scepter. "You can see in every direction. Three hundred sixty degrees—this is amazing!"

"Anyone else want to look?" GranMa asked.

"Why torture yourself? Where will we go while our apparitions have fun with GranPa?" Michael's disappointed voice asked.

"Don't be distraught. You'll have the apparitions' memories of this weekend to share with your parents. We needed to bring Gavin to Diggory Town so he can grow. He counts on us now that . . . " GranMa didn't continue. Her eyes hit the floor as the impact of her words filled the room with deafening quiet.

Several minutes passed. Eyes began to jet around the room, looking for something to do as the disquieting silence choked them. Even Gavin's gurgling quieted at the ugly silence. When Michael couldn't stand it anymore, he said, "So what do you think my *real self* will be doing this weekend?"

GranMa was grateful for the noise. "You can do anything you'd like as long as it's not dangerous."

Isabel's head gave an involuntary shake and her lungs took an unusually long breath, which caught GranMa's attention. Michael cast a side-glance Isabel's way.

How could she know? he thought. *Oh, she doesn't know. I'm just being paranoid.*

GranMa moved from the red couch to the green couch to relieve Gavin from his restraints. "I think I'll just spend the weekend enjoying my youngest GranBaby. Isn't that right, pumpkin? Give GranMa kisses." And big, slobbering wet kisses ran across GranMa's face. Noah crunched his face in disgust. He was certain that a little bit of snot had made its way into those kisses.

"Before I cut you children loose, I want to have a meeting with you in my chamber. We need to have an open discussion to answer any questions, or concerns, you might have. At this point, I feel you are doing especially well for your ages. However, I don't want to delude myself. I need to make sure you are doing as well as I think you are doing. I also want to make sure you feel you know what you need to know, to do what must be done. Is that clear? A battle is brewing in

Diggory Town, and I fear it will not be long before we must put your skills to the test."

"How do you know it won't be long?" Michael asked.

"The Skelly has contacted me. This is a sure sign that he feels he has the upper hand. He likes to use intimidation tactics, because he thinks it weakens his foe." Then GranMa recanted the night at the Archives.

"I'll show him how weak I am." Noah flexed his muscular arm, and gave it a punch for good measure. GranMa tried not to laugh at the funny image of a boy with arms shaped like a man's. He was turning into a little Atlas.

"This is no time for us to be over confident," GranMa said. "Pride always comes before the fall. I suggest we approach this with humbled confidence. Over prepare, and always assume you are losing even when you are winning. An overly confident warrior quits fighting too soon, and that could create a gap in your battle strategy that you may not be able to close. A worthy opponent doesn't need much room to overtake you. Whether we approve of The Skelly or not, he is a skilled adversary. He can take you out in the blink of an eye. Never forget that!"

With youthful indignation, Noah said, "I don't know, GranMa, we're pretty tough."

"Let me put this in terms you can understand, Noah. Football. Super Bowl forty-two: the New England Patriots had a perfect season—no losses. They were ab-so-lutely sure they were going to win because they had beaten the Giants earlier in the season. They spent the week before the Super Bowl flexing their arms for the media, but you know where the Giants flexed their arms?" GranMa asked.

"No," Noah said.

"On the playing field," GranMa said. "New York Giants seventeen, New England Patriots fourteen. The Giants had lost six out of eighteen games that season, but New England had won all eighteen of their games. The Giants won sixty-seven percent of the time, as opposed to the Patriots winning one hundred percent of the time. Why did the Patriots lose the Super Bowl?" GranMa asked.

"Because the Patriots believed they already had the Super Bowl won," Noah replied, "but the Giants believed they had to go out and *earn* the win."

"Humble hearts, Noah, that's what happened—the Giants had humble hearts," GranMa said.

"You're right, GranMa. I just know you're right. I'm going to fight like I'm losing," Noah announced. "I'm going to fight like a Giant."

"Good boy. We're here!"

The children exited the bus and walked with GranMa towards the Square. As they passed the bronze stature of the lion and the woman, Alexis asked, "GranMa, what do you know about Anita Whittaker?"

Isabel cringed at Alexis's question.

"She's my GranMother, and I was about Isabel's age when she took me to Diggory Town. I can tell you she made the best blueberry anything, of anyone, anywhere. I loved her blueberry pancakes and muffins, but nothing compared with her blueberry pie. Mmmm . . . hot with vanilla ice cream. Yummy! I can't smell blueberries and not think of her." GranMa's voice floated back to those walking behind her as they made their way through the Square and up the seventy steps. "She was a Responsible One. There can only be one in Diggory Town at a time. When she died, I became the Responsible One."

"How did she die?" Michael asked.

"Oh, that's a long story—" GranMa started, but was quickly interrupted by Isabel.

"Mimi was never a Responsible One. Why not?" Isabel burned to know the answer to this question, but more importantly, she didn't want GranMa telling that long story.

"It cannot be passed from mother to daughter." GranMa said as they reached the top of the long staircase.

As soon as the lion's head opened the door, Noah said, "Tell me about Mimi and Diggory Town. What was she like when she was here?"

The floodgates had been opened. GranMa wasn't prepared for the types of questions being asked. She was expecting to be asked about wars, battles, and gifts, but she would answer any question that burned in their hearts . . . no matter how uncomfortable it made her.

"Mimi in Diggory Town . . . hmmm . . . Mimi in Diggory Town." GranMa stumbled over the words. Her hands wrung, and her eyes couldn't find a place to settle.

"Mimi, Mimi, Mimi . . . ah . . . " GranMa sighed and tapped her bottom lip.

Hope came off her perch to play with Gavin. "Hi kids!" the always happy Hope said, picking up Gavin and walking away to spend precious time with a precious baby.

"It's not a trick question!" Noah laughed.

It wasn't long before four grinning faces where watching GranMa squirm and bite on her lower lip as she struggled for a truthful—and appropriate—response.

"Mimi . . . where do I begin . . . ? Hmmm . . . " GranMa paced, crossed her arms, and twisted her lips.

"I suggest you start at the beginning," Michael mused as GranMa squirmed.

"I guess I have to start with Tedde and Spencer if I am going to tell you about Mimi."

"Tedde and Spencer! Wow, I wouldn't have guessed that." Alexis shook her head. "Wow!"

"Well, if you'd all be quiet for a moment, maybe we'll know why we begin with them," Isabel, *The Bossy One*, suggested.

GranMa smiled at Isabel's direct, take-charge, demeanor. Every day, Isabel became more and more like GranMa. She was happy to follow the crowd, but if a leader was required, and one did not appear to be present, Isabel would gladly take charge.

"Go ahead, GranMa, tell the story. These knuckleheads are ready to listen."

"Thank you, Isabel." The movement in GranMa's chest betrayed the laughter she tried to suppress. While GranMa composed herself, the children pulled some of the overstuffed Queen Anne chairs from around the chamber up to GranMa's desk. Each chair was upholstered in a shimmering, regal fabric that depicted different scenes in Diggory Town history. Isabel sat lazily upon a scene from the Battle of Trafleka. Noah sat upon Tulum with his legs hanging over the arm of the chair. Alexis sat like a lady upon a scene from the Battle of Shame, and Michael sat squarely upon a scene from Ek Balam.

GranMa began. "Tedde was a high priestess at Ek Balam. You may know Ek Balam as an ancient Mayan ruin in *That World*. In *This World*, Ek Balam was a peaceful civilization ruled by a beautiful priestess, and her daringly handsome brother, Spencer." The children repositioned themselves and got comfortable for the long tale. They tucked their feet under their legs and curled on the large chairs to listen and relax, as GranMa's voice began to take them to another place and time.

"Spencer was not only a prince and a warrior; he was also a great athlete," GranMa's melodic voice continued. "The Queen of Ek Balam was Mimi. Her youngest daughter, Auntie Melissa, and Melissa's husband, Uncle Tim, were the chancellors of Ek Balam. As chancellors, their jobs were to manage government and maintain order for the citizens of Diggory Town. They functioned much like a governor or a mayor might function in *That World*.

"Mimi was happy to sit back and let her family rule the city. They were good, fair, and kind keepers of a peaceful nation. Because of their loving ways, they were highly respected by the citizens they ruled. When needed, they were fearless warriors capable of defeating any army; however, it was not their way to battle without good purpose. For the most part, diplomacy was how they handled matters of state. That was until they met Sam Dybbuk from Santa Fe."

GranMa's melodic voice took the children to Ek Balam. They slumbered into a dreamlike state, until before them stood a magnificent city with bright red stucco temples accented in turquoise and red hues. Freestanding statues and statues carved into the walls of the temples told stories of the city's amazing past. Everywhere was the statue of the Black Jaguar for which the city had been named—Ek Balam, Mayan for Black Jaguar.

Almost blinding were the white-paved streets that connected El Torres (The Tower) to the South Plaza. The Ek Balam before the children's eyes didn't look like an ancient ruin. This Ek Balam was a palatial city, and the hub of agriculture for the kingdom. Lush green fields of vegetables and cotton surrounded the city as white roads from every direction led to the Central Plaza. In the Central Plaza stood three large ceremonial structures used for public affairs, and ceremonies of state. Shrines to valiant warriors were built on the tops of temples. This was an influential city serving the worlds as the provincial capital.

From the forum Mimi had named Tarsus, which was part of El Torres, Tedde could see all of Ek Balam. Because of the superior engineering skills of her architects, her voice could be heard across the city when she stood in any of the many speaking forums. Speaking in normal tones, she could stand in certain locations of the hundred foot tall, five hundred and seventeen foot long, and two hundred foot wide temple and speak to her citizens. Her masterful architects had designed buildings that naturally functioned as microphones, amplifiers, and speakers. But the forum of Tarsus was where she felt most confident.

Smaller temples throughout the city housed her technologically advanced people. However, many years of peace had caused their survival instincts to wane. They did not feel threatened the day Sam Dybbuk magically walked onto the ball court. He had accidentally found the transporter in the ruins of Arroyo Hondo, New Mexico that would transport him from *That World* to *This World*. Spencer didn't stop to figure out who the stranger was that waltzed onto his Pitz court until after he scored the winning point.

As the captain of the Pitz team, it was Spencer's job to maintain the integrity of the game. It would not do for the ruler of the region to have a less than a winning Pitz team. Being the strongest, best performing athlete in the region had as much to do with his preparation as a warrior as it had to do with the sport itself.

Once a month, just before the full moon, Spencer would arrange a competition to entertain his sister, Tedde, and GranMother, Mimi. Each lady would sit in a temple at opposite ends of the five hundred forty-five foot long two hundred twenty-five foot wide ball court. Because of the fabulous acoustics, they could whisper to each other, and be clearly heard. Fortunately, or unfortunately, they could also be heard by anyone else on the court.

The game was simple. Not using your hands or feet, the goal was to make the ball pass through one of two vertical stone rings that were placed on opposite sides of center court. A ball player could not hit the ball more than twice in a row. Each player had a teammate directly behind him or her, to provide backup. Each team started the game at opposite ends of the court. A referee threw the ball onto the court, and then players hit it back and forth using their hips, heads, thighs, and upper arms. The goal of getting the ball through hoops set along the side walls of the court was particularly challenging since the hoops were approximately six feet in the air. It took a strong and agile athlete to score in this game, because opponents were making every effort to stop you from scoring. Spencer found this sport was exactly what he needed to stay in shape for battle. Imagine his surprise when Sam Dybbuk stumbled onto his court half dazed, and half amazed.

Spencer head butted the heavy Pitz ball into the hoop before addressing the situation. "Whoa! What's this guy doing on the court? Where did he come from?" Spencer looked to the referee with his hands extended out in a *what-to-heck* fashion.

The dazed man wondered around the center court, rubbing his eyes in disbelief. Sam spun to view thousands of fans seated around the court gawking at him. He kept rubbing and rubbing his eyes in an effort to make the illusions go away. Surely, it was the desert sun playing tricks on his mind. This was the result of excavating Arroyo Hondo for several days, and being ill prepared for the harsh conditions. Excavating a thousand-year-old pueblo required more effort than he'd anticipated. Insufficient hydrating, and a constant sun beating down on a man, is surely what led to the hallucinations. He had no idea how real a hallucination could seem.

Spencer approached the perspiring, shirtless, dark-skinned man. "Sir, can I help you?"

"Sure, you can bring me some water. I'll sit for a few minutes, and in no time at all, you'll go away," Sam responded in a voice well suited to his good looks.

The other team members were cautiously approaching, but Spencer put his arms out at his side, signaling them to keep their distance. "I'll handle this if someone will bring me the water bucket."

A four foot ten inches tall, star struck, young, beautiful Mayan girl handed her prince the bucket he requested. His six foot four shadow towered over her in absurd contrast. "Thank you," his flirtatious voice whispered to the girl, who could not take her eyes off the sweaty, muscular warrior.

"Sir, have you any idea where you are?" Spencer asked as he handed the man a ladle of cool, fresh water.

Sam's lips tingled. The water drifted past his dry, parched lips, cooling his burning throat. "Ahh, thank you, my kind illusion. I will be all the more happy when you leave. My back is killing me. My muscles are about to burst through my skin," he announced as he raised his arms over his head and flexed his magnificent, overworked muscles.

By now, Mimi was on her feet to get a better look at the handsome stranger who had made his way into her world. "My . . . he's a beautiful specimen!" Her hand quickly covered her lips as the words left her mouth. She was so dazzled by his rugged good looks that she forgot she was standing in the temple used for political speeches, concerts, theater, and of course Pitz. Her voice carried to the crowd that now cheered their beautiful, blushing queen.

"Oh my! I don't know what I was thinking." She giggled. The crowd quieted to hear her every word.

"I believe you think I am handsome," Sam responded. "It's too bad you're an illusion. You are a rather attractive specimen yourself." He stared at her young, slender build that mocked her age as her deep, dark brown eyes called to the man that lived inside of Sam. She was obviously of importance, dressed regally in a black and red silk Elizabethan gown. The high collar of the doublet jacket rode along her cheekbones, calling notice to her lovely face. The red silk underskirt brought out the color of the red rubies placed sparingly in her Oriental Circlet Tiara.

"Sir, this is my GranMother, and my queen. If you would like to keep your head attached to your neck, I suggest you choose your words more carefully." Spencer positioned himself for a fight.

"If *you* haven't noticed, sir, I am rather athletic myself. I am certain this would be an interesting fight if you were made of flesh and blood," Sam said as he took a jab at Spencer. He was surprised when he connected, but not nearly as surprised as he was when Spencer delivered the blow that rendered him unconscious.

"Spencer!" Mimi shouted. "That's enough! I have managed to make a big enough fool of the both of us. Please bring this helpless soul to the infirmary. We will provide him medical attention, and I will attempt to mend what is left of my dignity." Mimi moved from her throne as her loyal subjects bowed in respect. Even with their heads lowered, and several yards between them, the subjects could not miss the school girl grin that had planted itself upon her face.

Without betraying the dignity of her title, Mimi hurried herself down the seventy steps to the bottom of the temple. The black skirt of her Victorian gown flowed behind her. She made the long walk to the enormous building known as the South Plaza, and climbed the seventy steps that led to the infirmary.

As she entered the infirmary, Mimi felt excitement building in her chest. How silly, she thought, a woman of her age and stature, acting like a school girl about to receive her first kiss. She sat in the chair near Sam's hospital bed, and stayed for a couple of hours waiting for him to regain consciousness.

"I trust you are feeling better," Mimi said to the half-dazed, recovering man. She ran a cool washcloth across his face.

"Oh my goodness, my head is killing me. Is that young man's hand made of lead?" he asked as he propped himself on one elbow and rubbed his head.

"No, but be happy you did not have the opportunity to hit him in the head, or you would now have a broken hand." Mimi laughed as she responded to Sam. "Please forgive my GranSon, Spencer. He's a good man who was honoring his foolish GranMother. And your name sir . . . "

"Well, he is a lucky man that he would have such a beautiful grandmother to cast his eyes upon each day. My name is Sam, Sam Dybbuk," he said, flirting with Mimi until suddenly he realized what had just happened to him. "What the heck!" he yelled. "I know this is just an illusion or some kind of witchcraft. Back off!"

"I can assure you, sir, witchcraft is the last thing you will find here!" Mimi became indignant at the accusation.

"Then why in the midst of working diligently, excavating Arroyo Hondo, *BAM*, I'm in the middle of who knows what?" Sam demanded an explanation.

Mimi extended her right hand, "My name is Carol. Most people call me Mimi because that's what my granchildren call me. I am the Queen of Ek Balam. If you'll calm yourself, I will be happy to explain what I believe has just happened to you. Tell me what you were doing before you found yourself in the middle of my GranSon's Pitz game."

Sam ignored her hand, "Oh, no you don't! I have no idea who you are, and I'm not telling you anything."

Mimi pulled her hand back, and looked deep into Sam's dark brown eyes. She continued to look until she could see her own reflection in his pupils. "Listen carefully to what I have to say, Sam." The melody of her voice was irresistible. "We can help you, but only if you tell us where you came from. We are an ancient people. Our ways are probably more advanced than anything you have experienced. If you let us, we can get you back to your people." Mimi smiled sweetly, and Sam found himself getting lost in her brown eyes. It wasn't long before he was exposing every detail of the last week of his life.

"I am working on my doctorate. I'm a post graduate student studying archeology and anthropology. Which means I will soon be a

Doctor of Philosophy in Anthropology, with concentrations in Archaeology." His chest puffed out, and a smile stretched across his face.

"I'm sorry," Mimi responded. "I don't know what you mean. I don't believe we have anything like that here."

"Archaeology is the study of human cultures through the recovery, documentation, and analysis of material remains, and environmental data. It includes architecture, artifacts, biofacts, human remains, and landscapes." Sam's words flowed from his mouth like honey laced with just the slightest bit of arrogance.

"Yeck! Human remains!" So far, the Queen was not impressed. "Oh, I mean . . . do tell."

Sam smiled. "Anthropology is the study of humanity. Its origins are based in the natural sciences, the humanities, and the social sciences."

"Simply stated," Mimi interrupted, "you spend your day digging up old, rotted things, and then you try to figure out what kind of social structure existed around these old, rotted things. Is that what you are trying to say?" Mimi asked with her nose turned in disgust.

Sam chuckled. "Well, since you put it that way."

Mimi found herself getting lost in his smile. *Sam Dybbuk may be an arrogant man, but in many ways, he is quite charming,* she thought.

"Why would you want to do this?" she asked.

"The goals of archaeology are to document and explain the origins and development of human culture, understand cultural history, chronicle its evolution, and study human behavior and ecology." Sam lifted his eyebrows and nodded his head as his bright smile widened.

"Still nothing," Mimi responded. "Do you think if you dig up my remains a hundred years from now, you'll be able to tell from my old bones just how confounded I am today? I have to tell you, Sam, I can't think of one reason a person might want to do such a thing, except out of curiosity."

Captivated by her, and longing for her approval, he continued. "If we establish patterns in human behavior, and determine natural trends in evolutionary behavior, then it is likely we can predict the future of social patterns. Essentially, we are linking all human beings across place and time."

"This is a science?" she asked.

"Most definitely," he replied.

"Beyond historical facts, does it produce anything?" she asked.

"Well . . . there are social implications," he responded.

"Well, Sam, in Ek Balam, we like to live harmoniously in the present. We don't worry too much about social structure. We have one rule: be good to each other. We don't have to study it; we just do it." She smiled.

"I fear I am not explaining my job very well. The bottom line is, if we understand where people come from culturally, then perhaps we can understand the social impact it has on today's life. It will also help us chronicle the results of intelligent behavior. Archeology is just a way for contemporary people to read the minds of ancient people. We can figure out what they were thinking by examining how they lived, and what they've done." Sam shrugged as he wondered why she wasn't more interested in what controlled human behavior.

"I guess so. However, it seems to me that this is nothing more than the study of human behavior with regards to its historical and social impact. You must be very interested in how people live, and the things they acquire. But what will you gain by knowing these things?" Mimi remarked and, without waiting for a response, asked, "Would you like something to eat?"

"I *am* interested in human behavior, especially with regards to social structure. I like the idea that *one* person is ultimately the ruler of everything, and thank you, I'm very hungry. I might as well get comfortable; I am beginning to fear that you are not an illusion."

"Well, if your life is reality-based, and I fear it is, then you are not going to like what I have to say." Mimi paused and bit her lip. Her eyes narrowed in on him as she pondered what motivated Sam. Did she know enough about him to divulge one of Ek Balam's secrets, or was she opening its doors to evil? With hesitation she said, "I suspect you may have stumbled upon an ancient spirit that brought you here."

"Oh, I think I know what you are about to say!" Sam got off the bed and took a seat on the red couch near his bed. For the first time, he took a good look around the infirmary. High walls and tall windows decorated with gold and red curtains that gave way to the magnificent views. Silk comforters, and overstuffed beds, created decadence beyond any hospital ward he had ever seen. If a man were to be sick . . . this was the place to do it.

"No, Sam, you don't know what I'm about to say." Mimi paused, still sizing up this handsome man. "This is a special kingdom. It is unusual for us to have visitors. People from your world don't live here, and they don't belong here." Mimi offered Sam some fruit and breakfast cakes from the infirmary serving cart.

"Is everything in your world beautiful? The plates and cups are exquisite. The serving cart is more ornate than any serving cart I've ever seen." Sam was doing a little sizing up of his own while he took his first taste of the unusual fruit Mimi had offered him. "Yum! This is excellent. What is it? It taste like sweet strawberries, mango, and banana all in one, but it's crunchy and looks like an apple."

"It is the love fruit. You do not have this in your world?" Mimi asked.

"Sometimes I wonder if we have any kind of love in my world. But no, we do not have a fruit as wonderful as this." His Adam's apple moved while he stared blindly into his hands.

Mimi found herself wanting to hug this lonely, hardworking, handsome man. Instead, she went to get him a cup of tea, hoping it would sooth his heavy heart. "Here you go, Sam," she said as she offered him the tea. His fingers slid across her hand as she passed him the cup.

"You are a kind, beautiful woman. Women like you exist in my world too, but they are hard to find," he said as a thankful smile spread across his face.

Mimi flinched, realizing she was losing her composure. "Well, Sam, we will try and find a way to get you back to your world. As soon as we do, we can send you back. I am sure there are people wondering where you are."

"My mother died giving birth to me, and my father never forgave me for that. I've always had to take care of myself; provide for myself; create a world for myself. I doubt anyone is wondering about me."

"I'm so sorry, Sam. That's hardly a fair thing to blame on a child."

"Oh, I did all right. I didn't understand my father at first, but things got better once I did. I threw myself into my studies and my work as soon as I was old enough. It was the only way to avoid his wrath, and perhaps gain a little of his approval. He didn't want to hate me; he just couldn't find a way not to. I guess as a young man, I forgot to stop working long enough to make a life for myself. It is unlikely anyone is missing me. You are the nicest thing that has ever happened to me."

Mimi's eyes sparkled as reluctant lips spread across her face. "We're glad you're here, but we must get you back. I don't know what will become of a *man* who stays in *This World*. Our ways are not your ways, and I doubt you will have the ability to understand, or exist, in our world. I do not mean to be insulting, but I fear a lack of understanding could be harmful to you, and you have been harmed enough." She gently squeezed his arm. "We will get you safely home, Sam. I need to discuss this matter with my Chancellors. I will come back to see you later, so you rest for now. The nurses and doctors will get you anything you need."

"Brittani and Aaron, please come here," Mimi called across the infirmary to her wary GranDaughters. "Sam, my GranDaughters are in charge of the kingdom's medical facilities. They will be happy to take care of you. Girls, this is Sam Dybbuk. Please tend to his needs, and then clear your calendars this afternoon. I need you to come to the Council Temple. I am calling a meeting this afternoon to discuss how we get Mr. Dybbuk back to *That World*."

"It's a pleasure to meet you, Mr. Dybbuk," both GranDaughters lied.

"It's nice to meet you too. Do you do everything together and on cue?" Sam chuckled.

Aaron smiled back. "We're sisters, Mr. Dybbuk. We tend to think alike, when we're not arguing."

"Let me know if you need anything, Mr. Dybbuk." Brittani turned on her heels to catch up with Mimi.

"I'm sorry, Mr. Dybbuk. It's not like my sister to be so abrupt," Aaron said as she glared over her shoulder.

"That's all right, I'm sure she didn't mean it. You both have significant positions in your country—"

"Kingdom," Aaron corrected.

"Pardon me?" he said.

"Kingdom, Mr. Dybbuk. We are a kingdom composed of many provinces, and communities, that are *generally* self-governing, but ultimately, they are ruled by one authority. *We* are a kingdom, and the name of that kingdom is Diggory Town. We are in the province of Ek Balam."

"Kingdom," Sam corrected himself. "I'm sure your sister has a lot on her mind and isn't thrilled with my being here, adding to her workload. I have to say, you look more like beautiful Amazon Warriors than doctors. So what is it you do?" Sam inquired while observing her muscular shoulders and forearms.

"Actually, I am a nurse, and Brittani is a medical research scientist by trade. Our primary responsibilities these days are to manage the healthcare for our citizens. You know, make sure they have what they need, medically speaking," Aaron explained.

"But you were invited to attend the council meeting," he observed.

"Sure, everyone on the council is a warrior first. Our job, first and foremost, is to protect the citizens. We *look* like warriors because we *are* warriors."

"Interesting," he said.

"Now you get some rest. We can talk later. I'm going to prepare for the council meeting," Aaron said, looking over her shoulder.

"One more thing?" Sam pushed for more information.

"Okay, one more thing, and then you rest!" Aaron said while continuing to glance over her shoulder.

"Who is your king, and why isn't he with his queen?" Sam's eyes were focused on Aaron as he tried to figure out who ruled the kingdom.

"Hahaha . . . it doesn't work like that here, Mr. Dybbuk. There is no ruler in our land. No one person is more important than any other. Each job is special. A society cannot survive without everyone doing their job well, and treating each other with respect. Imagine civilization without a farmer. That farmer shovels manure to get his crops to grow. Do you think he is less important than our priestess?" Aaron asked.

"Of course he is!" Sam responded.

"No, my dear Mr. Dybbuk, he is not! Without his effort, our civilization could not continue. His job is important, and the queen and the priestess have the utmost respect for him, and all the people *they* serve. In our world, the bigger your title, the more you owe the citizens. I am expected to give my life to save them, Mr. Dybbuk, not vice versa. They appreciate us because we appreciate them. It is my honor, and *privilege*, to be *their* servant.

"My GranMother is not an empress. She is a queen. Why? Because she likes the title, and the people like having a queen. It makes them feel secure to think someone is in charge, but her heart belongs to the people. Their needs rule her actions, not vice versa. Tedde is a priestess because she likes the idea much in the same way little girls like to be princesses. Make no mistake about this, Mr. Dybbuk, Tedde is a warrior, not a princess, and Spencer is a warrior, not a prince. You would do well to *not* meet them in battle." Aaron's eyes narrowed to engage Sam, but she could not help throwing an occasional glance over her shoulder.

"Then why are you and Brittani without titles?" Sam asked.

"Mr. Dybbuk, that would be two more things. I will answer this question, and then I must go. Brittani and I serve under my mother, who is the most responsible of all the warriors. She is not a priestess, a queen, or an empress. She is a warrior who will eventually hold the title of the Responsible One. Loosely speaking, you could think of her as a president, or a prime minister who answers to the Ultimate Ruler. After my mother, my sister and I are the second and third most powerful warriors in our king—"

"Ah ha!" Sam interrupted. "There is an Ultimate Ruler. So you have a king! Can I meet him?"

Aaron laughed. "You will meet him some day, my dear Mr. Dybbuk. We all will. Now get some rest." Aaron turned and walked away.

As Sam listened to the hurried clicks of Aaron's heels, he hoisted himself back onto the bed, all the while thinking about what she had said . . . so many unanswered questions. How could a civilization exist without a leader? What a ridiculous idea! He had spent his life studying human behavior and its historical impact. Nations only survived because they had great leaders. He needed to find out about this dictator, this *Ultimate Ruler*. Maybe there was a place for Sam in Diggory Town. Maybe *he* could have all the power and possessions he wanted. But what would it cost him? There was no such thing as something for nothing. *Everything* has a price.

Sam kept an eye on Aaron as she walked away. He was certain she would be the weak link. Talkers always are, he thought. But he was wrong.

Chapter 20   The Other Prophecy

Aaron hurried to get to the door, anxious to find out what had triggered her sister's temper. If Brittani had a demon, it was her temper. Aaron had to get to Brittani before Brittani's temper got the best of her.

Earlier, when Mimi headed out the door of the infirmary, someone caught her arm. "What on Earth? Spencer, you scared me!"

"Sorry, Meem! I wanted to catch you before the council meeting. Why did you lie to Mr. Dybbuk about the transporter?"

"Ah, that! Honey, we don't know this man. He appears harmless, but consider where he came from. He was digging in a burial site because he's spent a lifetime learning about dead bones, burial sites, and old cultures. We have to wonder if there were evil spirits waiting for a man such as Sam to come along. And we have to ask ourselves, did he *stumble* on the transporter, or was he looking for it? If he did stumble upon the transporter, did something evil lead him to it? We don't know enough about him to share the transporter link between the worlds. We don't even share this information with our citizens. We cannot afford to share this knowledge with a stranger. A transporter, in the wrong hands, could lead to the destruction of humanity." Mimi was right. Mimi was *always* right.

"We need to get to this meeting and see about finding the transporter he used. I created more than one at Arroyo Honda. Where's your Aunt Dale? She's good at finding transporters. The sooner we get Sam Dybbuk's eyes out of our kingdom, the better."

"Well, he sure had an eye for you!" Spencer laughed and Mimi blushed.

Brittani threw the door to the infirmary open. "Well, I think he's come here to shoot arrows, but they're not Cupid's!" The fire in Brittani's eyes told Mimi she was on a war path.

"What's got into you, my dear girl? It's not like you to be so judgmental. As a matter of fact, when it comes to men and affairs of the heart, you could use a little more discretion!" Mimi retorted.

"Hey! This is weird! I'm in the middle of a fight between my GranMother and my cousin," Spencer said.

"Oh, shut up, you dimwit! I'm not happy about this guy, Dybbuk." Brittani muffled her voice with all the effectiveness of a freight train.

"Who put that bee in your armor?" Spencer sneered.

Mimi stood in silence with her head cocked. She waited for Brittani to approach her with the same venom. "Are you going to continue to let your temper control you? The only reason your mother is the number one warrior is because she doesn't lack control. If not for your temper, *you* would be in charge. Now, are you done losing your temper?" Mimi asked Brittani.

"Yes, I'm done! I just don't like anyone moving in on my *GranMother!*" The fire still blazed in Britt's eyes, but she forced a gentler tone in her voice.

Spencer placed his hand over his chest, as if he could keep it from rising and falling. "Oh, this is rich! Brittani is jealous of Mimi's new boyfriend."

The door flew open once more. "What the heck!" The shock in Aaron's voice was unmistakable. However, it didn't compare with the shock on her face as Spencer hit the floor.

"What's wrong with you, Brittani?" Mimi yelled as she positioned herself over Spencer.

"He came looking for that one, so I gave it to him!" Spencer lay on the ground for a few moments thinking about what he would do next.

"He'll be fine! Meem, I don't trust this guy Dybbuk! I can't tell you why, but my warrior instincts tell me to eliminate him." Brittani laughed at Spencer as he rubbed his jaw and lifted himself on one elbow. "I'm sorry, Spence." She extended her hand to help him up.

"Are you kidding? I couldn't be more impressed," Spencer managed to spit out through a jaw loosened by his cousin's effective punch.

"Spencer, you were hit by a girly-girl, ha ha ha!" Aaron sang with glee.

"No, I was hit by a warrior." Spencer smiled and took Brittani's extended hand.

Mimi needed to refocus her GranChildren. "I can't believe your nonsense! Have you forgotten why this happened? Honestly, it's hard to believe you kids are in charge of protecting a kingdom! Let's get back to Sam Dybbuk!"

"What happened, Britt?" Aaron asked. "I don't understand your behavior. He acts like a nice enough guy. But even if he's not, we haven't had enough interaction with him to assess his motives. What gives?"

"You know what Ma said about instincts being the only friend a warrior has. Ignoring our instincts could lead to our doom." Brittani was sure this would lead the others to obvious conclusions.

"She also said, if we overreact, or act too quickly, it will lead to the doom of others. Those others may be innocents." Aaron responded.

Spencer thought for a moment and then added, "You're both right. Let's just move cautiously. Besides, Mimi seems to be interested in learning a little more about this man that she finds so handsome."

Mimi felt the heat rising in her cheeks. "That's enough nonsense from the three of you. I will see you in the council in one hour." As Mimi turned, her cloak snapped in the air, closing the subject. Her heels clicked away with an indignant cadence as she moved down the hall. "I hate kids!" she mumbled, loud enough for them to hear.

"Do you think she hates us?" Spencer asked no one in particular.

"Only enough to give her life for us," Brittani responded.

"What would we do without her?" Aaron asked.

"I don't want to think about it." Spencer's throat tightened. "Let's just get ready for the council meeting."

Suddenly, the GranChildren were jerked back to the present by GranMa's voice. "You are about to see something you have only seen once before. The last time you traveled into the past with me, in my grief, I allowed you to see me at Aaron's death. I took you into the past without giving you proper warning. I cannot be in two places at once, you will be in my chamber, but I will be in the past. I will not see you, and I cannot hear you, because I will no longer be in the present. You will see this day exactly as it occurred. Do not do anything foolish, and do not disturb the past or the present, or I will be stuck in the past forever."

"Is this dangerous?" Isabel asked.

"Yes."

"Can I go with you?" Alexis begged.

"No, Alexis, and don't even ask, Noah," GranMa smiled.

"But I just want to . . . " Noah said.

"I know what you want, but I don't need your protection. I appreciate your willingness to save me, but you protect me best by making sure nothing gets disturbed."

"Okay, GranMa, but what should we do if someone besides us tries to disturb you? Let's say, oh, I don't know, maybe The Skelly shows up . . . " Noah was proud that he finally had the upper hand with GranMa, but his bubble soon burst when GranMa responded.

"If he shows up . . . kill me and then your mothers, to ensure you will never be born. If he absorbs your powers, everyone is doomed. It is better that we only doom ourselves."

Michael said, "The Skelly won't be showing up. He doesn't exist yet. Right, GranMa?"

GranMa nodded then immediately began taking the kids back in time.

With the potential for doom hanging over their heads, it was difficult to focus on GranMa's melodic voice. Eventually, she was able to take them to another place. The streets from the infirmary in the South Plaza to the Council Temple in the Central Plaza were a brilliant white. Although only their minds were in Ek Balam, the children felt like they were invisibly walking behind GranMa. Unseen and unfazed by the citizens they passed, the children were astonished by the majesty and magnificence of the city. Directly north of the South Plaza, they could see the hundred foot tall El Torres, the Temple of the Priestess. To the west were impressive smaller temples that housed the city's people. To the east, where they were headed, lay three medium-sized temples of the Central Plaza. The turquoise and red hues that decorated city kept the white from being blinding. Statues of current and fallen heroes adorned the city, but it was the ones on top of the temples that caught the children's eyes.

"Look. There's Papa. He's posed like the cowboy in that painting in GranMa's office in *That World*." Noah pointed to the statue on top of the Public Affairs building, which lay in the southeast corner of the Central Plaza.

"Who do you think that is?" Isabel whispered to Michael as she pointed to the grand and noble-looking statue on top of the Council Temple. The largest of the three temples stood alone on the west side of the Plaza.

"I don't know, but he looks like a leader. Maybe he's *the* leader," Michael said.

"You mean . . . " Isabel wasn't sure she agreed when her voice drifted off.

"If he's not the number one leader, then he's two or three. A statue like that has to make him a man of some importance," Michael said.

"There's something familiar about him. I feel like we should know who he is." Isabel moved closer to Michael, not wanting to raise her voice.

"He's somebody, all right," Michael said of the warrior statue with the gold-faced mask.

Alexis moved close to Isabel and Michael, so they could hear her whisper, "Did you notice the lady on the Public Affairs Temple isn't complete? Her head hasn't been carved."

"HEY!" Alexis jumped when Noah shouted for no apparent reason. "Just as I thought, if they can't see us, then they probably can't hear us. You're whispering for nothing. Michael, you should have been the one to figure that out," Noah said.

"It's true. You should have." Isabel's big brown eyes twinkled at Michael.

"I know! Could it be that Noah is getting smarter than me?"

"Not likely!" Isabel giggled.

"HEY!" Noah shouted again, only this time with purpose. "That's just plain mean!"

"Sorry," Isabel said insincerely as they followed GranMa up the seventy steps of the Council Temple.

Once inside the Council Temple, the children were surprised by the indiscriminate, overly plain decor. A large, round, black marble table stood in the middle of the room surrounded by twenty-four chairs. Twenty-three of the chairs were sturdy but modest. Alexis could not help but notice the large twenty-fourth chair with deeply-carved wood, and heavy legs embedded with crystal balls that mimicked the paperweights on GranMa's desk. Nothing besides torches hung on the polished gray marble walls—not a window in sight. Even the floors were a rough, bland, unpolished gray marble.

GranMa took the seat to the right of the ornate chair. With the exception of the words, Siege Perilous, which were engraved in the table in front of the ornate chair, there were no markings on the table. Anita "Grammy" Whittaker sat to the left of ornate chair. Seating themselves in orderly fashion to the left of Grammy were Papa, Mimi, Uncle Jon, Uncle Dennis, Amy, Mindy, Auntie Melissa, Uncle Tim, Tedde, Spencer, Katie, Nicky, Jackson, Brittani, four empty seats, Aaron, two empty seats, GranMa, and back to the empty, ornate chair. Not everyone from the Ancient Council had been seated.

"What do we know?" Grammy asked.

"He's from *That World* and he studies human history and culture by examining dead bodies and deteriorating remnants of their past," Mimi said.

"He seems to think every culture has to have a hierarchy like a king, president, or dictator," Aaron added.

"Why does he think he's here?" Grammy asked.

"He has no idea; it's as much a mystery to him as it is to us," Mimi said.

"What brought him here?" Grammy asked.

"We don't know," Mimi said.

"Then we cannot take him back until we do. If we send him back, and he is an evil spirit from our world, then we will unleash a danger in *That World* like it has never known. Remember World War I?" Everyone nodded their heads. "Millions died before we could stop the carnage. World War II was even worse, but World War III will be the war that ends all wars. Everyone will die," Grammy said, as Mimi hung her head so low it almost hit the table.

"Put your head up, Carol Ann!" Grammy Whittaker demanded of her daughter. "The transporters you created had nothing to do with World War I. We were able to transport well before your work was complete. If anything, your transporters do a better job of filtering out those who mean to do harm.

"I can't help it," Mimi (Carol Ann) lamented. "I think I could have done something differently."

"We all could have done something differently. But you didn't create evil. It existed well before you ever came along. My goodness . . . you're pretty full of yourself if you think you have that kind of power." Grammy smiled.

"Well, she does have the power to bring a man to his knees with her good looks," Spencer teased, giving Mimi an exaggerated wink. Everyone at the table agreed that Mimi was beautiful, and anything but evil.

"We should all be a little more selfless, like you. You bark like a rabid dog, but you act like a saint. I would say you are one of his divine works." Uncle Jon reached over and placed his hand in his mother's hand. Everyone at the table cast approving looks and smiles her way. A crimson color flushed across her face, blending nicely with her lipstick.

"All right, Carol Ann, since Mr. Dybbuk has an interest in you, I'll leave it up to you to discover the truth about this man," Grammy said. "The rest of you stay low, but keep a keen eye for anything suspicious. Tell Mr. Dybbuk we're working on a plan to get him home. Jon, aren't you and your friend Bill Hight living in Albuquerque?"

"Yes."

"Then get yourself up to Arroyo Hondo, and see if you can figure out what transport was used to get Mr. Dybbuk here. Be careful at the ruin. It could be a trap and you'll be alone. Make sure Dale knows when you're going so she can ensure you get out safely. You'll have three hours from the time you get onsite; if she doesn't hear from you in that period, she'll gather a team to find you. You okay with that, Dale?"

"Yes, I'm pretty familiar with the area. I can get him out if something goes wrong," GranMa said.

"Jon," Grammy said, "don't mingle with the locals. It's better if they don't know you are there. If anything goes wrong, we may be placing them in grave danger by an act as simple as speaking with them."

"The rest of you, do what you can to find out about Mr. Dybbuk. But don't be too obvious. Carol Ann will let us know if he's getting wise to us. Brittani, *you* stay away from him," Grammy said.

"But Grammy . . . " The look on Grammy's face stopped Brittani in her tracks.

Grammy looked to Katie and Nicky. "I know you two can't speak at the table, but do you have any information you think I should know? We can speak in the hall."

They both shook their heads.

"Unless someone has a better idea, or anything to add, this meeting is over," Grammy said. Everyone shook their heads, and the meeting adjourned.

GranMa lingered behind, and when everyone but Grammy had left the room, she said, "I've finished reading the sealed books."

"And?" Grammy asked.

GranMa's chest shuddered. Tears teetered on her lower lids. "I will do what is asked of me." Her voice cracked.

Grammy pulled GranMa into her arms. "I'm happy to hear you say this. We are running out of time, and his time has come. I am not mystified by our guest. He is the one of prophecy. She is what will cause him to crumble; 'he will be tormented by love.'" Grammy quoted the prophecy without flinching.

GranMa shuddered. "When it starts, I will face him alone."

"You must face him *with* me. There is only one way this can end." Grammy pulled GranMa tighter to her chest, and the tears that resisted their flow could no longer be held back by GranMa. "She will die too." Grammy whispered past the lump in her throat into GranMa's ear.

"I know," GranMa mumbled through her tears. "This is a horrible fate."

Grammy pushed GranMa back to look into her eyes. "Not if we succeed. If we succeed, it means world peace and eternity. This is a small price for peace and eternity. Do not let the little things cause you to stumble and take your eye off the bigger picture."

"I would hardly call this a little thing, and if we fail, then what have I done?"

"I'm an old lady who has lived a miraculous life," Grammy said. "And it would end eventually anyway. She is a courageous woman who has led a remarkable life. We have no regrets. If you do not try, then we have already failed. But we will not fail, and she and I can never die."

"How is it you can never die?" GranMa asked.

"Everything we are lives in you and those who will call us their ancestors. The day for making our ancestors proud comes near. The question is, will we make them proud?"

"Has she ever read the prophecy?" GranMa asked.

"No. She has no idea that she will write the history that changes the world."

"Why not?"

"Accepting prophecy is difficult enough when you are not the reason so many will die. Imagine if she knew."

"What will happen if she doesn't fall in love with him?"

"There are two prophecies. One belongs to our ruler, and the other belongs to his," Grammy said. "I suspect if she doesn't fall in love with him, then his prophecy will prevail."

"I wonder what it says."

"I don't know. But I'm certain we don't want it to come true."

"Should we try to find it?" GranMa asked.

"Finding the other prophecy is second only to fulfilling our own. If we find his prophecy, we will know exactly what he is trying to accomplish, and stopping him will be easier. However, if he finds ours . . . well, let's make sure that doesn't happen," Grammy insisted as they left the room.

There was a long silence as they walked out of the Council Temple. When they reached the stairs, Grammy said, "My one regret is I will not get to meet the Children of Prophecy in *This World*. What will you tell them about me?"

"I will tell them about your blueberry pies."

Grammy chuckled. "Why would you tell them about my blueberry pies?"

"Because after you are gone, blueberries will never taste the same."

The children found themselves back in GranMa's chamber listening to the happy sounds of the baby destined to rebuild the future.

Chapter 21 What's in a Name?

The children wanted more of the Mimi story, but GranMa decided they'd heard enough. She told them to think about their past and spend some time in the Historical Archives. "There is much you should know, but now I must trust you to teach yourselves. Truly great warriors don't repeat the past—they create the future. But if we don't learn from history, we are doomed to repeat it. I don't know who first said these words, but truer words have never been spoken. Now off with you children." She flicked her hand in the direction of the door. "I need to get busy playing with the only GranChild who doesn't give me back talk."

"Yet!" Alexis snickered.

"Yes," GranMa acknowledged, "you do start getting fresh at a very early age."

Goodbye hugs and kisses where exchanged. Once outside in the crisp air, the children agreed there was more to that council meeting than met the eye.

"Why do you suppose she didn't give us the whole story?" Michael asked as the children walked through the daily hustle and bustle of the Square.

"I don't know," Alexis said, and the other two shrugged.

Michael said, "Haven't you noticed GranMa doesn't do things haphazardly? Her actions appear random, but they seldom are. There is plenty of information in what she doesn't say. She's pointing us in a direction, but I'm not sure what it is. Isabel, you spend a lot of time in the Historical Archives; what do you do in there?"

"Well, I just . . . um . . . you know . . . read . . . I read stuff."

"What stuff?" Noah asked, more interested now that Michael had her squirming.

"You know . . . historical stuff."

Michael cast a doubtful eye her way, but it was Noah who said, "Then you should be able to help us find the historical *stuff* that GranMa wants us to know."

"Well, maybe Mrs. Bryer can help us. She's as old as Mimi, so she must have been around in those days," Alexis said.

"I don't know if we can trust her," Isabel said.

"What's to trust? She's a librarian. What's she going to do, beat us up with books? Jeez, let's ease up on the paranoia," Noah suggested.

"Let's not!" Isabel snapped back.

"Isabel is right. GranMa said something is going to happen soon. The last thing we want to do is lighten up, and you should know that better than anyone. Our enemies are not showing signs of lightening up, because if they had, your mother would still be here."

Michael's bitter words cut through Noah. Something that felt like anger, but hurt like pain, grew in the pit of Noah's stomach. "Let's not go there, Michael, since we're on the same team!"

"Sorry, I'm *really* sorry. That was low. I don't know what got into me." Michael begged for forgiveness.

"Anxiety," Alexis offered.

"I'm sure that was it." Noah's glare didn't match his words. "It's okay. I know you'd never say anything that stupid on purpose."

Michael was glad when they started up the seventy steps to the Historical Archives. Anything to get Noah's burrowing glares off him.

"I'll find Mrs. Bryer," Isabel said. She had decided that if Mrs. Bryer was the traitor, it was better to have her confidence. You can't see your enemy slip up if you're not close to them.

The other children went about the business of randomly searching for answers in the mountains of books that lay before them, each thinking this task was harder than finding the Loch Ness Monster.

"Ah, there you are, Mrs. Bryer," Isabel said to the startled woman with the wiry gray hair, neatly pressed dress, and practical flat shoes.

"How are you, my dear?" Mrs. Bryer asked over her spectacles that were too narrow for her diamond-shaped face. "I'm so used to seeing your smiling face inside these walls that the place feels dreary when you're gone."

"Thank you for saying that. It *is* starting to feel like home away from home."

"How can I help you, my dear?" Mrs. Bryer spoke with a rolling voice that sounded more sophisticated than the position she held.

"I'm looking for a book that records the history of Sam Dybbuk and my Great GranMother Mimi."

"Well, no one has asked for that series in a very long time. May I ask what you are looking for? Perhaps I can help since I knew your Great GranMother and Sam very well."

"Just looking to see what she was like." Isabel smiled. "He was a great love in her life, right?"

"Yesss," Mrs. Bryer said with a crooked smile as she stood from her desk. "Follow me."

"I just *love* love stories. Don't you?" Isabel asked.

"Yesss."

"Have you ever been in love?"

"Only once," Mrs. Bryer said abruptly.

"Oh, how wonderful. Did you marry him?"

"No."

"Oh! I'm sorry. What happened?" Isabel asked, fully aware that her question was inappropriate.

"He loved another."

"Oh, I thought since you are *Mrs*. Bryer . . . "

"We all don't get to marry those we love, my dear. Some of us must settle," Mrs. Bryer said as she reached high on a dusty shelf at the end of the archives. "Here." She shoved the thick, dusty, red leather book into Isabel's hands, and then went back to her desk without another word.

Isabel looked down upon the old book and ran her fingers across the binding. "The Days of Mimi," it read in gold script. She opened the book to the index and moved her eyes down the page, looking for the right section. Even though she was becoming adept at speed-reading, this book was far too large for her to try to read every page. There it was: "Chapter 38, Broken Love."

"Got it!" Isabel yelled across the Archives. Mrs. Bryer shot out of her seat to purse her finger over her lips and give Isabel the stink eye.

"Sorry," Isabel yelled to Mrs. Bryer, who narrowed her eyes even more at the irony.

In her library voice, Isabel said to her cousins, "Come with me. There's a reading room on the other side of the Archives that they use for guest speakers. Not that they ever have any." She shrugged.

The reading room was more than comfortable, and it was a shame that it hardly ever got used. Overstuffed couches and large reading desks in niches spread around the room for private group readings. In the center of the room were three couches so large that two people could easily stretch out on one. In the middle of the couches stood an equally large, square coffee table that sat just in front of a lovely fireplace. A candle-filled chandelier hung above the coffee table, lighting the entire room, including the portrait above the fireplace.

"Who do you suppose that is?" Noah asked of the scarred, handsome young face that stared back at him.

"I haven't been able to figure it out. Mrs. Bryer shrugged when I asked her," Isabel said.

"I wonder what the story is behind that scar on his right cheek," Michael added.

"I think it adds to his dark good looks rather than takes away. Don't you think?" Alexis asked.

No one answered. They just nodded their heads.

"Okay, let's get to this story. We don't have much time. I'm just going to try and pick up where GranMa left off," Isabel said as she thumbed through the pages, mumbling to herself. "Blah blah blah . . . Ah here's what we want." She began to read.

The days turned to weeks, weeks to months, and they were no closer to figuring out why, or how, Sam had come to find the kingdom. It didn't matter much to Mimi, or Sam, as they had fallen deeply in love. Sam loved Mimi with every fiber in his being, and she loved him equally. There was only one thing that caused Sam to stumble in Mimi's eyes: he seemed to love the things that the kingdom had to offer as much as he loved her. She attributed his behavior to his meager childhood, and assumed she took for granted all the lovely things around her while he appreciated them. Only one thing concerned Mimi, and that was his fascination with how the kingdom had no notable leader.

"How can leadership be random?" he asked.

"It is not random," Mimi responded. "The most qualified person is responsible to deal with whatever areas require their attention. If there is no clear leader, then it is up to the Responsible One to make sure the matter is handled."

"Nonsense, my beautiful queen. I use the term loosely since that seems to be how things are managed here," he teased as he gazed into her deep, dark eyes, and placed the gentlest kiss upon her lips.

"Ahhh," Isabel and Alexis chimed.

"Oh, brother!" the boys retaliated, and were reproached with the disapproving eyes of the girls.

"I do love you, Sam," Mimi whispered as he held her close in his arms. "I would give you anything I could."

"Well, you are a queen." He laughed back as he ran his fingers through her soft hair, which, until he'd arrived, was hardly ever left down. Then he picked her up by her tiny waist and swung her around the room in a lover's dance.

"Why does your silly kingdom only have one name?" he asked with sudden curiosity. "It never occurred to me before, but how do you tell one place from another if they all have the same name?"

"Well, my dear Sam, that is because we only have *one* kingdom. We have communities like Tulum, Ek Balam, and Cherith."

"Yes, but those are just neighborhoods."

"If it makes you happy, I shall decree the area just north of Cherith be named Dybbuk's Point." She delighted in the gift she'd given the man who gave her so much joy.

The handsome man gloated, "Does that make it mine?" He laughed.

"Dybbuk's Point belongs to us," she responded.

"And you and I are the King and Queen of Dybbuk's Point," he mused.

"No, silly. Dybbuk's Point will be named after you because it pleases you so much, but it belongs to everyone."

Sam pulled her close, but he was not smiling.

Not even Isabel was aware that she had just taken her brother, sister, and cousin back in time. The book ended abruptly and she closed it as if all she had done was read them a story.

"Darn, it will take forever to find the next volume in this series," Michael said. "That librarian, Mrs. Bryer, isn't very good at her job. There's no order to her insanity. It seems all she does is throw books on a shelf without regard to where they belong. She doesn't know how to manage information very well."

"That's very true." For the first time, Isabel became aware of what a terrible job Mrs. Bryer was doing as a librarian. She wondered why she hadn't noticed it before.

"It's almost time to go home anyway. Let's go see if we can weasel the end of this story out of GranMa?" Michael suggested.

They hurried to GranMa's chamber. Breathless when they hit the top stair, they heard the lion head's low growl and the door opened.

"So what happened to Mimi and Sam Dybbuk?" Isabel blurted out, because she couldn't wait to hear the end of this beautiful love story.

GranMa didn't miss a beat, and ended the story for the children. "Mimi did not survive Sam Dybbuk. His desires for what he thought were the finer things in life—his greed for money, his lust for power—all this was greater than his love for Mimi. Eventually, her love for him was not enough to save his soul.

"Greed is one of the seven deadly sins for a reason," GranMa continued. "Sam's desire for knowledge was noble, and it led him to search for truth. But while in Arroyo Honda, he dug in the ceremonial chamber of a burial site, and there he found skeletal remains that offered eternal life. He had no idea where this evil spirit was leading him. He was lured into darkness with the promise of having everything. All he needed to do was overthrow the Ultimate Ruler and become the High Priest. He shook hands with the devil without considering the possibility of a better way. Had he found the truth, he would have known that the price for eternal life, and all that is good, is simply to love. Love lasts forever, and honoring love is the price you must pay for a happy life. With all his education, he had missed the one thing that could have saved him. Now he is left in the darkness he created."

"Is there any way for him to redeem his own soul?" Alexis would not accept this ending.

"My darling girl, there are some roads you cannot come back from. That is why you must not go down these roads in haste, or without understanding. Everything has a price. Understand the cost of every action before you take it. If it appears too good to be true, then it is probably not good, and it is probably not true. You will be wise to learn this lesson early."

"GranMa, Sam Dybbuk is The Skelly." Michael wasn't asking a question. He was stating a fact that caused his cousins' jaws to slack.

"My dear Michael—" GranMa paused for a moment to gaze upon his mature and noble face, "—information is both your blessing and your curse. For this reason, you must lead wisely, and understand that timing is everything. Look upon your cousins' faces. Do they look a little surprised to you? And yes, the day he took Mimi's life his body began to deteriorate. Eventually, it was little more than a skeleton, and his soul began to slip away. That's when he started absorbing the souls of others, and the locals renamed him, The Skelly."

"Actually, GranMa, my cousins look like they're gonna puke," Michael responded.

"Then the next time you have information to share, you may want to be a little more sensitive about when and how you deliver it."

"So what happened to Mimi?" Isabel wanted to know.

GranMa cupped Isabel's beautiful little face and wiped the tears rolling down her rosy little cheeks. "I think all your heart is truly prepared to know is that Mimi lives safely in *That World*, and it is our job to make sure she stays that way. I will tell you this, after he killed her, he carved her image into the serpent's eye at El Torres. His love for her is the only thing his memory cannot shake. It is the only human emotion he has left, and it torments him. Stay away from El Torres; it is no longer safe."

"What did he kill her with? What was the *thing* that killed her?" Isabel asked the question even Noah knew the answer to, but she didn't want to believe.

"Love," GranMa said in a whisper laced with resentment.

"Then why did he kill her?" Isabel's voice was muffled through her tears.

"Greed," GranMa said.

"That makes no sense," Alexis remarked. "What does money have to do with this?"

"All of you still don't get this, do you?" GranMa asked with a tone that made her irritation unmistakable. Each child gazed across their shoes, as if the answers lay there.

"What do you think I've been trying to teach you?" GranMa let the uncomfortable silence continue to unnerve them. "Make eye contact with me!" GranMa barked.

"GranMa, we've all read it. 'The love of money is the root of all evil.' Greed, money—we get it." Michael didn't shift his eyes when GranMa glared at him. He stared right back into hers.

"Okay," GranMa whispered as she sucked deep and then blew out a breath. "I can see I still have work to do."

"Oh, no you don't!" Noah blurted with alarm. He had played dumb long enough, and wasn't about to risk another one of GranMa's lectures. "It's not about money, love, things, or even control. It all wraps up into one word. Greed! Money isn't a bad thing, love isn't a bad thing, and even taking control isn't a bad thing if you have the skills to do what needs to be done. Greed is about wanting *all* the money, *all* the things, *all* the control, and *all* the love."

"How can wanting love be bad?" That didn't make sense to Isabel; none of this did.

"Maybe love is the wrong word. I should use worship, adore, idolize—something ego driven like that. You know, the kind of guys who don't feel good about themselves, so they have to create false worship in order to feel adored," Noah corrected himself.

"Wow. You're pretty deep for a Neanderthal," Michael said. "I always thought of you as muscle and mass, and now *you're* making *me* look brainless. I'll have to rethink your intellect." Michael gave Noah a jab in the shoulder. "You're pretty smart."

Alexis defended Noah. "Hey, leave my brother alone. I always knew he was hiding genius behind that muscle. I will admit he's good at hiding it." She smiled.

Chapter 22   Dissonant

If the Battle of Destiny was as imminent as GranMa had implied, the kids were in trouble. They'd made little progress determining who the traitor was among them, and winning the battle would be near impossible if The Skelly had access to their battle strategy. No one thought the Ballams, or Mrs. Bryer, could provide that kind of information to The Skelly, but how could they know for sure? They didn't even know if they were on the right track. Based upon what they did know, anyone could be the snitch. Moreover, if they were wrong about their suspicions, they had wasted valuable time tracking the wrong people. An error this grave could lead to their doom, which was why they had to kick their efforts up a notch at the dress shop.

Mrs. Ballam was beside herself. It had been many years since she had a reason to do anything special in her shop besides chitchat. Oh sure, there was an occasional dress sale, and she made an honest living replenishing, altering, or mending the daily attire for the good people of Diggory Town. But today was special. Tedde and Spencer had been coming in regularly for formalwear fittings. Today was an especially exciting day. She was finished with the alterations, and for the first time, she would see the final fittings together.

Spencer was not nearly as excited as Mrs. Ballam. He dreaded the thought of wearing that ridiculous suit one more time. He especially hated the thought of Tedde seeing him in it. *Man, I'll never be able to live this one down*, he thought as he strode around the corner.

"How do you look in the suit?" Tedde asked as she walked beside her brother in the full, warm, morning sunlight.

"Lovely." Spencer moaned. "I look like a fruitcake, if you must know."

"C'mon, it can't be that bad."

"Let's just say I'm glad the kids won't be seeing me in it." But no sooner had the words flew out of his mouth, and there before him stood the four beaming faces.

Without as much as a hello, the words began racing out of Alexis's mouth. "Oh, I can't tell you how excited I am to see you in the suit. It's been years since there was a ball in Diggory Town. I know there won't be a *real* ball, but just the idea, and the place is abuzz, everyone is talking—"

"Talking? No one's supposed to *know*!" Spencer moaned again.

"Oh, dang—*no one* is supposed to know." Tedde did not share Alexis's excitement.

Michael, who was not prone to gossiping, said, "You're kidding, right? It's the dress shop—a major distribution center for fables, stories, and telling of tales, real or imagined. We're lucky it's been quiet this long."

Tedde took a deep breath, forced air out her lower lip, causing the small hairs surrounding her face to fly, and then she rolled her eyes. "Well," she said, "the only person we need to hide this from is GranMa. I guess it's okay that everyone is abuzz on the last day of fittings."

Even though Mrs. Ballam greeted them at the door, Isabel rang the shop bell.

"You just love ringing that bell, don't you, dear?" Mrs. Ballam said, not expecting an answer. "Oh, you are going to be so excited when you see how yummy Spencer looks."

"Yummy, huh?" Noah said while poking Michael in the ribs.

"Please make them leave." Spencer's whisper begged into Tedde's ear.

"Forget about them, Spencer. This may be our last chance to figure out if the Ballams are involved with The Skelly. The more eyes, the better," Tedde mumbled back. "Besides, I look great in my dress."

Spencer laid his head as far back as it would go, and grasped the top of his head as if expecting it to explode. He took a deep breath, but couldn't stop the moan his mouth made.

"Headache, dear?" Mrs. Ballam asked.

"Something like that," Spencer lied.

"Do you want to dress at the same time, or do you want to make a private grand entrance?" Mrs. Ballam beamed with anticipation.

"Private grand entrance!" Tedde said.

At the exact same time, Spencer said, "Same time!"

"Well, I think I'll let you two work this out," sweet Mrs. Ballam squeaked.

"Please, Tedde . . . I'm being a pretty good sport. Can we keep my humiliation down to a minimum? I said *please*!"

"How bad can it be, Spencer?"

Just then, Mr. Ballam came out from the back room and ran smack into the middle of Tedde and Spencer's conversation. Without missing a beat he said, "Oh, it's bad! It's really bad! Sorry, son," he said, giving Spencer a consolatory pat on the back.

"All right. We'll do it your way," Tedde conceded, while avoiding Spencer's eyes.

Mr. Ballam began removing the horrible suit from the mannequin. All the finishing touches were complete, including the jasper buttons. "It's going to look funny around here without that suit on the mannequin. It's been sitting in that corner for years," he said as he moved the mannequin out of the way and shoved it into the corner.

"Then maybe you should keep it," Spencer was quick to respond.

"Not a chance!" Mr. Ballam whispered under his breath as he handed the suit to Spencer. He didn't hesitate to look directly into Spencer's eyes, but Mr. Ballam's eyes were apologetic, not judgmental.

"I could have sworn that mannequin moaned when Mr. Ballam shoved it against the wall," Alexis whispered to Isabel.

"Don't be ridiculous. You are Alexis in Diggory Town, not Alice in Wonderland. Sometimes you let your imagination run away with you. Noah, stop messing with stuff!" Isabel. *The Bossy One*, snapped at her brother, who had by now moved just about everything in the store.

"Well, what are we supposed to do? It's taking them forever," Noah complained.

"Look at Michael. He's just patiently sitting there, spinning that hand mirror and observing," Isabel pointed out.

"Michael was *born* forty years old," Noah said. "He doesn't *need* fun."

Michael ignored Noah's comments, because he wasn't just sitting there observing patiently. The mirror he appeared to be goofing with was reflecting the mannequin, just waiting for it to move again. Maybe it was his imagination, but maybe it wasn't.

"I'm ready!" Tedde sang, loud enough for Spencer to hear from his dressing room. She peeped out the curtain. "I'm readyyyy!" her singing voice prompted Spencer once again.

"HEY! SPENCER! I SAID . . . I'm readyyyy!" she said, shouting the first four words, but singing the last two.

"I heard you! Give me a minute! I can't get the shirt buttoned because all the darn ruffles are in my way. Lucky for me this giant clown size lapel will hide most of the shirt," he mumbled in sarcastic, mildly resentful tones. "I'm ready. You go first. I'll follow right behind."

Tedde gracefully exited her dressing room. The glimmering full skirt of her royal blue gown with slight leprechaun green stripes groaned its way past the curtain. A crisscross bodice wrapped itself tightly around her waist as a sparse distribution of jasper beads, sparkling like stars, rolled up over her shoulders and down the scalloped V pattern until they met in the middle of her back. Pleats, skillfully woven into the shoulders, forced the fabric to puff as high as her jawline, then gathered tightly just before her elbows. A smooth finish decorated her forearms, ending with jasper bracelets sewn into the fabric at the wrists. The delicate, dazzling, leprechaun green pinstripes were barely noticeable as they peeked in and out of the billows of fabric that cascaded to the floor. Tedde enjoyed the awestruck faces mesmerized by her beauty. She barely noticed Spencer had failed to make his appearance.

After several moments, his long, large, royal blue and shiny leprechaun green pinstriped leg stepped out from behind the curtain. It was immediately followed by his tailcoat made mostly of the same material, except for the humongous, shiny, almost blinding leprechaun green lapel, and Napoleon collar that touched just below his ears. As if to point out the ridiculous contrast between the two outfits, leprechaun green piping was placed along every possible seam of Spencer's suit.

Everyone stood in stunned silence for what felt to Spencer like eternity. Hands cupping her prideful face, Mrs. Ballam finally spoke.

"Oh. My. Dear. It simply takes my breath away! We must find you the perfect hat," Mrs. Ballam said.

In his most feminine voice, Noah said, "Oh. My. Dear. I think we simply must."

It was then that Michael lost the battle with the muscles in his throat that strained to hold back the laughter. It continued far too long, with both boys holding their stomachs to fight off the aches. Isabel and Alexis could hardly do more than purse their lips in sympathetic frowns. Mr. Ballam had the good judgment to leave the room when he sensed the end was near for poor Spencer.

Still, with all his humiliation in full bloom, it was Spencer who noticed Mrs. Ballam's quivering lips. For a moment, he thought ignoring the pained expression might be the best course of action, but he could not ignore her pain. It occurred to Spencer that the uncomfortable moment would soon pass for him, but her pained expression would leave its mark on Mrs. Ballam for a long time.

"I guess you guys should be forgiven because you just don't know how things are done in Diggory Town." He looked directly at the boys, casting his eyes repeatedly in the direction of Mrs. Ballam's broken heart. Then he turned towards the mirror and pulled on his collar, as if he looked as good as Mrs. Ballam wanted him to.

"I guess it's hard to be insulted by morons. I'm going to ignore your stupidity because of your age, but when I attract *all* the attention at the ball, you'll be eating your laughter. Don't you think so, Mrs. Ballam?"

A smile of forgiveness came across her face. "Well, Spencer, they are just boys. We can't expect them to have sophisticated taste, now can we? Maybe you shouldn't be so harsh on them," Mrs. Ballam said with renewed pride.

Tedde's heart swelled. Her generous brother had once again come to the rescue of a broken heart. But her moment of prideful affection was short lived, because Michael suddenly lunged at the mannequin, tackling what lay hidden inside.

Mr. Ballam ran from the back room when he heard the crash of the breaking mannequin. He was shocked to see a woman, who resembled Hope, sitting sprawled and startled on the floor.

Mrs. Ballam pulled her sword out from under the counter. "Dissonant." She spat the name, as if a vile taste would not leave her mouth. "You have picked the wrong person to test today!" She raised her sword.

"NO, DOTTIE!" Mr. Ballam shouted before Mrs. Ballam lowered her sword. "We will learn nothing if you kill her."

"Please kill me!" Dissonant pleaded. "I would rather be dead then continue my life of servitude to that hideous, evil woman."

"What are you talking about?" Mrs. Ballam asked.

The stunned children looked on in disbelief, as the normally frail woman took command of the spy in their midst.

"She has my mistress!" the woman whose physique matched Hope's replied.

"Who has the professor?" Mrs. Ballam demanded.

"The librarian has Professor Panaid. She has been her prisoner for years. I did this to save my mistress," Dissonant confessed.

"I DON'T BELIEVE YOU!" Mrs. Ballam yelled. "GET UP!"

"Dottie, she could be telling the truth. It would explain why the professor disappeared so suddenly," Mr. Ballam offered.

The broken woman explained, "We were captured just outside Tulum as we were leaving the training camp. Mrs. Bryer saw her opportunity to aid her one true love. The Skelly told her if she truly loved him, she would kill her husband. She killed her husband before our eyes. Then he said if I did not do what I was told, my mistress would share his fate. My mistress begged me to let her give her life, but I could not. I have been a slave to The Skelly's puppet ever since. He controls the librarian with a promise of love that she will never receive."

"Whose husband? What puppet? What are you talking about?" Mr. Ballam asked.

"Mrs. Bryer, the puppet, killed Mr. Bryer to prove her love to The Skelly, the puppet master. Please try and follow the story, dear," Mrs. Ballam said in her normally sweet tone, but the tone was not shared with Dissonant. "I don't believe you!" Mrs. Ballam barked at Dissonant. "You'd better come up with a better story before I use my scissors to cut short the length of your lying tongue."

"Of course you don't believe me!" Dissonant said. "Why do you think we were chosen by The Skelly? My mistress is well aware of the suspicions that are cast her way. Her introverted ways, and the mistakes of her past, make her an easy target. But that doesn't make her guilty. She proved herself in the Battle of Trafleka, but in the eyes of some, she will never be redeemed. I suppose it is her lot in life to be judged this harshly by those who have not been given the authority to judge." Dissonant's head fell, and her voice trailed. "Perhaps we are both better off dead."

Mrs. Ballam felt empathy for the two, because she understood what it meant to be misjudged. Many mistook her for a silly old lady. "I am not a fool, Dissonant," Mrs. Ballam said in her sympathetic voice, as Dissonant's head lowered farther. "I am also not prone to being judgmental. Given these two facts, you will be granted your first wish to rescue your mistress, if being rescued is what she needs. If this is a trap, you will be granted your second wish, and before the day is over—you will *both* be dead."

Isabel's eyes looked as if someone had placed two magnifying glasses in front of them. Could this be the same Mrs. Ballam she loved to tease? She would not be mocking her again now that she had seen the power of what lay under Mrs. Ballam's counter. In the space of a moment, Isabel had learned what Mr. Ballam had always known. Above Mrs. Ballam's counter was a sweet, social, silly, creative old lady. What lay beneath was the powerful sword of a competent warrior.

Isabel broke her stunned silence by saying, "I guess this explains why the Historical Archives are always a mess. Looks like Beatrice is too busy spying to properly do her job." Isabel no longer felt the need to call Mrs. Bryer by her surname.

"Okay, dears," Mrs. Ballam said in her sweetest voice, "let's get this regalia off and get into our warrior clothes. Before the day is over, there will be blood, and I don't want it on my hard work. Toot sweet!" she said in her chipper voice while clapping her hands.

Mr. Ballam smiled from ear to ear. If there were two things he absolutely loved, they were Mrs. Ballam and a good fight.

"What do we do with her, and what is she?" Michael asked, pulling Dissonant up by her arm in a restraining manner.

"She goes with us to the Chamber. Hope will be interested to see you. Won't she, Dissonant? Tell the children why," Mrs. Ballam said.

"Hope and I are fraternal twins. Normally, there can only be one Responsible One Guardian alive at any given time. Some mystery of fate caused us to be born at the same time. When Hope was made the Responsible One Guardian, I became jealous and vengeful. I joined the wrong side out of spite. But fortunately, I found Professor Panaid. Together, we learned that we all have a relevant place in the world. But before my lesson was learned, I had harmed the relationship with my sister beyond repair. There are roads you can never come back from . . . but I didn't know that then." Tears teetered at the edges of Dissonant's eyes. Isabel almost believed her.

Eager to get out of his formalwear, Spencer was the first to step out from behind the dressing room curtain. "C'mon, Ted, it's a big day for us. Get that stuff off and let's get going."

"Almost done. Do you think today is *the* day?" Tedde asked from behind the curtain. She couldn't see the white faces of the children, but the silence said it all, as the sudden tension hurled itself around the room. "Okay, let's go," Tedde said, not bothering to look at anyone, nor did she press for an answer to her question.

Michael kept his grip on Dissonant, and the others followed him out the door. Mrs. Ballam grabbed her sword and Mr. Ballam had changed into battle gear. Isabel was the last to leave the shop, and without so much as a thought, she rang the bell.

The journey on the way to GranMa's chamber was spent in silent thought, as each wondered what the next hour would bring. The merciless midday sun beat down upon them, creating beads of perspiration that mixed with nervous perspiration. Tension hung over them like a smothering blanket. Soon they would be tested. Never before had a failing grade carried such weight.

Their armor tinged, mocking their anxiety, as they climbed the seventy stairs. "Don't be afraid," Mr. Ballam said. "We have all prepared for this day. We know what to expect. Do what you have been trained to do. You have fought this battle a hundred times in your heads, your hearts, and in practice. Spencer, did you train them to win?"

"Of course I did!" He tried to put a smile in his voice.

"Well, there you go! Nothing to fear!" Mr. Ballam said. "But remember to fight like you're losing until you know you have won."

"You're pretty sure of yourself," Alexis said.

Leading the group up the stairs, Mr. Ballam stopped at about stair forty, as if someone had thrown an invisible wall in his path. "If you are not sure of yourself," he said as he searched each pair of eyes, "then you shouldn't be here. Look around. Is there anyone here you feel you are not capable of saving?" No one said a word. "Then fight as if their lives depend on it, because they do. Love is the most powerful weapon I bring to a battle. I suggest you do the same. Alexis, can you save Tedde?"

"YES, I CAN!" she shouted in an odd but inspiring way.

"Is there anyone here who does not feel they can save Tedde, or anyone else on these stairs?" Everyone stood silent. "If you continue to follow me, I will assume it is because you are confident you will not fail. If one of you believes we cannot win, then I ask you to go back down the stairs. We cannot use you today." Mr. Ballam turned and resumed the long climb to GranMa's chamber.

Everyone was present when they heard GranMa say, "Open," before they ever knocked.

"Dissonant?" Hope asked from her perch. "I thought you were dead!"

"You mean you *hoped* I was dead."

"You're my sister, no matter how loathing your behavior."

"I'm here because I am a traitor," Dissonant said.

"And?" This was not news to Hope.

"You will never forgive me, but that won't stop me from trying to gain your forgiveness." Dissonant's eyes did not leave her sister's. She no longer felt the need for shame. She had paid the price for her actions. All she required now was forgiveness.

Nevertheless, layers of sarcasm sat upon Hope's tongue as she retorted, "So you come to me as a traitor demanding forgiveness. That's an approach I would have never considered."

Her voice just above a whisper, Dissonant said, "Redemption is a fickle fate."

"It is a fate only required by the wicked and the weak," Tedde spat, not making contact with what she was sure were GranMa's disapproving eyes.

Weighted by sincerity, Dissonant responded to Tedde's attack. "Then let's pray you never need it, my dear."

"Look, you two can wrestle for the title of 'Most Injured Sister' later," Spencer said. "We have more pressing issues to deal with right now. Tell GranMa what you know, Dissonant."

Dissonant laid out The Skelly's plan of attack on the Square, and of taking possession of the four Chambers. He thought if he took control of the Square and its Chambers he would cripple most of the kingdom.

"His plan is to kill Gavin. He's waiting for an opportunity to overtake the Square when he is sure Gavin is with you." She nodded towards GranMa. "My job was to collect information that could help him form a battle strategy. I thought by making myself tiny and flying into the mannequin at the dress shop, I would be in the best place to gather information. I knew that much of the information would be embellished stories, but I also knew that Dottie would filter the nonsense when she discussed the day's gossip with Ed. At night, I would fly out of the mannequin and report to the horrible librarian. If she felt I wasn't working hard enough, she would come to the shop looking for me. She would bring pieces of my mistress's blonde hair as a warning."

"I thought the old kook was just talking to herself because she was cooped up in the Archives all day," Mr. Ballam said. "How did you get into the mannequin?"

"There was a hole in the head of the mannequin. You didn't put a hat on it, and because I'm tiny and can fly, I just parted the hair on the wig and slipped inside the mannequin."

"I knew we should have had a hat for that suit!" Mrs. Ballam snapped her fingers. "Darn it!"

"Anyway . . . " Dissonant said, casting an incredulous look at Mrs. Ballam, "my job is to report any information that may help The Skelly develop a battle plan. In return, my mistress will be set free."

"You don't *really* believe he'd ever set her free . . . do you?" Hope asked.

"No, but I thought it would buy me some time to figure something out. I was about to give up hope that I would ever find a way to save her. When I was finally caught, I was relieved, not frightened."

GranMa listened without saying a word, but she had not heard anything she felt was useful. "Why should I believe anything you say?" GranMa asked.

"I am willing to give you my life in return for you rescuing my mistress. I may not be *the* Guardian, but I am *a* Guardian. This is what we are born to do. I give my life gladly for only *the promise* that you will rescue her, as she has rescued me."

"How did she rescue you?" Hope asked.

"Together, we learned that revenge is a mountainous burden to bear. My jealousy was crushing me, and it cost me you. I no longer want anything for you but good things. I don't expect you to believe me, nor do I *need* you to believe me. I know what is in my heart. The weight of hatred has been lifted. The goodness I feel comes from my knowing what I am. Not by what you *think* I am. I have been rescued from myself and my own dark sins. I was a victim at my own hand, but I am finally free of the darkness that suffocated me. I don't expect you to trust me, and I don't know what I can do to change your mind."

Hope swallowed. She wanted to believe her sister, but she couldn't afford to be wrong. She turned toward GranMa and said nothing in reply.

GranMa tapped her scepter, which soon became a sword. She moved close enough to feel Dissonant's breath. Their eyes locked as GranMa put the sword to Dissonant's throat. "You would pay the price for her freedom?" GranMa asked.

Dissonant's eyes stayed locked to GranMa's as she knelt, letting the cold blade make a shallow cut into her neck. Tiny pearls of blood reflected in the blade as Dissonant nodded her head, her eyes absent of fear.

"I have looked into these eyes before," GranMa said. "My Hope has honest, loyal eyes such as these." GranMa removed her sword from under Dissonant's chin, flicked the blood from her blade, and moved back to her desk. "Tell me." She waved her hand to the chair in front of her. "What would *you* suggest we do?"

Grateful for GranMa's kindness, Dissonant seated herself. "I suggest you tell me only what you want The Skelly to believe. He cannot torture out of me what I do not know. I will feed Mrs. Bryer the information you provide. Do not tell me if it is truthful or not. In return, I will trust you to rescue my mistress."

"We will save you both," GranMa said. "Dottie and Ed, it will be your responsibility to make sure they are rescued. Take whatever you need to ensure their safety and yours. Spencer will make sure you have enough manpower. Dissonant, tell the librarian I will be moving Gavin this evening, and I will *not* be using a transport. How many spies are in my army?" GranMa asked.

"At least a hundred," Dissonant responded.

"Are they any of my leaders?" GranMa asked.

"Not to my knowledge."

"So they're in the ranks," GranMa clarified.

"Yes, but not in the ranks of the one they call Jon. His men are loyal to him, which makes the risk of exposure too high. If any of The Skelly's spies are caught, it will compromise the others. They know infiltrating Jon's ranks is next to impossible, which makes it too risky."

"You are certain that Jon's men have not been compromised?" Spencer asked.

"Yes, I'm positive."

"Could you identify potential spies in my ranks?" Spencer asked.

"They are not significant enough, nor are they brave enough, to challenge your warriors. The cowards were forced into your ranks to monitor the actions of your warriors, but they are by no means loyal to The Skelly. He has thousands of followers, but few are loyal to him, or his cause. The spies in your ranks are no longer of consequence, but no, I would not be able to identify any of the spies."

"So we'll be up against thousands?" Spencer asked.

"Probably. Remember he has to call them from far and wide. It would be difficult to hide thousands in one location, so his men are spread out."

"What is the likelihood of them surrounding us?" Spencer asked.

"It's possible. But I doubt he'd have time to organize a battle plan if you move quickly."

"We'll need to alert the militia. They'll have to protect the Square," Spencer said to Tedde.

"Exactly how many thousands?" Tedde asked Dissonant.

"Depends how many he can round up. Could be two thousand, could be ten."

"What is your best guess of how he will approach this battle?" GranMa asked.

"It will depend on how many are with you. He will definitely want one of the children dead. It's the only way he can break the prophecy."

GranMa looked around the room as Dissonant spoke, but the children did not flinch. There was an eerie calm about them—the kind of calm that lays its hands on all-powerful warriors. They were not without fear, nor were they controlled by it.

"Killing *you* will only add to his pleasure," Dissonant continued, "so he'll be following you and Gavin. I would anticipate a three to one ratio of his men following you. If you are with a hundred men, he will have three hundred men. Capturing the Square is of monumental importance to him. He will send his remaining troops to take the Square. Given such short notice, I would anticipate two thousand or fewer men. This is my best guess."

"He is not the only one with short notice. Dottie, how soon will the rumor mill know that something has happened in your shop?" GranMa asked.

"My guess is the news of unusual activity is on its way as we speak," Mrs. Ballam replied.

"That means Beatrice will be contacting The Skelly soon. We need to impede her efforts. Isabel, you will go to the Archives and do whatever you must to delay her from contacting The Skelly. We'll send for you when we have a strategy in place. I'll need a couple of hours to get this underway, but you can be sure that, before the sun sets tonight, you will all have blood on your swords."

Chapter 23   To The Temptress

GranMa rolled out the map of the kingdom across her desk. The four paperweights that Alexis had long suspected were crystal balls split in half were nothing more than paperweights. GranMa placed one on each corner of the map and voiced her thoughts to no one in particular.

"I wonder where the evil demon is."

A youthful male finger drifted its way across the map. "He's here."

GranMa didn't have to look up to know that the finger belonged to Michael. Nor was she surprised that he knew where to find The Skelly. She cupped her hand over his and said, "I knew the day you watched your mother die that you would go looking for him. I watched and worried about you daily. Especially the night you challenged the man at the campfire." She turned his hand over to see the fresh scar that lay the width of his palm. "Your hand has healed nicely."

"You were there?" Michael asked incredulously.

"Yes. I was especially worried because Spencer wasn't tracking you that night. But you were very impressive."

Michael shot Spencer a confused look. "You've been tracking me too?"

Spencer shrugged. "I didn't know GranMa was tracking you. What can I say? We were worried."

Michael looked back to GranMa. "I can't believe you didn't stop me."

"An untested warrior is worthless. Watching you from afar, I learned so much. You used every bit of information at your disposal. Without fear, you approached anyone who could lead you to your destination. Every time you lifted your sword, you were dancing with fire, yet getting one step closer to winning the Battle of Destiny. I had no intention of interfering with your journey unless I thought you were in harm's way. As your journey would prove, the only person in harm's way was the one who got in yours. Why did you not kill the man at the campfire?"

"I had been tracking The Skelly secretly and I was exhausted. Between practicing with Spencer, my life in *That World*, and other distractions in *This World*, there was little time for me to sleep. I stumbled into that man's camp by accident."

"How do you stumble into a campfire?" Spencer asked.

"I didn't. The fire wasn't started when I first got there. It was dark. The man stood alarmed when I accidentally walked into his campsite. I gained his confidence and, before long, we were preparing a supper together. I let him do all the talking. Men like him always talk too much. In no time at all, his words were guiding me to The Skelly's hideout. He didn't mean to tell me where to find The Skelly. But with what I already knew, and the little bits of information he dropped, it wasn't long before I figured out an approximate area. Then something happened that I don't understand. He looked at my sword and said, 'YOU!' He pulled his sword, and in the time it takes to spit, we were dueling. He was a pretty good swordsman, but the night deceived him. He thought he had put his sword through me, but instead, it went along my side and it slid inside my palm." Michael turned his left hand over to show his healed wound to everyone. "I took the opportunity to fake a fatal injury and slipped away."

"Why didn't you finish him off?" Alexis asked.

"Didn't you hear the part where his sword slipped through my hand? If I hadn't faked a serious injury, he might have followed me. I'm sure he thought I was on my way to dying. Based on my conversations with him, he was nothing more than a mercenary. He didn't care about The Skelly, or his cause. He was in it for the money, so the putrid man meant nothing to me."

"Michael, this is the man I killed. Just before I killed him, he told me he worshipped The Skelly," Noah said.

Michael responded, "Most of The Skelly's followers are only in it for personal gain. They'd cut The Skelly's throat if they thought they could get away with it. Greed makes for a lonely existence. They don't care about anyone but themselves. He'd tell you he worships GranMa if he thought it were to his advantage. I believe his greed, and the greed of others like him, will always be to *our* advantage."

"Dissonant, I want you to go to Beatrice and tell her that I'll be taking Gavin and the children to the cave at Three Sisters. We'll be passing through Cherith. Tell her there will be one hundred of us."

Dissonant rose from her seat and glanced at her sister. Hope longed to hold her sister in an embrace of forgiveness, but she had been fooled by Dissonant before.

When the door closed behind Dissonant, GranMa said, "Ed and Dottie, I charge you with either saving or killing her. The choice will be entirely up to her and the decisions she makes."

Dottie and Ed both nodded, understanding what GranMa meant. As the door closed behind the Ballams, GranMa turned her attention to the children.

"Like The Skelly, we have little time to prepare. However, we have the advantage of controlling the battle location. We will also take advantage of the element of surprise. He will see a hundred of us heading to Three Sisters. He will not see the two hundred who will trap him from behind."

"Why don't we have six hundred warriors follow him?" Noah asked.

"Because we need as many warriors as possible protecting the Square. If he captures the Square, we are doomed. He will have, and control, full access to the kingdom.

"I would give anything to not be taking you children into battle today. But each of you has more than proven that you are ready. I am not taking untested warriors into battle. Today, The Skelly comes for Gavin's life. He is who The Skelly longs to absorb, but he will be stopped by more than children. He will be stopped by warriors."

"Do you have a battle plan?" Noah asked.

"It is the one we have practiced over and over again," GranMa said.

Noah furrowed his eyebrows. "We didn't practice a battle plan."

"Weren't you listening?" Michael asked. "We are going to Three Sisters, your favorite place."

"Oh, this is going to be a piece of cake!" Noah said. "I'll go get Isabel."

"Don't bother. She's not going," GranMa said.

"What?" Noah asked.

"I said she's not going!" GranMa didn't have to add, "and that's final," because everyone knew that it was. What they didn't know was that GranMa was saying her final goodbye. Before the midnight moon hung in a crisp, bright, moonlit sky, Uncle Jon would be barely clinging to life, and GranMa would be letting it go.

Chapter 24 How Warriors are Measured

Even the noise from the flourish of activity could not drown the shouts between GranMa and Isabel.

"You are not going into this battle!" GranMa screamed at Isabel.

"Why not? Am I not as brave as Noah, as good and accurate with a bow as Alexis, as swift with my sword as Michael? Do you think so little of me?"

"You are *not* going into this battle because *I* am the Responsible One, and until something happens to change that, *you* will not be going into this battle." GranMa let the silence hang over the room while she waited for her heart to stop racing and the pounding in her ears to cease. Once she felt her body calm, she asked, "Do you know why leaders and medics are the primary targets in a battle?"

"This is not the time for one of your insightful lectures!" Acrimonious words flew from Isabel's mouth. "I need to demonstrate courage, and fight with my sister, brother, and cousin! You remember courage, don't you, GranMa?"

GranMa ignored Isabel's insolent remark and spoke in a controlled manner. "When you kill a medic, it is said to be the equivalent of killing twenty of your enemy. Without a medic to save the wounded, twenty additional wounded warriors will die because no medic will be there to save them. When you kill a leader, you will kill at least a hundred warriors in the confusion caused by no leadership."

GranMa's eyes narrowed and she drove her finger into Isabel's chest. "That's why you're not going into battle today!" GranMa had spoken, and that was that.

Isabel smiled and pulled on GranMa's finger.

"This isn't a joking matter," GranMa said, and pulled her hand away.

Isabel looked into her granmother's eyes. "I know. But I just can't bear to leave you this way."

GranMa placed her hand on Isabel's shoulder. "You must accept your place in *This World*. Some day you will fight, but that is not your job today."

"What is my job today?" Isabel's voice cracked.

"In battle, your mother and aunt were warriors and medics, but you are not a medic. I think you know what your job is today, and perhaps from this day forth. Today, only you know if you can do what must be done," GranMa said, and then waited a moment for Isabel to ponder her options before she continued.

"It seems cold, I know. But the burdens of the job are incredible, and many days it will break your heart. The best advice I can give you is try to never do anything wrong, and always listen carefully to the advice you receive. Wisdom sometimes comes from the smallest voices. I have to go, but you know what to do from here." GranMa hugged Isabel with a bigger, warmer, more heartfelt embrace than usual. A brokenhearted Isabel knew exactly what this last embrace meant. GranMa whispered her final, "I love you."

By the time GranMa had finished with Isabel, Spencer had gathered the troops that would be going with her to Three Sisters. Tedde waited for her outside the Archives with Star.

"Tedde, I need you to stay here, and keep an eye on Isabel. I do not want her engaged in the attack on the Square, but I do want her watching the start of it. She still has much to learn. To see a real battle in action will provide her with more useful information than training ever could. Once the battle gets heated, she must go back to my office in *That World*. Tell her to use the transport in the Archives, and she is not to fight. She knows why."

"What if she won't go?"

"You tell her it is time for her to face the measure of her courage. The time has come to give an answer . . . even if the answer is no."

"But—" Before Tedde could finish her question, GranMa stopped her.

"There's no but, Tedde. She will understand, and she will go. Your job is to prepare and lead the militia to protect and defend the *inside* of the Square. Uncle Jon will attack the enemy from *outside* the Square. We'll have them surrounded. It's a perfect trap. Spencer should be with Uncle Jon as we speak. They are dividing the troops into those who follow Spencer to trap The Skelly's men that will be behind me, and those who will fight with Jon. Two skirmishes in one battle, same strategy: divide and conquer. I don't have to tell you the importance of what we do today. Give me a hug and have faith in the Ultimate Ruler."

"I don't have your faith, GranMa," Tedde said.

"And I can't give it to you. Faith is the gift you must give to yourself. I imagine you will continue to be humbled until you do. You are not here by accident. I don't believe in accidents. You are here for a purpose. Learn if you are here to learn. Teach if you are here to teach. Do that for which *you* have been chosen. You have been called, and you will continue to be humbled until you answer the call," GranMa said.

"Sorry, GranMa, that's all voodoo and pixy magic to me. I don't believe in that stuff either."

"Where do you think you will go if you die today?" GranMa asked.

"Nowhere. It's just over," Tedde said.

"Then make sure you don't die today, because I want you with me when I take my place in his kingdom." GranMa tiptoed to kiss and hug her tall, beautiful, muscular niece. "I'll see you in the kingdom," she whispered, then turned, mounted Star, and rode to join the others at the north gate.

GranMa brought Star to the front of the brigade, where he joined Lightning, Debbie, and Frank.

"How'd Isabel take it?" Noah asked as he leaned forward on Frank.

"With the wisdom of a masterful warrior!" GranMa said in a boastful tone. Then she leaned forward to look at Alexis on Lightning, and Michael on Debbie.

"Are you ready?" GranMa asked of the three, who responded with definite head nods. They could feel the excitement pounding in their veins, anxiety screaming in their heads, and determination being etched into their hearts. Today was either the end of their journey, or the beginning of their conquest. But no matter the results, they were committed to the Battle of Destiny.

"Hope?" GranMa yelled into the hot, late afternoon air. Hope flew to the backpack on GranMa's chest. She inserted her arms into the straps of the baby carrier, which looked like a backpack, only worn in the front.

"This is humiliating!" Hope said, reducing her size and wiggling her way into the baby carrier.

"You've done worse," GranMa commented as she helped Hope struggle into place.

"Don't remind me!" Hope laughed.

"How fast will you be able to get out of this thing with your wings shoved into this pack?" GranMa asked.

"I don't know. Let me give it a try." Hope grunted and groaned, but found herself hopelessly stuck in the baby carrier.

"Let me help." Alexis moved closer to GranMa, leaned far left, and twisted in a ridiculous way on her saddle. Leaning across GranMa, she smoothed out Hope's wings in the baby carrier.

Someday, Alexis thought as her hands covetously touched Hope's wings. "Try it now!"

Hope slipped out of the carrier without a single grunt or groan. "Thanks, Mom," she said to Alexis with a grand smile. "Now please tuck me in again. Put Gavin's little baseball cap on my head, and pull it down to cover my face, tuck my hair under it, and we'll be on our way."

Alexis slid her envious hands over Hope's feathery, silky wings one more time, completed the rest of the instructions, and then GranMa shouted, "Take your formation!" Debbie and Lightning moved to the lead, squaring off in front of GranMa. Frank moved to the back and aligned himself with the horse ridden by a girl who looked an awful lot like Isabel. One hundred saddled warriors formed in rows of four behind Noah and the girl. This was a typical defensive formation. Should an attack occur, the horsemen in rows of four would split in two and surround the young child, keeping the strongest warriors closet to the child as a final line of defense. However, today was not typical.

"Anyone who feels they cannot face the evil demon, or his men, now is the time to fall out of formation." GranMa waited.

No one fell out of formation, but one man asked, "Any last minute advice before we enter the battle?"

"Yes, and this is *very* important! When the battle starts, and your adrenaline takes over—don't forget to breathe! Forward!" she commanded as she pushed her right hand through the air. For the first time in Diggory Town, she cast her eyes upon Michael's Ninja Stick, strapped to its special harness on Debbie's saddle. The dry, cracked, ash-colored piece of bamboo Michael had found in Grandma's back yard in *That World,* which had fulfilled all his five-year-old ninja fantasies, was a magnificent gold weapon here. Perhaps it was not accidental that a wide-eyed five-year-old boy in *That World* happened upon a bamboo stick, whose origins Grandma could not explain.

"Michael, how does your stick work?" GranMa shouted ahead.

"It's fabulous, GranMa. But I have to be able to swing it to get the most impact. When I swing this thing, it's like a weapon of mass destruction; it cuts down everything in its path. I haven't found a material it can't penetrate. But I'm still learning how to use it."

"Then be careful with it. I don't want you hurting one of us. I must say, it's as fine a weapon as I have ever seen," GranMa smiled as she thought about the weapon she once knew as Aaron's Rod.

"I promise I'll be careful," Michael said.

"Where's Elvis?" GranMa asked.

"You know about Elvis?" Michael asked in astonishment.

"I know about *everything.*" GranMa chuckled. "Like I know she's somewhere in the woods following us. Make sure she stays hidden. I don't want her alarming The Skelly."

"Okay," Michael agreed.

"I told you you'd get caught." Alexis smirked at Michael.

Michael gave her the stink eye and said, "Be careful, or I'll have an accident in the battle." He tapped his Ninja Stick, and a big, wide grin pasted across his face. Both teased to try to lift the tension from the air. As they moved farther into the woods, the walls of anxiety began closing in.

Like every good warrior, and surely every warrior that followed in these ranks, their senses were on high alert. Every smell, every sound, and every movement mattered. Even their taste and touch seemed to be walking on a high wire as their mouths dried, and their skin crawled. They were about to engage in the sinister dance of war, and they had no idea what they were in for. Ironically, cutting through the thick air of anxiety was the confidence that came with being fully prepared.

GranMa brought down the Dome of Silence. "They are here. I can smell them." Her voice echoed down the long line of horsemen. "I'm lifting the Dome of Silence so I can hear them when they start the attack. Act as if you are caught off guard and make them chase us. Pay attention to Noah, and follow his lead. I want them chasing us up the Third Sister, and cornering us in the cave. Spencer will follow behind with his troops. Then we will have The Skelly and his men trapped." She lifted the invisible dome as everyone pretended to chitchat on a leisurely, yet cautious, ride. If they appeared too unconcerned, that *also* would alert The Skelly.

"I hear his men rustling," GranMa whispered to Michael and Alexis. "Get ready to run!"

With hearts pounding, muscles tensing, lungs constricting as if they could not to get enough air, each warrior tightened their thighs, transferring to their steeds an equal disquiet. "Hold them," GranMa said in a voice just above a whisper. "Hold them," she repeated. "We don't want our horses giving us away. The Skelly is very observant. If he thinks we're on to him, our plan will fail. Wait, wait . . . " Alexis and Michael kept Lightning and Debbie in place, but their steps had changed cadence from leisurely to clopping side steps.

"RUN!" GranMa shouted. Reins snapped across the necks of each horse and the line of four separated into two on each side of GranMa. The plan was working as the cadence of the horses changed into the anxious roar of a fearful chase. The heat from an ending day created hot wind gusts and perspiration, as the massive muscles shook the ground with desperation. This part of the strategy was owned by the horses and the riding skills of the warriors. Before long, the responsibility would shift into the hands of each warrior.

Hope was banged around in the carrier as GranMa and Noah moved forward to align with Michael and Alexis. "Take flight!" Noah shouted above the boom of the pounding horses.

"We're not leaving you!" GranMa shouted back.

"You're slowing us down! Your horses were meant to fly! They can't keep up with us!" Noah yelled with a strained, breathless voice. "Frank wants to run, but Star is the lead horse! Let Frank set the pace! You and Star go!"

With only seconds to think, GranMa took flight. Alexis and Michael followed, confusing The Skelly's men. However, it wasn't long before The Skelly and his Protectors also took flight.

A mixture of controlled panic and adrenaline pushed the warriors toward the Third Sister. Spencer and his men followed at a safe distance. He couldn't afford to get too close. But falling too far behind could put the children, GranMa, and her troops in significant danger. Spencer's thoughts were also with Uncle Jon, who would exact his own form of revenge today. Jon's rage would be satisfied this day, but the pain of losing his best friend, Bill, would never end. A hundred men would fall at his sword, but a million could not ease Uncle Jon's sorrow. By the end of the day, Uncle Jon would barely be clinging to life, but justice would be served.

Back at the Square, Jon prepared to position his men behind The Skelly's men. Isabel and Tedde stood beneath the watchtower, discussing the battle to come.

"I want you to watch from up there." Tedde pointed up. "If the battle takes a turn for the worse, I want you out of the watchtower and in the transport. Even if we are winning, I want you leaving as soon as the battle engages in full force. The time has come to face the measure of *your* courage. You must give an answer, even if the answer is no."

Isabel's dark, troubled eyes shot a confused look into Tedde's.

"No," Tedde responded slowly, "I don't know what it means. I only know you are troubled. I may not agree with GranMa's faith, but I have always agreed with her thinking. She did not lead you astray. A person has to trust and believe in something. I trust and believe in her."

"That's a pretty big burden you place on GranMa's shoulders—being responsible for your sacred trust," Isabel said accusingly.

"She doesn't seem to mind. Her faith is big enough for both of us."

"Then I need to grow mine quickly. I will try desperately to have enough of the faith you require. Now go! You have a battle to fight," Isabel said with authority. She gave her cousin a hug and a kiss on the cheek that lasted a little longer than usual.

Tedde's lack of concern was the telltale sign that Tedde was ignorant of the awful fate that awaited GranMa. *There is a blessing in this kind of ignorance*, Isabel thought. She climbed her way to the watchtower with a sense of doom.

Once she reached the top of the tower, she looked to the sky, knowing the first sign that the end was near would not be there. The last sentence of the first sealed book read, "On the day when the Alpha declares the Omega, Lightning will come from the sky." She did not find within its pages who would live or die on a clear day like today. It only said that three of the Five would prove themselves during the Battle of Destiny. She cast a worried look down from the tower, to see Tedde dressed for full battle. Tedde was not one of the Five.

Racing down the seventy stairs and yelling to the twelve statues, Tedde shouted, "STATUS!"

"They are coming," the twelve statues announced. "The militia is ready. The walls are secure, and the one they call Jon is on his way. The Skelly's army will be here in ten minutes."

With unwavering courage, Tedde took her post, knowing there would be many casualties. However, most would belong to The Skelly's and Uncle Jon's men. Jon would ensure that the militia suffered few losses. Tedde would eventually leave her post, and join her uncle just in time to kill the man who would thrust his sword into Uncle Jon's back.

Preparing to join the battle, Spencer rode at a steady pace, careful not move too fast, or too slow. He and these men were a crucial part of the battle plan. Timing was everything. He could feel sweat mixed with the dust running into his tired, dark eyes. There was no way to wipe the sweat off. His forearms were covered with the impenetrable, odd silver material. His men were confident in the leader who sat high upon his steed.

I could get there a lot faster if I could just fly, Spencer thought. But his place was with these men, and he could not suffer the luxury of *his* hero complex. He was not an army of one. He would stay with the men who trusted him to execute the strategy he created with GranMa. From his position, he could see that she, Alexis, and Michael had flown to the top of the Third Sister. They were probably in the cave by now.

The Skelly and his Protectors had them trapped. Believing he had the upper hand, GranMa kept The Skelly distracted by firing upon them.

"Let's not waste all our arrows on The Skelly. Stop shooting at him, and let's see what he does. Give Noah a few more minutes to get up the hill, and then we'll start distracting him again." GranMa and Alexis kept a keen eye on The Skelly while Michael looked around.

Alexis leaned against the boulder that lay just under the waterfall. She said to GranMa, "How come you've never taken us in here before?"

"For the most part, the Third Sister is a gentle soul, but there's a little volcano that lies inside of her. When it erupts, it's pretty violent inside this cave. I try and stay outside of this area because it's not safe."

"But it's beautiful from the inside looking out," Alexis said.

"That's how she tricks you into believing you're safe. But trust me; you're not. First, you'll get lulled by the Temptress, and next you'll be tricked by the beauty of the cave, and then, WHAM!"

Alexis jumped.

"She erupts. I love it in here," GranMa continued, "but I don't do anything to rattle the Third Sister. Of all the Sisters, it is she who controls the environment, and yields the most power."

"But the others look bigger."

"Do not be fooled by appearances. She is the smallest and the most ferocious. A tiger is prettier and smaller than an elephant. Which would you rather meet in the jungle?"

"Point taken," Alexis said, then turned her eyes back into the cave to see her inquisitive cousin. Hope flew over him like a hovering mother protecting her curious toddler.

"This place is amazing," Michael said, as he came back from the tunnel leading deep into the cave. "Did you know there's a river of molten lava that leads to a lake of fire?"

"Yes, I did. That is precisely why I have never taken you here before," GranMa responded, ducking from an arrow that splashed through the waterfall, ultimately making its way to the boulder. "They are getting aggressive. I think they're ready to attack. It's time for us to return fire again," GranMa said, and the three leaned up against the boulder, positioning their bows.

"Stay away from the Lake of Fire," GranMa said to Michael as, without turning her head, she released another arrow. "The Third Sister is the Keeper of the Lake, and she harnesses all the evil there. Perhaps it is why she erupts. I imagine it is a constant vigil to protect the world from impending evil. It must wear her down," GranMa said. Once more, she pulled her bow, and the arrow whizzed through the water and past The Skelly's head.

Noah had finally made it to the mountain. He was well prepared for this climb, and he hoped his men were ready for the challenge. Noah shouted to his men, "We're going to shoot down upon them and move around the mountain at the same time! They won't be able to move as fast as we can with arrows going past their heads! Our horses cannot go any farther. The mountain is too steep! We will make a steady climb while we keep shooting arrows. When I see Spencer in the background, we'll advance to the top quickly!" Noah's eyes flashed upon Spencer and his warriors. As if looking through a crystal ball with a clear center and blurred edges, Noah could see them climbing the mountain, but he knew there was no way Spencer could be there by now. His eyes focused on Spencer's face, and he watched Spencer issuing orders as he rode behind the Skulls.

Noah shook his head to clear his vision. What trickery was being played upon him? He rubbed his face and eyes, and regrouped his thoughts upon what was real. He went on as if the vision had not played before his eyes. "It looks like there are more evil Skulls than we anticipated!" he shouted. "I think there are five hundred, not three hundred! Be careful! We may be the ones walking into a trap!"

Noah dismounted, and gave Frank a good slap on the rump. But instead of riding away from the approaching Skulls, Frank turned and stampeded towards them. As the leader of the horses, the others followed suit. In the confusion the horses created, Noah and his men were given the opportunity to advance up the hill. Frank had given more to the battle than Noah had anticipated.

Noah looked into the distance. He could see the dust rising from Spencer and his warriors. He was uncertain if this vision was real, but the timing was right. He proceeded as if what he was seeing was real. It was time to drag the Skulls up the mountain, and it was important to distract them from noticing Spencer. "Go! Go! Go!" Noah yelled. Arrows flew from Skelly's men, but few hit their targets. By the time Noah landed at the top of the mountain, he had lost fewer than ten men. The Skelly's troops, on the other hand, had suffered significant losses. The plan was working.

GranMa did not have to see Noah. As soon as The Skelly and his Protectors took for the sky, she was certain that Noah was there. The Skelly was not a coward, nor was he interested in anything as honorable as a fair fight.

"Let's go! Pull your swords!" GranMa shouted. "Michael, where's Ninja Stick?"

"On Debbie! I don't know how to control it!" he shouted. "It would be dangerous to use it here!"

Alexis moved forward with trepidation. For the first time, she would watch men lying in pools of blood, see flesh ripped open, and hear bones crack under the weight of her sword. Today, she would taste the blood of war. The battle would soon be over, but she would never forget what it was like to feel flesh rip, or hear the sounds of the dead and dying. Their screams would haunt her in the aftermath of spat blood, broken bones, sliced tendons, and trampled souls. The smell of urine excreted by the dead and mixing with the blood of the dead and the dying would forever rest within her soul. She would wonder if defending those she loved made her more human, or more beast. These are the burdens of every warrior who fights an enemy they don't understand. She would do what needed to be done. But it would cost her more than she could afford to pay. By the end of the day, she would understand implicitly the meaning of testing the human spirit.

Chapter 25   Destiny

Michael made his way out of the cave, and was backed to the edge of the mountain with ten swords bearing down on him. He was holding his own, but his energy was waning. He could not hold off ten warriors for much longer. "NINJA STICK!" He shouted out of desperation, and Debbie was soon flying above him. Much to his surprise, Ninja Stick released itself from its harness in the saddle, and to the astonishment of the evil Skulls, planted itself firmly in his hand.

Taking advantage of his startled enemy, Michael swung the stick over his head. Within seconds, the stick was empowered with momentum as Michael lowered it, cutting the swords out of the hands of his attackers. With a second pass of the stick, the attackers were lying near their swords, painting the ground blood red. Michael advanced to the center of the battle. The Skulls fell back for fear of his omnipotent weapon. He was now on the offensive. Short jabs of his powerful stick made short order of his enemy. Pools of blood gathered at his feet as the half-dead moaned and writhed in agony. From the corner of his eye, he could see his cousins moving from a defensive to an attacking position. Many fell under Alexis's skillful sword, but Spencer wasn't getting there fast enough.

"Alexis!" Michael yelled above the din. "We need more time! We're not going to last. The men are tiring." He looked beyond Alexis to see GranMa losing ground as she fought three.

"Alexis!" GranMa called. "Time is on your hands!"

Alexis continued to swing her sword and cut the filthy flesh of many Skulls. But when she raised her sword for an uppercut into the gut of a taller enemy, she noticed the unique stone on her arm violently changing colors. Michael stepped in to assist her with the giant of a man. It was then that she noticed the stone on his sword sitting in its sheath, and changing in the same violent way.

Time is on my hands, she thought. "Yes, but what can I do with it?" she yelled in a panic.

"What?" Michael yelled back to her.

"Time is on my hands! It's on my hands!" She looked on the other wrist, where the arms of the watch were moving violently. "Time is on my hands! Look at the stone in your sword!" she hollered over her shoulder to Michael.

"What does that mean?" His voice strained above the din.

Alexis remembered the shock she received from the stone in Isabel's scepter. Thinking it must have to do with the stones touching, she moved her wrist down to Michael's sword. Explosive sparks flew in all directions.

"Knock it off, Alexis. You're going to kill us!" Michael's eyes caught a glimpse of the evil Skelly surveying the battle from the air. He saw The Skelly move closer, and watched his bloody face and eyes narrow as Alexis moved her wrist closer to his sword. Michael realized she was on to something.

"Alexis, try again!" he said.

She remembered GranMa's chamber. *Control it, don't let it control you.* This time, she moved slower as Michael fought off their attackers.

Time began to slow until it almost stood still. Swords swung in slow motion—even GranMa's and Noah's, but not Michael's and Alexis's. They had full control of time, but they couldn't figure out how to take advantage of it. If they moved, they lost contact. Michael could see The Skelly moving out of range. He was waiting for Michael and Alexis's time control power to weaken, and eventually it did.

But not before giving Spencer enough time to join the battle.

Spencer's arrival caused the Skulls to become more ferocious, and time control had taken a toll on Michael and Alexis. Yet, even in a weakened state, Alexis did not waiver in her courage. With Ninja Stick in his left hand, Michael continued to yield his sword fearlessly with his right. They came face to face with their greatest fears with even greater resolve. GranMa moved closer to fight alongside Alexis, her sword swirling through the air, slaying Skulls at its touch.

"Alexis," GranMa cried over the battle roar, "follow me!"

GranMa drew Alexis to a crevasse in the cave. It would not be long before they were spotted. GranMa had to act quickly. She put her sword to her side and began to speak in a lowered voice. Alexis strained to hear GranMa's words over the din.

"Alexis, this is not your battle," GranMa said as she gently stroked Alexis's face. "You have a greater battle to fight, and you must do it with the person who will succeed me."

When Alexis began to protest, GranMa lifted her hand for silence, and Alexis had no choice but to stand there and listen.

"You are the smallest, but like Hope, you are the greatest weapon of all the warriors. I once believed you were to succeed me. But I soon discovered your true place in Diggory Town. You are the new Guardian, and your job will be of great purpose. You fought in this battle only because I needed to be sure you were prepared to be the Final Guardian of the Final Responsible One. You have proven yourself. You must go now. She waits for you on the other side of Bus No. 3. Hurry! You must not die here, or it will mean the end of prophecy, and time."

With her heart breaking, GranMa hugged Alexis, and felt the bony changes in her shoulder blades that accompanied wings. "It will be a long time before we meet again in Diggory Town. Remember— speak no word of this in *That World*. Your voice is not protected there. It would cost you your life, as well as the lives of others in both worlds. When you see the Final Responsible One, only ask if she wants you to protect her—nothing more."

Alexis understood. This was not the Omega Battle. *This* was the Battle of Destiny. There would be many survivors, but GranMa would not be one of them. Alexis's warrior spirit could not stop her tears. She thought she would be the last of the Five to see GranMa in *This World*. When Alexis felt GranMa channeling her back to *That World*, she shouted, "I chose to love you, GranMa!"

With their hearts united in the mist, GranMa shouted back, "I chose to love you too!"

The last thing Alexis saw as she left Diggory Town was GranMa drawing her sword, and returning to a victorious battle that she would not survive. The first thing Alexis saw when she returned to

GranMa's office in *That World* was Isabel. Her back to Alexis, she stared into the painting above the fluffy, red couch.

Without turning, Isabel spoke. "I remember the first time you took me through this painting. When we came back, GranMa said, 'Always look for the tree that is a prisoner to the ice. That is your transporter home.' It's odd that no matter how hot it gets around the schoolhouse, the tree is always a prisoner to the ice. Sometimes, I feel like a prisoner. How is the battle going?"

"We're holding our own," Alexis said.

"And GranMa?"

"She's GranMa. She holds her own. She sent me here to ask *the* question. It's time for you to decide if I am the Final Guardian, because I need to know. Do you want me to protect you as the Final Responsible One?" Alexis wiped the remaining tears from her face.

Isabel did not reply. She stood staring blankly into the painting, as if somehow the answer were hidden there.

"Izzy?" Alexis said.

Isabel bowed her head and fiddled with the fabric of her dress. It was the red dress. The one GranMa had allowed her to have against GranMa's better judgment. It was a symbol of trust that Izzy would do the right things. Make the right judgments even when they went against Isabel's nature, or good reason. She made delicate circles with her fingertips, feeling the softness and vulnerability of the fabric. Any match, any knife, any dye could easily ruin the dress. It was not perfect like the other dress. It did not possess any special skills like the other dress. It was the red dress that left her vulnerable. The dress whose only weapon was the girl wearing it.

Izzy turned to find Alexis's eyes bearing down on her. She lowered her head to avoid the piercing look that wanted to see inside her soul.

Alexis pulled her sister close and cradled little Izzy's head. With her head upon her sister's shoulder, Izzy felt her chest tighten more with each shallow breath. Her tongue grew thick on the back of her throat while her temples pulsed, her ears rang, and her heart pounded. She could feel each blood cell rushing through her veins, trying to keep her alive. It would be better for her if only they would stop. Quietly, she listened to the sounds of guilt consuming her before she whispered the, "Yes," that sealed Michael's destiny.

It was the reason he watched the sword plunge forward that took his GranMother's life, and it was the reason the faint trace of a woman appeared in the smoke of the chimney in the painting labeled—

"The Way it Was"
1901 - 1939